CHARLES DICKENS

SELECTED SHORT FICTION

Edited with an introduction and notes by
Deborah A. Thomas
and four original illustrations by
Hablôt K. Browne ('Phiz'),
George Cattermole and
George Cruikshank

D0180566

PENGUIN BOOKS

PENGUIN BOOKS

Published by the Penguin Group
Penguin Books Ltd, 27 Wrights Lane, London W8 5TZ, England
Penguin Books USA Inc., 375 Hudson Street, New York, New York 10014, USA
Penguin Books Australia Ltd, Ringwood, Victoria, Australia
Penguin Books Canada Ltd, 10 Alcorn Avenue, Toronto, Ontario, Canada M4V 3B2
Penguin Books (NZ) Ltd, 182–190 Wairau Road, Auckland 10, New Zealand

Penguin Books Ltd, Registered Offices: Harmondsworth, Middlesex, England

This selection first published in the Penguin English Library 1976
Reprinted in Penguin Classics 1985
9 10 8

Introduction and notes copyright © Deborah A. Thomas, 1976
All rights reserved

Printed in England by Clays Ltd, St Ives plc
Set in Monotype Fournier

PENGUIN CLASSICS

SELECTED SHORT FICTION

CHARLES DICKENS was born at Portsmouth on 7 February 1812, the second of eight children. Dickens's childhood experiences were similar to those depicted in *David Copperfield*. His father, who was a government clerk, was imprisoned for debt and Dickens was sent to work at the age of twelve. The memories of this period were to haunt him until his death. He taught himself shorthand and became a reporter of parliamentary debates for the *Morning Chronicle*. He began to publish sketches in various periodicals, which were subsequently republished as *Sketches by Boz*. *The Pickwick Papers* were published in 1836–7 and after a slow start became a publishing phenomenon and Dickens's characters the centre of a popular cult. Part of the secret of his success was the method of cheap serial publication, which Dickens used for all his novels. He began *Oliver Twist* in 1837, followed by *Nicholas Nickleby* (1838–9) and *The Old Curiosity Shop* (1840–41). After finishing *Barnaby Rudge* (1841) Dickens set off for America; he went full of enthusiasm for the young republic but, in spite of a triumphant reception, he returned disillusioned. His experiences are recorded in *American Notes* (1842). *Martin Chuzzlewit* (1843–4) did not repeat its predecessors' success but this was quickly redressed by the huge popularity of the *Christmas Books*, of which the first *A Christmas Carol*, appeared in 1843. *Dombey and Son* (1846–8) and *David Copperfield* (1849–50) were more serious in theme and more carefully planned than his early novels. In this later work Dickens's social criticism became more radical and his comedy more savage. *Bleak House*, published in 1852–3, was followed by *Hard Times* (1854), *Little Dorrit* (1855–7), *A Tale of Two Cities* (1859), *Great Expectations* (1860–61) and *Our Mutual Friend* (1864–5). His last novel, *The Mystery of Edwin Drood*, was never completed and Dickens died on 9 June 1870. Public grief at his death was considerable and he was buried in the Poets' Corner of Westminster Abbey.

DEBORAH A. THOMAS is an Associate Professor of English at Villanova University in Villanova, Pennsylvania. She is the author of *Dickens and the Short Story* (1982).

CONTENTS

CONTENTS

CHARLES DICKENS

A NOTE BY ANGUS CALDER

CHARLES DICKENS was born at Portsmouth on 7 February 1812. He was the second of the eight children of John Dickens, a clerk in the Naval Pay Office, whose mother had been in service to Lord Crewe. Although John Dickens was hard-working, he was rarely able to live within his income, and this brought a series of crises upon his family, which lived under the shadow of menacing social insecurity.

John Dickens's work took him from place to place, so that Charles spent his early childhood in Portsmouth, London, and Chatham. He was happiest at Chatham, where he attended a school run by a young Baptist minister, who recognized his abilities and paid him special attention. In 1823 the family moved to London, faced with financial disaster, and, to help out, a relative of Mrs Dickens offered Charles work in a blacking business which he managed. Two days before his twelfth birthday the boy began work at a factory at Hungerford Stairs, labelling bottles for six shillings a week.

Shortly before this, John Dickens had been arrested for debt, and soon the whole family, except for Charles, who was found lodgings, joined him in the Marshalsea Debtors' Prison. The double blow – his menial job and the family shame – gave Charles a shock which transformed him. In later years he told only his wife and his closest friend, John Forster, of these experiences, which haunted him till his death.

After three months in prison, John Dickens was released by process of having himself declared an Insolvent Debtor, but it was not until weeks later that he withdrew Charles from work and sent him to school, where he did well. At fifteen, Charles began work in the office of a firm of Gray's Inn attorneys. Sensing a vocation elsewhere, he taught himself shorthand, and eighteen months later began to work as a freelance reporter in the court of Doctors' Commons.

In 1829 or 1830 he fell passionately in love with Maria Beadnell, the daughter of a banker. Their affair staggered fruitlessly on until the summer of 1833. Meanwhile, he began to report parliamentary debates, and won himself a high reputation for speed and accuracy. His first *Sketches by Boz* appeared in magazines soon after he was twenty-one. In 1834 he joined the reporting staff of the *Morning Chronicle*. A well-received volume of his *Sketches* appeared on his twenty-fourth birthday.

His growing reputation secured him a commission from the publishers, Chapman and Hall, to provide the text to appear in monthly instalments beside sporting plates by a popular artist, Seymour. He 'thought of Mr Pickwick'. Two days after the first number appeared he married Catherine Hogarth, the daughter of a fellow-journalist, on the prospect. Although early sales were disappointing, *Pickwick Papers* (1836–7) soon became a publishing phenomenon, and Dickens's characters the centre of a popular cult. Part of the secret was the method of cheap serial publication, which Dickens used for all his subsequent novels (some, however, being serialized in weekly magazines edited by himself), and which was copied by other writers.

While *Pickwick* was still running, Dickens began *Oliver Twist* (1837). *Nicholas Nickleby* (1838–9) provided him with a third success, and sales of *The Old Curiosity Shop* (1840–41) reached 100,000. After finishing *Barnaby Rudge* (1841), Dickens set off with his wife for the United States. He went full of enthusiasm for the young republic, but returned heartily disillusioned, in spite of a triumphant reception. His experiences are recorded in *American Notes* (1842).

His first setback came when *Martin Chuzzlewit* (1843–4) did not repeat the extraordinary success of its predecessors, though he promptly inaugurated his triumphant series of *Christmas Books* with *A Christmas Carol* (1843). He now travelled abroad, first to Italy (1844–5) and then to Switzerland and Paris (1846). During a brief interlude in England he projected, not another novel, but a paper, the *Daily News*. This first appeared in January 1846, but Dickens resigned after only seventeen days as editor.

His next novel, *Dombey and Son* (1846–8), was more wholly serious and more carefully planned than his early work. In *David Copperfield* (1849–50), he explored his own childhood and youth, thinly disguised. In the 1850s he increased his already intense interest in public affairs. He founded *Household Words*, a weekly magazine which combined entertainment with social purpose; it was succeeded in 1859 by *All the Year Round*, which sold as many as 300,000 copies. *Bleak House* (1852–3) and *Hard Times* (1854) have strong social themes, and *Little Dorrit* (1855–7) continues Dickens's bitter public denunciation of the whole framework of government and administration which had mismanaged the Crimean War.

In 1858 he separated from his wife. Although Kate, a shadowy, slow person, had given him ten children, she had never suited his exuberant temperament very well. He befriended a young actress, Ellen Ternan, who may have become his mistress. He was now living mainly in Kent, at Gad's Hill, near his boyhood home of Chatham. *A Tale of Two Cities* (1859), *Great Expectations* (1860–61), and *Our Mutual Friend* (1864–5) completed his life's main work of fourteen major novels. By the mid 1860s his health was failing, partly under the strain of his successful but exhausting public readings from his own work, which had begun in 1858. An immensely profitable but physically shattering series of readings in America (1867–8) speeded his decline, and he collapsed during a 'farewell' series in England. His last novel, *Edwin Drood* (1870), was never completed; he suffered a stroke after a full day's work at Gad's Hill on 8 June 1870 and died the following day. Lamentation was demonstrative and universal, and he was buried in the Poets' Corner of Westminster Abbey.

Dickens's extreme energy was not exhausted by his unique success as a novelist. His weekly journalism made heavy demands on his time after 1850, and he constantly turned to the stage, first in many amateur theatricals, given privately or for charity, where he produced and took leading roles with great brilliance, and, later, in his public readings. His concern with social reform in his novels and journalism was matched by an active personal interest in several charitable projects.

Furthermore, as Lionel Trilling puts it, 'the mere record of his conviviality is exhausting'. His typical relaxation was a long walk at great speed, and he was dedicated to any and every sort of game or jollification. In the early days of his success, observers were sometimes displeased by his flamboyant dress and a hint of vulgarity in his manners, but he had powerful, magnetizing eyes and overwhelming charm. Beneath his high spirits, friends could detect a permanent emotional insecurity and restlessness, which flavours the tragi-comic world of his novels.

Two biographies stand out among many: John Forster's *Life* (1872–4, many times reprinted); and Edgar Johnson's *Charles Dickens, His Tragedy and Triumph* (London: Gollancz, 1953), which embodies material neglected or suppressed by Forster. Readers interested in Dickens's methods as a novelist will be enlightened by John Butt's and Kathleen Tillotson's *Dickens at Work* (London: Methuen, 1957). There are innumerable specialized studies of his work, life and views. A magazine exclusively devoted to the subject, *The Dickensian*, is published three times a year by the Dickens Fellowship.

INTRODUCTION

LIKE an unfamiliar side dish ignored by diners intent on sirloin steak, Dickens's short fiction, apart from his *Christmas Books*, has often been overlooked.[1] Those who do turn their attention to it frequently find it baffling. Many of the assorted stories and sketches which Dickens produced throughout his career defy conventional categorization and now lie buried in remote corners of his collected works. The preternatural occurrences in tales like 'The Signalman', the impressionistic fusion of sensations in sketches like 'The Calais Night-Mail', and remarkable monologues like those in *Mrs Lirriper's Lodgings* and *Mrs Lirriper's Legacy* are seldom remembered in discussions of similar, although often less striking, elements in Dickens's novels. With the single exception of *A Christmas Carol*, the samples of Dickens's seemingly minor work which the modern reader most often encounters – the pieces collected in *Sketches by Boz* and the tales introduced into *Pickwick Papers* – are amongst his earliest compositions, and inevitably reflect the occasionally unsteady hand of the developing artist. Consequently, faced with the infinite variety of Dickens's better known writings from *Pickwick Papers* to *The Mystery of Edwin Drood*, few people have explored these unfamiliar pieces in any depth. Sylvère Monod's passing comment that 'his shorter stories . . . however intrinsically interesting, seemed to me to belong to another literary genre [than his novels] and to deserve a separate study'[2] is a rare tribute to the value of Dickens's short fiction in its own right. Nevertheless, this material is sometimes very lively, and evidently occupied an important place in Dickens's thoughts.

According to Percy Fitzgerald, one of his young associates, Dickens 'always seemed to hanker after the short story'.[3] As

1. Dickens's *Christmas Books* (*A Christmas Carol*, *The Chimes*, *The Cricket on the Hearth*, *The Battle of Life*, and *The Haunted Man*) have been edited in two volumes for the Penguin English Library by Michael Slater.

2. *Dickens the Novelist* (Norman, Okla.: University of Oklahoma Press, 1968), p. xiii.

3. *Memories of Charles Dickens with an Account of 'Household Words' and 'All the Year Round' and of the Contributors Thereto* (London: Simpkin, Marshall, Hamilton, Kent, 1913), p. 113.

Dickens learned relatively early, however, his public did not share this inclination. *Master Humphrey's Clock*, a journal, like Goldsmith's *Bee*, containing a miscellaneous assortment of short pieces, suffered a marked drop in sales, so he transformed one tale into a full-length novel (*The Old Curiosity Shop*) and thereafter confined his writing to novels, except on special occasions. The most special of such occasions was Christmas, which presented Dickens with the opportunity to indulge once again in literature like the fairy tales he had enjoyed in childhood. His close friend and biographer John Forster observed about Dickens's *Christmas Books*: 'No one was more intensely fond than Dickens of old nursery tales, and he had a secret delight in feeling that he was here only giving them a higher form.' Moreover, the five *Christmas Books* which Dickens produced in the 1840s were by no means his only outlet for short fiction. In 1850, he inaugurated *Household Words*, a weekly periodical succeeded in 1859 by *All the Year Round*, which he edited until his death in 1870; they provided him with an excuse not only for additional Christmas pieces but also for less seasonal subjects, like the workings of memory and the manifestations of the macabre, which emerge in many of his novels in less concentrated form. In some cases, as Harry Stone has perceptively argued, they gave him a chance to experiment with techniques of rendering the operation of the mind – at times verging upon stream-of-consciousness narration – which he felt his readers would not accept in novels.[4] Lack of inhibition is often dangerous, and some of Dickens's short creations might be gladly wished away, but others show a literary master brilliantly indulging in the very essence of his art.

The sketch entitled 'A Christmas Tree', for example, explicitly reveals this sense of liberation. Above all, as the narrator declares, Christmas is the time for an imaginative vacation:

4. 'Dickens and Interior Monologue', *Philological Quarterly*, vol. 38 (1959), pp. 59–60. Stone notes that the hallucinative opening of *The Mystery of Edwin Drood* is more conventionally organized and punctuated than some of Dickens's earlier, occasional writings in *Household Words* and *All the Year Round* and contends persuasively that, even in his last and in many ways experimental novel, Dickens was deliberately refraining from complete use of stylistic devices which he had previously employed in his short fiction: 'He decided to sacrifice technique for the sake of intelligibility, verisimilitude for the sake of easing the reader's way' (p. 59).

And I *do* come home at Christmas. We all do, or we all should. We all come home, or ought to come home, for a short holiday – the longer, the better – from the great boarding-school, where we are for ever working at our arithmetical slates, to take, and give a rest. As to going a visiting, where can we not go, if we will; where have we not been, when we would; starting our fancy from our Christmas Tree!

The 'fancy' which starts 'from our Christmas Tree' flies rapidly 'Away into the winter prospect' and into the realm of 'Winter Stories – Ghost Stories, or more shame for us – round the Christmas fire'. It flows in and out of narrative *personae*. The unspecified first-person singular speaker of the initial portion of the sketch becomes a nervous observer of ghosts: 'We are a middle-aged nobleman, and we make a generous supper with our host and hostess and their guests'; 'we always travel with pistols'; 'we are dead now'. The symbolic homecoming 'from the great boarding-school, where we are for ever working at our arithmetical slates' follows a fusion of recollections of toys and tales 'upon the branches of the Christmas Tree of our own young Christmas days', and the supernatural 'going a visiting' ultimately fades into seasonal emotion with an allusion to the birth in Bethlehem for which the holiday is named: 'In every cheerful image and suggestion that the season brings, may the bright star that rested above the poor roof, be the star of all the Christian world!' The motivation, the ingredients, the vitality, and the difficulties of Dickens's short fiction are here in embryo.

The key word in this context is 'fancy' – the vague but vital quality which triumphs over utilitarian practicality in Dickens's novel *Hard Times*. The term appears repeatedly in his writing, not as a clearly defined critical concept as in Wordsworth and Coleridge but rather as an infallible panacea for a debilitating overdose of fact. Fancy, for Dickens, was roughly synonymous with imagination. However, the meanings which he attached to this protean word range, among a host of others, from temporarily escaping the workaday world to softening it with feeling, or transforming it into something strange and new through the power of a contemplative, creative eye. As Dickens himself willingly acknowledged, fancy is fundamental to his concept of literature, and it appears in one or more of these senses in his work of any length. As he explained in one of his rare defences of his art:

It does not seem to me to be enough to say of any description that it is the exact truth. The exact truth must be there; but the merit or art in the narrator, is the manner of stating the truth. As to which thing in literature, it always seems to me that there is a world to be done. And in these times, when the tendency is to be frightfully literal and catalogue-like – to make the thing, in short, a sort of sum in reduction that any miserable creature can do in that way – I have an idea (really founded on the love of what I profess), that the very holding of popular literature through a kind of popular dark age, may depend on such fanciful treatment.

Significantly, this credo is quoted in Forster's *Life of Charles Dickens* in the context of what the discerning but staid biographer called Dickens's tendency to 'let himself loose' in passages of 'mere description' and in shorter and thus to Forster less important works. Dickens himself seems to have valued his short fiction precisely because it gave opportunities to express fancy in concentration.

Not all of the results, at least to modern palates, are felicitous. A few of Dickens's short pieces contain an even higher proportion of pathos than his description of the demise of the unfortunate Little Nell. In other short pieces, however, Dickens's penetration of the secrets of the human psyche far surpasses anything in his longer work.

The creative exuberance which led him to experiment so freely and so diversely poses special problems for an editor; the pieces included here by no means exhaust the subject of Dickens's short fiction. If a reader's appetite should become sufficiently whetted to evoke Oliver Twist's anxious question, he can rest contented that there is certainly 'more'. I have limited my choice to three general types so that readers may readily examine Dickens's recurring concerns and relate these concerns to elements in his novels. Nonetheless, this selection demonstrates in varying ways the essential characteristics of all Dickens's writing – his unsurpassed gift of comedy, his deepening awareness of human tragedy, and his belief, often emphasized in pieces associated with Christmas, in the value of human compassion.

Just as compassionate and non-compassionate impulses some-times defy rational description, so Dickens's short fiction often resists ordinary labels. Edgar Allan Poe's celebrated dictum that in a well-constructed tale 'there should be no word written, of which the tendency, direct or indirect, is not to the one pre-established design' (*Graham's Magazine*, May 1842) is seldom an adequate explanation of these brief excursions of a novelist whose 'out-standing, unmistakable mark', according to George Orwell, 'is the *unnecessary detail*'.[5] In many cases, as 'A Christmas Tree' demon-strates, even the seemingly simple distinction between realistic reporting and fanciful creation becomes an extremely complex issue. Consequently, I have used the term 'short fiction' rather than 'short story' with its connotations, many derived from Poe, of rigidly plotted tightness and compression.

The headings – 'Tales of the Supernatural', 'Impressionistic Sketches', and 'Dramatic Monologues' – of the three categories are arbitrary ones, chosen solely to facilitate discussion. The cate-gories themselves are likewise arbitrary and imprecise, but provide a useful perspective on an astonishingly variable scene.

The 'Tales of the Supernatural', which form the first category, openly encourage astonishment. For Dickens, as for numerous other writers in the Gothic tradition, tales could legitimately transcend the limits of ordinary physical reality. As an individual, Dickens had little patience with spiritualists or 'rappers' like his one-time friend William Howitt,[6] but, as a writer and an editor, he spared no pains upon occasion to produce the right involuntary shiver. Forster noted that 'Among his good things should not be omitted his telling of a ghost story', and Dickens himself exclaimed in a letter in 1851 to Mrs Gaskell, a contributor to *Household Words* and *All the Year Round* whom he admired for her talented writing of similar tales: 'Ghost-stories, illustrating particular states of

5. 'Charles Dickens', in *The Collected Essays, Journalism and Letters of George Orwell*, ed. Sonia Orwell and Ian Angus (Harmondsworth: Penguin, 1970), vol. 1, p. 493.

6. Harry Stone discusses the controversy between Dickens and Howitt as well as the Christmas number which resulted from it in 'The Unknown Dickens: With a Sampling of Uncollected Writings', in *Dickens Studies Annual*, ed. Robert B. Partlow, Jr, vol. 1 (Carbondale, Ill.: Southern Illinois University Press, 1970), pp. 1–22, 275–6.

mind and processes of the imagination, are common-property, I always think – except in the manner of relating them, and O who can rob some people of *that*!' Dickens's literary admiration in this realm of the ordinarily inexplicable was not confined to the subject of ghosts. When the noted illustrator and fanatic teetotaller George Cruikshank altered the story of 'Hop o' My Thumb' to show the evils of inebriation, Dickens exploded in outrage. 'Fairy-tales', he declared in an article called 'Frauds on the Fairies', are 'nurseries of fancy' and 'In a utilitarian age, of all other times, it is a matter of grave importance that Fairy tales should be respected' (*Household Words*, 1 October 1853). In view of the importance of such preternatural tales in Dickens's thinking, his own experiments warrant particular attention.

The demonic aura of Fagin in *Oliver Twist* and the fairy-tale illusions of Pip in *Great Expectations* are only two of the extranatural metaphors and motifs which proliferate in all of Dickens's work. With the exception of the *Christmas Books*, however, he had little opportunity to focus on such features save in a few short pieces like those included here. The narrator of 'A Christmas Tree' noted that ghost stories are particularly appropriate 'round the Christmas fire'; 'The Story of the Goblins who stole a Sexton', at the height of the Christmas celebration at Dingley Dell in the very centre of *Pickwick Papers*, emerges from just such a setting. Like the *Christmas Books* which it anticipates, this story of Gabriel Grub's metamorphosis from hate to love of mankind, achieved through supernatural means, is a form of fairy tale;[7] as in the *Christmas Books*, the potential terror of the supernatural agents is intentionally undercut by Dickens's humour. 'The Baron of Grogzwig', from the sixth chapter

7. The connection between this tale and *A Christmas Carol* has been discussed by John Butt in 'Dickens's Christmas Books', *Pope, Dickens and Others* (Edinburgh: Edinburgh University Press, 1969), pp. 134–5. Harry Stone has argued that the *Carol* as well as the other Christmas Books should be viewed as fairy tales; for example, see 'Dickens' Artistry and *The Haunted Man*', *The South Atlantic Quarterly*, vol. 61 (1962), pp. 492–505. Michael Slater's General Critical Introduction to his Penguin English Library edition of the *Christmas Books* (Harmondsworth: Penguin, 1971) offers a valuable survey of their background and characteristics; Robert L. Patten's Introduction to *Pickwick Papers* (Harmondsworth: Penguin, 1972), also in this series, contains an important analysis of the function of 'The Story of the Goblins who stole a Sexton' as well as the other tales introduced within the context of *Pickwick*.

of *Nicholas Nickleby*, follows a similar pattern, although here, perhaps prophetically in view of Dickens's own later domestic difficulties, the note of humour seems slightly strained. In 'To Be Read at Dusk' and the more skilful and mature 'Signalman', on the contrary, the chilling sensation on a reader's spine is all important; events move imperceptibly and disturbingly from the ordinary to the extraordinary world. 'A Confession Found in a Prison in the Time of Charles the Second', written by Dickens for his abortive *Master Humphrey's Clock*, introduces no supernatural agents. Nevertheless, as in some of the sensational tales in *Pickwick Papers*, its grimly implausible details seem designed to evoke the sensation of the 'uncanny' which Freud derives from 'a conflict of judgement whether things which have been "surmounted" and are regarded as incredible are not, after all, possible'.[8] Of all of Dickens's short fiction, such tales of terror come closest to the genre which Poe made famous; indeed in a review of an American edition of *Master Humphrey's Clock*, Poe described 'A Confession Found in a Prison in the Time of Charles the Second' as 'a paper of remarkable power' (*Graham's Magazine*, May 1841). The common denominator of these five tales is a temporary, in Dickens's terminology 'fanciful', flight from the ordinary, humdrum events of life. Admittedly, 'The Story of the Goblins who stole a Sexton' and, to an even greater degree, 'The Baron of Grogzwig' are inferior to *A Christmas Carol*, and, of the three designedly terrifying tales, perhaps only 'The Signalman' ranks with the masterpieces in this vein by writers such as Poe, LeFanu, and Lovecraft. Viewed as individual compositions, the significance of these tales by Dickens may be easily overlooked. Viewed as a group, as recurring exercises in an obviously escapist vein which Dickens particularly valued, and as concentrated manifestations of strains which run throughout his novels, they should not be casually dismissed.

Fancies prompted by Christmas trees, or other suitable stimuli, are by no means confined to 'Winter Stories', and a large number of Dickens's best short pieces, like 'A Christmas Tree' itself, simply capture a perceptive first-person observer's responses to and

8. 'The "Uncanny" ', in *Collected Papers*, authorized translation under the supervision of Joan Riviere, vol. IV (1925; reprinted, London: Hogarth Press, 1953), p. 404.

thoughts about his own immediate situation. Like the eighteenth-century descriptive essays from which they stem, these writings sometimes seem to be neither fiction nor non-fiction; Steele himself felt it necessary to note in the *Tatler* (no. 172) his 'libertine manner of writing by way of essay'. No editor could exclude such pieces, some of which are brilliantly imaginative; that would be the kind of Podsnappish gesture which Dickens himself would have ridiculed. Extended descriptions in Dickens's novels such as that of the fog at the beginning of *Bleak House* are fantastically heightened versions of the literal settings which lie behind them, and the same transforming power flowed readily into Dickens's sketches. Mario Praz has suggested that for Dickens 'the road which presented itself most naturally . . . was that of the essay on things observed', although, in Praz's words, the kind of observation which such pieces contain is far from simply factual – 'I said "things observed": but things observed through a peculiar distorting lens, fantastically distorted . . . Dickens's world is akin to that of Doré, of Hugo, of Breughel, and of the gargoyles on Gothic cathedrals.'[9] More recently, J. Hillis Miller has argued that any reading of the seemingly journalistic reportings in *Sketches by Boz* inevitably hovers between the view of them as figurative and the view of them as realistic representation:

What had seemed 'realistic' comes to be seen as figurative, and the radically fictive quality of the *Sketches* as a whole comes into the open. Back and forth between these two interpretations the reader oscillates. Neither takes precedence over the other, but the meaning of the text is generated by the mirage of alternation between them. [10]

In essence, the *Sketches* are not an imitation but an interpretation of the familiar world. These *Sketches* and the even more sophisticated versions which Dickens contributed later to *Household Words* and *All the Year Round* offer an incomparable laboratory in which to explore the boundaries of fiction, and the best products of Dickens's own experiments in this laboratory are too valuable to

9. *The Hero in Eclipse in Victorian Fiction*, trans. Angus Davidson (London: Oxford University Press, 1956), pp. 171, 172.

10. 'The Fiction of Realism: *Sketches by Boz, Oliver Twist*, and Cruikshank's Illustrations', in *Dickens Centennial Essays*, ed. Ada Nisbet and Blake Nevius (Berkeley: University of California Press, 1971), p. 116.

ignore. The selections included here under the heading 'Impressionistic Sketches' are fictive in the sense that their primary purpose is not an objective description of particular scenes but a recreation of these scenes through the eyes of an observant and thoughtful bystander. Like Monet's paintings of Rouen cathedral, they take their nature from the particular moment and particular mood in which they have been seen.

In the extracts from *Sketches by Boz*, for example, we see everyday events and people as this bystander sees them; we perceive their entertaining and striking qualities only as they have already been perceived. It is no accident that we occasionally spot this figure in the actual process of creating pictures. In 'Seven Dials', he pauses to put together the elements of a grim 'still life':

> Brokers' shops, which would seem to have been established by humane individuals, as refuges for destitute bugs, interspersed with announcements of day-schools, penny theatres, petition-writers, mangles, and music for balls or routs, complete the 'still life' of the subject; and dirty men, filthy women, squalid children, fluttering shuttlecocks, noisy battledores, reeking pipes, bad fruit, more than doubtful oysters, attenuated cats, depressed dogs, and anatomical fowls, are its cheerful accompaniments.

Dickens's style of description is down-to-earth but purposefully distorted. The speaker's vision is rooted in the noise, dirt, and odour of a London slum, but, as he gazes, the scene becomes more than a verbal photograph of urban decay. As in Dickens's mature treatments of London and its inhabitants, human beings are reduced to the level of things, while non-human things assume lives of their own.[11] 'Squalid children' fall into the same category as 'fluttering shuttlecocks'; 'dirty men' exist on the same level as 'reeking pipes'. Insects become as 'destitute' as the neighbourhood which they infest and seek refuge in secondhand stores. 'More than doubtful' oysters may not only give pause to a prospective purchaser but also wonder themselves how they came to be in such a place. 'Anatomical fowls' appear ready to give up their existence

11. For a further discussion of this aspect of Dickens's style, see Dorothy Van Ghent, 'The Dickens World: A View from Todgers's', *Sewanee Review*, vol. 58 (1950), reprinted in *The Dickens Critics*, ed. George H. Ford and Lauriat Lane, Jr. (Ithaca, N.Y.: Cornell University Press, 1961), pp. 213–14.

and lay themselves out to be dissected. Dickens's intention in this passage is largely playful – perhaps too playful, as his heavy-handed use of the word 'cheerful' suggests – and the picture thus created is an elementary illustration of the letting 'loose' at times of 'mere description' about which Forster complained. In later sketches such as 'The Calais Night-Mail', this imaginative heightening through verbal play becomes strikingly more polished.

Throughout these pieces, the point of view of the thoughtful observer is used. Sometimes, as in 'The Election for Beadle' from *Sketches by Boz*, his tone bears traces of condescension; more often, especially in later pieces, it is wryly sympathetic and nostalgic. In *Sketches by Boz* (the title of a collection of short writings first published between 1833 and 1836) the *persona* of Boz appears fortuitous, and a reader is given relatively little information about this personage himself. Nonetheless, Dickens evidently found the stance of the idly speculative bystander congenial. He returned to it in the 1850s when his editorship of *Household Words* gave him an opportunity for further pieces in this vein, and the unspecified narrator of sketches from *Household Words* like 'Lying Awake', 'Our School', and 'A Flight' is unmistakably an older and more experienced Boz. Still later, in the figure of the Uncommercial Traveller in *All the Year Round*, Dickens initiated another series of sketches narrated by an even more polished version of this now familiar voice: 'Figuratively speaking, I travel for the great house of Human Interest Brothers, and have rather a large connection in the fancy goods way. Literally speaking, I am always wandering here and there . . .' This wandering, observant narrator, of course, bears a close affinity to Dickens himself who was an energetic explorer of familiar and unfamiliar sights. Many of these 'Impressionistic Sketches' contain fragments of autobiography; some of them, such as 'Dullborough Town' and 'Nurse's Stories' are often used as sources of information about Dickens's happy years in Chatham before his family moved to London, where financial improvidence brought his father temporarily to a debtor's prison, forced Dickens at the age of twelve to work for a few indelibly unhappy months in a blacking warehouse, and terminated for ever his childhood sense of security and freedom from care. However, there are obvious hazards in uncritically reading such pieces as mere confessions – Dickens came to Chatham at the age of five while the Uncommercial Traveller describes Dullborough Town as the location of 'scenes among which my earliest days were passed' – and available evidence indicates that Dickens manipulated material from his own life to strengthen the voice of his narrator.

The piece entitled 'Our School' illustrates this point. Just as Elia's apparent recollections in 'Christ's Hospital Five-and-Thirty Years Ago' fuse Lamb's own memories with those of his friend Coleridge, so the picture in 'Our School' is not a completely accurate representation of its author's past. Forster observes that much of 'Our School' is modelled upon Dickens's own experience at Wellington House Academy, but he also remarks that Dickens did not attain the academic distinctions which the narrator of this sketch attributes to himself. In addition, the narrator contrasts 'Our School' with his earlier 'Preparatory Day-School', talks about friends who boarded at 'Our School', avoids any mention of his own living arrangements, and thus suggests that he too was a boarder, although Dickens explained to Forster that he had been a day student at Wellington House Academy. These subtle differences between Dickens's own experience and the experience which he portrays appear to show that his intention was to depict a thoughtful personality remembering a typical experience. The background of the piece is that of a normal, perfectly adjusted schoolboy; there is no suggestion that this schoolboy, like Dickens himself, might recently have escaped from a psychologically harrowing occupation or that his father, just out of prison, could barely afford his education. Part of this contrast undoubtedly stems from Dickens's lifelong reluctance to discuss his early misery in the blacking warehouse, but, two years earlier, he had fictionalized that very episode in *David Copperfield*. The reason behind his portrayal of such a natural childhood in this sketch seems to be literary strategy more than personal compulsion. The narrator's nostalgia is that of any adult remembering happy days, and he includes details of his bygone academic achievements and his apparent lack of family complications to make the sketch more convincing.

Thus Dickens's goal in such pieces is not accurate documentation but the achievement of particular effects, and, like 'A Christmas Tree', some of the resulting sketches openly declare their freedom from the confines of literality. Boz begins 'A Visit to Newgate' with the assurance 'that we do not intend to fatigue the reader with any statistical accounts of the prison', and, in 'City of London Churches', the Uncommercial Traveller specifically disavows any antiquarian concern with facts for their own sake:

> I never wanted to know the names of the churches to which I went, and to this hour I am profoundly ignorant in that particular of at least nine-tenths of them ... No question did I ever ask of living creature concerning these churches, and no answer to any antiquarian question on the subject that I ever put to books, shall harass the reader's soul. A full half of my pleasure in them arose out of their mystery; mysterious I found them; mysterious they shall remain for me.

Again and again in these pieces, the first-person speaker speculates upon places and their inhabitants – discerning amusement in unpromising material, transforming commonplace events into something notable and strange.

As the title of one piece, 'Meditations in Monmouth-Street', suggests, the narrator sometimes allows us to follow the progress of his thinking and occasionally captures the very moment when this thinking bursts the confines of actuality:

> We have gone on speculating in this way, until whole rows of coats have started from their pegs, and buttoned up, of their own accord, round the waists of imaginary wearers; lines of trousers have jumped down to meet them; waistcoats have almost burst with anxiety to put themselves on; and half an acre of shoes have suddenly found feet to fit them, and gone stumping down the street ...

Dickens's fascination with interior mental processes emerges strikingly in the short writings. The extended description of the thoughts of the criminal 'spending his last night on earth' which enters Boz's mind in 'A Visit to Newgate' anticipates the macabre vignettes in 'Lying Awake', a description moving, in its insomniac narrator's words, by 'association of ideas' through a 'train of thoughts as I lay awake'. In this remarkable piece, as Harry Stone has pointed out,[12] Dickens experiments with techniques similar to those of the modern interior monologue; his experiments become

12. 'Dickens and Interior Monologue', *Philological Quarterly*, vol. 38 (1959), pp. 62–4.

even more daring as the Uncommercial Traveller fuses fragments of a popular song with his recollections of boyhood reading and his current reactions to a rough crossing of the English Channel in 'The Calais Night-Mail':

> What may be the speciality of these waves as they come rushing on, I cannot desert the pressing demands made upon me by the gems she wore, to inquire, but they are charged with something about Robinson Crusoe, and I think it was in Yarmouth Roads that he first went a seafaring and was near foundering (what a terrific sound that word had for me when I was a boy!) in his first gale of wind. Still, through all this, I must ask her (who *was* she I wonder!) for the fiftieth time, and without ever stopping. Does she not fear to stray, So lone and lovely through this bleak way, And are Erin's sons so good or so cold, As not to be tempted by more fellow-creatures at the paddle-box or gold? Sir Knight I feel not the least alarm, No son of Erin will offer me harm, For though they love fellow-creature with umbrella down again and golden store, Sir Knight they what a tremendous one love honour and virtue more: For though they love Stewards with a bull's eye bright, they'll trouble you for your ticket, sir — rough passage to-night!

The subject of such pieces is not only the impressions of their narrator but the twists and turnings of his mind as these impressions are formed.

Moreover, Dickens's experiments with first-person narrative as a tool for revealing mental processes were by no means confined to his impressionistic sketches, and the virtuoso pieces grouped under the heading of 'Dramatic Monologues' contain some of his most fascinating explorations of the inner sources of human nature. Dickens's skill at creating characters is proverbial; some, like Scrooge, have made their way into the dictionary. As readers have noted with some dismay, however, the outstanding characters in Dickens's novels often seem to dwarf their surroundings. Virginia Woolf's acid comment that 'Dickens made his books blaze up, not by tightening the plot or sharpening the wit, but by throwing another handful of people upon the fire'[13] contains some truth. G. K. Chesterton observed more charitably, 'the units of Dickens, the primary elements, are not the stories, but the characters who

13. '*David Copperfield*', *Collected Essays*, vol. I (London: Hogarth Press, 1966), p. 194.

affect the stories – or, more often still, the characters who do not affect the stories'.[14] Chesterton's remark is overstated; individuals as diverse as Pip in *Great Expectations* and Pecksniff in *Martin Chuzzlewit* have a strong effect on the plots of the novels in which they appear. Nevertheless, it is difficult to deny the fundamental role of characterization in Dickens's art, and many of the people whom Dickens creates possess astonishing vocal powers. Characters like Mrs Gamp in *Martin Chuzzlewit* and Flora Finching in *Little Dorrit* exist largely in terms of what they say. Curiously enough, Flora and Mrs Gamp often seem to talk not to their ostensible listeners but to themselves, and their absorption in their own words appears, in less extreme form, in other figures in Dickens's novels. George H. Ford has commented, in a discussion of *David Copperfield*, 'There are times when Dickens's characters do not seem to be talking to each other but *at* each other, like people at parties in America, especially at crowded cocktail parties, where conversation is made up of a cacophony of non-intersecting soliloquies, each speaker isolated and alone.'[15] In the monologues which comprise the third major category of Dickens's short fiction, this sense of isolated soliloquy is intensified. Plot recedes into the background, other characters disappear into the wings, leaving a solitary obsessive conversationalist of the type contained in Dickens's novels.

In marked contrast to the observant personality who presides over the impressionistic sketches, narrators like Doctor Marigold and the 'blighted public character' of 'His Brown-Paper Parcel' are unique individuals. Unlike the first-person speakers in uncanny pieces such as 'The Signalman' and 'A Confession Found in a Prison in the Time of Charles the Second', these narrators are not simply vehicles for revealing some abnormal or unnatural event. Rather, they are preoccupied with bringing their distinctive existences into general view. Mrs Lirriper, the widowed keeper of a London boarding house, introduces herself in her second monologue in a passage that briefly rivals the free associations of Joyce's Molly Bloom:

14. *Charles Dickens* (London: Methuen, 1906), p. 82.
15. 'Introduction', to *David Copperfield* (Boston, 1958), reprinted in *The Dickens Critics*, ed. George H. Ford and Lauriat Lane, Jr (Ithaca, N.Y.: Cornell University Press, 1961), pp. 354–5.

Being here before your eyes my dear in my own easy-chair in my own quiet room in my own Lodging House Number Eighty-one Norfolk-street Strand London situated midway between the City and St James's – if anything is where it used to be with these hotels calling themselves Limited but called Unlimited by Major Jackman rising up everywhere and rising up into flagstaffs where they can't go any higher, but my mind of those monsters is give me a landlord's or landlady's wholesome face when I come off a journey and not a brass plate with an electrified number clicking out of it which it's not in nature can be glad to see me and to which I don't want to be hoisted like molasses at the Docks and left there telegraphing for help with the most ingenious instruments but quite in vain – being here my dear I have no call to mention that I am still in the Lodgings as a business hoping to die in the same and if agreeable to the clergy partly read over at Saint Clement's Danes and concluded in Hatfield churchyard when lying once again by my poor Lirriper ashes to ashes and dust to dust.

Whether their words flow glibly like Doctor Marigold's or stumble hesitantly like George Silverman's, their utterances reveal the texture of their minds. We see not only the daily events of their lives, but also their unconscious foibles and faults. The affectations and self-interestedness of the incomparable waiter in *Somebody's Luggage* are minor weaknesses, but those of his irrepressible younger counterpart in the railroad refreshment room at Mugby Junction verge upon juvenile delinquency. The Boy at Mugby thoroughly enjoys preying upon society, and he revels in his chosen occupation as 'a most highly delicious lark'. He depicts his exploits with such gusto, nevertheless, that it is impossible to deny him the kind of sympathy which Dickens himself must have felt when he signed a letter to his friend Thomas Beard 'The Boy (at Mugby)'. In such pieces, Dickens approaches the problem of conflicting evaluations of a speaker's words explored by his contemporary Robert Browning in some of his best poems, and he encourages 'the tension between sympathy and moral judgement' which Robert Langbaum has described as the hallmark of the dramatic monologue.[16] Like a comic version of the duke in Browning's 'My Last Duchess', the Boy at Mugby possesses, in Langbaum's terms,

16. *The Poetry of Experience: The Dramatic Monologue in Modern Literary Tradition* (1957; reprinted New York: Norton, 1963), p. 85.

a 'hard core of character fiercely loyal to itself';[17] he displays his outrageous attitude with such unfaltering confidence that a reader hesitates to condemn him as he deserves. Other narrators of these monologues by Dickens are not so zestfully reprehensible. Mrs Lirriper's wandering thoughts, minor jealousies, and uneducated errors are a far cry from the Boy's high-spirited determination to 'Keep the Public Down'. Whatever response Dickens's speakers ultimately elicit, however, their words reveal their own fanciful and idiosyncratic perspective on their audience's everyday world.

These extraordinary monologues are often bypassed in critical examinations of Dickens because of the unusual circumstances under which most of them were written. Except for 'George Silverman's Explanation', all the ones included in this selection appeared in the extra Christmas numbers of *All the Year Round*. These special publications, which Dickens began with *Household Words*, were initially simple affairs; the number for 1850, in which 'A Christmas Tree' appeared, is merely a regular issue whose contents deal with the subject of Christmas. Subsequently, however, the Christmas number became a separate and increasingly elaborate publication, and Dickens gradually hit upon a scheme, which Scheherazade might well have envied, for enclosing contributions by other authors within his own words. His procedure was to outline a principal narrative which formed usually, but not always, the first and last chapters of the Christmas number; this framing narrative gave some excuse for interpolated pieces from other contributors and occasionally from Dickens himself. By 1862, this basic format had become well established, and *Somebody's Luggage*, the Christmas number for this year, playfully pokes fun at Dickens's contributors and his own activities as editor of *All the Year Round*; as he wrote to Wilkie Collins, it was designed as 'a comic defiance of the difficulty of a Xmas No., with an unexpected end to it'.

The difficulties which Dickens experienced in producing his Christmas numbers still plague those who wish to evaluate his contributions; they are usually reprinted out of their original contexts in editions of Dickens's collected works, where they sometimes seem oddly constructed and mysterious. Consequently, the

17. ibid, p. 83.

selections reprinted here are presented as self-contained portions of larger works. They consist of the framework and one of the two pieces which Dickens introduced into *Somebody's Luggage* as well as the frameworks of *Mrs Lirriper's Lodgings*, *Mrs Lirriper's Legacy*, and *Doctor Marigold's Prescriptions*. 'Main Line. The Boy at Mugby' is one of his additions at the end of the major narrative of *Mugby Junction* (his other added piece, 'No. 1 Branch Line. The Signalman', is included under 'Tales of the Supernatural'). In these dazzling contributions, Dickens triumphed over the annual challenges of the Christmas number.

Moreover, Dickens's work in this genre was not confined solely to the Christmas season. Near the end of his career, in a characterization created before his second visit for initial publication in America, he used the form, even more skilfully, for George Silverman's hauntingly equivocal explanation. The repeated efforts of this narrator not to be 'worldly' have led only to misunderstanding and injustice, and his monologue is a last, despairing effort to explain his own altruistic intentions. At the same time, his remarks and behaviour suggest that he is neurotic, unsocial and self-centred. He is selfishly oblivious to the feelings of the women whose friendship and love he rejects; he is condoning a serious deception when he voluntarily relinquishes his claim to the inheritance appropriated by his self-proclaimed guardian – but this does not disturb him. As in Browning's 'Andrea del Sarto', where the speaker attributes his problems both to his own loving sacrifice and the failure of others to understand him, we see what George Silverman believes and also what he manifests about himself.

His self-portrait at the farmhouse near the ruined Hoghton Towers, as he observes a youthful birthday celebration which he has refused to attend, illustrates these two facets of his personality:

Ah! If they could have seen me next day in the ruin, watching for the arrival of the cart full of merry young guests; if they could have seen me at night, gliding out from behind the ghostly statue, listening to the music and the fall of dancing feet, and watching the lighted farm-house windows from the quadrangle when all the ruin was dark; if they could have read my heart as I crept up to bed by the back way, comforting myself with the reflection, 'They will take no hurt from me,' – they would not have thought mine a morose or an unsocial nature!

On first glance, this series of imagined pictures merely demonstrates Silverman's growing diffidence and his willingness to sacrifice his own happiness to protect those for whom he cares, but, on second glance, the words of his description reveal disturbing connotations. The young girl whom he admires, and avoids because he tells himself that she might catch the fever of which his parents died, would hardly have felt easy if she could have seen him 'gliding out from behind the ghostly statue', peeping at her birthday festivities from the darkened ruin, and furtively creeping up the stairs to his bed. Had the farmer who scolds him for not being sociable literally been able to read the boy's heart, he undoubtedly would have wondered why George Silverman did not discuss his fear of contamination openly, or at least find a brighter alternative to the party than Hoghton Towers after dark. Silverman himself considers the episode a significant one, and he uses it as an analogy for the later life which he recalls at college:

I can see others in the sunlight; I can see our boats' crews and our athletic young men on the glistening water, or speckled with the moving lights of sunlit leaves; but I myself am always in the shadow looking on. Not unsympathetically, – God forbid! – but looking on, alone, much as I looked at Sylvia from the shadows of the ruined house, or looked at the red gleam shining through the farmer's windows, and listened to the fall of dancing feet, when all the ruin was dark that night in the quadrangle.

The thought of himself as 'always in the shadow looking on' indicates the angle from which he gathers his impressions of life. Like a *voyeur*, he shrinks from involvement yet maintains that he intends no harm.

Ultimately, however, the conflicting evaluations evoked by this monologue are juxtaposed so subtly that they cannot be definitively resolved. Silverman presents his view of his life persuasively, and final judgement of his personality remains in doubt; awareness of his limitations is balanced by compassion for his dilemma. In this work, Dickens has presented one of his favourite and generally admirable situations – that of self-sacrificing renunciation[18] – but

18. George H. Ford, *Dickens and His Readers: Aspects of Novel-Criticism since 1836* (1955; reprinted New York: Norton, 1965), p. 67 and note. I have discussed this monologue at greater length in 'The Equivocal Explanation of

he has intentionally complicated a reader's understanding of this situation through his chosen narrative technique. Like Conrad's Jim, Dickens's Silverman seems designed to remain an enigmatic reflection of the ambiguity of human existence.

From Gabriel Grub's reformed conviction that 'it was a very decent and respectable sort of world after all' to George Silverman's anguished perception that the world he so steadfastly renounces is neither understanding nor just, the short writings included here reveal Dickens's increasingly pessimistic preoccupation with the problems of dwelling in society and the divisions within the individual self. Viewed from one direction, they reflect the growing loss of illusions familiar to readers of his later novels, yet they also reveal startling flashes of comic, holiday exuberance with late characters from the Christmas numbers like the Boy at Mugby and Mrs Lirriper or Doctor Marigold, the inherently generous lover of material possessions, conceived just after the sombre manifestations of human greed in *Our Mutual Friend*. Forster remarked about Doctor Marigold's monologue that 'It expressed, as perfectly as anything he has ever done, that which constitutes in itself very much of the genius of all his writing, the wonderful neighbourhood in this life of ours, of serious and humorous things; the laughter close to the pathos, but never touching it with ridicule.' In varying ways, this assessment suggests the most important element of his friend's short fiction. Here, far more freely than in his novels, Dickens felt himself able to unleash the unique combination of talents which formed 'the genius of all his writing', to arouse pathos, to evoke laughter, and to attempt to hold the two in equilibrium. Here he showed most intensely the quality of fancy, which he never firmly defined yet sensed as a primary aspect of his art. Thus, he felt quite free to escape momentarily from actuality or soften it with emotion, to transform fact through the power of a perceiving eye, and to experiment with techniques of narrating perspectives on the ordinary world. In the process, he explored corners of the human mind – penetrating, as

Dickens' George Silverman', *Dickens Studies Annual*, ed. Robert B. Partlow, Jr, vol. III (Carbondale, Ill.: Southern Illinois University Press, 1974), pp. 134–43, 239–40.

all our nightmares and daydreams do, beyond the realm of possible experience, capturing evanescent impressions of the moment, demonstrating the way in which our personalities are inexorably manifested in our words. At their best, the results not only illuminate the novels that have paradoxically overshadowed them; they are multicoloured lights which are fascinating in themselves.

SELECT BIBLIOGRAPHY

THE standard biographies of Dickens are those by Edgar Johnson, *Charles Dickens: His Tragedy and Triumph*, 2 vols. (New York: Simon and Schuster, 1952) and John Forster, *The Life of Charles Dickens*, ed. J. W. T. Ley (London: Cecil Palmer, 1928). The most complete version of Dickens's letters is the three-volume edition, *The Letters of Charles Dickens* edited by Walter Dexter (London: Nonesuch Press, 1938) as part of the limited Nonesuch Edition of Dickens's works. A much more comprehensive collection of the letters is being published; it is the Pilgrim Edition, edited by Madeline House and Graham Storey, who are joined by Kathleen Tillotson in the third volume, and published by the Clarendon Press, Oxford. Volumes 1 (1965), 2 (1969), and 3 (1974), covering the years 1820–43, have so far been published. The following studies offer useful insights from diverse directions into the subject of Dickens's short fiction.

BARRY D. BART, '"George Silverman's Explanation"', *Dickensian*, vol. 60 (1964), pp. 48–51.

JOHN BUTT, 'Dickens's Christmas Books', *Pope, Dickens and Others* (Edinburgh: Edinburgh University Press, 1969), pp. 127–48.

JOHN BUTT and KATHLEEN TILLOTSON, *Dickens at Work* (London: Methuen, 1957). This is a discussion of Dickens's methods of composition which includes a chapter dealing with his revisions to *Sketches by Boz*.

G. K. CHESTERTON, *Charles Dickens* (London: Methuen, 1906).

P[HILIP] A. W. COLLINS, 'Queen Mab's Chariot Among the Steam Engines: Dickens and "Fancy"', *English Studies*, vol. 42 (1961), pp. 78–90.

PHILIP COLLINS, *Dickens and Crime*, 2nd ed. (1964; reprinted Bloomington Ind.: Indiana University Press, 1968).

PERCY FITZGERALD, *Memories of Charles Dickens with an Account of 'Household Words' and 'All the Year Round' and of the Contributors Thereto* (London: Simpkin, Marshall, Hamilton, Kent, 1913).

DUDLEY FLAMM, 'The Prosecutor Within: Dickens's Final Explanation', *Dickensian*, vol. 66 (1970), pp. 16–23 (a discussion of 'George Silverman's Explanation').

GEORGE H. FORD, *Dickens and His Readers: Aspects of Novel-Criticism since 1836* (1955; reprinted New York: Norton, 1965).

GEORGE H. FORD, 'Introduction' to *David Copperfield* (Boston, 1958), reprinted in *The Dickens Critics*, ed. George H. Ford and Lauriat Lane, Jr (Ithaca, N.Y.: Cornell University Press, 1961), pp. 349–65.

SIGMUND FREUD, 'The "Uncanny"', *Collected Papers*, authorized translation under the supervision of Joan Riviere, vol. IV (1925; reprinted London: Hogarth Press, 1953), pp. 368–407.

VIRGIL GRILLO, *Charles Dickens' 'Sketches by Boz': End in the Beginning* (Boulder, Col.: Colorado Associated University Press, 1974).

GERALD G. GRUBB, 'The Personal and Literary Relationships of Dickens and Poe', *Nineteenth-Century Fiction*, vol. 5 (1950) part 1, pp. 1–22; part 2, pp. 101–20; part 3, pp. 209–21.

ROBERT HAMILTON, 'The Creative Eye: Dickens as Essayist', *Dickensian*, vol. 64 (1968), pp. 36–42.

BARBARA HARDY, 'Dickens's Storytellers', *Dickensian*, vol. 69 (1973), 71–78 (primarily about Dickens's novels but relevant to his short fiction).

WENDELL V. HARRIS, 'English Short Fiction in the Nineteenth Century', *Studies in Short Fiction*, vol. 6 (1968), pp. 1–93.

ROBERT LANGBAUM, *The Poetry of Experience: The Dramatic Monologue in Modern Literary Tradition* (1957; reprinted New York: Norton, 1963).

J. HILLIS MILLER, 'The Fiction of Realism: *Sketches by Boz, Oliver Twist*, and Cruikshank's Illustrations', *Dickens Centennial Essays*, ed. Ada Nisbet and Blake Nevius (Berkeley: University of California Press, 1971), pp. 85–153.

SYLVÈRE MONOD, *Dickens romancier* (Paris: Hachette, 1953); translated and revised by the author as *Dickens the Novelist* (Norman, Okla.: University of Oklahoma Press, 1968).

GEORGE ORWELL, 'Charles Dickens', *The Collected Essays, Journalism and Letters of George Orwell*, ed. Sonia Orwell and Ian Angus, vol. 1 (Harmondsworth: Penguin, 1970), pp. 454–504.

ROBERT L. PATTEN, '"The Story-weaver at His Loom": Dickens and the Beginning of *The Old Curiosity Shop*', *Dickens the Craftsman*, ed. Robert B. Partlow, Jr (Carbondale, Ill.: Southern Illinois University Press, 1970), pp. 44–64, 191–3, 205.

ROBERT L. PATTEN (ed.), Charles Dickens, *The Posthumous Papers of The Pickwick Club* (Harmondsworth: Penguin, 1972).

MARIO PRAZ, *The Hero in Eclipse in Victorian Fiction*, translated by Angus Davidson (London: Oxford University Press, 1956).

MICHAEL SLATER (ed.), Charles Dickens, *The Christmas Books*, 2 vols. (Harmondsworth: Penguin, 1971).

HARRY STONE, 'Dickens's Tragic Universe: "George Silverman's Explanation"', *Studies in Philology*, vol. 55 (1958), pp. 86–97.

HARRY STONE, 'Dickens and Interior Monologue', *Philological Quarterly*, vol. 38 (1959), pp. 52–65.

HARRY STONE, 'Dickens' Artistry and *The Haunted Man*', *South Atlantic Quarterly*, vol. 61 (1962), pp. 492–505.

HARRY STONE (ed.), *Charles Dickens' Uncollected Writings from 'Household Words' 1850–1859*, 2 vols. (Bloomington, Ind.: Indiana University Press, 1968). This is an important collection of Dickens's 'composite' writings as well as a valuable source of information about his editorial policies and the periodical context which gave rise to much of his short fiction.

HARRY STONE, 'The Unknown Dickens: With a Sampling of Uncollected Writings', *Dickens Studies Annual*, ed. Robert B. Partlow, Jr, vol. I (Carbondale, Ill.: Southern Illinois University Press, 1970), pp. 1–22, 275–6.

HARVEY PETER SUCKSMITH, 'The Secret of Immediacy: Dickens' Debt to the Tale of Terror in *Blackwood's*', *Nineteenth-Century Fiction*, vol. 26 (1971), pp. 145–57.

DEBORAH ALLEN THOMAS, 'The Equivocal Explanation of Dickens' George Silverman', *Dickens Studies Annual*, ed. Robert B. Partlow, Jr, vol. III (Carbondale, Ill.: Southern Illinois University Press, 1974), pp. 134–43, 239–40.

DEBORAH A[LLEN] THOMAS, 'Contributors to the Christmas Numbers of *Household Words* and *All the Year Round*, 1850–1867', *Dickensian*, part 1, vol. 69 (1973), pp. 163–72; part 2, vol. 70 (1974), pp. 21–29.

SELECT BIBLIOGRAPHY

DOROTHY VAN GHENT, 'The Dickens World: A View from Todgers's,' *Sewanee Review*, vol. 58 (1950), pp. 419–38; reprinted in *The Dickens Critics*, ed. George H. Ford and Lauriat Lane, Jr (Ithaca, N.Y.: Cornell University Press, 1961), pp. 213–32.

VIRGINIA WOOLF, '*David Copperfield*', *Collected Essays*, vol. I (London: Hogarth Press, 1966), pp. 191–5.

Excerpts from Chesterton's and Orwell's discussions of Dickens and part of Poe's review of *The Old Curiosity Shop* (excluding his discussion of the machinery of *Master Humphrey's Clock*) are reprinted in *The Dickens Critics*, edited by George H. Ford and Lauriat Lane, Jr (Ithaca, N.Y.: Cornell University Press, 1961). Portions of Orwell's and Chesterton's treatments of Dickens appear in *Charles Dickens: A Critical Anthology*, edited by Stephen Wall (Harmondsworth: Penguin, 1970), along with Virginia Woolf's essay, and selections from Forster's *Life of Charles Dickens*, Van Ghent's 1953 study of *The English Novel: Form and Function* (analysing the style of *Great Expectations*), Butt and Tillotson's *Dickens at Work*, Stone's 'Dickens and Interior Monologue', and Monod's *Dickens the Novelist* (dealing with *David Copperfield*).

A NOTE ON THE TEXT

THE pieces presented here, which span Dickens's literary career, stem from a variety of locations. Some were collected and revised in successive editions during his lifetime; others were allowed to lapse into obscurity and added to his collected works only after his death in 1870.

'The Story of the Goblins who stole a Sexton' and 'The Baron of Grogzwig' are taken from the 1867 texts of *Pickwick Papers* and *Nicholas Nickleby* which Dickens prepared for the Charles Dickens Edition of his writings, the edition which incorporates his last, although sometimes haphazard, revisions before his death. The selections from *Sketches by Boz* and *The Uncommercial Traveller* as well as from *American Notes, and Reprinted Pieces* ('A Christmas Tree', 'A Flight', 'Our School', and 'Lying Awake') are also based on the Charles Dickens Edition (1868). The texts of 'To Be Read at Dusk' and 'George Silverman's Explanation' are those of the first editions – the *Keepsake* (1852) and the *Atlantic Monthly* (1868). 'George Silverman's Explanation' was serialized in the January, February, and March 1868 issues of the *Atlantic Monthly*, and the breaks between parts are indicated here by asterisks. 'A Confession Found in a Prison in the Time of Charles the Second', with Cattermole's illustration, follows the text of the first volume edition of *Master Humphrey's Clock* (1840–41).

The selections from *Somebody's Luggage*, *Mrs Lirriper's Lodgings*, *Mrs Lirriper's Legacy*, *Doctor Marigold's Prescriptions*, and *Mugby Junction* are based on the texts of the extra Christmas numbers of *All the Year Round*, 1862–6. As Harry Stone has pointed out in his edition of *Charles Dickens' Uncollected Writings from 'Household Words' 1850–1859*, Dickens modified these pieces along with some from *Household Words* for the special Diamond Edition of his works, published in the United States in 1867 at the time of a visit by Dickens,[1] and an argument might thus be made for adhering to this version. However, the *All the Year Round* texts

1. *Charles Dickens' Uncollected Writings from 'Household Words' 1850–1859* (Bloomington, Ind.: Indiana University Press, 1968), vol. II, p. 542.

containing Dickens's handwritten changes now located in the Berg Collection of the New York Public Library indicate that Dickens performed some drastic surgery in making his selections for the Diamond Edition. For example, the framework of *Doctor Marigold's Prescriptions* becomes a single monologue; the word 'prescriptions' vanishes from the title along with the humorous chapter headings – changes which weaken the joke about Marigold's medical skills on which the work is based; and the extended comic allusion to the *All the Year Round* format at the end of the first section disappears. It is difficult to appreciate these works fully apart from their original contexts, and a modern edition of the complete Christmas numbers from *Household Words* and *All the Year Round* is needed. In the meantime, the present selections are based on the first versions of these unusual pieces in order to recapture, as far as possible, their original vitality.

In each case, the specified text has been consistently followed, although a few obvious printer's errors have been silently corrected, and a few typographic conventions have been amended (for example, the full stops which Dickens placed after titles have been deleted). Likewise, in keeping with Penguin house-style, single quotation marks have been used first, and full stops after terms like Mr have been omitted. There is inconsistency between the various texts in such matters as italicization of foreign words and some spellings: these have been left in their original forms. Asterisked footnotes are originals.

I wish to express my thanks to the staff of the New York Public Library for its assistance as well as to Professor George H. Ford and Dr Michael Slater for their generously given advice in the preparation of this edition.

TALES OF THE SUPERNATURAL

The Goblin and the Sexton

The Story of the Goblins who stole a Sexton

'In an old abbey town, down in this part of the country, a long, long while ago – so long, that the story must be a true one, because our great grandfathers implicitly believed it – there officiated as sexton and grave-digger in the churchyard, one Gabriel Grub. It by no means follows that because a man is a sexton, and constantly surrounded by the emblems of mortality, therefore he should be a morose and melancholy man; your undertakers are the merriest fellows in the world; and I once had the honour of being on intimate terms, with a mute, who in private life, and off duty, was as comical and jocose a little fellow as ever chirped out a devil-may-care song, without a hitch in his memory, or drained off the contents of a good stiff glass without stopping for breath. But, notwithstanding these precedents to the contrary, Gabriel Grub was an ill-conditioned, cross-grained, surly fellow – a morose and lonely man, who consorted with nobody but himself, and an old wicker bottle which fitted into his large deep waistcoat pocket – and who eyed each merry face, as it passed him by, with such a deep scowl of malice and ill-humour, as it was difficult to meet, without feeling something the worse for.

'A little before twilight, one Christmas Eve, Gabriel shouldered his spade, lighted his lantern, and betook himself towards the old churchyard; for he had got a grave to finish by next morning, and, feeling very low, he thought it might raise his spirits, perhaps, if he went on with his work at once. As he went his way, up the ancient street, he saw the cheerful light of the blazing fires gleam through the old casements, and heard the loud laugh and the cheerful shouts of those who were assembled around them; he marked the bustling preparations for next day's cheer, and smelt the numerous savoury odours consequent thereupon, as they steamed up from the kitchen windows in clouds. All this was gall and wormwood[1] to the heart of Gabriel Grub; and when groups of children, bounded out of the houses, tripped across the road, and were met, before they could knock at the opposite door, by half a dozen curly-headed little rascals who crowded round them as they flocked up-stairs to spend the evening in their Christmas games, Gabriel smiled grimly, and clutched the handle of his spade with a firmer grasp, as he thought of measles, scarlet-fever, thrush, hooping-cough, and a good many other sources of consolation besides.

'In this happy frame of mind, Gabriel strode along: returning a short, sullen growl to the good-humoured greetings of such of his neighbours as now and then passed him: until he turned into the dark lane which led to the churchyard. Now, Gabriel had been looking forward to reaching the dark lane, because it was, generally speaking, a nice, gloomy, mournful place, into which the towns-people did not much care to go, except in broad day-light, and when the sun was shining; consequently, he was not a little in-dignant to hear a young urchin roaring out some jolly song about a merry Christmas, in this very sanctuary, which had been called Coffin Lane ever since the days of the old abbey, and the time of the shaven-headed monks. As Gabriel walked on, and the voice drew nearer, he found it proceeded from a small boy, who was hurrying along, to join one of the little parties in the old street, and who, partly to keep himself company, and partly to prepare himself for the occasion, was shouting out the song at the highest pitch of his lungs. So Gabriel waited until the boy came up, and then dodged him into a corner, and rapped him over the head with his lantern five or six times, to teach him to modulate his voice. And as the boy hurried away with his hand to his head, singing quite a different sort of tune, Gabriel Grub chuckled very heartily to himself, and entered the churchyard: locking the gate behind him.

'He took off his coat, put down his lantern, and getting into the unfinished grave, worked at it for an hour or so, with right good will. But the earth was hardened with the frost, and it was no very easy matter to break it up, and shovel it out; and although there was a moon, it was a very young one, and shed little light upon the grave, which was in the shadow of the church. At any other time, these obstacles would have made Gabriel Grub very moody and miserable, but he was so well pleased with having stopped the small boy's singing, that he took little heed of the scanty progress he had made, and looked down into the grave, when he had finished work for the night, with grim satisfaction: murmuring as he gathered up his things:

> 'Brave lodgings for one, brave lodgings for one,
> A few feet of cold earth, when life is done;
> A stone at the head, a stone at the feet,
> A rich, juicy meal for the worms to eat;
> Rank grass over head, and damp clay around,
> Brave lodgings for one, these, in holy ground!'

'"Ho! ho!" laughed Gabriel Grub, as he sat himself down on a flat tombstone which was a favourite resting-place of his; and drew forth his wicker bottle. "A coffin at Christmas! A Christmas Box. Ho! ho! ho!"

'"Ho! ho! ho!" repeated a voice which sounded close behind him.

'Gabriel paused, in some alarm, in the act of raising the wicker bottle to his lips: and looked round. The bottom of the oldest grave about him, was not more still and quiet, than the churchyard in the pale moonlight. The cold hoarfrost glistened on the tombstones, and sparkled like rows of gems, among the stone carvings of the old church. The snow lay hard and crisp upon the ground; and spread over the thickly-strewn mounds of earth, so white and smooth a cover, that it seemed as if corpses lay there, hidden only by their winding sheets. Not the faintest rustle broke the profound tranquillity of the solemn scene. Sound itself appeared to be frozen up, all was so cold and still.

'"It was the echoes," said Gabriel Grub, raising the bottle to his lips again.

'"It was *not*," said a deep voice.

'Gabriel started up, and stood rooted to the spot with astonishment and terror; for his eyes rested on a form that made his blood run cold.

'Seated on an upright tombstone, close to him, was a strange unearthly figure, whom Gabriel felt at once, was no being of this world. His long fantastic legs which might have reached the ground, were cocked up, and crossed after a quaint, fantastic fashion; his sinewy arms were bare; and his hands rested on his knees. On his short round body, he wore a close covering, ornamented with small slashes; a short cloak dangled at his back; the collar was cut into curious peaks, which served the goblin in lieu of ruff or neckerchief; and his shoes curled up at his toes into long points. On his head, he wore a broad-brimmed sugar-loaf hat, garnished with a single feather. The hat was covered with the white frost; and the goblin looked as if he had sat on the same tombstone very comfortably, for two or three hundred years. He was sitting perfectly still; his tongue was put out, as if in derision; and he was grinning at Gabriel Grub with such a grin as only a goblin could call up.

'"It was *not* the echoes," said the goblin.

'Gabriel Grub was paralysed, and could make no reply.

'"What do you do here on Christmas Eve?" said the goblin sternly.

'"I came to dig a grave, sir," stammered Gabriel Grub.

'"What man wanders among graves and churchyards on such a night as this?" cried the goblin.

'"Gabriel Grub! Gabriel Grub!" screamed a wild chorus of voices that seemed to fill the churchyard. Gabriel looked fearfully round – nothing was to be seen.

'"What have you got in that bottle?" said the goblin.

'"Hollands, sir," replied the sexton, trembling more than ever; for he had bought it of the smugglers, and he thought that perhaps his questioner might be in the excise department of the goblins.

'"Who drinks Hollands alone, and in a churchyard, on such a night as this?" said the goblin.

'"Gabriel Grub! Gabriel Grub!" exclaimed the wild voices again.

'The goblin leered maliciously at the terrified sexton, and then raising his voice, exclaimed:

'"And who, then, is our fair and lawful prize?"

'To this inquiry the invisible chorus replied, in a strain that sounded like the voices of many choristers singing to the mighty swell of the old church organ – a strain that seemed borne to the sexton's ears upon a wild wind, and to die away as it passed onward; but the burden of the reply was still the same, "Gabriel Grub! Gabriel Grub!"

'The goblin grinned a broader grin than before, as he said, "Well, Gabriel, what do you say to this?"

'The sexton gasped for breath.

'"What do you think of this, Gabriel?" said the goblin, kicking up his feet in the air on either side of the tombstone, and looking at the turned-up points with as much complacency as if he had been contemplating the most fashionable pair of Wellington's in all Bond Street.

'"It's – it's – very curious, sir," replied the sexton, half dead with fright: "very curious, and very pretty, but I think I'll go back and finish my work, sir, if you please."

'"Work!" said the goblin, "what work?"

'"The grave, sir; making the grave," stammered the sexton.

'"Oh, the grave, eh?" said the goblin; "who makes graves at a time when all other men are merry, and takes a pleasure in it?"

'Again the mysterious voices replied, "Gabriel Grub! Gabriel Grub!"

'"I'm afraid my friends want you, Gabriel," said the goblin, thrusting his tongue further into his cheek than ever – and a most astonishing tongue it was – "I'm afraid my friends want you, Gabriel," said the goblin.

'"Under favour, sir," replied the horror-stricken sexton, "I don't think they can, sir; they don't know me, sir; I don't think the gentlemen have ever seen me, sir."

'"Oh yes they have," replied the goblin; "we know the man with the sulky face and grim scowl, that came down the street to-night, throwing his evil looks at the children, and grasping his burying spade the tighter. We know the man who struck the boy in the envious malice of his heart, because the boy could be merry, and he could not. We know him, we know him."

'Here the goblin gave a loud shrill laugh, which the echoes returned twenty-fold: and throwing his legs up in the air, stood upon his head, or rather upon the very point of his sugar-loaf hat, on the narrow edge of the tombstone: whence he threw a somerset with extraordinary agility, right to the sexton's feet, at which he planted himself in the attitude in which tailors generally sit upon the shopboard.

'"I – I – am afraid I must leave you, sir," said the sexton, making an effort to move.

'"Leave us!" said the goblin, "Gabriel Grub going to leave us. Ho! ho! ho!"

'As the goblin laughed, the sexton observed, for one instant, a brilliant illumination within the windows of the church, as if the whole building were lighted up; it disappeared, the organ pealed forth a lively air, and whole troops of goblins, the very counterpart of the first one, poured into the churchyard, and began playing at leap-frog with the tombstones: never stopping for an instant to take breath, but "overing" the highest among them, one after the other, with the utmost marvellous dexterity. The first goblin was a most astonishing leaper, and none of the others could come near him; even in the extremity of his terror the sexton could not help observing, that while his friends were content to leap over the common-sized gravestones, the first one took the family vaults, iron railings and all, with as much ease as if they had been so many street posts.

'At last the game reached to a most exciting pitch; the organ played quicker and quicker; and the goblins leaped faster and faster: coiling themselves up, rolling head over heels upon the ground, and bounding over the tombstones like foot-balls. The sexton's brain whirled round with the rapidity of the motion he beheld, and his legs reeled beneath him, as the spirits flew before his eyes: when the goblin king, suddenly darting towards him, laid his hand upon his collar, and sank with him through the earth.

'When Gabriel Grub had had time to fetch his breath, which the rapidity of his descent had for the moment taken away, he found himself in what appeared to be a large cavern, surrounded on all sides by crowds of goblins, ugly and grim; in the centre of the room, on an elevated seat, was stationed his friend of the churchyard; and close beside him stood Gabriel Grub himself, without power of motion.

'"Cold to-night," said the king of the goblins, "very cold. A glass of something warm, here!"

'At this command, half a dozen officious goblins, with a perpetual smile upon their faces, whom Gabriel Grub imagined to be courtiers, on that account, hastily disappeared, and presently returned with a goblet of liquid fire, which they presented to the king.

'"Ah!" cried the goblin, whose cheeks and throat were transparent, as he tossed down the flame, "This warms one, indeed! Bring a bumper of the same, for Mr Grub."

'It was in vain for the unfortunate sexton to protest that he was not in the habit of taking anything warm at night; one of the goblins held him while another poured the blazing liquid down his throat; the whole assembly screeched with laughter as he coughed and choked, and wiped away the tears which gushed plentifully from his eyes, after swallowing the burning draught.

'"And now," said the king, fantastically poking the taper corner of his sugar-loaf hat into the sexton's eye, and thereby occasioning him the most exquisite pain: "And now, show the man of misery and gloom, a few of the pictures from our own great storehouse!"

'As the goblin said this, a thick cloud which obscured the remoter end of the cavern, rolled gradually away, and disclosed, apparently at a great distance, a small and scantily furnished, but neat and clean apartment. A crowd of little children were gathered round a bright fire, clinging to their mother's gown, and gambolling around her chair. The mother occasionally rose, and drew aside the window-curtain, as if to look for some expected object; a frugal meal was ready spread upon the table; and an elbow chair was placed near the fire. A knock was heard at the door: the mother opened it, and the children crowded round her, and clapped their hands for joy, as their father entered. He was wet and weary, and shook the snow from his garments, as the children crowded round him, and seizing his cloak, hat, stick, and gloves, with busy zeal, ran with them from the room. Then, as he sat down to his meal before the fire, the children climbed about his knee, and the mother sat by his side, and all seemed happiness and comfort.

'But a change came upon the view, almost imperceptibly. The scene was altered to a small bed-room, where the fairest and youngest child lay dying; the roses had fled from his cheek, and the light from his eye; and even as the sexton looked upon him with an interest he had never felt or known before, he died. His young brothers and sisters crowded round his little bed, and seized his tiny hand, so cold and heavy; but they shrunk back from its touch, and looked with awe on his infant face; for calm and tranquil as it was, and sleeping in rest and peace as the beautiful child seemed to be, they saw that he was dead, and they knew that he was an Angel looking down upon, and blessing them, from a bright and happy Heaven.

'Again the light cloud passed across the picture, and again the subject changed. The father and mother were old and helpless now, and the number of those about them was diminished more than half; but content and cheerfulness sat on every face, and beamed in every eye, as they crowded round the fireside, and told and listened to old stories of earlier and bygone days. Slowly and peacefully, the father sank into the grave, and, soon after, the sharer of all his cares and troubles followed him to a place of rest. The few, who yet survived them, knelt by their tomb, and watered the green turf which covered it, with their tears; then rose, and turned away: sadly and mournfully, but not with bitter cries, or despairing lamentations, for they knew that they should one day meet again; and once more they mixed with the busy world, and their content and cheerfulness were restored. The cloud settled upon the picture, and concealed it from the sexton's view.

'"What do you think of *that*?" said the goblin, turning his large face towards Gabriel Grub.

'Gabriel murmured out something about its being very pretty, and looked somewhat ashamed, as the goblin bent his fiery eyes upon him.

'"*You* a miserable man!" said the goblin, in a tone of excessive contempt. "You!" He appeared disposed to add more, but indignation choked his utterance, so he lifted up one of his very pliable legs, and flourishing it above his head a little, to insure his aim, administered a good sound kick to Gabriel Grub; immediately after which, all the goblins in waiting, crowded round the wretched sexton, and kicked him without mercy: according to the established and invariable custom of courtiers upon earth, who kick whom royalty kicks, and hug whom royalty hugs.

'"Show him some more!" said the king of the goblins.

'At these words, the cloud was dispelled, and a rich and beautiful landscape was disclosed to view – there is just such another, to this day, within half a mile of the old abbey town. The sun shone out from the clear blue sky, the water sparkled beneath his rays, and the trees looked greener, and the flowers more gay, beneath his cheering influence. The water rippled on, with a pleasant sound; the trees rustled in the light wind that murmured among their leaves; the birds sang upon the boughs; and the lark carolled on high, her welcome to the morning. Yes, it was morning: the bright, balmy morning of summer; the minutest leaf, the smallest blade of grass, was instinct with life. The ant crept forth to her daily toil, the butterfly fluttered and basked in the warm rays of the sun; myriads of insects spread their transparent wings, and revelled in their brief but happy existence. Man walked forth, elated with the scene; and all was brightness and splendour.

"'*You* a miserable man!" said the king of the goblins, in a more contemptuous tone than before. And again the king of the goblins gave his leg a flourish; again it descended on the shoulders of the sexton; and again the attendant goblins imitated the example of their chief.

'Many a time the cloud went and came, and many a lesson it taught to Gabriel Grub, who, although his shoulders smarted with pain from the frequent applications of the goblin's feet, looked on with an interest that nothing could diminish. He saw that men who worked hard, and earned their scanty bread with lives of labour, were cheerful and happy; and that to the most ignorant, the sweet face of nature was a never-failing source of cheerfulness and joy. He saw those who had been delicately nurtured, and tenderly brought up, cheerful under privations, and superior to suffering, that would have crushed many of a rougher grain, because they bore within their own bosoms the materials of happiness, content-ment, and peace. He saw that women, the tenderest and most fragile of all God's creatures, were the oftenest superior to sorrow, adversity, and distress; and he saw that it was because they bore, in their own hearts, an inexhaustible well-spring of affection and devotion. Above all, he saw that men like himself, who snarled at the mirth and cheerfulness of others, were the foulest weeds on the fair surface of the earth; and setting all the good of the world against the evil, he came to the conclusion that it was a very decent and respectable sort of world after all. No sooner had he formed it, than the cloud which closed over the last picture, seemed to settle on his senses, and lull him to repose. One by one, the goblins faded from his sight; and as the last one disappeared, he sunk to sleep.

'The day had broken when Gabriel Grub awoke, and found himself lying, at full length on the flat gravestone in the church-yard, with the wicker bottle lying empty by his side, and his coat, spade, and lantern, all well whitened by the last night's frost, scattered on the ground. The stone on which he had first seen the goblin seated, stood bolt upright before him, and the grave at which he had worked, the night before, was not far off. At first, he began to doubt the reality of his adventures, but the acute pain in his shoulders when he attempted to rise, assured him that the kicking of the goblins was certainly not ideal. He was staggered again, by observing no traces of footsteps in the snow on which the goblins had played at leap-frog with the gravestones, but he speedily accounted for this circumstance when he remembered that, being spirits, they would leave no visible impression behind them. So, Gabriel Grub got on his feet as well as he could, for the pain in his back; and brushing the frost off his coat, put it on and turned his face towards the town.

'But he was an altered man, and he could not bear the thought of returning to a place where his repentance would be scoffed at, and his reformation disbelieved. He hesitated for a few moments; and then turned away to wander where he might, and seek his bread elsewhere.

'The lantern, the spade, and the wicker bottle, were found, that day, in the churchyard. There were a great many speculations about the sexton's fate, at first, but it was speedily determined that he had been carried away by the goblins; and there were not wanting some very credible witnesses who had distinctly seen him whisked through the air on the back of a chestnut horse blind of one eye, with the hind-quarters of a lion, and the tail of a bear. At length all this was devoutly believed; and the new sexton used to exhibit to the curious, for a trifling emolument, a good-sized piece of the church weathercock which had been accidentally kicked off by the aforesaid horse in his aërial flight, and picked up by himself in the churchyard, a year or two afterwards.

'Unfortunately, these stories were somewhat disturbed by the unlooked-for reappearance of Gabriel Grub himself, some ten years afterwards, a ragged, contented, rheumatic old man. He told his story to the clergyman, and also to the mayor; and in course of time it began to be received, as a matter of history, in which form it has continued down to this very day. The believers in the weather-cock tale, having misplaced their confidence once, were not easily prevailed upon to part with it again, so they looked as wise as they could, shrugged their shoulders, touched their foreheads, and murmured something about Gabriel Grub having drunk all the Hollands, and then fallen asleep on the flat tombstone; and they affected to explain what he supposed he had witnessed in the goblin's cavern, by saying that he had seen the world, and grown wiser. But this opinion, which was by no means a popular one at any time, gradually died off; and be the matter how it may, as Gabriel Grub was afflicted with rheumatism to the end of his days, this story has at least one moral, if it teach no better one – and that is, that if a man turn sulky and drink by himself at Christmas time, he may make up his mind to be not a bit the better for it: let the spirits be never so good, or let them be even as many degrees beyond proof, as those which Gabriel Grub saw in the goblin's cavern.'

The Baron of Grogzwig

'THE Baron Von Koëldwethout, of Grogzwig in Germany, was as likely a young baron as you would wish to see. I needn't say that he lived in a castle, because that's of course; neither need I say that he lived in an old castle; for what German baron ever lived in a new one? There were many strange circumstances connected with this venerable building, among which, not the least startling and mysterious were, that when the wind blew, it rumbled in the chimneys, or even howled among the trees in the neighbouring forest; and that when the moon shone, she found her way through certain small loopholes in the wall, and actually made some parts of the wide halls and galleries quite light, while she left others in gloomy shadow. I believe that one of the baron's ancestors, being short of money, had inserted a dagger in a gentleman who called one night to ask his way, and it *was* supposed that these miraculous occurrences took place in consequence. And yet I hardly know how that could have been, either, because the baron's ancestor, who was an amiable man, felt very sorry afterwards for having been so rash, and laying violent hands upon a quantity of stone and timber which belonged to a weaker baron, built a chapel as an apology, and so took a receipt from Heaven, in full of all demands.

'Talking of the baron's ancestor puts me in mind of the baron's great claims to respect, on the score of his pedigree. I am afraid to say, I am sure, how many ancestors the baron had; but I know that he had a great many more than any other man of his time; and I only wish that he had lived in these latter days, that he might have had more. It is a very hard thing upon the great men of past centuries, that they should have come into the world so soon, because a man who was born three or four hundred years ago, cannot reasonably be expected to have had as many relations before him, as a man who is born now. The last man, whoever he is – and he may be a cobbler or some low vulgar dog for aught we know – will have a longer pedigree than the greatest nobleman now alive; and I contend that this is not fair.

'Well, but the Baron Von Koëldwethout of Grogzwig! He was a fine swarthy fellow, with dark hair and large moustachios, who rode a-hunting in clothes of Lincoln green, with russet boots on his feet, and a bugle slung over his shoulder, like the guard of a long stage. When he blew this bugle, four-and-twenty other gentlemen of inferior rank, in Lincoln green a little coarser, and russet boots with a little thicker soles, turned out directly; and away galloped the whole train, with spears in their hands like lackered area railings, to hunt down the boars, or perhaps encounter a bear: in which latter case the baron killed him first, and greased his whiskers with him afterwards.

'This was a merry life for the Baron of Grogzwig, and a merrier still for the baron's retainers, who drank Rhine wine every night till they fell under the table, and then had the bottles on the floor, and called for pipes. Never were such jolly, roystering, rollicking, merry-making blades, as the jovial crew of Grogzwig.

'But the pleasures of the table, or the pleasures of under the table, require a little variety; especially when the same five-and-twenty people sit daily down to the same board, to discuss the same subjects, and tell the same stories. The baron grew weary, and wanted excitement. He took to quarrelling with his gentlemen, and tried kicking two or three of them every day after dinner. This was a pleasant change at first; but it became monotonous after a week or so, and the baron felt quite out of sorts, and cast about, in despair, for some new amusement.

'One night, after a day's sport in which he had outdone Nimrod or Gillingwater,[1] and slaughtered "another fine bear", and brought him home in triumph, the Baron Von Koëldwethout sat moodily at the head of his table, eyeing the smoky roof of the hall with a discontented aspect. He swallowed huge bumpers of wine, but the more he swallowed, the more he frowned. The gentlemen who had been honoured with the dangerous distinction of sitting on his right and left, imitated him to a miracle in the drinking, and frowned at each other.

'"I will!" cried the baron suddenly, smiting the table with his right hand, and twirling his moustache with his left. "Fill to the Lady of Grogzwig!"

'The four-and-twenty Lincoln greens turned pale, with the exception of their four-and-twenty noses, which were unchangeable.

'"I said to the Lady of Grogzwig," repeated the baron, looking round the board.

'"To the Lady of Grogzwig!" shouted the Lincoln greens; and down their four-and-twenty throats went four-and-twenty imperial pints of such rare old hock, that they smacked their eight-and-forty lips, and winked again.

'"The fair daughter of the Baron Von Swillenhausen," said Koëldwethout, condescending to explain. "We will demand her in marriage of her father, ere the sun goes down tomorrow. If he refuse our suit, we will cut off his nose."

'A hoarse murmur arose from the company; every man touched, first the hilt of his sword, and then the tip of his nose, with appalling significance.

'What a pleasant thing filial piety is, to contemplate! If the daughter of the Baron Von Swillenhausen had pleaded a preoccupied heart, or fallen at her father's feet and corned[2] them in salt tears, or only fainted away, and complimented the old gentleman in frantic ejaculations, the odds are a hundred to one, but Swillenhausen castle would have been turned out at window, or rather the baron turned out at window, and the castle demolished. The damsel held her peace, however, when an early messenger bore the request of Von Koëldwethout next morning, and modestly retired to her chamber, from the casement of she watched the coming of the suitor and his retinue. She was no sooner assured that the horseman with the large moustachios was her proffered husband, than she hastened to her father's presence, and expressed her readiness to sacrifice herself to secure his peace. The venerable baron caught his child to his arms, and shed a wink of joy.

'There was great feasting at the castle, that day. The four-and-twenty Lincoln greens of Von Koëldwethout exchanged vows of eternal friendship with twelve Lincoln greens of Von Swillenhausen, and promised the old baron that they would drink his wine "Till all was blue"[3] – meaning probably until their whole countenances had acquired the same tint as their noses. Everybody slapped everybody else's back, when the time for parting came; and the Baron Von Koëldwethout and his followers rode gaily home.

'For six mortal weeks, the bears and boars had a holiday. The houses of Koëldwethout and Swillenhausen were united; the spears rusted; and the baron's bugle grew hoarse for lack of blowing.

'Those were great times for the four-and-twenty; but, alas! their high and palmy days had taken boots to themselves, and were already walking off.

'"My dear," said the baroness.

'"My love," said the baron.

'"Those coarse, noisy men –"

'"Which, ma'am?" said the baron starting.

'The baroness pointed, from the window at which they stood, to the courtyard beneath, where the unconscious Lincoln greens were taking a copious stirrup-cup, preparatory to issuing forth, after a boar or two.

'"My hunting train, ma'am," said the baron.

'"Disband them, love," murmured the baroness.

'"Disband them!" cried the baron, in amazement.

'"To please me, love," replied the baroness.

'"To please the devil, ma'am," answered the baron.

'Whereupon the baroness uttered a great cry, and swooned away at the baron's feet.

'What could the baron do? He called for the lady's maid, and roared for the doctor; and then, rushing into the yard, kicked the two Lincoln greens who were the most used to it, and cursing the others all round, bade them go – but never mind where, I don't know the German for it, or I would put it delicately that way.

'It is not for me to say by what means or by what degrees, some wives manage to keep down some husbands as they do, although I may have my private opinion on the subject, and may think that no Member of Parliament ought to be married, inasmuch as three married members out of every four, must vote according to their wives' consciences (if there be such things), and not according to their own. All I need say, just now, is, that the Baroness Von Koëldwethout somehow or other acquired great control over the Baron Von Koëldwethout, and that, little by little, and bit by bit, and day by day, and year by year, the baron got the worst of some disputed question, or was slily unhorsed from some old hobby; and that by the time he was a fat hearty fellow of forty-eight or there-abouts, he had no feasting, no revelry, no hunting train, and no hunting – nothing in short that he liked, or used to have; and that, although he was as fierce as a lion and as bold as brass, he was decidedly snubbed and put down, by his own lady, in his own castle of Grogzwig.

'Nor was this the whole extent of the baron's misfortunes. About a year after his nuptials, there came into the world a lusty young baron, in whose honour a great many fireworks were let off, and a great many dozens of wine drunk; but next year there came a young baroness, and next year another young baron, and so on, every year, either a baron or baroness (and one year both together), until the baron found himself the father of a small family of twelve. Upon every one of these anniversaries, the venerable Baroness Von Swillenhausen was nervously sensitive for the well-being of her child the Baroness Von Koëldwethout; and although it was not found that the good lady ever did anything material towards contributing to her child's recovery, still she made it a point of duty to be as nervous as possible at the castle at Grogzwig, and to divide her time between moral observations on the baron's housekeeping, and bewailing the hard lot of her unhappy daughter. And if the Baron of Grogzwig, a little hurt and irritated at this, took heart, and ventured to suggest that his wife was at least no worse off than the wives of other barons, the Baroness Von Swillenhausen begged all persons to take notice, that nobody but she, sympathized with her dear daughter's sufferings; upon which, her relations and friends remarked, that to be sure she did cry a great deal more than her son-in-law, and that if there were a hard-hearted brute alive, it was that Baron of Grogzwig.

'The poor baron bore it all, as long as he could, and when he could bear it no longer lost his appetite and his spirits, and sat himself gloomily and dejectedly down. But there were worse troubles yet in store for him, and as they came on, his melancholy and sadness increased. Times changed. He got into debt. The Grogzwig coffers ran low, though the Swillenhausen family had looked upon them as inexhaustible; and just when the baroness was on the point of making a thirteenth addition to the family pedigree, Von Koëldwethout discovered that he had no means of replenishing them.

'"I don't see what is to be done," said the baron. "I think I'll kill myself."

'This was a bright idea. The baron took an old hunting-knife from a cupboard hard by, and having sharpened it on his boot, made what boys call "an offer" at his throat.

'"Hem!" said the baron, stopping short. "Perhaps it's not sharp enough."

'The baron sharpened it again, and made another offer, when his hand was arrested by a loud screaming among the young barons and baronesses, who had a nursery in an upstairs tower with iron bars outside the window, to prevent their tumbling out into the moat.

'"If I had been a bachelor," said the baron sighing, "I might have done it fifty times over, without being interrupted. Hallo! Put a flask of wine and the largest pipe, in the little vaulted room behind the hall."

'One of the domestics, in a very kind manner, executed the baron's order in the course of half an hour or so, and Von Koëldwethout being apprised thereof, strode to the vaulted room, the walls of which, being of dark shining wood, gleamed in the light of the blazing logs which were piled upon the hearth. The bottle and pipe were ready, and, upon the whole, the place looked very comfortable.

'"Leave the lamp," said the baron.

'"Anything else, my lord?" inquired the domestic.

'"The room," replied the baron. The domestic obeyed, and the baron locked the door.

'"I'll smoke a last pipe," said the baron, "and then I'll be off." So, putting the knife upon the table till he wanted it, and tossing off a goodly measure of wine, the Lord of Grogzwig threw himself back in his chair, stretched his legs out before the fire, and puffed away.

'He thought about a great many things – about his present troubles and past days of bachelorship, and about the Lincoln greens, long since disappeared up and down the country, no one knew whither: with the exception of two who had been unfortunately beheaded, and four who had killed themselves with drinking. His mind was running upon bears and boars, when, in the process of draining his glass to the bottom, he raised his eyes, and saw, for the first time and with unbounded astonishment, that he was not alone.

'No, he was not; for, on the opposite side of the fire, there sat with folded arms a wrinkled hideous figure, with deeply sunk and bloodshot eyes, and an immensely long cadaverous face, shadowed by jagged and matted locks of coarse black hair. He wore a kind of tunic of a dull bluish colour, which, the baron observed, on regarding it attentively, was clasped or ornamented down the front, with coffin handles. His legs too, were encased in coffin plates as though in armour; and over his left shoulder he wore a short dusky cloak, which seemed made of remnant of some pall. He took no notice of the baron, but was intently eyeing the fire.

'"Halloa!" said the baron, stamping his foot to attract attention.

'"Halloa!" replied the stranger, moving his eyes towards the baron, but not his face or himself. "What now?"

'"What now!" replied the baron, nothing daunted by his hollow voice and lustreless eyes, "I should ask that question. How did you get here?"

'"Through the door," replied the figure.

'"What are you?" says the baron.

'"A man," replied the figure.

'"I don't believe it," says the baron.

'"Disbelieve it then," says the figure.

'"I will," rejoined the baron.

'The figure looked at the bold Baron of Grogzwig for some time, and then said familiarly,

'"There's no coming over you, I see. I'm not a man!"

'"What are you then?" asked the baron.

'"A genius," replied the figure.

'"You don't look much like one," returned the baron scornfully.

'"I am the Genius of Despair and Suicide," said the apparition. "Now you know me."

'With these words the apparition turned towards the baron, as if composing himself for a talk – and, what was very remarkable, was, that he threw his cloak aside, and displaying a stake, which was run through the centre of his body, pulled it out with a jerk, and laid it on the table, as composedly as if it had been a walking-stick.

'"Now," said the figure, glancing at the hunting-knife, "are you ready for me?"

'"Not quite," rejoined the baron; "I must finish this pipe first."

'"Look sharp then," said the figure.

'"You seem in a hurry," said the baron.

'"Why, yes, I am," answered the figure; "they're doing a pretty brisk business in my way, over in England and France just now, and my time is a good deal taken up."

'"Do you drink?" said the baron, touching the bottle with the bowl of his pipe.

'"Nine times out of ten, and then very hard," rejoined the figure, drily.

'"Never in moderation?" asked the baron.

'"Never," replied the figure, with a shudder, "that breeds cheerfulness."

'The baron took another look at his new friend, whom he thought an uncommonly queer customer, and at length inquired whether he took any active part in such little proceedings as that which he had in contemplation.

'"No," replied the figure evasively; "but I am always present."

'"Just to see fair, I suppose?" said the baron.

'"Just that," replied the figure playing with the stake, and examining the ferule.

'"Be as quick as you can, will you, for there's a young gentleman who is afflicted with too much money and leisure wanting me now, I find."

'"Going to kill himself because he has too much money!" exclaimed the baron, quite tickled: "Ha! ha! that's a good one." (This was the first time the baron had laughed for many a long day.)

'"I say," expostulated the figure, looking very much scared; "don't do that again."

'"Why not?" demanded the baron.

'"Because it gives me pain all over," replied the figure. "Sigh as much as you please; that does me good."

'The baron sighed mechanically, at the mention of the word; the figure, brightening up again, handed him the hunting-knife with the most winning politeness.

'"It's not a bad idea though," said the baron, feeling the edge of the weapon; "a man killing himself because he has too much money."

'"Pooh!" said the apparition, petulantly, "no better than a man's killing himself because he has none or little."

'Whether the genius unintentionally committed himself in saying this, or whether he thought the baron's mind was so thoroughly made up that it didn't matter what he said, I have no means of knowing. I only know that the baron stopped his hand, all of a sudden, opened his eyes wide, and looked as if quite a new light had come upon him for the first time.

'"Why, certainly," said Von Koëldwethout, "nothing is too bad to be retrieved."

'"Except empty coffers," cried the genius.

'"Well; but they may be one day filled again," said the baron.

'"Scolding wives," snarled the genius.

'"Oh! They may be made quiet," said the baron.

'"Thirteen children," shouted the genius.

'"Can't all go wrong, surely," said the baron.

'The genius was evidently growing very savage with the baron, for holding these opinions all at once; but he tried to laugh it off, and said if he would let him know when he had left off joking, he should feel obliged to him.

'"But I am not joking; I was never farther from it," remonstrated the baron.

'"Well, I am glad to hear that," said the genius, looking very grim, "because a joke, without any figure of speech, *is* the death of me. Come! Quit this dreary world at once."

'"I don't know," said the baron, playing with the knife; "it's a dreary one certainly, but I don't think yours is much better, for you have not the appearance of being particularly comfortable. That puts me in mind — what security have I, that I shall be any the better for going out of the world after all!" he cried, starting up; "I never thought of that."

'"Dispatch," cried the figure, gnashing its teeth.

'"Keep off!" said the baron. "I'll brood over miseries no longer, but put a good face on the matter, and try the fresh air and the bears again; and if that don't do, I'll talk to the baroness soundly, and cut the Von Swillenhausens dead." With this the baron fell into his chair, and laughed so loud and boisterously, that the room rang with it.

'The figure fell back a pace or two, regarding the baron meanwhile with a look of intense terror, and when he had ceased, caught up the stake, plunged it violently into its body, uttered a frightful howl, and disappeared.

'Von Koëldwethout never saw it again. Having once made up his mind to action, he soon brought the baroness and the Von Swillenhausens to reason, and died many years afterwards: not a rich man that I am aware of, but certainly a happy one: leaving behind him a numerous family, who had been carefully educated in bear- and boar-hunting under his own personal eye. And my advice to all men is, that if ever they become hipped and melancholy from similar causes (as very many men do), they look at both sides of the question, applying a magnifying glass to the best one; and if they still feel tempted to retire without leave, that they smoke a large pipe and drink a full bottle first, and profit by the laudable example of the baron of Grogzwig.'

A Confession Found in a Prison in the Time of Charles the Second

I HELD a lieutenant's commission in His Majesty's army and served abroad in the campaigns of 1677 and 1678. The treaty of Nimeguen being concluded, I returned home, and retiring from the service withdrew to a small estate lying a few miles east of London, which I had recently acquired in right of my wife.

This is the last night I have to live, and I will set down the naked truth without disguise. I was never a brave man, and had always been from my childhood of a secret sullen distrustful nature. I speak of myself as if I had passed from the world, for while I write this my grave is digging and my name is written in the black book of death.

Soon after my return to England, my only brother was seized with mortal illness. This circumstance gave me slight or no pain, for since we had been men we had associated but very little together. He was open-hearted and generous, handsomer than I, more accomplished, and generally beloved. Those who sought my acquaintance abroad or at home because they were friends of his, seldom attached themselves to me long, and would usually say in our first conversation that they were surprised to find two brothers so unlike in their manners and appearance. It was my habit to lead them on to this avowal, for I knew what comparisons they must draw between us, and having a rankling envy in my heart, I sought to justify it to myself.

We had married two sisters. This additional tie between us, as it may appear to some, only estranged us the more. His wife knew me well. I never struggled with any secret jealousy or gall when she was present but that woman knew it as well as I did. I never raised my eyes at such times but I found hers fixed upon me; I never bent them on the ground or looked another way, but I felt that she overlooked me always. It was an inexpressible relief to me when we quarrelled, and a greater relief still when I heard abroad that she was dead. It seems to me now as if some strange and terrible foreshadowing of what has happened since, must have hung over us then. I was afraid of her, she haunted me, her fixed and steady look comes back upon me now like the memory of a dark dream and makes my blood run cold.

She died shortly after giving birth to a child – a boy. When my brother knew that all hope of his own recovery was past, he called my wife to his bed-side and confided this orphan, a child of four years old, to her protection. He bequeathed to him all the property he had, and willed that in case of the child's death it should pass to my wife as the only acknowledgement he could make her for her care and love. He exchanged a few brotherly words with me deploring our long separation, and being exhausted, fell into a slumber from which he never awoke.

We had no children, and as there had been a strong affection between the sisters, and my wife had almost supplied the place of a mother to this boy, she loved him as if he had been her own. The child was ardently attached to her; but he was his mother's image in face and spirit and always mistrusted me.

I can scarcely fix the date when the feeling first came upon me, but I soon began to be uneasy when this child was by. I never roused myself from some moody train of thought but I marked him looking at me: not with mere childish wonder, but with something of the purpose and meaning that I had so often noted in his mother. It was no effort of my fancy, founded on close resemblance of feature and expression. I never could look the boy down. He feared me, but seemed by some instinct to despise me while he did so; and even when he drew back beneath my gaze – as he would when we were alone, to get nearer to the door – he would keep his bright eyes upon me still.

Perhaps I hide the truth from myself, but I do not think that when this began, I meditated to do him any wrong. I may have thought how serviceable his inheritance would be to us, and may have wished him dead, but I believe I had no thought of compassing his death. Neither did the idea come upon me at once, but by very slow degrees, presenting itself at first in dim shapes at a very great distance, as men may think of an earthquake or the last day – then drawing nearer and nearer and losing something of its horror and improbability – then coming to be part and parcel, nay nearly the whole sum and substance of my daily thoughts, and resolving itself into a question of means and safety; not of doing or abstaining from the deed.

While this was going on within me, I never could bear that the child should see me looking at him, and yet I was under a fascination which made it a kind of business with me to contemplate his slight and fragile figure and think how easily it might be done. Sometimes I would steal upstairs and watch him as he slept, but usually I hovered in the garden near the window of the room in which he learnt his little tasks, and there as he sat upon a low seat beside my wife, I would peer at him for hours together from behind a tree: starting like the guilty wretch I was at every rustling of a leaf, and still gliding back to look and start again.

Hard by our cottage, but quite out of sight, and (if there were any wind astir) of hearing too, was a deep sheet of water. I spent days in shaping with my pocket-knife a rough model of a boat, which I finished at last and dropped in the child's way. Then I withdrew to a secret place which he must pass if he stole away alone to swim this bauble, and lurked there for his coming. He came neither that day nor the next, though I waited from noon till nightfall. I was sure that I had him in my net for I had heard him prattling of the toy, and knew that in his infant pleasure he kept it by his side in bed. I felt no weariness or fatigue, but waited patiently, and on the third day he passed me, running joyously along, with his silken hair streaming in the wind and he singing – God have mercy upon me! – singing a merry ballad – who could hardly lisp the words.

I stole down after him, creeping under certain shrubs which grow in that place, and none but devils know with what terror I, a full-grown man, tracked the footsteps of that baby as he approached the water's brink. I was close upon him, had sunk upon my knee and raised my hand to thrust him in, when he saw my shadow in the stream and turned him round.

His mother's ghost was looking from his eyes. The sun burst forth from behind a cloud: it shone in the bright sky, the glistening earth, the clear water, the sparkling drops of rain upon the leaves. There were eyes in everything. The whole great universe of light was there to see the murder done. I know not what he said; he came of bold and manly blood, and child as he was, he did not crouch or fawn upon me. I heard him cry that he would try to love me – not that he did – and then I saw him running back towards the house. The next I saw was my own sword naked in my hand and he lying at my feet stark dead – dabbled here and there with blood but otherwise no different from what I had seen him in his sleep – in the same attitude too, with his cheek resting upon his little hand.

I took him in my arms and laid him – very gently now that he was dead – in a thicket. My wife was from home that day and would not return until the next. Our bed-room window, the only sleeping room on that side of the house, was but a few feet from the ground, and I resolved to descend from it at night and bury him in the garden. I had no thought that I had failed in my design, no thought that the water would be dragged and nothing found, that the money must now lie waste since I must encourage the idea that the child was lost or stolen. All my thoughts were bound up and knotted together, in the one absorbing necessity of hiding what I had done.

How I felt when they came to tell me that the child was missing, when I ordered scouts in all directions, when I gasped and trembled at everyone's approach, no tongue can tell or mind of man conceive. I buried him that night. When I parted the boughs and looked into the dark thicket, there was a glow-worm shining like the visible spirit of God upon the murdered child. I glanced down into his grave when I had placed him there and still it gleamed upon his breast: an eye of fire looking up to Heaven in supplication to the stars that watched me at my work.

I had to meet my wife, and break the news, and give her hope that the child would soon be found. All this I did – with some appearance, I suppose, of being sincere, for I was the object of no suspicion. This done, I sat at the bed-room window all day long and watched the spot where the dreadful secret lay.

It was in a piece of ground which had been dug up to be newly turfed, and which I had chosen on that account as the traces of my spade were less likely to attract attention. The men who laid down the grass must have thought me mad. I called to them continually to expedite their work, ran out and worked beside them, trod down the turf with my feet, and hurried them with frantic eagerness. They had finished their task before night, and then I thought myself comparatively safe.

I slept – not as men do who wake refreshed and cheerful, but I did sleep, passing from vague and shadowy dreams of being hunted down, to visions of the plot of grass, through which now a hand and now a foot and now the head itself was starting out. At this point I always woke and stole to the window to make sure that it was not really so. That done I crept to bed again, and thus I spent the night in fits and starts, getting up and lying down full twenty times and dreaming the same dream over and over again – which was far worse than lying awake, for every dream had a whole night's suffering of its own. Once I thought the child was alive and that I had never tried to kill him. To wake from that dream was the most dreadful agony of all.

The next day I sat at the window again, never once taking my eyes from the place, which, although it was covered by the grass, was as plain to me – its shape, its size, its depth, its jagged sides, and all – as if it had been open to the light of day. When a servant walked across it, I felt as if he must sink in; when he had passed I looked to see that his feet had not worn the edges. If a bird lighted there, I was in terror lest by some tremendous interposition it should be instrumental in the discovery; if a breath of air sighed across it, to me it whispered murder. There was not a sight or sound how ordinary mean or unimportant soever, but was fraught with fear. And in this state of ceaseless watching I spent three days.

On the fourth, there came to the gate one who had served with me abroad, accompanied by a brother officer of his whom I had never seen. I felt that I could not bear to be out of sight of the place. It was a summer evening, and I bade my people take a table and a flask of wine into the garden. Then I sat down *with my chair upon the grave*, and being assured that nobody could disturb it now, without my knowledge, tried to drink and talk.

They hoped that my wife was well – that she was not obliged to keep her chamber – that they had not frightened her away. What could I do but tell them with a faltering tongue about the child? The officer whom I did not know was a down-looking man and kept his eyes upon the ground while I was speaking. Even that terrified me! I could not divest myself of the idea that he saw something there which caused him to suspect the truth. I asked him hurriedly if he supposed that – and stopped. 'That the child had been murdered?' said he, looking mildly at me. 'Oh, no! what could a man gain by murdering a poor child?' *I* could have told him what a man gained by such a deed, no one better, but I held my peace and shivered as with an ague.

Mistaking my emotion they were endeavouring to cheer me with the hope that the boy would certainly be found – great cheer that was for me – when we heard a low deep howl, and presently there sprung over the wall two great dogs, who bounding into the garden repeated the baying sound we had heard before.

'Blood-hounds!' cried my visitors.

What need to tell me that! I had never seen one of that kind in all my life, but I knew what they were and for what purpose they had come. I grasped the elbows of my chair, and neither spoke nor moved.

'They are of the genuine breed,' said the man whom I had known abroad, 'and being out for exercise have no doubt escaped from their keeper.'

Both he and his friend turned to look at the dogs, who with their noses to the ground moved restlessly about, running to and fro, and up and down, and across, and round in circles, careering about like wild things, and all this time taking no notice of us, but ever and again lifting their heads and repeating the yell we had heard already, then dropping their noses to the ground again and tracking earnestly here and there. They now began to snuff the earth more eagerly than they had done yet, and although they were still very restless, no longer beat about in such wide circuits, but kept near to one spot, and constantly diminished the distance between themselves and me.

At last they came up close to the great chair on which I sat, and raising their frightful howl once more, tried to tear away the wooden rails that kept them from the ground beneath. I saw how I looked, in the faces of the two who were with me.

'They scent some prey,' said they, both together.

'They scent no prey!' cried I.

'In Heaven's name move,' said the one I knew, very earnestly, 'or you will be torn to pieces.'

'Let them tear me limb from limb, I'll never leave this place!' cried I. 'Are dogs to hurry men to shameful deaths? Hew them down, cut them in pieces.'

'There is some foul mystery here!' said the officer whom I did not know, drawing his sword. 'In King Charles's name assist me to secure this man.'

They both set upon me and forced me away, though I fought and bit and caught at them like a madman. After a struggle they got me quietly between them, and then, my God! I saw the angry dogs tearing at the earth and throwing it up into the air like water.

What more have I to tell? That I fell upon my knees and with chattering teeth confessed the truth and prayed to be forgiven. That I have since denied and now confess to it again. That I have been tried for the crime, found guilty, and sentenced. That I have not the courage to anticipate my doom or to bear up manfully against it. That I have no compassion, no consolation, no hope, no friend. That my wife has happily lost for the time those faculties which would enable her to know my misery or hers. That I am alone in this stone dungeon with my evil spirit, and that I die to-morrow!

To Be Read at Dusk

ONE, two, three, four, five. There were five of them.

Five couriers, sitting on a bench outside the convent on the summit of the Great St Bernard in Switzerland, looking at the remote heights, stained by the setting sun, as if a mighty quantity of red wine had been broached upon the mountain top, and had not yet had time to sink into the snow.

This is not my simile. It was made for the occasion by the stoutest courier, who was a German. None of the others took any more notice of it than they took of me, sitting on another bench on the other side of the convent door, smoking my cigar, like them, and – also like them – looking at the reddened snow, and at the lonely shed hard by, where the bodies of belated travellers, dug out of it, slowly wither away, knowing no corruption in that cold region.

The wine upon the mountain top soaked in as we looked; the mountain became white; the sky, a very dark blue; the wind rose; and the air turned piercing cold. The five couriers buttoned their rough coats. There being no safer man to imitate in all such proceedings than a courier, I buttoned mine.

The mountain in the sunset had stopped the five couriers in a conversation. It is a sublime sight, likely to stop conversation. The mountain being now out of the sunset, they resumed. Not that I had heard any part of their previous discourse; for, indeed, I had not then broken away from the American gentleman, in the travellers' parlour of the convent, who, sitting with his face to the fire, had undertaken to realize to me the whole progress of events which had led to the accumulation by the Honourable Ananias Dodger of one of the largest acquisitions of dollars ever made in our country.

'My God!' said the Swiss courier, speaking in French, which I do not hold (as some authors appear to do) to be such an all-sufficient excuse for a naughty word, that I have only to write it in that language to make it innocent; 'if you talk of ghosts –'

'But I *don't* talk of ghosts,' said the German.

'Of what then?' asked the Swiss.

'If I knew of what then,' said the German, 'I should probably know a great deal more.'

It was a good answer, I thought, and it made me curious. So, I moved my position to that corner of my bench which was nearest to them, and leaning my back against the convent-wall, heard perfectly, without appearing to attend.

'Thunder and lightning!' said the German, warming, 'when a certain man is coming to see you, unexpectedly; and, without his own knowledge, sends some invisible messenger, to put the idea of him in your head all day, what do you call that? When you walk along a crowded street -- at Frankfort, Milan, London, Paris – and think that a passing stranger is like your friend Heinrich, and then that another passing stranger is like your friend Heinrich, and so begin to have a strange foreknowledge that presently you'll meet your friend Heinrich – which you do, though you believed him at Trieste – what do you call *that*?'

'It's not uncommon either,' murmured the Swiss and the other three.

'Uncommon!' said the German. 'It's as common as cherries in the Black Forest. It's as common as maccaroni at Naples. And Naples reminds me! When the old Marchesa Senzanima shrieks at a card party on the Chiaja – as I heard and saw her, for it happened in a Bavarian family of mine, and I was overlooking the service that evening – I say, when the old Marchesa starts up at the card-table, white through her rouge, and cries, "My sister in Spain is dead! I felt her cold touch on my back!" – and when that sister *is* dead at the moment – what do you call that?'

'Or when the blood of San Gennaro liquefies at the request of the clergy – as all the world knows that it does regularly once a-year, in my native city,' said the Neapolitan courier after a pause, with a comical look, 'what do you call that?'

'*That!*' cried the German. 'Well! I think I know a name for that.'

'Miracle?' said the Neapolitan, with the same sly face.

The German merely smoked and laughed; and they all smoked and laughed.

'Bah!' said the German, presently. 'I speak of things that really do happen. When I want to see the conjurer, I pay to see a professed one, and have my money's worth. Very strange things do happen without ghosts. Ghosts! Giovanni Baptista, tell your story of the English bride. There's no ghost in that, but something full as strange. Will any man tell me what?'

As there was a silence among them, I glanced around. He whom I took to be Baptista was lighting a fresh cigar. He presently went on to speak. He was a Genoese, as I judged.

'The story of the English bride?' said he. 'Basta! one ought not to call so slight a thing a story. Well, it's all one. But it's true. Observe me well, gentlemen, it's true. That which glitters is not always gold; but what I am going to tell, is true.'

He repeated this more than once.

Ten years ago, I took my credentials to an English gentleman at Long's Hotel, in Bond Street, London, who was about to travel – it might be for one year, it might be for two. He approved of them; likewise of me. He was pleased to make inquiry. The testimony that he received was favourable. He engaged me by the six months, and my entertainment was generous.

He was young, handsome, very happy. He was enamoured of a fair young English lady, with a sufficient fortune, and they were going to be married. It was the wedding trip, in short, that we were going to take. For three months' rest in the hot weather (it was early summer then) he had hired an old palace on the Riviera, at an easy distance from my city, Genoa, on the road to Nice. Did I know that palace? Yes; I told him I knew it well. It was an old palace, with great gardens. It was a little bare, and it was a little dark and gloomy, being close surrounded by trees; but it was spacious, ancient, grand, and on the sea shore. He said it had been so described to him exactly, and he was well pleased that I knew it. For its being a little bare of furniture, all such places were. For its being a little gloomy, he had hired it principally for the gardens, and he and my mistress would pass the summer weather in their shade.

'So all goes well, Baptista?' said he.

'Indubitably, signor; very well.'

We had a travelling chariot for our journey, newly built for us, and in all respects complete. All we had was complete; we wanted for nothing. The marriage took place. They were happy. *I* was happy, seeing all so bright, being so well situated, going to my own city, teaching my language in the rumble to the maid, la bella Carolina, whose heart was gay with laughter: who was young and rosy.

The time flew. But I observed – listen to this, I pray! (and here the courier dropped his voice) – I observed my mistress sometimes brooding in a manner very strange; in a frightened manner; in an unhappy manner; with a cloudy, uncertain alarm upon her. I think that I began to notice this when I was walking up hills by the carriage side, and master had gone on in front. At any rate, I remember that it impressed itself upon my mind one evening in the South of France, when she called to me to call master back; and when he came back, and walked for a long way, talking encouragingly and affectionately to her, with his hand upon the open window, and hers in it. Now and then, he laughed in a merry way, as if he were bantering her out of something. By and by, she laughed, and then all went well again.

It was curious. I asked la bella Carolina, the pretty little one, Was mistress unwell? – No. Out of spirits? – No. Fearful of bad roads, or brigands? – No. And what made it more mysterious was, the pretty little one would not look at me in giving answer, but *would* look at the view.

But, one day she told me the secret.

'If you must know,' said Carolina, 'I find, from what I have overheard, that mistress is haunted.'

'How haunted?'

'By a dream.'

'What dream?'

'By a dream of a face. For three nights before her marriage, she saw a face in a dream – always the same face, and only One.'

'A terrible face?'

'No. The face of a dark, remarkable-looking man, in black, with black hair and a grey moustache – a handsome man, except for a reserved and secret air. Not a face she ever saw, or at all like a face she ever saw. Doing nothing in the dream but looking at her fixedly, out of darkness.'

'Does the dream come back?'

'Never. The recollection of it, is all her trouble.'

'And why does it trouble her?'

Carolina shook her head.

'That's master's question,' said la bella. 'She don't know. She wonders why, herself. But I heard her tell him, only last night, that if she was to find a picture of that face in our Italian house (which she is afraid she will), she did not know how she could ever bear it.'

Upon my word I was fearful after this (said the Genoese courier) of our coming to the old palazzo, lest some such ill-starred picture should happen to be there. I knew there were many there; and, as we got nearer and nearer to the place, I wished the whole gallery in the crater of Vesuvius. To mend the matter, it was a stormy dismal evening when we, at last, approached that part of the Riviera. It thundered; and the thunder of my city and its environs, rolling among the high hills, is very loud. The lizards ran in and out of the chinks in the broken stone wall of the garden, as if they were frightened; the frogs bubbled and croaked their loudest; the sea-wind moaned, and the wet trees dripped; and the lightning – body of San Lorenzo, how it lightened!

We all know what an old palazzo in or near Genoa is – how time and the sea air have blotted it – how the drapery painted on the outer walls has peeled off in great flakes of plaster – how the lower windows are darkened with rusty bars of iron – how the courtyard is overgrown with grass – how the outer buildings are dilapidated – how the whole pile seems devoted to ruin. Our palazzo was one of the true kind. It had been shut up close for months. Months? – years! It had an earthy smell, like a tomb. The scent of the orange-trees on the broad back terrace, and of the lemons ripening on the wall, and of some shrubs that grew around a broken fountain, had got into the house somehow, and had never been able to get out again. There it was, in every room, an aged smell, grown faint with confinement. It pined in all the cupboards and drawers. In the little rooms of communication between great rooms, it was stifling. If you turned a picture – to come back to the pictures – there it still was, clinging to the wall behind the frame, like a sort of bat.

The lattice-blinds were close shut, all over the house. There were two ugly grey old women in the house, to take care of it; one of them with a spindle, who stood winding and mumbling in the doorway, and who would as soon have let in the devil as the air. Master, mistress, la bella Carolina, and I, went all through the palazzo. I went first, though I have named myself last, opening the windows and the lattice-blinds, and shaking down on myself splashes of rain, and scraps of mortar, and now and then a dozing mosquito, or a monstrous, fat, blotchy, Genoese spider.

When I had let the evening light into a room, master, mistress, and la bella Carolina, entered. Then, we looked round at all the pictures, and I went forward again into another room. Mistress secretly had great fear of meeting with the likeness of that face – we all had; but there was no such thing. The Madonna and Bambino, San Francisco, San Sebastiano, Venus, Santa Caterina, Angels, Brigands, Friars, Temples at Sunset, Battles, White Horses, Forests, Apostles, Doges, all my old acquaintance many times repeated? – yes. Dark handsome man in black, reserved and secret, with black hair and grey moustache, looking fixedly at mistress out of darkness? – no.

At last we got through all the rooms and all the pictures, and came out into the gardens. They were pretty well kept, being rented by a gardener, and were large and shady. In one place, there was a rustic theatre, open to the sky, the stage a green slope: the coulisses, three entrances upon a side, sweet-smelling leafy screens. Mistress moved her bright eyes, even there, as if she looked to see the face come in upon the scene: but all was well.

'Now Clara,' master said, in a low voice, 'you see that it is nothing? You are happy.'

Mistress was much encouraged. She soon accustomed herself to that grim palazzo, and would sing, and play the harp, and copy the old pictures, and stroll with master under the green trees and vines, all day. She was beautiful. He was happy. He would laugh and say to me, mounting his horse for his morning ride before the heat:

'All goes well, Baptista!'

'Yes, signore, thank God; very well!'

We kept no company. I took la bella to the Duomo and Annunciata, to the Café, to the Opera, to the village Festa, to the Public Garden, to the Day Theatre, to the Marionetti. The pretty little one was charmed with all she saw. She learnt Italian – heavens! miraculously! Was mistress quite forgetful of that dream? I asked

Carolina sometimes. Nearly, said la bella – almost. It was wearing out.

One day master received a letter, and called me.

'Baptista!'

'Signore.'

'A gentleman who is presented to me will dine here today. He is called the Signor Dellombra. Let me dine like a prince.'

It was an odd name. I did not know that name. But, there had been many noblemen and gentlemen pursued by Austria on political suspicions, lately, and some names had changed. Perhaps this was one. Altro! Dellombra was as good a name to me as another.

When the Signor Dellombra came to dinner (said the Genoese courier in the low voice, into which he had subsided once before), I showed him into the reception-room, the great sala of the old palazzo. Master received him with cordiality, and presented him to mistress. As she rose, her face changed, she gave a cry, and fell upon the marble floor.

Then, I turned my head to the Signor Dellombra, and saw that he was dressed in black, and had a reserved and secret air, and was a dark remarkable-looking man, with black hair and a grey moustache.

Master raised mistress in his arms, and carried her to her own room, where I sent la bella Carolina straight. La bella told me afterwards that mistress was nearly terrified to death, and that she wandered in her mind about her dream, all night.

Master was vexed and anxious – almost angry, and yet full of solicitude. The Signor Dellombra was a courtly gentleman, and spoke with great respect and sympathy of mistress's being so ill. The African wind had been blowing for some days (they had told him at his Hôtel of the Maltese Cross), and he knew that it was often hurtful. He hoped the beautiful lady would recover soon. He begged permission to retire, and to renew his visit when he should have the happiness of hearing that she was better. Master would not allow of this, and they dined alone.

He withdrew early. Next day he called at the gate, on horseback, to inquire for mistress. He did so two or three times in that week.

What I observed myself, and what la bella Carolina told me, united to explain to me that master had now set his mind on curing mistress of her fanciful terror. He was all kindness, but he was sensible and firm. He reasoned with her, that to encourage such fancies was to invite melancholy, if not madness. That it rested with herself to be herself. That if she once resisted her strange weakness, so successfully as to receive the Signor Dellombra as an English lady would receive any other guest, it was for ever conquered. To make an end, the Signor came again, and mistress received him without marked distress (though with constraint and apprehension still), and the evening passed serenely. Master was so delighted with this change, and so anxious to conform it, that the Signor Dellombra became a constant guest. He was accomplished in pictures, books, and music; and his society, in any grim palazzo, would have been welcome.

I used to notice, many times, that mistress was not quite recovered. She would cast down her eyes and droop her head, before the Signor Dellombra, or would look at him with a terrified and fascinated glance, as if his presence had some evil influence or power upon her. Turning from her to him, I used to see him in the shaded gardens, or the large half-lighted sala, looking, as I might say, 'fixedly upon her out of darkness'. But, truly, I had not forgotten la bella Carolina's words describing the face in the dream.

After his second visit I heard master say:

'Now see, my dear Clara, it's over! Dellombra has come and gone, and your apprehension is broken like glass.'

'Will he – will he ever come again?' asked mistress.

'Again? Why, surely, over and over again! Are you cold?' (She shivered.)

'No, dear – but – he terrifies me: are you sure that he need come again?'

'The surer for the question, Clara!' replied master, cheerfully.

But, he was very hopeful of her complete recovery now, and grew more and more so every day. She was beautiful. He was happy.

'All goes well, Baptista?' he would say to me again.

'Yes, signore, thank God; very well.'

We were all (said the Genoese courier, constraining himself to speak a little louder), we were all at Rome for the Carnival. I had been out, all day, with a Sicilian, a friend of mine and a courier, who was there with an English family. As I returned at night to our hôtel, I met the little Carolina, who never stirred from home alone, running distractedly along the Corso.

'Carolina! What's the matter?'

'O Baptista! Oh, for the Lord's sake! where is my mistress?'

'Mistress, Carolina?'

'Gone since morning – told me, when master went out on his day's journey, not to call her, for she was tired with not resting in the night (having been in pain), and would lie in bed until the evening; then get up refreshed. She is gone! – she is gone! Master has come back, broken down the door, and she is gone! My beautiful, my good, my innocent mistress!'

The pretty little one so cried, and raved, and tore herself, that I could not have held her, but for her swooning on my arm as if she had been shot. Master came up – in manner, face, or voice, no more the master that I knew, than I was he. He took me (I laid the little one upon her bed in the hôtel, and left her with the chamberwomen), in a carriage, furiously through the darkness, across the desolate Campagna. When it was day, and we stopped at a miserable posthouse, all the horses had been hired twelve hours ago, and sent away in different directions. Mark me! – by the Signor Dellombra, who had passed there in a carriage, with a frightened English lady crouching in one corner.

I never heard (said the Genoese courier, drawing a long breath) that she was ever traced beyond that spot. All I know is, that she vanished into infamous oblivion, with the dreaded face beside her that she had seen in her dream.

'What do you call *that*?' said the German courier, triumphantly: 'Ghosts! There are no ghosts *there!* What do you call this, that I am going to tell you? Ghosts! There are no ghosts *here!*'

I took an engagement once (pursued the German courier) with an English gentleman, elderly and a bachelor, to travel through my country, my Fatherland. He was a merchant who traded with my country and knew the language, but who had never been there since he was a boy – as I judge, some sixty years before.

His name was James, and he had a twin-brother John, also a

bachelor. Between these brothers there was a great affection. They were in business together, at Goodman's Fields, but they did not live together. Mr James dwelt in Poland Street, turning out of Oxford Street, London. Mr John resided by Epping Forest.

Mr James and I were to start for Germany in about a week. The exact day depended on business. Mr John came to Poland Street (where I was staying in the house), to pass that week with Mr James. But, he said to his brother on the second day, 'I don't feel very well, James. There's not much the matter with me; but I think I am a little gouty. I'll go home and put myself under the care of my old housekeeper, who understands my ways. If I get quite better, I'll come back and see you before you go. If I don't feel well enough to resume my visit where I leave it off, why *you* will come and see *me* before you go.' Mr James, of course, said he would, and they shook hands – both hands, as they always did – and Mr John ordered out his old-fashioned chariot and rumbled home.

It was on the second night after that – that is to say, the fourth in the week – when I was awoke out of my sound sleep by Mr James coming into my bedroom in his flannel-gown, with a lighted candle. He sat upon the side of my bed, and looking at me, said:

'Wilhelm, I have reason to think I have got some strange illness upon me.'

I then perceived that there was a very unusual expression in his face.

'Wilhelm,' said he, 'I am not afraid or ashamed to tell you, what I might be afraid or ashamed to tell another man. You come from a sensible country, where mysterious things are inquired into, and are not settled to have been weighed and measured – or to have been unweighable and unmeasurable – or in either case to have been completely disposed of, for all time – ever so many years ago. I have just now seen the phantom of my brother.'

I confess (said the German courier) that it gave me a little tingling of the blood to hear it.

'I have just now seen,' Mr James repeated, looking full at me, that I might see how collected he was, 'the phantom of my brother John. I was sitting up in bed, unable to sleep, when it came into my room, in a white dress, and, regarding me earnestly, passed up to the end of the room, glanced at some papers on my writing-desk, turned, and, still looking earnestly at me as it passed the bed, went out at the door. Now, I am not in the least mad, and am not in the least disposed to invest that phantom with any external existence out of myself. I think it is a warning to me that I am ill; and I think I had better be bled.'

I got out of bed directly (said the German courier) and began to get on my clothes, begging him not to be alarmed, and telling him that I would go myself to the doctor. I was just ready, when we heard a loud knocking and ringing at the street door. My room being an attic at the back, and Mr James's being the second-floor room in the front, we went down to his room, and put up the window, to see what was the matter.

'Is that Mr James?' said a man below, falling back to the opposite side of the way to look up.

'It is,' said Mr James; 'and you are my brother's man, Robert.'

'Yes, sir. I am sorry to say, sir, that Mr John is ill. He is very bad, sir. It is even feared that he may be lying at the point of death. He wants to see you, sir. I have a chaise here. Pray come to him. Pray lose no time.'

Mr James and I looked at one another. 'Wilhelm,' said he, 'this is strange. I wish you to come with me!' I helped him to dress, partly there and partly in the chaise; and no grass grew under the horses' iron shoes between Poland Street and the Forest.

Now, mind! (said the German courier). I went with Mr James into his brother's room, and I saw and heard myself what follows.

His brother lay upon his bed, at the upper end of a long bed-chamber. His old housekeeper was there, and others were there: I think three others were there, if not four, and they had been with him since early in the afternoon. He was in white, like the figure – necessarily so, because he had his night-dress on. He looked like the figure – necessarily so, because he looked earnestly at his brother when he saw him come into the room.

But, when his brother reached the bed-side, he slowly raised himself in bed, and looking full upon him, said these words:

'JAMES, YOU HAVE SEEN ME BEFORE, TO-NIGHT – AND YOU KNOW IT!'

And so died!

*

I waited, when the German courier ceased, to hear something said of this strange story. The silence was unbroken. I looked round and the five couriers were gone: so noiselessly that the ghostly mountain might have absorbed them into its eternal snows. By this time, I was by no means in a mood to sit alone in that awful scene, with the chill air coming solemnly upon me – or, if I may tell the truth, to sit alone anywhere. So I went back into the convent-parlour, and, finding the American gentleman still disposed to relate the biography of the Honourable Ananias Dodger, heard it all out.

MUGBY JUNCTION

No. 1 Branch Line. The Signalman

'HALLOA! Below there!'

When he heard a voice thus calling to him, he was standing at the door of his box, with a flag in his hand, furled round its short pole. One would have thought, considering the nature of the ground, that he could not have doubted from what quarter the voice came; but, instead of looking up to where I stood on the top of the steep cutting nearly over his head, he turned himself about and looked down the Line. There was something remarkable in his manner of doing so, though I could not have said for my life, what. But, I know it was remarkable enough to attract my notice, even though his figure was foreshortened and shadowed, down in the deep trench, and mine was high above him, so steeped in the glow of an angry sunset that I had shaded my eyes with my hand before I saw him at all.

'Halloa! Below!'

From looking down the Line, he turned himself about again, and, raising his eyes, saw my figure high above him.

'Is there any path by which I can come down and speak to you?'

He looked up at me without replying, and I looked down at him without pressing him too soon with a repetition of my idle question. Just then, there came a vague vibration in the earth and air, quickly changing into a violent pulsation, and an oncoming rush that caused me to start back, as though it had force to draw me down. When such vapour as rose to my height from this rapid train, had passed me and was skimming away over the landscape, I looked down again, and saw him re-furling the flag he had shown while the train went by.

I repeated my inquiry. After a pause, during which he seemed to regard me with fixed attention, he motioned with his rolled-up flag towards a point on my level, some two or three hundred yards distant. I called down to him, 'All right!' and made for that point. There, by dint of looking closely about me, I found a rough zig-zag descending path notched out: which I followed.

The cutting was extremely deep, and unusually precipitate. It was made through a clammy stone that became oozier and wetter as I went down. For these reasons, I found the way long enough to give me time to recall a singular air of reluctance or compulsion with which he had pointed out the path.

When I came down low enough upon the zig-zag descent, to see him again, I saw that he was standing between the rails on the way by which the train had lately passed, in an attitude as if he were waiting for me to appear. He had his left hand at his chin, and that left elbow rested on his right hand crossed over his breast. His attitude was one of such expectation and watchfulness, that I stopped a moment, wondering at it.

I resumed my downward way, and, stepping out upon the level of the railroad and drawing nearer to him, saw that he was a dark sallow man, with a dark beard and rather heavy eyebrows. His post was in as solitary and dismal a place as ever I saw. On either side, a dripping-wet wall of jagged stone, excluding all view but a strip of sky; the perspective one way, only a crooked prolongation of this great dungeon; the shorter perspective in the other direction, terminating in a gloomy red light, and the gloomier entrance to a black tunnel, in whose massive architecture there was a barbarous, depressing, and forbidding air. So little sunlight ever found its way to this spot, that it had an earthy deadly smell; and so much cold wind rushed through it, that it struck chill to me, as if I had left the natural world.

Before he stirred, I was near enough to him to have touched him. Not even then removing his eyes from mine, he stepped back one step, and lifted his hand.

This was a lonesome post to occupy (I said), and it had riveted my attention when I looked down from up yonder. A visitor was a rarity, I should suppose; not an unwelcome rarity, I hoped? In me, he merely saw a man who had been shut up within narrow limits all his life,[1] and who, being at last set free, had a newly-awakened interest in these great works. To such purpose I spoke to him; but I am far from sure of the terms I used, for, besides that I am not happy in opening any conversation, there was something in the man that daunted me.

He directed a most curious look towards the red light near the tunnel's mouth, and looked all about it, as if something were missing from it, and then looked at me.

That light was part of his charge? Was it not?

He answered in a low voice: 'Don't you know it is?'

The monstrous thought came into my mind as I perused the fixed eyes and the saturnine face, that this was a spirit, not a man. I have speculated since, whether there may have been infection in his mind.

In my turn, I stepped back. But in making the action, I detected in his eyes some latent fear of me. This put the monstrous thought to flight.

'You look at me,' I said, forcing a smile, 'as if you had a dread of me.'

'I was doubtful,' he returned, 'whether I had seen you before.'

'Where?'

He pointed to the red light he had looked at.

'There?' I said.

Intently watchful of me, he replied (but without sound), Yes.

'My good fellow, what should I do there? However, be that as it may, I never was there, you may swear.'

'I think I may,' he rejoined. 'Yes. I am sure I may.'

His manner cleared, like my own. He replied to my remarks with readiness, and in well-chosen words. Had he much to do there? Yes; that was to say, he had enough responsibility to bear; but exactness and watchfulness were what was required of him, and of actual work – manual labour – he had next to none. To change that signal, to trim those lights, and to turn this iron handle now and then, was all he had to do under that head. Regarding those many long and lonely hours of which I seemed to make so much, he could only say that the routine of his life had shaped itself into that form, and he had grown used to it. He had taught himself a language down here – if only to know it by sight, and to have formed his own crude ideas of its pronunciation, could be called learning it. He had also worked at fractions and decimals, and tried a little algebra; but he was, and had been as a boy, a poor hand at figures. Was it necessary for him when on duty, always to remain in that channel of damp air, and could he never rise into the sunshine from between those high stone walls? Why, that depended upon times and circumstances. Under some conditions there would be less upon the Line than under others, and the same held good as to certain hours of the day and night. In bright weather, he did choose occasions for getting a little above these lower shadows; but, being at all times liable to be called by his electric bell, and at such times listening for it with redoubled anxiety, the relief was less than I would suppose.

He took me into his box, where there was a fire, a desk for an official book in which he had to make certain entries, a telegraphic instrument with its dial face and needles, and the little bell of which he had spoken. On my trusting that he would excuse the remark that he had been well educated, and (I hoped I might say without offence), perhaps educated above that station, he observed that instances of slight incongruity in such-wise would rarely be found wanting among large bodies of men; that he had heard it was so in workhouses, in the police force, even in that last desperate resource, the army; and that he knew it was so, more or less, in any great railway staff. He had been, when young (if I could believe it, sitting in that hut; he scarcely could), a student of natural philosophy, and had attended lectures; but he had run wild, misused his opportunities, gone down, and never risen again. He had no complaint to offer about that. He had made his bed, and he lay upon it. It was far too late to make another.

All that I have here condensed, he said in a quiet manner, with his grave dark regards divided between me and the fire. He threw in the word 'Sir', from time to time, and especially when he referred to his youth: as though to request me to understand that he claimed to be nothing but what I found him. He was several times interrupted by the little bell, and had to read off messages, and send replies. Once, he had to stand without the door, and display a flag as a train passed, and make some verbal communication to the driver. In the discharge of his duties I observed him to be remarkably exact and vigilant, breaking off his discourse at a syllable, and remaining silent until what he had to do was done.

In a word, I should have set this man down as one of the safest of men to be employed in that capacity, but for the circumstance that while he was speaking to me he twice broke off with a fallen colour, turned his face towards the little bell when it did NOT ring, opened the door of the hut (which was kept shut to exclude the unhealthy damp), and looked out towards the red light near the mouth of the tunnel. On both of those occasions, he came back to the fire with the inexplicable air upon him which I had remarked, without being able to define, when we were so far asunder.

Said I when I rose to leave him: 'You almost make me think that I have met with a contented man.'

(I am afraid I must acknowledge that I said it to lead him on.)

'I believe I used to be so,' he rejoined, in the low voice in which he had first spoken; 'but I am troubled, sir, I am troubled.'

He would have recalled the words if he could. He had said them, however, and I took them up quickly.

'With what? What is your trouble?'

'It is very difficult to impart, sir. It is very, very difficult to speak of. If ever you make me another visit, I will try to tell you.'

'But I expressly intend to make you another visit. Say, when shall it be?'

'I go off early in the morning, and I shall be on again at ten to-morrow night, sir.'

'I will come at eleven.'

He thanked me, and went out at the door with me. 'I'll show my white light, sir,' he said, in his peculiar low voice, 'till you have found the way up. When you have found it, don't call out! And when you are at the top, don't call out!'

His manner seemed to make the place strike colder to me, but I said no more than 'Very well.'

'And when you come down to-morrow night, don't call out! Let me ask you a parting question. What made you cry "Halloa! Below there!" to-night?'

'Heaven knows,' said I. 'I cried something to that effect –'

'Not to that effect, sir. Those were the very words. I know them well.'

'Admit those were the very words. I said them, no doubt, because I saw you below.'

'For no other reason?'

'What other reason could I possibly have!'

'You have no feeling that they were conveyed to you in any supernatural way?'

'No.'

He wished me good night, and held up his light. I walked by the side of the down Line of rails (with a very disagreeable sensation of a train coming behind me), until I found the path. It was easier to mount than to descend, and I got back to my inn without any adventure.

Punctual to my appointment, I placed my foot on the first notch of the zig-zag next night, as the distant clocks were striking eleven. He was waiting for me at the bottom, with his white light on. 'I have not called out,' I said, when we came close together; 'may I speak now?' 'By all means, sir.' 'Good night then, and here's my hand.' 'Good night, sir, and here's mine.' With that, we walked side by side to his box, entered it, closed the door, and sat down by the fire.

'I have made up my mind, sir,' he began, bending forward as soon as we were seated, and speaking in a tone but a little above a whisper, 'that you shall not have to ask me twice what troubles me. I took you for some one else yesterday evening. That troubles me.'

'That mistake?'

'No. That some one else.'

'Who is it?'

'I don't know.'

'Like me?'

'I don't know. I never saw the face. The left arm is across the face, and the right arm is waved. Violently waved. This way.'

I followed his action with my eyes, and it was the action of an arm gesticulating with the utmost passion and vehemence: 'For God's sake clear the way!'

'One moonlight night,' said the man, 'I was sitting here, when I heard a voice cry "Halloa! Below there!" I started up, looked from that door, and saw this Some one else standing by the red light near the tunnel, waving as I just now showed you. The voice seemed hoarse with shouting, and it cried, "Look out! Look out!" And then again "Halloa! Below there! Look out!" I caught up my lamp, turned it on red, and ran towards the figure, calling, "What's wrong? What has happened? Where?" It stood just outside the blackness of the tunnel. I advanced so close upon it that I wondered at its keeping the sleeve across its eyes. I ran right up at it, and had my hand stretched out to pull the sleeve away, when it was gone.'

'Into the tunnel,' said I.

'No. I ran on into the tunnel, five hundred yards. I stopped and held my lamp above my head, and saw the figures of the measured distance, and saw the wet stains stealing down the walls and trickling through the arch. I ran out again, faster than I had run in (for I had a mortal abhorrence of the place upon me), and I looked all round the red light with my own red light, and I went up the iron ladder to the gallery atop of it, and I came down again, and ran back here. I telegraphed both ways: "An alarm has been given. Is anything wrong?" The answer came back, both ways: "All well."'

Resisting the slow touch of a frozen finger tracing out my spine, I showed him how that this figure must be a deception of his sense of sight, and how that figures, originating in disease of the delicate nerves that minister to the functions of the eye, were known to have often troubled patients, some of whom had become conscious of the nature of their affliction, and had even proved it by experiments upon themselves. 'As to an imaginary cry,' said I, 'do but listen for a moment to the wind in this unnatural valley while we speak so low, and to the wild harp it makes of the telegraph wires!'

That was all very well, he returned, after we had sat listening for a while, and he ought to know something of the wind and the wires, he who so often passed long winter nights there, alone and watching. But he would beg to remark that he had not finished.

I asked his pardon, and he slowly added these words, touching my arm:

'Within six hours after the Appearance, the memorable accident on this Line happened, and within ten hours the dead and wounded were brought along through the tunnel over the spot where the figure had stood.'

A disagreeable shudder crept over me, but I did my best against it. It was not to be denied, I rejoined, that this was a remarkable coincidence, calculated deeply to impress his mind. But, it was unquestionable that remarkable coincidences did continually occur, and they must be taken into account in dealing with such a subject.

Though to be sure I must admit, I added (for I thought I saw that he was going to bring the objection to bear upon me), men of common sense did not allow much for coincidences in making the ordinary calculations of life.

He again begged to remark that he had not finished.

I again begged his pardon for being betrayed into interruptions.

'This,' he said, again laying his hand upon my arm, and glancing over his shoulder with hollow eyes, 'was just a year ago. Six or seven months passed, and I had recovered from the surprise and shock, when one morning, as the day was breaking, I, standing at that door, looked towards the red light, and saw the spectre again.' He stopped, with a fixed look at me.

'Did it cry out?'

'No. It was silent.'

'Did it wave its arm?'

'No. It leaned against the shaft of the light, with both hands before the face. Like this.'

Once more, I followed his action with my eyes. It was an action of mourning. I have seen such an attitude in stone figures on tombs.

'Did you go up to it?'

'I came in and sat down, partly to collect my thoughts, partly because it had turned me faint. When I went to the door again, daylight was above me, and the ghost was gone.'

'But nothing followed? Nothing came of this?'

He touched me on the arm with his forefinger twice or thrice, giving a ghastly nod each time:

'That very day, as a train came out of the tunnel, I noticed, at a carriage window on my side, what looked like a confusion of hands and heads, and something waved. I saw it, just in time to signal the driver, Stop! He shut off, and put his brake on, but the train drifted past here a hundred and fifty yards or more. I ran after it, and, as I went along, heard terrible screams and cries. A beautiful young lady had died instantaneously in one of the compartments, and was brought in here, and laid down on this floor between us.'

Involuntarily, I pushed my chair back, as I looked from the boards at which he pointed, to himself.

'True, sir. True. Precisely as it happened, so I tell it you.'

I could think of nothing to say, to any purpose, and my mouth was very dry. The wind and the wires took up the story with a long lamenting wail.

He resumed. 'Now, sir, mark this, and judge how my mind is troubled. The spectre came back, a week ago. Ever since, it has been there, now and again, by fits and starts.'

'At the light?'

'At the Danger-light.'

'What does it seem to do?'

He repeated, if possible with increased passion and vehemence, that former gesticulation of 'For God's sake clear the way!'

Then, he went on. 'I have no peace or rest for it. It calls to me, for many minutes together, in an agonized manner, "Below there! Look out! Look out!" It stands waving to me. It rings my little bell—'

I caught at that. 'Did it ring your bell yesterday evening when I was here, and you went to the door?'

'Twice.'

'Why, see,' said I, 'how your imagination misleads you. My eyes were on the bell, and my ears were open to the bell, and if I am a living man, it did NOT ring at those times. No, nor at any other time, except when it was rung in the natural course of physical things by the station communicating with you.'

He shook his head. 'I have never made a mistake as to that, yet, sir. I have never confused the spectre's ring with the man's. The ghost's ring is a strange vibration in the bell that it derives from nothing else, and I have not asserted that the bell stirs to the eye. I don't wonder that you failed to hear it. But *I* heard it.'

'And did the spectre seem to be there, when you looked out?'

'It WAS there.'

'Both times?'

He repeated firmly: 'Both times.'

'Will you come to the door with me, and look for it now?'

He bit his under-lip as though he were somewhat unwilling, but arose. I opened the door, and stood on the step, while he stood in the doorway. There, was the Danger-light. There, was the dismal mouth of the tunnel. There, were the high wet stone walls of the cutting. There, were the stars above them.

'Do you see it?' I asked him, taking particular note of his face.

His eyes were prominent and strained; but not very much more so, perhaps, than my own had been when I had directed them earnestly towards the same spot.

'No,' he answered. 'It is not there.'

'Agreed,' said I.

We went in again, shut the door, and resumed our seats. I was thinking how best to improve this advantage, if it might be called one, when he took up the conversation in such a matter of course way, so assuming that there could be no serious question of fact between us, that I felt myself in the weakest of positions.

'By this time you will fully understand, sir,' he said, 'that what troubles me so dreadfully, is the question, What does the spectre mean?'

I was not sure, I told him, that I did fully understand.

'What is its warning against?' he said, ruminating, with his eyes on the fire, and only by times turning them on me. 'What is the danger? Where is the danger? There is danger overhanging, some-where on the Line. Some dreadful calamity will happen. It is not to be doubted this third time, after what has gone before. But surely this is a cruel haunting of *me*. What can *I* do!'

He pulled out his handkerchief, and wiped the drops from his heated forehead.

'If I telegraph Danger, on either side of me, or on both, I can give no reason for it,' he went on, wiping the palms of his hands. 'I should get into trouble, and do no good. They would think I was mad. This is the way it would work: Message: "Danger! Take care!" Answer: "What Danger? Where?" Message: "Don't know. But for God's sake take care!" They would displace me. What else could they do?'

His pain of mind was most pitiable to see. It was the mental torture of a conscientious man, oppressed beyond endurance by an unintelligible responsibility involving life.

'When it first stood under the Danger-light,' he went on, putting his dark hair back from his head, and drawing his hands outward across and across his temples in an extremity of feverish distress, 'why not tell me where that accident was to happen – if it must happen? Why not tell me how it could be averted – if it could have been averted? When on its second coming it hid its face, why not

tell me instead: "She is going to die. Let them keep her at home"?
If it came, on those two occasions, only to show me that its warnings were true, and so to prepare me for the third, why not warn me plainly now? And I, Lord help me! A mere poor signalman on this solitary station! Why not go to somebody with credit to be believed, and power to act!'

When I saw him in this state, I saw that for the poor man's sake, as well as for the public safety, what I had to do for the time was, to compose his mind. Therefore, setting aside all question of reality or unreality between us, I represented to him that whoever thoroughly discharged his duty, must do well, and that at least it was his comfort that he understood his duty, though he did not understand these confounding Appearances. In this effort I succeeded far better than in the attempt to reason him out of his conviction. He became calm; the occupations incidental to his post as the night advanced, began to make larger demands on his attention; and I left him at two in the morning. I had offered to stay through the night, but he would not hear of it.

That I more than once looked back at the red light as I ascended the pathway, that I did not like the red light, and that I should have slept but poorly if my bed had been under it, I see no reason to conceal. Nor, did I like the two sequences of the accident and the dead girl. I see no reason to conceal that, either.

But, what ran most in my thoughts was the consideration how ought I to act, having become the recipient of this disclosure? I had proved the man to be intelligent, vigilant, painstaking, and exact; but how long might he remain so, in his state of mind? Though in a subordinate position, still he held a most important trust, and would I (for instance) like to stake my own life on the chances of his continuing to execute it with precision?

Unable to overcome a feeling that there would be something treacherous in my communicating what he had told me, to his superiors in the Company, without first being plain with himself and proposing a middle course to him, I ultimately resolved to offer to accompany him (otherwise keeping his secret for the present) to the wisest medical practitioner we could hear of in those parts, and to take his opinion. A change in his time of duty would come round next night, he had apprised me, and he would be off an hour or two after sunrise, and on again soon after sunset. I had appointed to return accordingly.

Next evening was a lovely evening, and I walked out early to enjoy it. The sun was not yet quite down when I traversed the field-path near the top of the deep cutting. I would extend my walk for an hour, I said to myself, half an hour on and half an hour back, and it would then be time to go to my signalman's box.

Before pursuing my stroll, I stepped to the brink, and mechanically looked down, from the point from which I had first seen him. I cannot describe the thrill that seized upon me, when, close at the mouth of the tunnel, I saw the appearance of a man, with his left sleeve across his eyes, passionately waving his right arm.

The nameless horror that oppressed me, passed in a moment, for in a moment I saw that this appearance of a man was a man indeed, and that there was a little group of other men standing at a short distance, to whom he seemed to be rehearsing the gesture he made. The Danger-light was not yet lighted. Against its shaft, a little low hut, entirely new to me, had been made of some wooden supports and tarpaulin. It looked no bigger than a bed.

With an irresistible sense that something was wrong – with a flashing self-reproachful fear that fatal mischief had come of my leaving the man there, and causing no one to be sent to overlook or correct what he did – I descended the notched path with all the speed I could make.

'What is the matter?' I asked the men.

'Signalman killed this morning, sir.'

'Not the man belonging to that box?'

'Yes, sir.'

'Not the man I know?'

'You will recognize him, sir, if you knew him,' said the man who spoke for the others, solemnly uncovering his own head and raising an end of the tarpaulin, 'for his face is quite composed.'

'O! how did this happen, how did this happen?' I asked, turning from one to another as the hut closed in again.

'He was cut down by an engine, sir. No man in England knew his work better. But somehow he was not clear of the outer rail. It was just at broad day. He had struck the light, and had the lamp in his hand. As the engine came out of the tunnel, his back was towards her, and she cut him down. That man drove her, and was showing how it happened. Show the gentleman, Tom.'

The man, who wore a rough dark dress, stepped back to his former place at the mouth of the tunnel:

'Coming round the curve in the tunnel, sir,' he said, 'I saw him at the end, like as if I saw him down a perspective-glass. There was no time to check speed, and I knew him to be very careful. As he didn't seem to take heed of the whistle, I shut it off when we were running down upon him, and called to him as loud as I could call.'

'What did you say?'

'I said, Below there! Look out! Look out! For God's sake clear the way!'

I started.

'Ah! it was a dreadful time, sir. I never left off calling to him. I put this arm before my eyes, not to see, and I waved this arm to the last; but it was no use.'

Without prolonging the narrative to dwell on any one of its curious circumstances more than on any other, I may, in closing it, point out the coincidence that the warning of the Engine-Driver included, not only the words which the unfortunate Signalman had repeated to me as haunting him, but also the words which I myself — not he — had attached, and that only in my own mind, to the gesticulation he had imitated.

IMPRESSIONISTIC SKETCHES

The Election for Beadle

A GREAT event has recently occurred in our parish. A contest of paramount interest has just terminated; a parochial convulsion has taken place. It has been succeeded by a glorious triumph, which the country – or at least the parish – it is all the same – will long remember. We have had an election; an election for beadle. The supporters of the old beadle system have been defeated in their stronghold, and the advocates of the great new beadle principles have achieved a proud victory.

Our parish, which, like all other parishes, is a little world of its own, has long been divided into two parties, whose contentions, slumbering for a while, have never failed to burst forth with unabated vigour, on any occasion on which they could by possibility be renewed. Watching-rates,[1] lighting-rates, paving-rates, sewer's-rates, church-rates, poor's-rates – all sorts of rates, have been in their turns the subjects of a grand struggle; and as to questions of patronage, the asperity and determination with which they have been contested is scarcely credible.

The leader of the official party – the steady advocate of the churchwardens, and the unflinching supporter of the overseers – is an old gentleman who lives in our row. He owns some half a dozen houses in it, and always walks on the opposite side of the way, so that he may be able to take in a view of the whole of his property at once. He is a tall, thin, bony man, with an interrogative nose, and little restless perking eyes, which appear to have been given him for the sole purpose of peeping into other people's affairs with. He is deeply impressed with the importance of our parish business, and prides himself, not a little, on his style of addressing the parishioners in vestry assembled. His views are rather confined than extensive; his principles more narrow than liberal. He has been heard to declaim very loudly in favour of the liberty of the press, and advocates the repeal of the stamp duty on newspapers, because the daily journals who now have a monopoly of the public, never give *verbatim* reports of vestry meetings. He would not appear egotistical for the world, but at the same time he must say, that there *are* speeches – that celebrated speech of his own, on the emoluments of the sexton, and the duties of the office, for instance – which might be communicated to the public, greatly to their improvement and advantage.

His great opponent in public life is Captain Purday, the old naval officer on half-pay, to whom we have already introduced our readers.[2] The captain being a determined opponent of the constituted authorities, whoever they may chance to be, and our other friend being their steady supporter, with an equal disregard of their individual merits, it will readily be supposed, that occasions for their coming into direct collision are neither few nor far between. They divided the vestry fourteen times on a motion for heating the church with warm water instead of coals: and made speeches about liberty and expenditure, and prodigality and hot water, which threw the whole parish into a state of excitement. Then the captain, when he was on the visiting committee, and his opponent overseer, brought forward certain distinct and specific charges relative to the management of the workhouse, boldly expressed his total want of confidence in the existing authorities, and moved for 'a copy of the recipe by which the paupers' soup was prepared, together with any documents relating thereto.' This the overseer steadily resisted; he fortified himself by precedent, appealed to the established usage, and declined to produce the papers, on the ground of the injury that would be done to the public service, if documents of a strictly private nature, passing between the master of the workhouse and the cook, were to be thus dragged to light on the motion of any individual member of the vestry. The motion was lost by a majority of two; and then the captain, who never allows himself to be defeated, moved for a committee of inquiry into the whole subject. The affair grew serious: the question was discussed at meeting after meeting, and vestry after vestry; speeches were made, attacks repudiated, personal defiances exchanged, explanations received, and the greatest excitement prevailed, until at last, just as the question was going to be finally decided, the vestry found that somehow or other, they had become entangled in a point of form, from which it was impossible to escape with propriety. So, the motion was dropped, and everybody looked extremely important, and seemed quite satisfied with the meritorious nature of the whole proceeding.

VOTE for SPRUGGINS Ten Small Children and a Wife

BUNG for BEADLE Five Small Children

HASTE to the POLL

George Cruikshank.

The Election for Beadle

This was the state of affairs in our parish a week or two since, when Simmons, the beadle, suddenly died. The lamented deceased had over-exerted himself, a day or two previously, in conveying an aged female, highly intoxicated, to the strong room of the workhouse. The excitement thus occasioned, added to a severe cold, which this indefatigable officer had caught in his capacity of director of the parish engine, by inadvertently playing over himself instead of a fire, proved too much for a constitution already enfeebled by age; and the intelligence was conveyed to the Board one evening that Simmons had died, and left his respects.

The breath was scarcely out of the body of the deceased functionary, when the field was filled with competitors for the vacant office, each of whom rested his claims to public support, entirely on the number and extent of his family, as if the office of beadle were originally instituted as an encouragement for the propagation of the human species. 'Bung for Beadle. Five small children!' – 'Hopkins for Beadle. Seven small children!!' – 'Timkins for Beadle. Nine small children!!!' Such were the placards in large black letters on a white ground, which were plentifully pasted on the walls, and posted in the windows of the principal shops. Timkins's success was considered certain: several mothers of families half promised their votes, and the nine small children would have run over the course, but for the production of another placard, announcing the appearance of a still more meritorious candidate. 'Spruggins for Beadle. Ten small children (two of them twins), and a wife!!!' There was no resisting this; ten small children would have been almost irresistible in themselves, without the twins, but the touching parenthesis about that interesting production of nature, and the still more touching allusion to Mrs Spruggins, must ensure success. Spruggins was the favourite at once, and the appearance of his lady, as she went about to solicit votes (which encouraged confident hopes of a still further addition to the house of Spruggins at no remote period), increased the general prepossession in his favour. The other candidates, Bung alone excepted, resigned in despair. The day of election was fixed; and the canvass proceeded with briskness and perseverance on both sides.

The members of the vestry could not be supposed to escape the contagious excitement inseparable from the occasion. The majority of the lady inhabitants of the parish declared at once for Spruggins; and the *quondam* overseer took the same side, on the ground that men with large families always had been elected to the office, and that although he must admit, that, in other respects, Spruggins was the least qualified candidate of the two, still it was an old practice, and he saw no reason why an old practice should be departed from. This was enough for the captain. He immediately sided with Bung, canvassed for him personally in all directions, wrote squibs on Spruggins, and got his butcher to skewer them up on conspicuous joints in his shop-front; frightened his neighbour, the old lady,[3] into a palpitation of the heart, by his awful denunciations of Spruggins's party; and bounced in and out, and up and down, and backwards and forwards, until all the sober inhabitants of the parish thought it inevitable that he must die of a brain fever, long before the election began.

The day of election arrived. It was no longer an individual struggle, but a party contest between the ins and outs. The question was, whether the withering influence of the overseers, the domination of the churchwardens, and the blighting despotism of the vestry-clerk, should be allowed to render the election of beadle a form – a nullity: whether they should impose a vestry-elected beadle on the parish, to do their bidding and forward their views, or whether the parishioners, fearlessly asserting their undoubted rights, should elect an independent beadle of their own.

The nomination was fixed to take place in the vestry, but so great was the throng of anxious spectators, that it was found necessary to adjourn to the church, where the ceremony commenced with due solemnity. The appearance of the churchwardens and overseers, and the ex-churchwardens and ex-overseers, with Spruggins in the rear, excited general attention. Spruggins was a little thin man, in rusty black, with a long pale face, and a countenance expressive of care and fatigue, which might either be attributed to the extent of his family or the anxiety of his feelings. His opponent appeared in a cast-off coat of the captain's – a blue coat with bright buttons: white trousers, and that description of shoes familiarly known by the appellation of 'high-lows'.[4] There was a serenity in the open countenance of Bung – a kind of moral dignity in his confident air – an 'I wish you may get it' sort of expression in his eye – which infused animation into his supporters, and evidently dispirited his opponents.

The ex-churchwarden rose to propose Thomas Spruggins for beadle. He had known him long. He had had his eye upon him closely for years; he had watched him with twofold vigilance for months. (A parishioner here suggested that this might be termed 'taking a double sight', but the observation was drowned in loud cries of 'Order!') He would repeat that he had had his eye upon him for years, and this he would say, that a more well-conducted, a more well-behaved, a more sober, a more quiet man, with a more well-regulated mind, he had never met with. A man with a larger family he had never known (cheers). The parish required a man who could be depended on ('Hear!' from the Spruggins side, answered by ironical cheers from the Bung party). Such a man he now proposed ('No', 'Yes'). He would not allude to individuals (the ex-churchwarden continued, in the celebrated negative style adopted by great speakers). He would not advert to a gentleman who had once held a high rank in the service of his majesty; he would not say, that that gentleman was no gentleman; he would not assert, that that man was no man; he would not say, that he was a turbulent parishioner; he would not say, that he had grossly misbehaved himself, not only on this, but on all former occasions; he would not say, that he was one of those discontented and treasonable spirits, who carried confusion and disorder wherever they went; he would not say, that he harboured in his heart envy, and hatred, and malice, and all uncharitableness.[5] No! He wished to have everything comfortable and pleasant, and therefore, he would say – nothing about him (cheers).

The captain replied in a similar parliamentary style. He would not say, he was astonished at the speech they had just heard; he would not say, he was disgusted (cheers). He would not retort the epithets which had been hurled against him (renewed cheering); he would not allude to men once in office, but now happily out of it, who had mismanaged the workhouse, ground the paupers, diluted the beer, slack-baked the bread, boned the meat, heightened the work, and lowered the soup (tremendous cheers). He would not ask what such men deserved (a voice, 'Nothing a-day, and find themselves!'). He would not say, that one burst of general indignation should drive them from the parish they polluted with their presence ('Give it him!'). He would not allude to the unfortunate man who had been proposed – he would not say, as the vestry's tool, but as Beadle. He would not advert to that individual's family; he would not say, that nine children, twins, and a wife, were very bad examples of pauper imitation (loud cheers). He would not advert in detail to the qualifications of Bung. The man stood before him, and he would not say in his presence, what he might be disposed to say of him, if he were absent. (Here Mr Bung telegraphed to a friend near him, under cover of his hat, by contracting his left eye, and applying his right thumb to the tip of his nose). It had been objected to Bung that he had only five children ('Hear, hear!' from the opposition). Well; he had yet to learn that the legislature had affixed any precise amount of infantine qualification to the office of beadle; but taking it for granted that an extensive family were a great requisite, he entreated them to look to facts, and compare *data*, about which there could be no mistake. Bung was 35 years of age. Spruggins – of whom he wished to speak with all possible respect – was 50. Was it not more than possible – was it not very probable – that by the time Bung attained the latter age, he might see around him a family, even exceeding in number and extent, that to which Spruggins at present laid claim (deafening cheers and waving of handkerchiefs)? The captain concluded, amidst loud applause, by calling upon the parishioners to sound the tocsin, rush to the poll, free themselves from dictation, or be slaves for ever.

On the following day the polling began, and we never have had such a bustle in our parish since we got up our famous anti-slavery petition, which was such an important one, that the House of Commons ordered it to be printed, on the motion of the member for the district. The captain engaged two hackney-coaches and a cab for Bung's people – the cab for the drunken voters, and the two coaches for the old ladies, the greater portion of whom, owing to the captain's impetuosity, were driven up to the poll and home again, before they recovered from their flurry sufficiently to know, with any degree of clearness, what they had been doing. The opposite party wholly neglected these precautions, and the consequence was, that a great many ladies who were walking leisurely up to the church – for it was a very hot day – to vote for Spruggins, were artfully decoyed into the coaches, and voted for Bung. The captain's arguments, too, had produced considerable effect: the attempted influence of the vestry produced a greater. A threat of exclusive dealing was clearly established against the vestry-clerk – a case of heartless and profligate atrocity. It appeared that the delinquent had been in the habit of purchasing six penn'orth of muffins, weekly, from an old woman who rents a small house in the parish, and resides among the original settlers; on her last weekly visit, a message was conveyed to her through the medium of the cook, couched in mysterious terms, but indicating with sufficient clearness, that the vestry-clerk's appetite for muffins, in future, depended entirely on her vote on the beadleship. This was sufficient: the stream had been turning previously, and the impulse thus administered directed its final course. The Bung party ordered one shilling's-worth of muffins weekly for the remainder of the old woman's natural life; the parishioners were loud in their exclamations; and the fate of Spruggins was sealed.

It was in vain that the twins were exhibited in dresses of the same pattern, and night-caps to match, at the church door: the boy in Mrs Spruggins's right arm, and the girl in her left – even Mrs Spruggins herself failed to be an object of sympathy any longer. The majority attained by Bung on the gross poll was four hundred and twenty-eight, and the cause of the parishioners triumphed.

Seven Dials

WE have always been of opinion that if Tom King and the Frenchman[1] had not immortalized Seven Dials,[2] Seven Dials would have immortalized itself. Seven Dials! the region of song and poetry – first effusions, and last dying speeches: hallowed by the names of Catnach and of Pitts[3] – names that will entwine themselves with costermongers, and barrel-organs, when penny magazines shall have superseded penny yards of song,[4] and capital punishment be unknown!

Look at the construction of the place. The gordian knot[5] was all very well in its way: so was the maze of Hampton Court: so is the maze at the Beulah Spa:[6] so were the ties of stiff white neckcloths, when the difficulty of getting one on, was only to be equalled by the apparent impossibility of ever getting it off again. But what involutions can compare with those of Seven Dials? Where is there such another maze of streets, courts, lanes, and alleys? Where such a pure mixture of Englishmen and Irishmen, as in this complicated part of London? We boldly aver that we doubt the veracity of the legend to which we have averted. We *can* suppose a man rash enough to inquire at random – at a house with lodgers too – for a Mr Thompson, with all but the certainty before his eyes, of finding at least two or three Thompsons in any house of moderate dimensions; but a Frenchman – a Frenchman in Seven Dials! Pooh! He was an Irishman. Tom King's education had been neglected in his infancy, and as he couldn't understand half the man said, he took it for granted he was talking French.

The stranger who finds himself in 'The Dials' for the first time, and stands Belzoni-like,[7] at the entrance of seven obscure passages, uncertain which to take, will see enough around him to keep his curiosity and attention awake for no inconsiderable time. From the irregular square into which he was plunged, the streets and courts dart in all directions, until they are lost in the unwholesome vapour which hangs over the house-tops, and renders the dirty perspective uncertain and confined; and lounging at every corner, as if they came there to take a few gasps of such fresh air as has found its way so far, but is too much exhausted already, to be enabled to force itself into the narrow alleys around, are groups of people, whose appearance and dwellings would fill any mind but a regular Londoner's with astonishment.

On one side, a little crowd has collected round a couple of ladies, who having imbibed the contents of various 'three-outs'[8] of gin and bitters in the course of the morning, have at length differed on some point of domestic arrangement, and are on the eve of settling the quarrel satisfactorily, by an appeal to blows, greatly to the interest of other ladies who live in the same house, and tenements adjoining, and who are all partisans on one side or other.

'Vy don't you pitch into her, Sarah?' exclaims one half-dressed

Seven Dials

matron, by way of encouragement. 'Vy don't you? if *my* 'usband had treated her with a drain last night, unbeknown to me, I'd tear her precious eyes out – a wixen!'

'What's the matter, ma'am?' inquires another old woman, who has just bustled up to the spot.

'Matter!' replies the first speaker, talking *at* the obnoxious combatant, 'matter! Here's poor dear Mrs Sulliwin, as has five blessed children of her own, can't go out a charing for one arternoon, but what hussies must be a comin', and 'ticing avay her oun' 'usband, as she's been married to twelve year come next Easter Monday, for I see the certificate ven I vas a drinkin' a cup o' tea vith her, only the werry last blessed Ven'sday as ever was sent. I 'appen'd to say promiscuously, "Mrs Sulliwin," says I—'

'What do you mean by hussies?' interrupts a champion of the other party, who has evinced a strong inclination throughout to get up a branch fight on her own account ('Hooroar,' ejaculates a pot-boy in parenthesis, 'put the kye-bosk on her,[9] Mary!'), 'What do you mean by hussies?' reiterates the champion.

'Niver mind,' replies the opposition expressively, 'niver mind; *you* go home, and, ven you're quite sober, mend your stockings.'

This somewhat personal allusion, not only to the lady's habits of intemperance, but also to the state of her wardrobe, rouses her utmost ire, and she accordingly complies with the urgent request of the bystanders to 'pitch in', with considerable alacrity. The scuffle becáme general, and terminates, in minor play-bill phraseology, with 'arrival of the policemen, interior of the station-house, and impressive *dénouement*.'

In addition to the numerous groups who are idling about the gin-shops and squabbling in the centre of the road, every post in the open space has its occupant, who leans against it for hours, with listless perseverance. It is odd enough that one class of men in London appear to have no enjoyment beyond leaning against posts. We never saw a regular bricklayer's labourer take any other recreation, fighting excepted. Pass through St Giles's in the evening of a week-day, there they are in their fustian dresses, spotted with brick-dust and whitewash, leaning against posts. Walk through Seven Dials on Sunday morning: there they are again, drab or light corduroy trousers, Blucher boots,[10] blue coats, and great yellow waistcoats, leaning against posts. The idea of a man dressing himself in his best clothes, to lean against a post all day!

The peculiar character of these streets, and the close resemblance each one bears to its neighbour, by no means tends to decrease the bewilderment in which the unexperienced wayfarer through 'the Dials' finds himself involved. He traverses streets of dirty, straggling houses, with now and then an unexpected court composed of buildings as ill-proportioned and deformed as the half-naked children that wallow in the kennels. Here and there, a little dark chandler's shop, with a cracked bell hung up behind the door to announce the entrance of a customer, or betray the presence of some young gentleman in whom a passion for shop tills has developed itself at an early age: others, as if for support, against some handsome lofty building, which usurps the place of a low dingy public-house; long rows of broken and patched windows expose plants that may have flourished when 'the Dials' were built, in vessels as dirty as 'the Dials' themselves; and shops for the purchase of rags, bones, old iron, and kitchen-stuff, vie in cleanliness with the bird-fanciers and rabbit-dealers, which one might fancy so many arks, but for the irresistible conviction that no bird in its proper senses, who was permitted to leave one of them, would ever come back again. Brokers' shops, which would seem to have been established by humane individuals, as refuges for destitute bugs, interspersed with announcements of day-schools, penny theatres, petition writers, mangles, and music for balls or routs, complete the 'still life' of the subject; and dirty men, filthy women, squalid children, fluttering shuttlecocks, noisy battledores, reeking pipes, bad fruit, more than doubtful oysters, attenuated cats, depressed dogs, and anatomical fowls, are its cheerful accompaniments.

If the external appearance of the houses, or a glance at their inhabitants, present but few attractions, a closer acquaintance with either is little calculated to alter one's first impression. Every room has its separate tenant, and every tenant is, by the same mysterious dispensation which causes a country curate to 'increase and multiply'[11] most marvellously, generally the head of a numerous family.

The man in the shop, perhaps, is in the baked 'jemmy'[12] line, or the fire-wood and hearth-stone line, or any other line which requires a floating capital of eighteen-pence or thereabouts: and he and his family live in the shop, and the small back parlour behind it. Then there is an Irish labourer and *his* family in the back kitchen, and a jobbing man – carpet-beater and so forth – with *his* family in the front one. In the front one-pair, there's another man with another wife and family, and in the back one-pair, there's 'a young 'oman as takes in tambour-work, and dresses quite genteel', who talks a good deal about 'my friend', and can't 'a-bear anything low'. The second floor front, and the rest of the lodgers, are just a second edition of the people below, except a shabby-genteel man in the back attic, who has his half-pint of coffee every morning from the coffee-shop next door but one, which boasts a little front den called a coffee-room, with a fire-place, over which is an inscription, politely requesting that, 'to prevent mistakes', customers will 'please to pay on delivery'. The shabby-genteel man is an object of some mystery, but as he leads a life of seclusion, and never was known to buy anything beyond an occasional pen, except half-pints of coffee, penny loaves, and ha'porths of ink, his fellow-lodgers very naturally suppose him to be an author; and rumours are current in the Dials, that he writes poems for Mr Warren.[13]

Now anybody who passed through the Dials on a hot summer's evening, and saw the different women of the house gossiping on the steps, would be apt to think that all was harmony among them, and that a more primitive set of people than the native Diallers could not be imagined. Alas! the man in the shop ill-treats his family; the carpet-beater extends his professional pursuits to his wife; the one-pair front has an undying feud with the two-pair front, in consequence of the two-pair front persisting in dancing over his (the one-pair front's) head, when he and his family have retired for the night; the two-pair back *will* interfere with the front kitchen's children; the Irishman comes home drunk every other night, and attacks everybody; and the one-pair back screams at everything. Animosities spring up between floor and floor; the very cellar asserts his equality. Mrs A 'smacks' Mrs B's child, for 'making faces'. Mrs B forthwith throws cold water over Mrs B's child for 'calling names'. The husbands are embroiled – the quarrel becomes general – an assault is the consequence, and a police-officer the result.

Meditations in Monmouth-Street

WE have always entertained a particular attachment towards Monmouth-street,[1] as the only true and real emporium for second-hand wearing apparel. Monmouth-street is venerable from its antiquity, and respectable from its usefulness. Holywell-street[2] we despise; the red-headed and red-whiskered Jews who forcibly haul you into their squalid houses, and thrust you into a suit of clothes, whether you will or not, we detest.

The inhabitants of Monmouth-street are a distinct class; a peaceable and retiring race, who immure themselves for the most part in deep cellars, or small back parlours, and who seldom come forth into the world, except in the dusk and coolness of the evening, when they may be seen seated, in chairs on the pavement, smoking their pipes, or watching the gambols of their engaging children as they revel in the gutter, a happy troop of infantine scavengers. Their countenances bear a thoughtful and a dirty cast, certain indications of their love of traffic; and their habitations are distinguished by that disregard of outward appearance and neglect of personal comfort, so common among people who are constantly immersed in profound speculations, and deeply engaged in sedentary pursuits.

We have hinted at the antiquity of our favourite spot. 'A Monmouth-street laced coat' was a by-word a century ago; and still we find Monmouth-street the same. Pilot greatcoats with wooden buttons, have usurped the place of the ponderous laced coats with full skirts; embroidered waistcoats with large flaps, have yielded to double-breasted checks with roll-collars; and three-corner hats of quaint appearance, have given place to the low crowns and broad brims of the coachman school; but it is the times that have changed, not Monmouth-street. Through every alteration and every change, Monmouth-street has still remained the burial-place of the fashions; and such, to judge from all present appearances, it will remain until there are no more fashions to bury.

We love to walk among these extensive groves of the illustrious dead, and to indulge in the speculations to which they give rise;

now fitting a deceased coat, then a dead pair of trousers, and anon the mortal remains of a gaudy waistcoat, upon some being of our own conjuring up, and endeavouring, from the shape and fashion of the garment itself, to bring its former owner before our mind's eye. We have gone on speculating in this way, until whole rows of coats have started from their pegs, and buttoned up, of their own accord, round the waists of imaginary wearers; lines of trousers have jumped down to meet them; waistcoats have almost burst with anxiety to put themselves on; and half an acre of shoes have suddenly found feet to fit them, and gone stumping down the street with a noise which has fairly awakened us from our pleasant reverie, and driven us slowly away, with a bewildered stare, an object of astonishment to the good people of Monmouth-street, and of no slight suspicion to the policemen at the opposite street corner.

We were occupied in this manner the other day, endeavouring to fit a pair of lace-up half-boots[3] on an ideal personage, for whom, to say the truth, they were full a couple of sizes too small, when our eyes happened to alight on a few suits of clothes ranged outside a shop-window, which it immediately struck us, must at different periods have belonged to, and been worn by, the same individual, and had now, by one of those strange conjunctions of circumstances which will occur sometimes, come to be exposed together for sale in the same shop. The idea seemed a fantastic one, and we looked at the clothes again with a firm determination not to be easily led away. No, we were right; the more we looked, the more we were convinced of the accuracy of our previous impression. There was the man's whole life written as legibly on those clothes, as if we had his autobiography engrossed on parchment before us.

The first was a patched and much-soiled skeleton suit; one of those straight blue cloth cases in which small boys used to be confined, before belts and tunics had come in, and old notions had gone out: an ingenious contrivance for displaying the full symmetry of a boy's figure, by fastening him into a very tight jacket, with an ornamental row of buttons over each shoulder, and then buttoning his trousers over it, so as to give his legs the appearance of being hooked on, just under the armpits. This was the boy's dress. It had belonged to a town boy, we could see; there was a shortness about the legs and arms of the suit; and a bagging at the knees, peculiar to the rising youth of London streets. A small day-school he had been at, evidently. If it had been a regular boys' school they wouldn't have let him play on the floor so much, and rub his knees so white. He had an indulgent mother too, and plenty of halfpence, as the numerous smears of some sticky substance about the pockets, and just below the chin, which even the salesman's skill could not succeed in disguising, sufficiently betokened. They were decent people, but not overburdened with riches, or he would not have so far out-grown the suit when he passed into those corduroys with the round jacket; in which he went to a boys' school, however, and learnt to write – and in ink of pretty tolerable blackness, too, if the place where he used to wipe his pen might be taken as evidence.

A black suit and the jacket changed into a diminutive coat. His father had died, and the mother had got the boy a message-lad's place in some office. A long-worn suit that one; rusty and thread-bare before it was laid aside, but clean and free from soil to the last. Poor woman! We could imagine her assumed cheerfulness over the scanty meal, and the refusal of her own small portion, that her hungry boy might have enough. Her constant anxiety for his welfare, her pride in his growth mingled sometimes with the thought, almost too acute to bear, that as he grew to be a man his old affection might cool, old kindnesses fade from his mind, and old promises be forgotten – the sharp pain that even then a careless word or a cold look would give her – all crowded on our thoughts as vividly as if the very scene were passing before us.

These things happen every hour, and we all know it; and yet we felt as much sorrow when we saw, or fancied we saw – it makes no difference which – the change that began to take place now, as if we had just conceived the bare possibility of such a thing for the first time. The next suit, smart but slovenly; meant to be gay, and yet not half so decent as the threadbare apparel; redolent of the idle lounge, and the blackguard companions, told us, we thought, that the widow's comfort had rapidly faded away. We could imagine that coat – imagine! we could see it; we *had* seen it a hundred times – sauntering in company with three or four other coats of the same cut, about some place of profligate resort at night.

We dressed, from the same shop-window in an instant, half a dozen boys of from fifteen to twenty; and putting cigars into their mouths, and their hands into their pockets, watched them as they sauntered down the street, and lingered at the corner, with the obscene jest, and the oft-repeated oath. We never lost sight of them, till they had cocked their hats a little more on one side, and swaggered into the public-house; and then we entered the desolate home, where the mother sat late in the night, alone; we watched her, as she paced the room in feverish anxiety, and every now and then opened the door, looked wistfully into the dark and empty street, and again returned, to be again and again disappointed. We beheld the look of patience with which she bore the brutish threat, nay, even the drunken blow; and we heard the agony of tears that gushed from her very heart, as she sank upon her knees in her solitary and wretched apartment.

A long period had elapsed, and a greater change had taken place, by the time of casting off the suit that hung above. It was that of a stout, broad-shouldered, sturdy-chested man; and we knew at once, as anybody would, who glanced at that broad-skirted green coat, with the large metal buttons, that its wearer seldom walked forth without a dog at his heels, and some idle ruffian, the very counterpart of himself, at his side. The vices of the boy had grown with the man, and we fancied his home then – if such a place deserve the name.

We saw the bare and miserable room, destitute of furniture, crowded with his wife and children, pale, hungry, and emaciated; the man cursing their lamentations, staggering to the tap-room, from whence he had just returned, followed by his wife and a sickly infant, clamouring for bread; and heard the street-wrangle and noisy recrimination that his striking her occasioned. And then imagination led us to some metropolitan workhouse, situated in the midst of crowded streets and alleys, filled with noxious vapours, and ringing with boisterous cries, where an old and feeble woman, imploring pardon for her son, lay dying in a close dark room, with no child to clasp her hand, and no pure air from heaven to fan her brow. A stranger closed the eyes that settled into a cold unmeaning glare, and strange ears received the words that murmured from the white and half-closed lips.

A coarse round frock, with a worn cotton neckerchief, and other articles of clothing of the commonest description, completed the history. A prison, and the sentence – banishment or the gallows. What would the man have given then, to be once again the contented humble drudge of his boyish years; to have restored to life, but for a week, a day, an hour, a minute, only for so long a time as would enable him to say one word of passionate regret to, and hear one sound of heartfelt forgiveness from, the cold and ghastly form that lay rotting in the pauper's grave! The children wild in the streets, the mother a destitute widow; both deeply tainted with the deep disgrace of the husband and father's name, and impelled by sheer necessity, down the precipice that had led him to a lingering death, possibly of many years' duration, thousands of miles away. We had no clue to the end of the tale; but it was easy to guess its termination.

We took a step or two further on, and by way of restoring the naturally cheerful tone of our thoughts, began fitting visionary feet and legs into a cellar-board full of boots and shoes, with a speed and accuracy that would have astonished the most expert artists in leather, living. There was one pair of boots in particular – a jolly, good-tempered, hearty-looking, pair of tops,[4] that excited our warmest regard; and we had got a fine, red-faced, jovial fellow of a market-gardener into them, before we had made their acquaintance half a minute. They were just the very thing for him. There were his huge fat legs bulging over the tops, and fitting them too tight to admit of his tucking in the loops he had pulled them on by; and his knee-cords[5] with an interval of stocking; and his blue apron tucked up round his waist; and his red neckerchief and blue coat, and a white hat stuck on one side of his head; and there he stood with a broad grin on his great red face, whistling away, as if any other idea but that of being happy and comfortable had never entered his brain.

This was the very man after our own heart; we knew all about him; we had seen him coming up to Covent-garden in his green chaise-cart, with the fat tubby little horse, half a thousand times; and even while we cast an affectionate look upon his boots, at that instant, the form of a coquettish servant-maid suddenly sprung into a pair of Denmark satin[6] shoes that stood beside them, and we at once recognized the very girl who accepted his offer of a ride, just on this side the Hammersmith suspension-bridge, the very last Tuesday morning we rode into town from Richmond.

A very smart female, in a showy bonnet, stepped into a pair of grey cloth boots, with black fringe and binding, that were studiously pointing out their toes on the other side of the top-boots, and seemed very anxious to engage his attention, but we didn't observe that our friend the market-gardener appeared at all captivated with these blandishments; for beyond giving a knowing wink when they first began, as if to imply that he quite understood their end and object, he took no further notice of them. His indifference, however, was amply recompensed by the excessive gallantry of a very old gentleman with a silver-headed stick, who tottered into a pair of large list shoes, that were standing in one corner of the board, and indulged in a variety of gestures expressive of his admiration of the lady in the cloth boots, to the immeasurable amusement of a young fellow we put into a pair of long-quartered pumps, who we thought would have split the coat that slid down to meet him, with laughing.

We had been looking on at this little pantomime with great satisfaction for some time, when, to our unspeakable astonishment, we perceived that the whole of the characters, including a numerous *corps de ballet* of boots and shoes in the back-ground, into which we had been hastily thrusting as many feet as we could press into the service, were arranging themselves in order for dancing; and some music striking up at the moment, to it they went without delay. It was perfectly delightful to witness the agility of the market-gardener. Out went the boots, first on one side, then on the other, then cutting, then shuffling, then setting to the Denmark satins, then advancing, then retreating, then going round, and then repeating the whole of the evolutions again, without appearing to suffer in the least from the violence of the exercise.

Nor were the Denmark satins a bit behindhand, for they jumped and bounded about, in all directions; and though they were neither so regular, nor so true to the time as the cloth boots, still, as they seemed to do it from the heart, and to enjoy it more, we candidly confess that we preferred their style of dancing to the other. But the old gentleman in the list shoes was the most amusing object in the whole party; for, besides his grotesque attempts to appear youthful, and amorous, which were sufficiently entertaining in themselves, the young fellow in the pumps managed so artfully that every time the old gentleman advanced to salute the lady in the cloth boots, he trod with his whole weight on the old fellow's toes, which made him roar with anguish, and rendered all the others like to die of laughing.

We were in the full enjoyment of these festivities when we heard a shrill, and by no means musical voice, exclaim, 'Hope you'll know me agin, imperence!'[7] and on looking intently forward to see from whence the sound came, we found that it proceeded, not from the young lady in the cloth boots, as we had first been inclined to suppose, but from a bulky lady of elderly appearance who was seated in a chair at the head of the cellar-steps, apparently for the purpose of superintending the sale of the articles arranged there.

A barrel-organ, which had been in full force close behind us, ceased playing; the people we had been fitting into the shoes and boots took to flight at the interruption; and as we were conscious that in the depth of our meditations we might have been rudely staring at the old lady for half an hour without knowing it, we took to flight too, and were soon immersed in the deepest obscurity of the adjacent 'Dials'.

A Visit to Newgate

'THE force of habit' is a trite phrase in everybody's mouth; and it is not a little remarkable that those who use it most as applied to others, unconsciously afford in their own persons singular examples of the power which habit and custom exercise over the minds of men, and of the little reflection they are apt to bestow on subjects with which every day's experience has rendered them familiar. If Bedlam could be suddenly removed like another Aladdin's palace,[1] and set down on the space now occupied by Newgate,[2] scarcely one man out of a hundred, whose road to business every morning lies through Newgate-street, or the Old Bailey,[3] would pass the building without bestowing a hasty glance on its small, grated windows, and a transient thought upon the condition of the unhappy beings immured in its dismal cells; and yet these same men, day by day, and hour by hour, pass and repass this gloomy depository of the guilt and misery of London, in one perpetual stream of life and bustle, utterly unmindful of the throng of wretched creatures pent up within it – nay, not even knowing, or if they do, not heeding, the fact, that as they pass one particular angle of the massive wall with a light laugh or a merry whistle, they stand within one yard of a fellow-creature, bound and helpless, whose hours are numbered, from whom the last feeble ray of hope has fled for ever, and whose miserable career will shortly terminate in a violent and shameful death. Contact with death even in its least terrible shape, is solemn and appalling. How much more awful is it to reflect on this near vicinity to the dying – to men in full health and vigour, in the flower of youth or the prime of life, with all their faculties and perceptions as acute and perfect as your own; but dying, nevertheless – dying as surely – with the hand of death imprinted upon them as indelibly – as if mortal disease had wasted their frames to shadows, and corruption had already begun!

It was with some such thoughts as these that we determined, not many weeks since, to visit the interior of Newgate – in an amateur capacity, of course; and, having carried our intention into effect, we proceed to lay its results before our readers, in the hope – founded more upon the nature of the subject, than on any presumptuous confidence in our own descriptive powers – that this paper may not be found wholly devoid of interest. We have only to premise, that we do not intend to fatigue the reader with any statistical accounts of the prison; they will be found at length in numerous reports of numerous committees, and a variety of authorities of equal weight. We took no notes, made no memoranda, measured none of the yards, ascertained the exact number of inches in no particular room: are unable even to report of how many apartments the gaol is composed.

We saw the prison, and saw the prisoners; and what we did see, and what we thought, we will tell at once in our own way.

Having delivered our credentials to the servant who answered our knock at the door of the governor's house, we were ushered into the 'office'; a little room, on the right-hand side as you enter, with two windows looking into the Old Bailey: fitted up like an ordinary attorney's office, or merchant's counting-house, with the usual fixtures – a wainscoted partition, a shelf or two, a desk, a couple of stools, a pair of clerks, an almanack, a clock, and a few maps. After a little delay, occasioned by sending into the interior of the prison for the officer whose duty it was to conduct us, that functionary arrived; a respectable-looking man of about two or three and fifty, in a broad-brimmed hat, and full suit of black, who, but for his keys, would have looked quite as much like a clergyman as a turnkey. We were disappointed; he had not even top-boots on. Following our conductor by a door opposite to that at which we had entered, we arrived at a small room, without any other furniture than a little desk, with a book for visitors' autographs, and a shelf, on which were a few boxes for papers, and casts of the heads and faces of the two notorious murderers, Bishop and Williams;4 the former, in particular, exhibiting a style of head and set of features, which might have afforded sufficient moral grounds for his instant execution at any time, even had there been no other evidence against him. Leaving this room also, by an opposite door, we found ourself in the lodge which opens on the Old Bailey; one side of which is plentifully garnished with a choice collection of heavy sets of irons, including those worn by the redoubtable Jack Sheppard – genuine; and those *said* to have been graced by the sturdy limbs of the no less celebrated Dick Turpin5 – doubtful. From this lodge, a heavy oaken gate, bound with iron, studded with nails of the same material, and guarded by another turnkey, opens on a few steps, if we remember right, which terminate in a narrow and dismal stone passage, running parallel with the Old Bailey, and leading to the different yards, through a number of tortuous and intricate windings, guarded in their turn by huge gates and gratings, whose appearance is sufficient to dispel at once the slightest hope of escape that any new comer may have entertained; and the very recollection of which, on eventually traversing the place again, involves one in a maze of confusion.

It is necessary to explain here, that the buildings in the prison, or in other words the different wards – form a square, of which the four sides abut respectively on the Old Bailey, the old College of Physicians (now forming a part of Newgate-market), the Sessions-house, and Newgate-street. The intermediate space is divided into several paved yards, in which the prisoners take such air and exercise as can be had in such a place. These yards, with the exception of that in which prisoners under sentence of death are confined (of which we shall presently give a more detailed description), run parallel with Newgate-street, and consequently from the Old Bailey, as it were, to Newgate-market. The women's side is in the right wing of the prison nearest the Sessions-house. As we were introduced into this part of the building first, we will adopt the same order, and introduce our readers to it also.

Turning to the right, then, down the passage to which we just now adverted, omitting any mention of intervening gates – for if we noticed every gate that was unlocked for us to pass through, and locked again as soon as we had passed, we should require a gate at every comma – we came to a door composed of thick bars of wood, through which were discernible, passing to and fro in a narrow yard, some twenty women: the majority of whom, however, as soon as they were aware of the presence of strangers, retreated to their wards. One side of this yard is railed off at a considerable distance, and formed into a kind of iron cage, about five feet ten inches in height, roofed at the top, and defended in front by iron bars, from which the friends of the female prisoners communicate with them. In one corner of this singular-looking den, was a yellow, haggard, decrepit old woman, in a tattered gown that had once been black, and the remains of an old straw bonnet, with faded ribbon of the same hue, in earnest conversation with a young girl – a prisoner, of course – of about two-and-twenty. It is impossible to imagine a more poverty-stricken object, or a creature so borne down in soul and body, by excess of misery and destitution as the old woman. The girl was a good-looking robust female, with a profusion of hair streaming about in the wind – for she had no bonnet on – and a man's silk pocket-handkerchief loosely thrown over a most ample pair of shoulders. The old woman was talking in that low, stifled tone of voice which tells so forcibly of mental anguish; and every now and then burst into an irrepressible sharp, abrupt cry of grief, the most distressing sound that ears can hear. The girl was perfectly unmoved. Hardened beyond all hope of redemption, she listened doggedly to her mother's entreaties, whatever they were: and, beyond inquiring after 'Jem', and eagerly catching at the few halfpence her miserable parent had brought her, took no more apparent interest in the conversation than the most unconcerned spectators. Heaven knows there were enough of them, in the persons of the other prisoners in the yard, who were no more concerned by what was passing before their eyes, and within their hearing, than if they were blind and deaf. Why should they be? Inside the prison, and out, such scenes were too familiar to them, to excite even a passing thought, unless of ridicule or contempt for feelings which they had long since forgotten.

A little farther on, a squalid-looking woman in a slovenly, thick-bordered cap, with her arms muffled in a large red shawl, the fringed ends of which straggled nearly to the bottom of a dirty white apron, was communicating some instructions to *her* visitor – her daughter evidently. The girl was thinly clad, and shaking with the cold. Some ordinary word of recognition passed between her and her mother when she appeared at the grating, but neither hope, condolence, regret, nor affection was expressed on either side. The mother whispered her instructions, and the girl received them with her pinched-up half-starved features twisted into an expression of careful cunning. It was some scheme for the woman's defence that she was disclosing, perhaps; and a sullen smile came over the girl's face for an instant, as if she were pleased: not so much at the probability of her mother's liberation, as at the chance of her 'getting off' in spite of her prosecutors. The dialogue was soon concluded; and with the same careless indifference with which they had approached each other, the mother turned towards the inner end of the yard, and the girl to the gate at which she had entered.

The girl belonged to a class – unhappily but too extensive – the very existence of which, should make men's hearts bleed. Barely past her childhood, it required but a glance to discover that she was one of those children, born and bred in neglect and vice, who have never known what childhood is: who have never been taught to love and court a parent's smile, or to dread a parent's frown. The thousand nameless endearments of childhood, its gaiety and its innocence, are alike unknown to them. They have entered at once upon the stern realities and miseries of life, and to their better nature it is almost hopeless to appeal in aftertimes, by any of the references which will awaken, if it be only for a moment, some good feeling in ordinary bosoms, however corrupt they may have become. Talk to *them* of parental solicitude, the happy days of childhood, and the merry games of infancy! Tell them of hunger and the streets, beggary and stripes, the gin-shop, the station-house, and the pawnbroker's, and they will understand you.

Two or three women were standing at different parts of the grating, conversing with their friends, but a very large proportion of the prisoners appeared to have no friends at all, beyond such of their old companions as might happen to be within the walls. So, passing hastily down the yard, and pausing only for an instant to notice the little incidents we have just recorded, we were conducted up a clean and well-lighted flight of stone stairs to one of the wards. There were several in this part of the building, but a description of one is a description of the whole.

It was a spacious, bare, whitewashed apartment, lighted, of course, by windows looking into the interior of the prison, but far more light and airy than one could reasonably expect to find in such a situation. There was a large fire with a deal table before it, round which ten or a dozen women were seated on wooden forms at dinner. Along both sides of the room ran a shelf; below it, at regular intervals, a row of large hooks were fixed in the wall, on each of which was hung the sleeping mat of a prisoner: her rug and blanket being folded up, and placed on the shelf above. At night, these mats are placed on the floor, each beneath the hook on which it hangs during the day; and the ward is thus made to answer the purposes both of a day-room and sleeping apartment. Over the fireplace, was a large sheet of pasteboard, on which were displayed a variety of texts from Scripture, which were also scattered about the room in scraps about the size and shape of the copy-slips which are used in schools. On the table was a sufficient provision of a kind of stewed beef and brown bread, in pewter dishes, which are kept perfectly bright, and displayed on shelves in great order and regularity when they are not in use.

The women rose hastily, on our entrance, and retired in a hurried manner to either side of the fireplace. They were all cleanly – many of them decently – attired, and there was nothing peculiar, either in their appearance or demeanour. One or two resumed the needlework which they had probably laid aside at the commencement of their meal; others gazed at the visitors with listless curiosity; and a few retired behind their companions to the very end of the room, as if desirous to avoid even the casual observation of the strangers. Some old Irish women, both in this and other wards, to whom the thing was no novelty, appeared perfectly indifferent to our presence, and remained standing close to the seats from which they had just risen; but the general feeling among the females seemed to be one of uneasiness during the period of our stay among them: which was very brief. Not a word was uttered during the time of our remaining, unless, indeed, by the wardswoman in reply to some question which we put to the turnkey who accompanied us. In every ward on the female side, a wardswoman is appointed to preserve order, and a similar regulation is adopted among the males. The wardsmen and wardswomen are all prisoners, selected for good conduct. They alone are allowed the privilege of sleeping on bedsteads; a small stump bedstead[6] being placed in every ward for that purpose. On both sides of the gaol, is a small receiving-room, to which prisoners are conducted on their first reception, and whence they cannot be removed until they have been examined by the surgeon of the prison.*

Retracing our steps to the dismal passage in which we found ourselves at first (and which, by-the-bye, contains three or four dark cells for the accommodation of refractory prisoners), we were led through a narrow yard to the 'school' – a portion of the prison set apart for boys under fourteen years of age. In a tolerable-sized room, in which were writing-materials and some copy-books, was the schoolmaster, with a couple of his pupils; the remainder having been fetched from an adjoining apartment, the whole were drawn up in line for our inspection. There were fourteen of them in all, some with shoes, some without; some in pinafores without jackets, others in jackets without pinafores, and one in scarce anything at all. The whole number, without an exception we believe, had been committed for trial on charges of pocket-picking; and fourteen

---

*The regulations of the prison relative to the confinement of prisoners during the day, their sleeping at night, their taking their meals, and other matters of gaol economy, have been all altered – greatly for the better – since this sketch was first published. Even the construction of the prison itself has been changed.

such terrible little faces we never beheld. – There was not one re-deeming feature among them – not a glance of honesty – not a wink expressive of anything but the gallows and the hulks, in the whole collection. As to anything like shame or contrition, that was en-tirely out of the question. They were evidently quite gratified at being thought worth the trouble of looking at; their idea appeared to be, that we had come to see Newgate as a grand affair, and that they were an indispensable part of the show; and every boy as he 'fell in' to the line, actually seemed as pleased and important as if he had done something excessively meritorious in getting there at all. We never looked upon a more disagreeable sight, because we never saw fourteen such hopeless creatures of neglect, before.

On either side of the school-yard is a yard for men, in one of which – that towards Newgate-street – prisoners of the more re-spectable class are confined. Of the other, we have little description to offer, as the different wards necessarily partake of the same character. They are provided, like the wards on the women's side, with mats and rugs, which are disposed of in the same manner dur-ing the day; the only very striking difference between their appear-ance and that of the wards inhabited by the females, is the utter absence of any employment. Huddled together on two opposite forms, by the fireside, sit twenty men perhaps; here, a boy in livery; there, a man in a rough great-coat and top-boots; farther on, a des-perate-looking fellow in his shirt sleeves, with an old Scotch cap upon his shaggy head; near him again, a tall ruffian, in a smock-frock; next to him, a miserable being of distressed appearance, with his head resting on his hand; – all alike in one respect, all idle and listless. When they do leave the fire, sauntering moodily about, lounging in the window, or leaning against the wall, vacantly swinging their bodies to and fro. With the exception of a man read-ing an old newspaper, in two or three instances, this was the case in every ward we entered.

The only communication these men have with their friends, is through two close iron gratings, with an intermediate space of about a yard in width between the two, so that nothing can be handed across, nor can the prisoner have any communication by touch with the person who visits him. The married men have a separate grating, at which to see their wives, but its construction is the same.

The prison chapel is situated at the back of the governor's house: the latter having no windows looking into the interior of the prison. Whether the associations connected with the place – the knowledge that here a portion of the burial service is, on some dreadful occasions, performed over the quick and not upon the dead – cast over it a still more gloomy and sombre air than art has imparted to it, we know not, but its appearance is very striking. There is something in a silent and deserted place of worship, solemn and impressive at any time; and the very dissimilarity of this one from any we have been accustomed to, only enhances the impression. The meanness of its appointments – the bare and scanty pulpit, with the paltry painted pillars on either side – the women's gallery with its great heavy curtain – the men's with its unpainted benches and dingy front – the tottering little table at the altar, with the commandments on the wall above it, scarcely legible through lack of paint, and dust and damp – so unlike the velvet and gilding, the marble and wood, of a modern church – are strange and striking. There is one object, too, which rivets the attention and fascinates the gaze, and from which we may turn horror-stricken in vain, for the recollection of it will haunt us, waking and sleeping, for a long time afterwards. Immediately below the reading-desk, on the floor of the chapel, and forming the most conspicuous object in its little area, is *the condemned pew*; a huge black pen, in which the wretched people, who are singled out for death, are placed on the Sunday preceding their execution, in sight of all their fellow-prisoners, from many of whom they may have been separated but a week before, to hear prayers for their own souls, to join in the responses of their own burial service, and to listen to an address, warning their recent companions to take example by their fate, and urging themselves, while there is yet time – nearly four-and-twenty hours – to 'turn, and flee from the wrath to come!'[8] Imagine what have been the feelings of the men whom that fearful pew has enclosed, and of whom, between the gallows and the knife, no mortal remnant may now remain! Think of the hopeless clinging to life to the last, and the wild despair, far exceeding in anguish the felon's death itself, by which they have heard the certainty of their speedy transmission to another world, with all their crimes upon their heads, rung into their ears by the officiating clergyman!

At one time – and at no distant period either – the coffins of the men about to be executed were placed in that pew, upon the seat by their side, during the whole service. It may seem incredible, but it is true. Let us hope that the increased spirit of civilization and humanity which abolished this frightful and degrading custom, may extend itself to other usages equally barbarous; usages which have not even the plea of utility in their defence, as every year's experience has shown them to be more and more inefficacious.

Leaving the chapel, descending to the passage so frequently alluded to, and crossing the yard before noticed as being allotted to prisoners of a more respectable description than the generality of men confined here, the visitor arrives at a thick iron gate of great size and strength. Having been admitted through it by the turnkey on duty, he turns sharp round to the left, and pauses before another gate; and, having passed this last barrier, he stands in the most terrible part of this gloomy building – the condemned ward.

The press-yard, well known by name to newspaper readers, from its frequent mention in accounts of executions, is at the corner of the building, and next to the ordinary's house, in Newgate-street: running from Newgate-street, towards the centre of the prison, parallel with Newgate-market. It is a long, narrow court, of which a portion of the wall in Newgate-street forms one end, and the gate the other. At the upper end, on the left-hand – that is, adjoining the wall in Newgate-street – is a cistern of water, and at the bottom a double grating (of which the gate itself forms a part) similar to that before described. Through these grates the prisoners are allowed to see their friends; a turnkey always remaining in the vacant space between, during the whole interview. Immediately on the right as you enter, is a building containing the press-room, day-room, and cells; the yard is on every side surrounded by lofty walls guarded by *chevaux de frise*; and the whole is under the constant inspection of vigilant and experienced turnkeys.

In the first apartment into which we were conducted – which was at the top of a staircase, and immediately over the press-room – were five-and-twenty or thirty prisoners, all under sentence of death, awaiting the result of the recorder's report – men of all ages and appearances, from a hardened old offender with swarthy face and grizzly beard of three days' growth, to a handsome boy, not fourteen years old, and of singularly youthful appearance even for that age, who had been condemned for burglary. There was nothing remarkable in the appearance of these prisoners. One or two decently-dressed men were brooding with a dejected air over the fire; several little groups of two or three had been engaged in conversation at the upper end of the room, or in the windows; and the remainder were crowded round a young man seated at a table, who appeared to be engaged in teaching the younger ones to write. The room was large, airy, and clean. There was very little anxiety or mental suffering depicted in the countenance of any of the men; — they had all been sentenced to death, it is true, and the recorder's report had not yet been made; but, we question whether there was a man among them, notwithstanding, who did not *know* that although he had undergone the ceremony, it never was intended that his life should be sacrificed. On the table lay a Testament, but there were no tokens of its having been in recent use.

In the press-room below, were three men, the nature of whose offence rendered it necessary to separate them, even from their companions in guilt. It is a long, sombre room, with two windows sunk into the stone wall, and here the wretched men are pinioned on the morning of their execution, before moving towards the scaffold. The fate of one of these prisoners was uncertain; some mitigatory circumstances having come to light since his trial, which had been humanely represented in the proper quarter. The other two had nothing to expect from the mercy of the crown; their doom was sealed; no plea could be urged in extenuation of their crime, and they well knew that for them there was no hope in this world. 'The two short ones,' the turnkey whispered, 'were dead men.'

The man to whom we have alluded as entertaining some hopes of escape, was lounging, at the greatest distance he could place between himself and his companions, in the window nearest to the door. He was probably aware of our approach, and had assumed an air of courageous indifference; his face was purposely averted towards the window, and he stirred not an inch while we were present. The other two men were at the upper end of the room. One of them, who was imperfectly seen in the dim light, had his back towards us, and was stooping over the fire, with his right arm on the mantel-piece, and his head sunk upon it. The other, was leaning on the sill of the farthest window. The light fell full upon him, and communicated to his pale, haggard face, and disordered hair, an appearance which, at that distance, was ghastly. His cheek rested upon his hand; and, with his face a little raised, and his eyes wildly staring before him, he seemed to be unconsciously intent on counting the chinks in the opposite wall. We passed this room again afterwards. The first man was pacing up and down the court with a firm military step – he had been a soldier in the foot-guards – and a cloth cap jauntily thrown on one side of his head. He bowed respectfully to our conductor, and the salute was returned. The other two still remained in the positions we have described, and were as motionless as statues.*

A few paces up the yard, and forming a continuation of the building, in which are the two rooms we have just quitted, lie the condemned cells. The entrance is by a narrow and obscure staircase leading to a dark passage, in which a charcoal stove casts a lurid tint over the objects in its immediate vicinity, and diffuses something like warmth around. From the left-hand side of this passage, the massive door of every cell on the story opens; and from it alone can they be approached. There are three of these passages, and three of these ranges of cells, one above the other; but in size, furniture and appearance, they are all precisely alike. Prior to the recorder's report being made, all the prisoners under sentence of death are removed from the day-room at five o'clock in the afternoon, and locked up in these cells, where they are allowed a candle until ten o'clock; and here they remain until seven next morning. When the warrant for a prisoner's execution arrives, he is removed to the cells and confined in one of them until he leaves it for the scaffold. He is at liberty to walk in the yard; but, both in his walks and in his cell, he is constantly attended by a turnkey who never leaves him on any pretence.

We entered the first cell. It was a stone dungeon, eight feet long by six wide, with a bench at the upper end, under which were a common rug, a bible, and prayer-book. An iron candlestick was fixed into the wall at the side; and a small high window in the back admitted as much air and light as could struggle in between a

*These two men were executed shortly afterwards. The other was respited during his Majesty's pleasure.

double row of heavy, cross iron bars. It contained no other furniture of any description.

Conceive the situation of a man, spending his last night on earth in this cell. Buoyed up with some vague and undefined hope of reprieve, he knew not why – indulging in some wild and visionary idea of escaping, he knew not how – hour after hour of the three preceding days allowed him for preparation, has fled with a speed which no man living would deem possible, for none but this dying man can know. He has wearied his friends with entreaties, exhausted the attendants with importunities, neglected in his feverish restlessness the timely warnings of his spiritual consoler; and, now that the illusion is at last dispelled, now that eternity is before him and guilt behind, now that his fears of death amount almost to madness, and an overwhelming sense of his helpless, hopeless state rushes upon him, he is lost and stupefied, and has neither thoughts to turn to, nor power to call upon, the Almighty Being, from whom alone he can seek mercy and forgiveness, and before whom his repentance can alone avail.

Hours have glided by, and still he sits upon the same stone bench with folded arms, heedless alike of the fast decreasing time before him, and the urgent entreaties of the good man at his side. The feeble light is wasting gradually, and the deathlike stillness of the street without, broken only by the rumbling of some passing vehicle which echoes mournfully through the empty yards, warns him that the night is waning fast away. The deep bell of St Paul's strikes – one! He heard it; it has roused him. Seven hours left! He paces the narrow limits of his cell with rapid strides, cold drops of terror starting on his forehead, and every muscle of his frame quivering with agony. Seven hours! He suffers himself to be led to his seat, mechanically takes the bible which is placed in his hand, and tries to read and listen. No: his thoughts will wander. The book is torn and soiled by use – and like the book he read his lessons in, at school, just forty years ago! He has never bestowed a thought upon it, perhaps, since he left it as a child: and yet the place, the time, the room – nay, the very boys he played with, crowd as vividly before him as if they were scenes of yesterday; and some forgotten phrase, some childish word, rings in his ears like the echo of one uttered but a minute since. The voice of the clergyman recalls him to himself. He is reading from the sacred book its solemn promises of pardon for repentance, and its awful denunciation of obdurate men. He falls upon his knees and clasps his hands to pray. Hush! what sound was that? He starts upon his feet. It cannot be two yet. Hark! Two quarters have struck; – the third – the fourth. It is! Six hours left. Tell him not of repentance! Six hours' repentance for eight times six years of guilt and sin! He buries his face in his hands, and throws himself on the bench.

Worn with watching and excitement, he sleeps, and the same unsettled state of mind pursues him in his dreams. An insupportable load is taken from his breast; he is walking with his wife in a pleasant field, with the bright sky above them, and a fresh and boundless prospect on every side – how different from the stone walls of Newgate! She is looking – not as she did when he saw her for the last time in that dreadful place, but as she used when he loved her – long, long ago, before misery and ill-treatment had altered her looks, and vice had changed his nature, and she is leaning upon his arm, and looking up into his face with tenderness and affection – and he does *not* strike her now, nor rudely shake her from him. And oh! how glad he is to tell her all he had forgotten in that last hurried interview, and to fall on his knees before her and fervently beseech her pardon for all the unkindness and cruelty that wasted her form and broke her heart! The scene suddenly changes. He is on his trial again: there are the judge and jury, and prosecutors, and witnesses, just as they were before. How full the court is – what a sea of heads – with a gallows, too, and a scaffold – and how all those people stare at *him*! Verdict, 'Guilty'. No matter; he will escape.

The night is dark and cold, the gates have been left open, and in an instant he is in the street, flying from the scene of his imprisonment like the wind. The streets are cleared, the open fields are gained and the broad wide country lies before him. Onward he dashes in the midst of darkness, over hedge and ditch, through mud and pool, bounding from spot to spot with a speed and lightness, astonishing even to himself. At length he pauses; he must be safe from pursuit now; he will stretch himself on that bank and sleep till sunrise.

A period of unconsciousness succeeds. He wakes, cold and

wretched. The dull grey light of morning is stealing into the cell, and falls upon the form of the attendant turnkey. Confused by his dreams, he starts from his uneasy bed in momentary uncertainty. It is but momentary. Every object in the narrow cell is too frightfully real to admit of doubt or mistake. He is the condemned felon again, guilty and despairing; and in two hours more will be dead.

A Christmas Tree

I HAVE been looking on, this evening, at a merry company of children assembled round that pretty German toy, a Christmas Tree. The tree was planted in the middle of a great round table, and towered high above their heads. It was brilliantly lighted by a multitude of little tapers; and everywhere sparkled and glittered with bright objects. There were rosy-cheeked dolls, hiding behind the green leaves; and there were real watches (with movable hands, at least, and an endless capacity of being wound up) dangling from innumerable twigs; there were French-polished tables, chairs, bed-steads, wardrobes, eight-day clocks, and various other articles of domestic furniture (wonderfully made, in tin, at Wolverhampton), perched among the boughs, as if in preparation for some fairy house-keeping; there were jolly, broad-faced little men, much more agreeable in appearance than many real men – and no wonder, for their heads took off, and showed them to be full of sugar-plums; there were fiddles and drums; there were tambourines, books, work-boxes, paint-boxes, sweetmeat-boxes, peep-show boxes, and all kinds of boxes; there were trinkets for the elder girls, far brighter than any grown-up gold and jewels; there were baskets and pin-cushions in all devices; there were guns, swords, and banners; there were witches standing in enchanted rings of pasteboard, to tell for-tunes; there were teetotums, humming-tops, needle-cases, pen-wipers, smelling-bottles, conversation-cards, bouquet-holders; real fruit, made artificially dazzling with gold leaf; imitation apples, pears, and walnuts, crammed with surprises; in short, as a pretty child, before me, delightedly whispered to another pretty child, her bosom friend, 'There was everything, and more.' This motley collection of odd objects, clustering on the tree like magic fruit, and flashing back the bright looks directed towards it from every side – some of the diamond-eyes admiring it were hardly on a level with the table, and a few were languishing in timid wonder on the bosoms of pretty mothers, aunts, and nurses – made a lively realization of the fancies of childhood; and set me thinking how all the trees that grow and all the things that come into existence on the earth, have their wild adornments at that well-remembered time.

Being now at home again, and alone, the only person in the house awake, my thoughts are drawn back, by a fascination which I do not care to resist, to my own childhood. I begin to consider, what do we all remember best upon the branches of the Christmas Tree of our own young Christmas days, by which we climbed to real life.

Straight, in the middle of the room, cramped in the freedom of its growth by no encircling walls or soon-reached ceiling, a shadowy tree arises; and, looking up into the dreamy brightness of its top – for I observe in this tree the singular property that it appears to grow downward towards the earth – I look into my youngest Christmas recollections!

All toys at first, I find. Up yonder, among the green holly and red berries, is the Tumbler with his hands in his pockets, who wouldn't lie down, but whenever he was put upon the floor, persisted in rolling his fat body about, until he rolled himself still, and brought those lobster eyes of his to bear upon me – when I affected to laugh very much, but in my heart of hearts was extremely doubtful of him. Close beside him is that infernal snuff-box, out of which sprang a demoniacal Counsellor in a black gown, with an obnoxious head of hair, and a red cloth mouth, wide open, who was not to be endured on any terms, but could not be put away either; for he used suddenly, in a highly magnified state, to fly out of Mammoth Snuff-boxes in dreams, when least expected. Nor is the frog with cobbler's wax on his tail, far off; for there was no knowing where he wouldn't jump; and when he flew over the candle, and came upon one's hand with that spotted back – red on a green ground – he was horrible. The cardboard lady in a blue-silk skirt, who was stood up against the candlestick to dance, and whom I see on the same branch, was milder, and was beautiful; but I can't say as much for the larger cardboard man, who used to be hung against the wall and pulled by a string; there was a sinister expression in that nose of his; and when he got his legs round his neck (which he very often did), he was ghastly, and not a creature to be alone with.

When did that dreadful Mask first look at me? Who put it on, and why was I so frightened that the sight of it is an era in my life? It is not a hideous visage in itself; it is even meant to be droll; why then were its stolid features so intolerable? Surely not because it hid the wearer's face. An apron would have done as much; and though I should have preferred even the apron away, it would not have been absolutely insupportable, like the mask. Was it the immovability of the mask? The doll's face was immovable, but I was not afraid of *her*. Perhaps that fixed and set change coming over a real face, infused into my quickened heart some remote suggestion and dread of the universal change that is to come on every face, and make it still? Nothing reconciled me to it. No drummers, from whom proceeded a melancholy chirping on the turning of a handle; no regiment of soldiers, with a mute band, taken out of a box, and fitted, one by one, upon a stiff and lazy little set of lazy-tongs; no old woman, made of wires and a brown-paper composition, cutting up a pie for two small children; could give me a permanent comfort, for a long time. Nor was it any satisfaction to be shown the Mask, and see that it was made of paper, or to have it locked up and be assured that no one wore it. The mere recollection of that fixed face, the mere knowledge of its existence anywhere, was sufficient to awake me in the night all perspiration and horror, with, 'O I know it's coming! O the mask!'

I never wondered what the dear old donkey with the panniers – there he is! was made of, then! His hide was real to the touch, I recollect. And the great black horse with the round red spots all over him – the horse that I could even get upon – I never wondered what had brought him to that strange condition, or thought that such a horse was not commonly seen at Newmarket. The four horses of no colour, next to him, that went into the waggon of cheeses, and could be taken out and stabled under the piano, appear to have bits of fur-tippet for their tails, and other bits for their manes, and to stand on pegs instead of legs, but it was not so when they were brought home for a Christmas present. They were all right, then; neither was their harness unceremoniously nailed into their chests, as appears to be the case now. The tinkling works of the music-cart, I *did* find out, to be made of quill tooth-picks and wire; and I always thought that little tumbler in his shirt sleeves, perpetually swarming up one side of a wooden frame, and coming down, head foremost, on the other, rather a weak-minded person – though good-natured; but the Jacob's Ladder, next him, made of little squares of red wood, that went flapping and clattering over one another, each developing a different picture, and the whole enlivened by small bells, was a mighty marvel and a great delight.

Ah! The Doll's house! – of which I was not proprietor, but where I visited. I don't admire the Houses of Parliament half so much as that stone-fronted mansion with real glass windows, and door-steps, and a real balcony – greener than I ever see now, except at watering-places; and even they afford but a poor imitation. And though it *did* open all at once, the entire house-front (which was a blow, I admit, as cancelling the fiction of a staircase), it was but to shut it up again, and I could believe. Even open, there were three distinct rooms in it: a sitting-room and bed-room, elegantly furnished, and best of all, a kitchen, with uncommonly soft fire-irons, a plentiful assortment of diminutive utensils – oh, the warming-pan! – and a tin man-cook in profile, who was always going to fry two fish. What Barmecide[1] justice have I done to the noble feasts wherein the set of wooden platters figured, each with its own peculiar delicacy, as a ham or turkey, glued tight on to it, and garnished with something green, which I recollect as moss! Could all the Temperance Societies of these later days, united, give me such a tea-drinking as I have had through the means of yonder little set of blue crockery, which really would hold liquid (it ran out of the small wooden cask, I recollect, and tasted of matches), and which made tea, nectar. And if the two legs of the ineffectual little sugar-tongs did tumble over one another, and want purpose, like Punch's hands,[2] what does it matter? And if I did once shriek out, as a poisoned child, and strike the fashionable company with consternation, by reason of having drunk a little teaspoon, inadvertently dissolved in too hot tea, I was never the worse for it, except by a powder!

Upon the next branches of the tree, lower down, hard by the green roller and miniature gardening-tools, how thick the books begin to hang. Thin books, in themselves, at first, but many of them, and with deliciously smooth covers of bright red or green. What fat black letters to begin with! 'A was an archer, and shot at a frog.' Of course he was. He was an apple-pie also, and there he is! He was a good many things in his time, was A, and so were most of his friends, except X, who had so little versatility, that I never knew him to get beyond Xerxes or Xantippe – like Y, who was always confined to a Yacht or a Yew Tree; and Z condemned for ever to be a Zebra or a Zany. But, now, the very tree itself changes, and becomes a bean-stalk – the marvellous bean-stalk up which Jack climbed to the Giant's house! And now, those dreadfully interesting, double-headed giants, with their clubs over their shoulders, begin to stride along the boughs in a perfect throng, dragging knights and ladies home for dinner by the hair of their heads. And Jack – how noble, with his sword of sharpness, and his shoes of swiftness! Again those old meditations come upon me as I gaze up at him; and I debate within myself whether there was more than one Jack (which I am loth to believe possible), or only one genuine original admirable Jack, who achieved all the recorded exploits.[3]

Good for Christmas time is the ruddy color of the cloak, in which – the tree making a forest of itself for her to trip through, with her basket – Little Red Riding-Hood comes to me one Christmas Eve to give me information of the cruelty and treachery of that dissembling Wolf who ate her grandmother, without making any impression on his appetite, and then ate her, after making that ferocious joke about his teeth.[4] She was my first love. I felt that if I could have married Little Red Riding-Hood, I should have known perfect bliss. But, it was not to be; and there was nothing for it but to look out the Wolf in the Noah's Ark there, and put him late in the procession on the table, as a monster who was to be degraded. O the wonderful Noah's Ark! It was not found seaworthy when put in a washing-tub, and the animals were crammed in at the roof, and needed to have their legs well shaken down before they could be got in, even there – and then, ten to one but they began to tumble out at the door, which was but imperfectly fastened with a wire latch – but what was *that* against it! Consider the noble fly, a size or two smaller than the elephant: the lady-bird, the butterfly – all triumphs of art! Consider the goose, whose feet were so small, and whose balance was so indifferent, that he usually tumbled forward, and knocked down all the animal creation. Consider Noah and his family, like idiotic tobacco-stoppers; and how the leopard stuck to warm little fingers; and now the tails of the larger animals used gradually to resolve themselves into frayed bits of string!

Hush! Again a forest, and somebody up in a tree – not Robin Hood, not Valentine, not the Yellow Dwarf (I have passed him and all Mother Bunch's wonders,[5] without mention), but an Eastern King with a glittering scimitar and turban. By Allah! two Eastern Kings, for I see another, looking over his shoulder! Down upon the grass, at the tree's foot, lies the full length of a coal-black Giant, stretched asleep, with his head in a lady's lap; and near them is a glass box, fastened with four locks of shining steel, in which he keeps the lady prisoner when he is awake. I see the four keys at his girdle now. The lady makes signs to the two kings in the tree, who softly descend. It is the setting-in of the bright Arabian Nights.

Oh, now all common things become uncommon and enchanted to me. All lamps are wonderful; all rings are talismans. Common flower-pots are full of treasure, with a little earth scattered on the top; trees are for Ali Baba to hide in; beef-steaks are to throw down into the Valley of Diamonds, that the precious stones may stick to them, and be carried by the eagles to their nests, whence the traders, with loud cries, will scare them. Tarts are made, according to the recipe of the Vizier's son of Bussorah, who turned pastry-cook after he was set down in his drawers at the gate of Damascus; cobblers are all Mustaphas, and in the habit of sewing up people cut into four pieces, to whom they are taken blindfold.

Any iron ring let into stone is the entrance to a cave which only waits for the magician, and the little fire, and the necromancy, that will make the earth shake. All the dates imported come from the same tree as that unlucky date, with whose shell the merchant knocked out the eye of the genie's invisible son. All olives are of the stock of that fresh fruit, concerning which the Commander of the Faithful overheard the boy conduct the fictitious trial of the fraudulent olive merchant; all apples are akin to the apple purchased (with two others) from the Sultan's gardener for three sequins, and which the tall black slave stole from the child. All dogs are associated with the dog, really a transformed man, who jumped upon the baker's counter, and put his paw on the piece of bad money. All rice recalls the rice which the awful lady, who was a ghoule, could only peck by grains, because of her nightly feasts in the burial-place. My very rocking-horse, – there he is, with his nostrils turned completely inside-out, indicative of Blood! – should have a peg in his neck, by virtue thereof to fly away with me, as the wooden horse did with the Prince of Persia, in the sight of all his father's Court.

Yes, on every object that I recognize among those upper branches of my Christmas Tree, I see this fairy light! When I wake in bed, at daybreak, on the cold dark winter mornings, the white snow dimly beheld, outside, through the frost on the window-pane, I hear Dinarzade. 'Sister, sister, if you are yet awake, I pray you finish the history of the Young King of the Black Islands.' Scheherazade replies, 'If my lord the Sultan will suffer me to live another day, sister, I will not only finish that, but tell you a more wonderful story yet.' Then, the gracious Sultan goes out, giving no orders for the execution, and we all three breathe again.[6]

At this height of my tree I begin to see, cowering among the leaves – it may be born of turkey, or of pudding, or mince pie, or of these many fancies, jumbled with Robinson Crusoe on his desert island,[7] Philip Quarll among the monkeys,[8] Sandford and Merton with Mr Barlow,[9] Mother Bunch, and the Mask – or it may be the result of indigestion, assisted by imagination and over-doctoring – a prodigious nightmare. It is so exceedingly indistinct, that I don't know why it's frightful – but I know it is. I can only make out that it is an immense array of shapeless things, which appear to be planted on a vast exaggeration of the lazy-tongs that used to bear the toy soldiers, and to be slowly coming close to my eyes, and receding to an immeasurable distance. When it comes closest, it is worst. In connection with it I descry remembrances of winter nights incredibly long; of being sent early to bed, as a punishment for some small offence, and waking in two hours, with a sensation of having been asleep two nights; of the laden hopelessness of morning ever dawning; and the oppression of a weight of remorse.

And now, I see a wonderful row of little lights rise smoothly out of the ground, before a vast green curtain. Now, a bell rings – a magic bell, which still sounds in my ears unlike all other bells – and music plays, amidst a buzz of voices, and a fragrant smell of orange-peel and oil. Anon, the magic bell commands the music to cease, and the great green curtain rolls itself up majestically, and The Play begins! The devoted dog of Montargis[10] avenges the death of his master, foully murdered in the Forest of Bondy; and a humorous Peasant with a red nose and a very little hat, whom I take from this hour forth to my bosom as a friend (I think he was a Waiter or an Hostler at a village Inn, but many years have passed since he and I have met), remarks that the sassigassity of that dog is indeed surprising; and evermore this jocular conceit will live in my remembrance fresh and unfading, overtopping all possible jokes, unto the end of time. Or now, I learn with bitter tears how poor Jane Shore,[11] dressed all in white, and with her brown hair hanging down, went starving through the streets; or how George Barnwell killed the worthiest uncle that ever man had,[12] and was afterwards so sorry for it that he ought to have been let off. Comes swift to comfort me, the Pantomime[13] – stupendous Phenomenon! – when clowns are shot from loaded mortars into the great chandelier, bright constellation that it is; when Harlequins, covered all over with scales of pure gold, twist and sparkle, like amazing fish; when Pantaloon (whom I deem it no irreverence to compare in my own mind to my grandfather) puts red-hot pokers in his pocket, and cries 'Here's somebody coming!' or taxes the Clown with petty larceny, by saying, 'Now, I sawed you do it!' when Everything is capable, with the greatest ease, of being changed into Anything; and 'Nothing is, but thinking makes it so'.[14] Now, too, I perceive my first experience of the dreary sensation – often to return in after-life – of being unable, next day, to get back to the dull, settled world; of wanting to live for ever in the bright atmosphere I have quitted; of doting on the little Fairy, with the wand like a celestial Barber's Pole, and pining for a Fairy immortality along with her. Ah, she comes back, in many shapes, as my eye wanders down the branches of my Christmas Tree, and goes as often, and has never yet stayed by me!

Out of this delight springs the toy-theatre,[15] – there it is, with its familiar proscenium, and ladies in feathers, in the boxes! – and all its attendant occupation with paste and glue, and gum, and water colors, in the getting-up of The Miller and his Men, and Elizabeth, or the Exile of Siberia. In spite of a few besetting accidents and failures (particularly an unreasonable disposition in the respectable Kelmar, and some others, to become faint in the legs, and double up, at exciting points of the drama), a teeming world of fancies so suggestive and all-embracing, that, far below it on my Christmas Tree, I see dark, dirty, real Theatres in the day-time, adorned with these associations as with the freshest garlands of the rarest flowers, and charming me yet.

But hark! The Waits are playing, and they break my childish sleep! What images do I associate with the Christmas music as I see them set forth on the Christmas Tree? Known before all the others, keeping far apart from all the others, they gather round my little bed. An angel, speaking to a group of shepherds in a field; some travellers, with eyes uplifted, following a star; a baby in a manger; a child in a spacious temple, talking with grave men; a solemn figure, with a mild and beautiful face, raising a dead girl by the hand; again, near a city gate, calling back the son of a widow, on his bier, to life; a crowd of people looking through the opened roof of a chamber where he sits, and letting down a sick person on a bed, with ropes; the same, in a tempest, walking on the water to a ship; again, on a sea-shore, teaching a great multitude; again, with a child upon his knee, and other children round; again, restoring sight to the blind, speech to the dumb, hearing to the deaf, health to the sick, strength to the lame, knowledge to the ignorant; again, dying upon a Cross, watched by armed soldiers, a thick darkness coming on, the earth beginning to shake, and only one voice heard, 'Forgive them, for they know not what they do.'[16]

Still, on the lower and maturer branches of the Tree, Christmas associations cluster thick. School-books shut up; Ovid and Virgil silenced; the Rule of Three,[17] with its cool impertinent inquiries, long disposed of; Terence and Plautus[18] acted no more, in an arena of huddled desks and forms, all chipped, and notched, and inked; cricket-bats, stumps, and balls, left higher up, with the smell of trodden grass and the softened noise of shouts in the evening air; the tree is still fresh, still gay. If I no more come home at Christmas time, there will be boys and girls (thank Heaven!) while the World lasts; and they do! Yonder they dance and play upon the branches of my Tree, God bless them, merrily, and my heart dances and plays too!

And I *do* come home at Christmas. We all do, or we all should. We all come home, or ought to come home, for a short holiday – the longer, the better – from the great boarding-school, where we are for ever working at our arithmetical slates, to take, and give a rest. As to going a visiting, where can we not go, if we will; where have we not been, when we would; starting our fancy from our Christmas Tree!

Away into the winter prospect. There are many such upon the tree! On, by low-lying, misty grounds, through fens and fogs, up long hills, winding dark as caverns between thick plantations, almost shutting out the sparkling stars; so, out on broad heights, until we stop at last, with sudden silence, at an avenue. The gate-bell has a deep, half-awful sound in the frosty air; the gate swings open on its hinges; and, as we drive up to a great house, the glancing lights grow larger in the windows, and the opposing rows of trees seem to fall solemnly back on either side, to give us place. At intervals, all day, a frightened hare has shot across this whitened turf; or the distant clatter of a herd of deer trampling the hard frost, has, for the minute, crushed the silence too. Their watchful eyes beneath the fern may be shining now, if we could see them, like the icy dewdrops on the leaves; but they are still, and all is still. And so, the lights growing larger, and the trees falling back before us, and closing up again behind us, as if to forbid retreat, we come to the house.

There is probably a smell of roasted chestnuts and other good comfortable things all the time, for we are telling Winter Stories – Ghost Stories, or more shame for us – round the Christmas fire; and we have never stirred, except to draw a little nearer to it. But, no matter for that. We came to the house, and it is an old house, full of great chimneys where wood is burnt on ancient dogs upon the hearth, and grim portraits (some of them with grim legends, too) lower distrustfully from the oaken panels of the walls. We are a middle-aged nobleman, and we make a generous supper with our host and hostess and their guests – it being Christmas-time, and the old house full of company – and then we go to bed. Our room is a very old room. It is hung with tapestry. We don't like the portrait of a cavalier in green, over the fireplace. There are great black beams in the ceiling, and there is a great black bedstead, supported at the foot by two great black figures, who seem to have come off a couple of tombs in the old baronial church in the park, for our particular accommodation. But, we are not a superstitious nobleman, and we don't mind. Well! we dismiss our servant, lock the door, and sit before the fire in our dressing-gown, musing about a great many things. At length we go to bed. Well! we can't sleep. We toss and tumble, and can't sleep. The embers on the hearth burn fitfully and make the room look ghostly. We can't help peeping out over the counterpane, at the two black figures and the cavalier – that wicked-looking cavalier – in green. In the flickering light they seem to advance and retire: which, though we are not by any means a superstitious nobleman, is not agreeable. Well! we get nervous – more and more nervous. We say 'This is very foolish, but we can't stand this; we'll pretend to be ill, and knock up somebody.' Well! we are just going to do it, when the locked door opens, and there comes in a young woman, deadly pale, and with long fair hair, who glides to the fire, and sits down in the chair we have left there, wringing her hands. Then, we notice that her clothes are wet. Our tongue cleaves to the roof of our mouth, and we can't speak; but, we observe her accurately. Her clothes are wet; her long hair is dabbled with moist mud; she is dressed in the fashion of two hundred years ago; and she has at her girdle a bunch of rusty keys. Well! there she sits, and we can't even faint we are in such a state about it. Presently she gets up, and tries all the locks in the room with the rusty keys, which won't fit one of them; then, she fixes her eyes on the portrait of the cavalier in green, and says, in a low, terrible voice, 'The stags know it!' After that, she wrings her hands again, passes the bedside, and goes out at the door. We hurry on our dressing-gown, seize our pistols (we always travel with pistols), and are following, when we find the door locked. We turn the key, look out into the dark gallery; no one there. We wander away, and try to find our servant. Can't be done. We pace the gallery till daybreak; then return to our deserted room, fall asleep, and are awakened by our servant (nothing ever haunts *him*) and the shining sun. Well! we make a wretched breakfast, and all the company say we look queer. After breakfast, we go over the house with our host, and then we take him to the portrait of the cavalier in green, and then it all comes out. He was false to a young housekeeper once attached to that family, and famous for her beauty, who drowned herself in a pond, and whose body was discovered, after a long time, because the stags refused to drink of the water. Since which, it has been whispered that she traverses the house at midnight (but goes especially to that room where the cavalier in green was wont to sleep) trying the old locks with the rusty keys. Well! we tell our host of what we have seen, and a shade comes over his features, and he begs it may be hushed up; and so it is. But, it's all true; and we said so, before we died (we are dead now) to many responsible people.

There is no end to the old houses, with resounding galleries, and dismal state-bedchambers, and haunted wings shut up for many years, through which we may ramble, with an agreeable creeping up our back, and encounter any number of ghosts, but (it is worthy of remark perhaps) reducible to a very few general types and classes; for, ghosts have little originality, and 'walk' in a beaten track. Thus, it comes to pass, that a certain room in a certain old hall, where a certain bad lord, baronet, knight, or gentleman, shot himself, has certain planks in the floor from which the blood *will not* be taken out. You may scrape and scrape, as the present owner has done, or plane and plane, as his father did, or scrub and scrub, as his grandfather did, or burn and burn with strong acids, as his great-grandfather did, but, there the blood will still be – no redder and no paler – no more and no less – always just the same. Thus, in such another house there is a haunted door, that never will keep open; or another door that never will keep shut; or a haunted sound of a spinning-wheel, or a hammer, or a footstep, or a cry, or a sigh, or a horse's tramp, or the rattling of a chain. Or else, there is a turret-clock, which, at the midnight hour, strikes thirteen when the head of the family is going to die; or a shadowy, immovable black carriage which at such a time is always seen by somebody, waiting near the great gates in the stable-yard. Or thus, it came to pass how Lady Mary went to pay a visit at a large wild house in the Scottish Highlands, and, being fatigued with her long journey, retired to bed early, and innocently said, next morning, at the breakfast-table, 'How odd, to have so late a party last night, in this remote

place, and not to tell me of it, before I went to bed!' Then, everyone asked Lady Mary what she meant? Then, Lady Mary replied,
'Why, all night long, the carriages were driving round and round
the terrace, underneath my window!' Then, the owner of the house
turned pale, and so did his Lady, and Charles Macdoodle of
Macdoodle signed to Lady Mary to say no more, and every one was
silent. After breakfast, Charles Macdoodle told Lady Mary that it
was a tradition in the family that those rumbling carriages on the
terrace betokened death. And so it proved, for, two months afterwards, the Lady of the mansion died. And Lady Mary, who was a
Maid of Honour at Court, often told this story to the old Queen
Charlotte; by this token that the old King[19] always said, 'Eh, eh?
What, what? Ghosts, ghosts? No such thing, no such thing!' And
never left off saying so, until he went to bed.

Or, a friend of somebody's whom most of us know, when he
was a young man at college, had a particular friend, with whom he
made the compact that, if it were possible for the Spirit to return
to this earth after its separation from the body, he of the twin who
first died, should reappear to the other. In course of time, this compact was forgotten by our friend; the two young men having pro-
gressed in life, and taken diverging paths that were wide asunder.
But, one night, many years afterwards, our friend being in the
North of England, and staying for the night in an inn, on the
Yorkshire Moors, happened to look out of bed; and there, in
the moonlight, leaning on a bureau near the window, stedfastly
regarding him, saw his old college friend! The appearance being
solemnly addressed, replied, in a kind of whisper, but very audibly,
'Do not come near me. I am dead. I am here to redeem my promise.
I come from another world, but may not disclose its secrets!' Then,
the whole form becoming paler, melted, as it were, into the moonlight, and faded away.

Or, there was the daughter of the first occupier of the picturesque
Elizabethan house, so famous in our neighbourhood. You have
heard about her? No! Why, *She* went out one summer evening at
twilight, when she was a beautiful girl, just seventeen years of age,
to gather flowers in the garden; and presently came running, terrified, into the hall to her father, saying, 'Oh, dear father, I have
met myself!' He took her in his arms, and told her it was fancy, but

she said, 'Oh no! I met myself in the broad walk, and I was pale and gathering withered flowers, and I turned my head, and held them up!' And, that night, she died; and a picture of her story was begun, though never finished, and they say it is somewhere in the house to this day, with its face to the wall.

Or, the uncle of my brother's wife was riding home on horse-back, one mellow evening at sunset, when, in a green lane close to his own house, he saw a man standing before him, in the very centre of the narrow way. 'Why does that man in the cloak stand there!' he thought. 'Does he want me to ride over him?' But the figure never moved. He felt a strange sensation at seeing it so still, but slackened his trot and rode forward. When he was so close to it, as almost to touch it with his stirrup, his horse shied, and the figure glided up the bank, in a curious, unearthly manner – backward, and without seeming to use its feet – and was gone. The uncle of my brother's wife, exclaiming, 'Good Heaven! It's my cousin Harry, from Bombay!' put spurs to his horse, which was suddenly in a profuse sweat, and, wondering at such a strange behaviour, dashed round to the front of his house. There, he saw the same figure, just passing in at the long French window of the drawing-room, open-ing on the ground. He threw his bridle to a servant, and hastened in after it. His sister was sitting there, alone. 'Alice, where's my cousin Harry?' 'Your cousin Harry, John?' 'Yes. From Bombay. I met him in the lane just now, and saw him enter here, this instant.' Not a creature had been seen by any one; and in that hour and minute, as it afterwards appeared, this cousin died in India.

Or, it was a certain sensible old maiden lady, who died at ninety-nine, and retained her faculties to the last, who really did see the Orphan Boy; a story which has often been incorrectly told, but, of which the real truth is this – because it is, in fact, a story belonging to our family – and she was a connexion of our family. When she was about forty years of age, and still an uncommonly fine woman (her lover died young, which was the reason why she never married, though she had many offers), she went to stay at a place in Kent, which her brother, an Indian-Merchant, had newly bought. There was a story that this place had once been held in trust, by the guardian of a young boy; who was himself the next heir, and who killed the young boy by harsh and cruel treatment. She knew nothing of that. It has been said that there was a Cage in her bed-room in which the guardian used to put the boy. There was no such thing. There was only a closet. She went to bed, made no alarm whatever in the night, and in the morning said composedly to her maid when she came in, 'Who is the pretty forlorn-looking child who has been peeping out of that closet all night?' The maid replied by giving a loud scream, and instantly decamping. She was sur-prised; but she was a woman of remarkable strength of mind, and she dressed herself and went down stairs, and closeted herself with her brother. 'Now, Walter,' she said, 'I have been disturbed all night by a pretty, forlorn-looking boy, who has been constantly peeping out of that closet in my room, which I can't open. This is some trick.' 'I am afraid not, Charlotte,' said he, 'for it is the legend of the house. It is the Orphan Boy. What did he do?' 'He opened the door softly,' said she, 'and peeped out. Sometimes, he came a step or two into the room. Then, I called to him, to encourage him, and he shrunk, and shuddered, and crept in again, and shut the door.' 'The closet has no communication, Charlotte,' said her brother, 'with any other part of the house, and it's nailed up.' This was undeniably true, and it took two carpenters a whole forenoon to get it open, for examination. Then, she was satisfied that she had seen the Orphan Boy. But, the wild and terrible part of the story is, that he was also seen by three of her brother's sons, in succession, who all died young. On the occasion of each child being taken ill, he came home in a heat, twelve hours before, and said, Oh, Mamma, he had been playing under a particular oak-tree, in a certain meadow, with a strange boy – a pretty, forlorn-looking boy, who was very timid, and made signs! From fatal experience, the parents came to know that this was the Orphan Boy, and that the course of that child whom he chose for his little playmate was surely run.

Legion is the name of[20] the German castles, where we sit up alone to wait for the Spectre – where we are shown into a room, made comparatively cheerful for our reception – where we glance round at the shadows, thrown on the blank walls by the crackling fire – where we feel very lonely when the village innkeeper and his pretty daughter have retired, after laying down a fresh store of wood upon the hearth, and setting forth on the small table such supper-cheer as a cold roast capon, bread, grapes, and a flask of old

Rhine wine – where the reverberating doors close on their retreat, one after another, like so many peals of sullen thunder – and where, about the small hours of the night, we come into the knowledge of divers supernatural mysteries. Legion is the name of the haunted German students, in whose society we draw yet nearer to the fire, while the schoolboy in the corner opens his eyes wide and round, and flies off the footstool he has chosen for his seat, when the door accidentally blows open. Vast is the crop of such fruit, shining on our Christmas Tree; in blossom, almost at the very top; ripening all down the boughs!

Among the later toys and fancies hanging there – as idle often and less pure – be the images once associated with the sweet old Waits, the softened music in the night, ever unalterable! Encircled by the social thoughts of Christmas time, still let the benignant figure of my childhood stand unchanged! In every cheerful image and suggestion that the season brings, may the bright star that rested above the poor roof, be the star of all the Christian World! A moment's pause, O vanishing tree, of which the lower boughs are dark to me as yet, and let me look once more! I know there are blank spaces on thy branches, where eyes that I have loved, have shone and smiled; from which they are departed. But, far above, I see the raiser of the dead girl, and the Widow's Son; and God is good! If Age be hiding for me in the unseen portion of thy downward growth, O may I, with a grey head, turn a child's heart to that figure yet, and a child's trustfulness and confidence!

Now, the tree is decorated with bright merriment, and song, and dance, and cheerfulness. And they are welcome. Innocent and welcome be they ever held, beneath the branches of the Christmas Tree, which cast no gloomy shadow! But, as it sinks into the ground, I hear a whisper going through the leaves. 'This, in commemoration of the law of love and kindness, mercy and compassion. This, in remembrance of Me!'[21]

A Flight

WHEN Don Diego de – I forget his name – the inventor of the last
new Flying Machines, price so many francs for ladies, so many
more for gentlemen – when Don Diego, by permission of Deputy
Chaff Wax[1] and his noble band, shall have taken out a Patent for
the Queen's dominions, and shall have opened a commodious
Warehouse in an airy situation; and when all persons of any
gentility will keep at least a pair of wings, and be seen skimming
about in every direction; I shall take a flight to Paris (as I soar
round the world) in a cheap and independent manner. At present,
my reliance is on the South Eastern Railway Company, in whose
Express Train here I sit, at eight of the clock on a very hot morning, under the very hot roof of the Terminus at London Bridge, in
danger of being 'forced' like a cucumber or a melon, or a pine-
apple – And talking of pine-apples, I suppose there never were so
many pine-apples in a Train as there appear to be in this Train.

Whew! The hot-house air is faint with pine-apples. Every French
citizen or citizeness is carrying pine-apples home. The compact
little Enchantress in the corner of my carriage (French actress,
to whom I yielded up my heart under the auspices of that brave
child, 'MEAT-CHELL',[2] at the St James's Theatre the night before
last) has a pine-apple in her lap. Compact Enchantress's friend, con-
fidante, mother, mystery, Heaven knows what, has two pine-apples
in her lap, and a bundle of them under the seat. Tobacco-smoky
Frenchman in Algerine wrapper, with peaked hood behind, who
might be Abd-el-Kader[3] dyed rifle-green, and who seems to be
dressed entirely in dirt and braid, carries pine-apples in a covered
basket. Tall, grave, melancholy Frenchman, with black Vandyke
beard, and hair close-cropped, with expansive chest to waistcoat,
and compressive waist to coat: saturnine as to his pantaloons, calm
as to his feminine boots, precious as to his jewellery, smooth and
white as to his linen: dark-eyed, high-foreheaded, hawk-nosed –
got up, one thinks, like Lucifer or Mephistopheles, or Zamiel,[4]
transformed into a highly genteel Parisian – has the green end of a
pine-apple sticking out of his neat valise.

Whew! If I were to be kept here long, under this forcing-frame, wonder what would become of me – whether I should be forced into a giant, or should sprout or blow into some other phenomenon! Compact Enchantress is not ruffled by the heat – she is always composed, always compact. O look at her little ribbons, frills, and edges, at her shawl, at her gloves, at her hair, at her bracelets, at her bonnet, at everything about her! How is it accomplished! What does she do to be so neat? How is it that every trifle she wears belongs to her, and cannot choose but be a part of her? And even Mystery, look at *her*! A model. Mystery is not young, not pretty, though still of an average candle-light passability; but she does such miracles in her own behalf, that, one of these days, when she dies, they'll be amazed to find an old woman in her bed, distantly like her. She was an actress once, I shouldn't wonder, and had a Mystery attendant on herself. Perhaps, Compact Enchantress will live to be a Mystery, and to wait with a shawl at the side-scenes, and to sit opposite Mademoiselle in railway carriages, and smile and talk subserviently, as Mystery does now. That's hard to believe!

Two Englishmen, and now our carriage is full. First Englishman, in the monied interest – flushed, highly respectable – Stock Exchange, perhaps – City, certainly. Faculties of second Englishman entirely absorbed in hurry. Plunges into the carriage, blind. Calls out of window concerning his luggage, deaf. Suffocates himself under pillows of great coats, for no reason, and in a demented manner. Will receive no assurance from any porter whatsoever. Is stout and hot, and wipes his head, and makes himself hotter by breathing so hard. Is totally incredulous respecting assurance of Collected Guard, that 'there's no hurry'. No hurry! And a flight to Paris in eleven hours!

It is all one to me in this drowsy corner, hurry or no hurry. Until Don Diego shall send home my wings, my flight is with the South Eastern Company. I can fly with the South Eastern, more lazily, at all events, than in the upper air. I have but to sit here thinking as idly as I please, and be whisked away. I am not accountable to anybody for the idleness of my thoughts in such an idle summer flight; my flight is provided for by the South Eastern and is no business of mine.

The bell! With all my heart. It does not require *me* to do so much as even to flap my wings. Something snorts for me, something shrieks for me, something proclaims to everything else that it had better keep out of my way, – and away I go.

Ah! The fresh air is pleasant after the forcing-frame, though it does blow over these interminable streets, and scatter the smoke of this vast wilderness of chimneys. Here we are – no, I mean there we were, for it has darted far into the rear – in Bermondsey where the tanners live. Flash! The distant shipping in the Thames is gone. Whirr! The little streets of new brick and red tile, with here and there a flagstaff growing like a tall weed out of the scarlet beans, and, everywhere, plenty of open sewer and ditch for the promotion of the public health, have been fired off in a volley. Whizz! Dust-heaps, market-gardens, and waste grounds. Rattle! New Cross Station. Shock! There we were at Croydon. Bur-r-r-r! The tunnel.

I wonder why it is that when I shut my eyes in a tunnel I begin to feel as if I were going at an Express pace the other way. I am clearly going back to London now. Compact Enchantress must have forgotten something, and reversed the engine. No! After long darkness, pale fitful streaks of light appear. I am still flying on for Folkestone. The streaks grow stronger – become continuous – become the ghost of day – become the living day – became I mean – the tunnel is miles and miles away, and here I fly through sunlight, all among the harvest and the Kentish hops.

There is a dreamy pleasure in this flying. I wonder where it was, and when it was, that we exploded, blew into space somehow, a Parliamentary Train,[5] with a crowd of heads and faces looking at us out of cages, and some hats waving. Monied Interest says it was at Reigate Station. Expounds to Mystery how Reigate Station is so many miles from London, which Mystery again develops to Compact Enchantress. There might be neither a Reigate nor a London for me, as I fly away among the Kentish hops and harvest. What do *I* care?

Bang! We have let another Station off, and fly away regardless. Everything is flying. The hop-gardens turn gracefully towards me, presenting regular avenues of hops in rapid flight, then whirl away. So do the pools and rushes, haystacks, sheep, clover in full bloom delicious to the sight and smell, corn-sheaves, cherry orchards, apple-orchards, reapers, gleaners, hedges, gates, fields that taper off into little angular corners, cottages, gardens, now and then a church. Bang, bang! A double-barrelled Station! Now a wood, now a bridge, now a landscape, now a cutting, now a— Bang! a single-barrelled Station – there was a cricket-match somewhere with two white tents, and then four flying cows, then turnips – now the wires of the electric telegraph are all alive, and spin, and blurr their edges, and go up and down, and make the intervals between each other most irregular: contracting and expanding in the strangest manner. Now we slacken. With a screwing, and a grinding, and a smell of water thrown on ashes, now we stop!

Demented Traveller, who has been for two or three minutes watchful, clutches his great coats, plunges at the door, rattles it, cries 'Hi!' eager to embark on board of impossible packets, far inland. Collected Guard appears. 'Are you for Tunbridge, sir?' 'Tunbridge? No. Paris.' 'Plenty of time, sir. No hurry. Five minutes here, sir, for refreshment.' I am so blest (anticipating Zamiel, by half a second) as to procure a glass of water for Compact Enchantress.

Who would suppose we had been flying at such a rate, and shall take wing again directly? Refreshment-room full, platform full, porter with watering-pot deliberately cooling a hot wheel, another porter with equal deliberation helping the rest of the wheels bountifully to ice cream. Monied Interest and I re-entering the carriage first, and being there alone, he intimates to me that the French are 'no go' as a Nation. I ask why? He says, that Reign of Terror of theirs was quite enough. I ventured to inquire whether he remembers anything that preceded said Reign of Terror? He says not particularly. 'Because,' I remark, 'the harvest that is reaped, has sometimes been sown.' Monied Interest repeats, as quite enough for him, that the French are revolutionary, – 'and always at it.'

Bell. Compact Enchantress, helped in by Zamiel, (whom the stars confound!) gives us her charming little side-box look, and smites me to the core. Mystery eating sponge-cake. Pine-apple atmosphere faintly tinged with suspicions of sherry. Demented Traveller flits past the carriage, looking for it. Is blind with agitation, and can't see it. Seems singled out by Destiny to be the only unhappy creature in the flight, who has any cause to hurry himself.

Is nearly left behind. Is seized by Collected Guard after the Train is in motion, and bundled in. Still, has lingering suspicions that there must be a boat in the neighbourhood, and *will* look wildly out of window for it.

Flight resumed. Corn-sheaves, hop-gardens, reapers, gleaners, apple-orchards, cherry-orchards, Stations single and double-barrelled, Ashford. Compact Enchantress (constantly talking to Mystery, in an exquisite manner) gives a little scream; a sound that seems to come from high up in her precious little head; from behind her bright little eyebrows. 'Great Heaven, my pine-apple! My Angel! It is lost!' Mystery is desolated. A search made. It is not lost. Zamiel finds it. I curse him (flying) in the Persian manner. May his face be turned upside down, and jackasses sit upon his uncle's grave!

Now fresher air, now glimpses of unenclosed Down-land with flapping crows flying over it whom we soon outfly, now the Sea, now Folkestone at a quarter after ten. 'Tickets ready, gentlemen!' Demented dashes at the door. 'For Paris, sir?' No hurry.

Not the least. We are dropped slowly down to the Port, and sidle to and fro (the whole Train) before the insensible Royal George Hotel, for some ten minutes. The Royal George takes no more heed of us than its namesake under water at Spithead, or under earth at Windsor, does. The Royal George's dog lies winking and blinking at us, without taking the trouble to sit up; and the Royal George's 'wedding party' at the open window (who seem, I must say, rather tired of bliss) don't bestow a solitary glance upon us, flying thus to Paris in eleven hours. The first gentleman in Folkestone is evidently used up, on this subject.

Meanwhile, Demented chafes. Conceives that every man's hand is against him, and exerting itself to prevent his getting to Paris. Refuses consolation. Rattles door. Sees smoke on the horizon, and 'knows' it's the boat gone without him. Monied Interest resentfully explains that *he* is going to Paris too. Demented signifies that if Monied Interest chooses to be left behind, *he* don't.

'Refreshments in the Waiting-Room, ladies and gentlemen. No hurry, ladies and gentlemen, for Paris. No hurry whatever!'

Twenty minutes' pause, by Folkestone clock, for looking at Enchantress while she eats a sandwich, and at Mystery while she eats of everything there that is eatable, from pork-pie, sausage, jam, and gooseberries, to lumps of sugar. All this time, there is a very waterfall of luggage, with a spray of dust, tumbling slantwise from the pier into the steamboat. All this time, Demented (who has no business with it) watches it with starting eyes, fiercely requiring to be shown *his* luggage. When it at last concludes the cataract, he rushes hotly to refresh – is shouted after, pursued, jostled, brought back, pitched into the departing steamer upside down, and caught by mariners disgracefully.

A lovely harvest day, a cloudless sky, a tranquil sea. The piston-rods of the engines so regularly coming up from below, to look (as well they may) at the bright weather, and so regularly almost knocking their iron heads against the cross beam of the skylight, and never doing it! Another Parisian actress is on board, attended by another Mystery. Compact Enchantress greets her sister artist – Oh, the Compact One's pretty teeth! – and Mystery greets Mystery. *My* Mystery soon ceases to be conversational – is taken poorly, in a word, having lunched too miscellaneously – and goes below. The remaining Mystery then smiles upon the sister artists (who, I am afraid, wouldn't greatly mind stabbing each other), and is upon the whole ravished.

And now I find that all the French people on board begin to grow, and all the English people to shrink. The French are nearing home, and shaking off a disadvantage, whereas we are shaking it on. Zamiel is the same man, and Abd-el-Kader is the same man, but each seems to come into possession of an indescribable confidence that departs from us – from Monied Interest, for instance, and from me. Just what they gain, we lose. Certain British 'Gents' about the steersman, intellectually nurtured at home on parody of everything and truth of nothing, become subdued, and in a manner forlorn; and when the steersman tells them (not exultingly) how he has 'been upon this station now eight year, and never see the old town of Bullum yet,' one of them, with an imbecile reliance on a reed, asks him what he considers to be the best hotel in Paris?

Now, I tread upon French ground, and am greeted by the three charming words, Liberty, Equality, Fraternity, painted up (in letters a little too thin for their height) on the Custom-house wall – also by the sight of large cocked hats, without which demonstrative head-gear nothing of a public nature can be done upon this soil. All the rabid Hotel population of Boulogne howl and shriek outside a distant barrier, frantic to get at us. Demented, by some unlucky means peculiar to himself, is delivered over to their fury, and is presently seen struggling in a whirlpool of Touters – is somehow understood to be going to Paris – is, with infinite noise, rescued by two cocked hats, and brought into Custom-house bondage with the rest of us.

Here, I resign the active duties of life to an eager being, of preternatural sharpness, with a shelving forehead and a shabby snuff-colored coat, who (from the wharf) brought me down with his eye before the boat came into port. He darts upon my luggage, on the floor where all the luggage is strewn like a wreck at the bottom of the great deep; gets it proclaimed and weighed as the property of 'Monsieur a traveller unknown;' pays certain francs for it, to a certain functionary behind a Pigeon Hole, like a pay-box at a Theatre (the arrangements in general are on a wholesale scale, half military and half theatrical); and I suppose I shall find it when I come to Paris – he says I shall. I know nothing about it, except that I pay him his small fee, and pocket the ticket he gives me, and sit upon a counter, involved in the general distraction.

Railway station. 'Lunch or dinner, ladies and gentlemen. Plenty of time for Paris. Plenty of time!' Large hall, long counter, long strips of dining-table, bottles of wine, plates of meat, roast chickens, little loaves of bread, basins of soup, little caraffes of brandy, cakes, and fruit. Comfortably restored from these resources, I begin to fly again.

I saw Zamiel (before I took wing) presented to Compact Enchantress and Sister Artist, by an officer in uniform, with a waist like a wasp's, and pantaloons like two balloons. They all got into the next carriage together, accompanied by the two Mysteries. They laughed. I am alone in the carriage (for I don't consider Demented anybody) and alone in the world.

Fields, windmills, low grounds, pollard-trees, windmills, fields, fortifications, Abbeville, soldiering and drumming. I wonder where England is, and when I was there last – about two years ago, I should say. Flying in and out among these trenches and batteries, skimming the clattering drawbridges, looking down into the stagnant ditches, I become a prisoner of state, escaping. I am con-

fined with a comrade in a fortress. Our room is in an upper story.
We have tried to get up the chimney, but there's an iron grating
across it, imbedded in the masonry. After months of labour, we
have worked the grating loose with the poker, and can lift it up.
We have also made a hook, and twisted our rugs and blankets into
ropes. Our plan is, to go up the chimney, hook our ropes to the
top, descend hand over hand upon the roof of the guard-house far
below, shake the hook loose, watch the opportunity of the senti-
nel's pacing away, hook again, drop into the ditch, swim across it,
creep into the shelter of the wood. The time is come – a wild and
stormy night. We are up the chimney, we are on the guard-house
roof, we are swimming in the murky ditch, when lo! 'Qui v'là?' a
bugle, the alarm, a crash! What is it? Death? No, Amiens.

More fortifications, more soldiering and drumming, more basins
of soup, more little loaves of bread, more bottles of wine, more
caraffes of brandy, more time for refreshment. Everything good,
and everything ready. Bright, unsubstantial-looking, scenic sort of
station. People waiting. Houses, uniforms, beards, moustaches,
some sabots, plenty of neat women, and a few old-visaged children.
Unless it be a delusion born of my giddy flight, the grown-up
people and the children seem to change places in France. In general,
the boys and girls are little old men and women, and the men and
women lively boys and girls.

Bugle, shriek, flight resumed. Monied Interest has come into my
carriage. Says the manner of refreshing is 'not bad', but considers
it French. Admits great dexterity and politeness in the attendants.
Thinks a decimal currency may have something to do with their
despatch in settling accounts, and don't know but what it's sensible
and convenient. Adds, however, as a general protest, that they're a
revolutionary people – and always at it.

Ramparts, canals, cathedral, river, soldiering and drumming,
open country, river, earthenware manufactures, Creil. Again ten
minutes. Not even Demented in a hurry. Station, a drawing-room
with a verandah: like a planter's house. Monied Interest considers
it a band-box, and not made to last. Little round tables in it, at one
of which the Sister Artists and attendant Mysteries are established
with Wasp and Zamiel, as if they were going to stay a week.

Anon, with no more trouble than before, I am flying again, and lazily wondering as I fly. What has the South Eastern done with all the horrible little villages we used to pass through, in the *Diligence*? What have they done with all the summer dust, with all the winter mud, with all the dreary avenues of little trees, with all the ramshackle postyards, with all the beggars (who used to turn out at night with bits of lighted candle, to look in at the coach windows), with all the long-tailed horses who were always biting one another, with all the big postilions in jack-boots – with all the mouldy cafés that we used to stop at, where a long mildewed tablecloth, set forth with jovial bottles of vinegar and oil, and with a Siamese arrangement of pepper and salt, was never wanting? Where are the grass-grown little towns, the wonderful little market-places all unconscious of markets, the shops that nobody kept, the streets that nobody trod, the churches that nobody went to, the bells that nobody rang, the tumble-down old buildings plastered with many-colored bills that nobody read? Where are the two-and-twenty weary hours of long long day and night journey, sure to be either insupportably hot or insupportably cold? Where are the pains in my bones, where are the fidgets in my legs, where is the Frenchman with the nightcap who never *would* have the little coupé-window down, and who always fell upon me when he went to sleep, and always slept all night snoring onions?

A voice breaks in with 'Paris! Here we are!'

I have overflown myself, perhaps, but I can't believe it. I feel as if I were enchanted or bewitched. It is barely eight o'clock yet – it is nothing like half-past – when I have had my luggage examined at that briskest of Custom-houses attached to the station, and am rattling over the pavement in a hackney cabriolet.

Surely, not the pavement of Paris? Yes, I think it is, too. I don't know any other place where there are all these high houses, all these haggard-looking wine shops, all these billiard tables, all these stocking-makers with flat red or yellow legs of wood for signboard, all these fuel shops with stacks of billets painted outside, and real billets sawing in the gutter, all these dirty corners of streets, all these cabinet pictures over dark doorways representing discreet matrons nursing babies. And yet this morning – I'll think of it in a warm-bath.

Very like a small room that I remember in the Chinese baths

upon the Boulevard, certainly; and, though I see it through the steam, I think that I might swear to that peculiar hot-linen basket, like a large wicker hour-glass. When can it have been that I left home? When was it that I paid 'through to Paris' at London Bridge, and discharged myself of all responsibility, except the preservation of a voucher ruled into three divisions, of which the first was snipped off at Folkestone, the second aboard the boat, and the third taken at my journey's end? It seems to have been ages ago. Calculation is useless. I will go out for a walk.

The crowds in the streets, the lights in the shops and balconies, the elegance, variety, and beauty of their decorations, the number of the theatres, the brilliant cafés with their windows thrown up high and their vivacious groups at little tables on the pavement, the light and glitter of the houses turned as it were inside out, soon convince me that it is no dream; that I am in Paris, howsoever I got here. I stroll down to the sparkling Palais Royal, up the Rue de Rivoli, to the Place Vendôme. As I glance into a print-shop window Monied Interest, my late travelling companion, comes upon me, laughing with the highest relish of disdain. 'Here's a people!' he says, pointing to Napoleon in the window and Napoleon on the column. 'Only one idea all over Paris! A monomania!' Humph! I THINK I have seen Napoleon's match? There WAS a statue, when I came away, at Hyde Park Corner,[6] and another in the City, and a print or two in the shops.

I walk up to the Barrière de l'Etoile, sufficiently dazed by my flight to have a pleasant doubt of the reality of everything about me; of the lively crowd, the overhanging trees, the performing dogs, the hobby-horses, the beautiful perspectives of shining lamps: the hundred and one enclosures, where the singing is, in gleaming orchestras of azure and gold, and where a star-eyed Houri comes round with a box for voluntary offerings. So, I pass to my hotel, enchanted; sup, enchanted; go to bed, enchanted; pushing back this morning (if it really were this morning) into the remoteness of time, blessing the South Eastern Company for realizing the Arabian Nights in these prose days, murmuring, as I wing my idle flight into the land of dreams, 'No hurry, ladies and gentlemen, going to Paris in eleven hours. It is so well done, that there really is no hurry!'

Our School

WE went to look at it, only this last Midsummer, and found that the Railway had cut it up root and branch. A great trunk-line had swallowed the playground, sliced away the schoolroom, and pared off the corner of the house: which, thus curtailed of its proportions, presented itself, in a green stage of stucco, profilewise towards the road, like a forlorn flat-iron without a handle, standing on end.

It seems as if our schools were doomed to be the sport of change. We have faint recollections of a Preparatory Day-School, which we have sought in vain, and which must have been pulled down to make a new street, ages ago. We have dim impressions, scarcely amounting to a belief, that it was over a dyer's shop. We know that you went up steps to it; that you frequently grazed your knees in doing so; that you generally got your leg over the scraper, in trying to scrape the mud off a very unsteady little shoe. The mistress of the Establishment holds no place in our memory; but, rampant on one eternal door-mat, in an eternal entry long and narrow, is a puffy pug-dog, with a personal animosity towards us, who triumphs over Time. The bark of that baleful Pug, a certain radiating way he had of snapping at our undefended legs, the ghastly grinning of his moist black muzzle and white teeth, and the insolence of his crisp tail curled like a pastoral crook, all live and flourish. From an otherwise unaccountable association of him with a fiddle, we conclude that he was of French extraction, and his name *Fidèle*. He belonged to some female, chiefly inhabiting a back-parlor, whose life appears to us to have been consumed in sniffing, and in wearing a brown beaver bonnet. For her, he would sit up and balance cake upon his nose, and not eat it until twenty had been counted. To the best of our belief we were once called in to witness this performance; when, unable, even in his milder moments, to endure our presence, he instantly made at us, cake and all.

Why a something in mourning, called 'Miss Frost', should still connect itself with our preparatory school, we are unable to say. We retain no impression of the beauty of Miss Frost – if she were beautiful; or of the mental fascinations of Miss Frost – if she were accomplished; yet her name and her black dress hold an enduring place in our remembrance. An equally impersonal boy, whose name has long since shaped itself unalterably into 'Master Mawls', is not to be dislodged from our brain. Retaining no vindictive feeling towards Mawls – no feeling whatever, indeed – we infer that neither he nor we can have loved Miss Frost. Our first impression of Death and Burial is associated with this formless pair. We all three nestled awfully in a corner one wintry day, when the wind was blowing shrill, with Miss Frost's pinafore over our heads; and Miss Frost told us in a whisper about somebody being 'screwed down'. It is the only distinct recollection we preserve of these impalpable creatures, except a suspicion that the manners of Master Mawls were susceptible of much improvement. Generally speaking, we may observe that whenever we see a child intently occupied with its nose, to the exclusion of all other subjects of interest, our mind reverts, in a flash, to Master Mawls.

But, the School that was Our School before the Railroad came and overthrew it, was quite another sort of place. We were old enough to be put into Virgil when we went there, and to get Prizes for a variety of polishing on which the rust has long accumulated. It was a School of some celebrity in its neighbourhood – nobody could have said why – and we had the honor to attain and hold the eminent position of first boy. The master was supposed among us to know nothing, and one of the ushers was supposed to know everything. We are still inclined to think the first-named supposition perfectly correct.

We have a general idea that its subject had been in the leather trade, and had bought us – meaning Our School – of another proprietor who was immensely learned. Whether this belief had any real foundation, we are not likely ever to know now. The only branches of education with which he showed the least acquaintance, were, ruling and corporally punishing. He was always ruling ciphering-books with a bloated mahogany ruler, or smiting the palms of offenders with the same diabolical instrument, or viciously drawing a pair of pantaloons tight with one of his large hands, and caning the wearer with the other. We have no doubt whatever that this occupation was the principal solace of his existence.

A profound respect for money pervaded Our School, which was, of course, derived from its Chief. We remember an idiotic goggle-eyed boy, with a big head and half-crowns without end, who suddenly appeared as a parlor-boarder, and was rumoured to have come by sea from some mysterious part of the earth where his parents rolled in gold. He was usually called 'Mr' by the Chief, and was said to feed in the parlor on steaks and gravy; likewise to drink currant wine. And he openly stated that if rolls and coffee were ever denied him at breakfast, he would write home to that unknown part of the globe from which he had come, and cause himself to be recalled to the regions of gold. He was put into no form or class, but learnt alone, as little as he liked – and he liked very little – and there was a belief among us that this was because he was too wealthy to be 'taken down'. His special treatment, and our vague association of him with the sea, and with storms, and sharks, and Coral Reefs occasioned the wildest legends to be circulated as his history. A tragedy in blank verse was written on the subject – if our memory does not deceive us, by the hand that now chronicles these recollections – in which his father figured as Pirate, and was shot for a voluminous catalogue of atrocities: first imparting to his wife the secret of the cave in which his wealth was stored, and from which his only son's half-crowns now issued. Dumbledon (the boy's name) was represented as 'yet unborn' when his brave father met his fate; and the despair and grief of Mrs Dumbledon at that calamity was movingly shadowed forth as having weakened the parlor-boarder's mind. This production was received with great favor, and was twice performed with closed doors in the dining-room. But, it got wind, and was seized as libellous, and brought the unlucky poet into severe affliction. Some two years afterwards, all of a sudden one day, Dumbledon vanished. It was whispered that the Chief himself had taken him down to the Docks, and re-shipped him for the Spanish Main; but nothing certain was ever known about his disappearance. At this hour, we cannot thoroughly disconnect him from California.

Our School was rather famous for mysterious pupils. There was another – a heavy young man, with a large double-cased silver watch, and a fat knife the handle of which was a perfect tool-box – who unaccountably appeared one day at a special desk of his own, erected close to that of the Chief, with whom he held familiar converse. He lived in the parlor, and went out for his walks, and never took the least notice of us – even of us, the first boy – unless to give us a deprecatory kick, or grimly to take our hat off and throw it away, when he encountered us out of doors, which unpleasant ceremony he always performed as he passed – not even condescending to stop for the purpose. Some of us believed that the classical attainments of this phenomenon were terrific, but that his penmanship and arithmetic were defective, and he had come there to mend them; others, that he was going to set up a school, and had paid the Chief 'twenty-five pound down', for leave to see Our School at work. The gloomier spirits even said that he was going to buy US; against which contingency, conspiracies were set on foot for a general defection and running away. However, he never did that. After staying for a quarter, during which period, though closely observed, he was never seen to do anything but make pens out of quills, write small hand in a secret portfolio, and punch the point of the sharpest blade in his knife into his desk all over it, he too disappeared, and his place knew him no more.

There was another boy, a fair, meek boy, with a delicate complexion and rich curling hair, who, we found out, or thought we found out (we have no idea now, and probably had none then, on what grounds, but it was confidentially revealed from mouth to mouth), was the son of a Viscount who had deserted his lovely mother. It was understood that if he had his rights, he would be worth twenty thousand a year. And that if his mother ever met his father, she would shoot him with a silver pistol, which she carried, always loaded to the muzzle, for that purpose. He was a very suggestive topic. So was a young Mulatto, who was always believed (though very amiable) to have a dagger about him somewhere. But, we think they were both outshone, upon the whole, by another boy who claimed to have been born on the twenty-ninth of February, and to have only one birthday in five years. We suspect this to have been a fiction – but he lived upon it all the time he was at Our School.

The principal currency of Our School was slate pencil. It had some inexplicable value, that was never ascertained, never reduced to a standard. To have a great hoard of it, was somehow to be rich. We used to bestow it in charity, and confer it as a precious boon upon our chosen friends. When the holidays were coming, contributions were solicited for certain boys whose relatives were in India, and who were appealed for under the generic name of 'Holiday-stoppers', – appropriate marks of remembrance that should enliven and cheer them in their homeless state. Personally, we always contributed these tokens of sympathy in the form of slate-pencil, and always felt that it would be a comfort and a treasure to them.

Our School was remarkable for white mice. Red-polls, linnets, and even canaries, were kept in desks, drawers, hat-boxes, and other strange refuges for birds; but white mice were the favourite stock. The boys trained the mice, much better than the masters trained the boys. We recall one white mouse, who lived in the cover of a Latin dictionary, who ran up ladders, drew Roman chariots, shouldered muskets, turned wheels, and even made a very creditable appearance on the stage as the Dog of Montargis.[1] He might have achieved greater things, but for having the misfortune to mistake his way in a triumphal procession to the Capitol, when he fell into a deep inkstand, and was dyed black and drowned. The mice were the occasion of some most ingenious engineering, in the construction of their houses and instruments of performance. The famous one belonged to a company of proprietors, some of whom have since made Railroads, Engines, and Telegraphs; the chairman has erected mills and bridges in New Zealand.

The usher at Our School, who was considered to know everything as opposed to the Chief, who was considered to know nothing, was a bony, gentle-faced, clerical-looking young man in rusty black. It was whispered that he was sweet upon one of Maxby's sisters (Maxby lived close by, and was a day pupil), and further that he 'favoured Maxby'. As we remember, he taught Italian to Maxby's sisters on half-holidays. He once went to the play with them, and wore a white waistcoat and a rose: which was considered among us equivalent to a declaration. We were of opinion on that occasion, that to the last moment he expected Maxby's father to ask him to dinner at five o'clock, and therefore neglected his own dinner at half-past one, and finally got none. We exaggerated in our imaginations the extent to which he punished Maxby's father's cold meat at supper; and we agreed to believe that he was elevated with wine and water when he came home. But, we all liked him; for he had a good knowledge of boys, and would have made it a much better school if he had had more power. He was writing master, mathematical master, English master, made out the bills, mended the pens, and did all sorts of things. He divided the little boys with the Latin master (they were smuggled through their rudimentary books, at odd times when there was nothing else to do), and he always called at parents' houses to inquire after sick boys, because he had gentlemanly manners. He was rather musical, and on some remote quarter-day had bought an old trombone; but a bit of it was lost, and it made the most extraordinary sounds when he sometimes tried to play it of an evening. His holidays never began (on account of the bills) until long after ours; but, in the summer vacations he used to take pedestrian excursions with a knapsack; and at Christmas time, he went to see his father at Chipping Norton, who we all said (on no authority) was a dairy-fed-pork-butcher. Poor fellow! He was very low all day on Maxby's sister's wedding-day, and afterwards was thought to favour Maxby more than ever, though he had been expected to spite him. He has been dead these twenty years. Poor fellow!

Our remembrance of Our School, presents the Latin master as a colorless doubled-up near-sighted man with a crutch, who was always cold, and always putting onions into his ears for deafness, and always disclosing ends of flannel under all his garments, and almost always applying a ball of pocket-handkerchief to some part of his face with a screwing action round and round. He was a very good scholar, and took great pains where he saw intelligence and a desire to learn: otherwise, perhaps not. Our memory presents him (unless teased into a passion) with as little energy as color – as having been worried and tormented into monotonous feebleness – as having had the best part of his life ground out of him in a Mill of boys. We remember with terror how he fell asleep one sultry afternoon with the little smuggled class before him, and awoke not when the footstep of the Chief fell heavy on the floor; how the Chief aroused him, in the midst of a dread silence, and said, 'Mr Blinkins, are you ill, sir?' how he blushingly replied, 'Sir, rather so'; how the Chief retorted with severity, 'Mr Blinkins, this is no place to be ill in' (which was very, very true), and walked back solemn as the ghost in Hamlet,[2] until, catching a wandering eye, he caned that boy for inattention, and happily expressed his feelings towards the Latin master through the medium of a substitute.

There was a fat little dancing-master who used to come in a gig, and taught the more advanced among us hornpipes (as an accomplishment in great social demand in after life); and there was a brisk little French master who used to come in the sunniest weather, with a handleless umbrella, and to whom the Chief was always polite, because (as we believed), if the Chief offended him, he would instantly address the Chief in French, and for ever confound him before the boys with his inability to understand or reply.

There was besides, a serving man, whose name was Phil. Our retrospective glance presents Phil as a shipwrecked carpenter, cast away upon the desert island of a school, and carrying into practice an ingenious inkling of many trades. He mended whatever was broken, and made whatever was wanted. He was general glazier, among other things, and mended all the broken windows – at the prime cost (as was darkly rumoured among us) of ninepence, for every square charged three-and-six to parents. We had a high opinion of his mechanical genius, and generally held that the Chief 'knew something bad of him', and on pain of divulgence enforced Phil to be his bondsman. We particularly remember that Phil had a sovereign contempt for learning: which engenders in us a respect for his sagacity, as it implies his accurate observation of the relative positions of the Chief and the ushers. He was an impenetrable man, who waited at table between whiles, and throughout 'the half' kept the boxes in severe custody. He was morose, even to the Chief, and never smiled, except at breaking-up, when, in acknowledgment of the toast, 'Success to Phil! Hooray!' he would slowly carve a grin out of his wooden face, where it would remain until we were all gone. Nevertheless, one time when we had the scarlet fever in the school, Phil nursed all the sick boys of his own accord, and was like a mother to them.

There was another school not far off, and of course Our School could have nothing to say to that school. It is mostly the way with schools, whether of boys or men. Well! the railway has swallowed up ours, and the locomotives now run smoothly over its ashes.

> 'So fades and languishes, grows dim and dies,
>   All that this world is proud of,'[3]

– and is not proud of, too. It had little reason to be proud of Our School, and has done much better since in that way, and will do far better yet.

Lying Awake

'MY uncle lay with his eyes half closed, and his nightcap drawn almost down to his nose. His fancy was already wandering, and began to mingle up the present scene with the crater of Vesuvius, the French Opera, the Coliseum at Rome, Dolly's Chop-house in London, and all the farrago of noted places with which the brain of a traveller is crammed; in a word, he was just falling asleep.'[1]

Thus, that delightful writer, WASHINGTON IRVING, in his Tales of a Traveller. But, it happened to me the other night to be lying: not with my eyes half closed, but with my eyes wide open; not with my nightcap drawn almost down to my nose, for on sanitary principles I never wear a nightcap: but with my hair pitchforked and touzled all over the pillow; not just falling asleep by any means, but glaringly, persistently, and obstinately, broad awake. Perhaps, with no scientific intention or invention, I was illustrating the theory of the Duality of the Brain; perhaps one part of my brain, being wakeful, sat up to watch the other part which was sleepy. Be that as it may, something in me was as desirous to go to sleep as it possibly could be, but something else in me *would not* go to sleep, and was as obstinate as George the Third.

Thinking of George the Third – for I devote this paper to my train of thoughts as I lay awake: most people lying awake sometimes, and having some interest in the subject – put me in mind of BENJAMIN FRANKLIN, and so Benjamin Franklin's paper on the art of procuring pleasant dreams, which would seem necessarily to include the art of going to sleep, came into my head. Now, as I often used to read that paper when I was a very small boy, and as I recollect everything I read then, as perfectly as I forget everything I read now, I quoted 'Get out of bed, beat up and turn your pillow, shake the bed-clothes well with at least twenty shakes, then throw the bed open and leave it to cool; in the meanwhile, continuing undrest, walk about your chamber. When you begin to feel the cold air unpleasant, then return to your bed, and you will soon fall asleep, and your sleep will be sweet and pleasant.'² Not a bit of it! I performed the whole ceremony, and if it were possible for me to be more saucer-eyed than I was before, that was the only result that came of it.

Except Niagara. The two quotations from Washington Irving and Benjamin Franklin may have put it in my head by an American association of ideas; but there I was, and the Horse-shoe Fall was thundering and tumbling in my eyes and ears, and the very rainbows that I left upon the spray when I really did last look upon it, were beautiful to see. The night-light being quite as plain, however, and sleep seeming to be many thousand miles further off than Niagara, I made up my mind to think a little about Sleep; which I no sooner did than I whirled off in spite of myself to Drury Lane Theatre, and there saw a great actor and dear friend of mine (whom I had been thinking of in the day) playing Macbeth, and heard him apostrophising 'the death of each day's life',³ as I have heard him many a time, in the days that are gone.

But, Sleep. I *will* think about Sleep. I am determined to think (this is the way I went on) about Sleep. I must hold the word Sleep, tight and fast, or I shall be off at a tangent in half a second. I feel myself unaccountably straying, already, into Clare Market. Sleep. It would be curious, as illustrating the equality of sleep, to inquire how many of its phenomena are common to all classes, to all degrees of wealth and poverty, to every grade of education and ignorance. Here, for example, is her Majesty Queen Victoria in her palace, this present blessed night, and here is Winking Charley, a sturdy vagrant, in one of her Majesty's jails. Her Majesty has fallen, many thousands of times, from that same Tower, which *I* claim a right to tumble off now and then. So has Winking Charley. Her Majesty in her sleep has opened or prorogued Parliament, or has held a Drawing Room, attired in some very scanty dress, the deficiencies and improprieties of which have caused her great uneasiness. I, in my degree, have suffered unspeakable agitation of mind from taking the chair at a public dinner at the London Tavern in my night-clothes, which not all the courtesy of my kind friend and host MR BATHE[4] could persuade me were quite adapted to the occasion. Winking Charley has been repeatedly tried in a worse condition. Her Majesty is no stranger to a vault or firmament, of a sort of floorcloth, with an indistinct pattern distantly resembling eyes, which occasionally obtrudes itself on her repose. Neither am I. Neither is Winking Charley. It is quite common to all three of us to skim along with airy strides a little above the ground; also to hold, with the deepest interest, dialogues with various people, all represented by ourselves; and to be at our wit's end to know what they are going to tell us; and to be indescribably astonished by the secrets they disclose. It is probable that we have all three committed murders and hidden bodies. It is pretty certain that we have all desperately wanted to cry out, and have had no voice; that we have all gone to the play and not been able to get in; that we have all dreamed much more of our youth than of our later lives; that – I have lost it! The thread's broken.

And up I go. I, lying here with the night-light before me, up I go, for no reason on earth that I can find out, and drawn by no links that are visible to me, up the Great Saint Bernard! I have lived in Switzerland, and rambled among the mountains; but, why I should go there now, and why up the Great Saint Bernard in preference to any other mountain, I have no idea. As I lie here broad awake, and with every sense so sharpened that I can distinctly hear distant noises inaudible to me at another time, I make that journey, as I really did, on the same summer day, with the same happy party – ah! two since dead, I grieve to think – and there is the same track, with the same black wooden arms to point the way, and there are the same storm-refuges here and there; and there is the same snow falling at the top, and there are the same frosty mists, and there is the same intensely cold convent with its ménagerie smell, and the same breed of dogs fast dying out, and the same breed of jolly young monks whom I mourn to know as humbugs, and the same convent parlour with its piano and the sitting round the fire, and the same supper, and the same lone night in a cell, and the same bright fresh morning when going out into the highly rarefied air was like a plunge into an icy bath. Now, see here what comes along; and why does this thing stalk into my mind on the top of a Swiss mountain!

It is a figure that I once saw, just after dark, chalked upon a door in a little back lane near a country church – my first church. How young a child I may have been at the time I don't know, but it horrified me so intensely – in connexion with the churchyard, I suppose, for it smokes a pipe, and has a big hat with each of its ears sticking out in a horizontal line under the brim, and is not in itself more oppressive than a mouth from ear to ear, a pair of goggle eyes, and hands like two bunches of carrots, five in each, can make it – that it is still vaguely alarming to me to recall (as I have often done before, lying awake) the running home, the looking behind, the horror, of its following me; though whether disconnected from the door, or door and all, I can't say, and perhaps never could. It lays a disagreeable train. I must resolve to think of something on the voluntary principle.

The balloon ascents of this last season. They will do to think about, while I lie awake, as well as anything else. I must hold them tight though, for I feel them sliding away, and in their stead are the Mannings, husband and wife, hanging on the top of Horsemonger Lane Jail.[5] In connexion with which dismal spectacle, I recall this curious fantasy of the mind. That, having beheld that execution, and having left those two forms dangling on the top of the entrance gateway – the man's, a limp, loose suit of clothes as if the man had gone out of them; the woman's, a fine shape, so elaborately corseted and artfully dressed, that it was quite unchanged in its trim appearance as it slowly swung from side to side – I never could, by my uttermost efforts, for some weeks, present the outside of that prison to myself (which the terrible impression I had received continually obliged me to do) without presenting it with the two figures still hanging in the morning air. Until, strolling past the gloomy place one night, when the street was deserted and quiet, and actually seeing that the bodies were not there, my fancy was persuaded, as it were, to take them down and bury them within the precincts of the jail, where they have lain ever since.

The balloon ascents of last season. Let me reckon them up. There were the horse, the bull, the parachute, and the tumbler hanging on – chiefly by his toes, I believe – below the car. Very wrong, indeed, and decidedly to be stopped. But, in connexion with these and similar dangerous exhibitions, it strikes me that that portion of the public whom they entertain, is unjustly reproached. Their pleasure is in the difficulty overcome. They are a public of great faith, and are quite confident that the gentleman will not fall off the horse, or the lady off the bull or out of the parachute, and that the tumbler has a firm hold with his toes. They do not go to see the adventurer vanquished, but triumphant. There is no parallel in public combats between men and beasts, because nobody can answer for the particular beast – unless it were always the same beast, in which case it would be a mere stage-show, which the same public would go in the same state of mind to see, entirely believing in the brute being beforehand safely subdued by the man. That they are not accustomed to calculate hazards and dangers with any nicety, we may know from their rash exposure of themselves in overcrowded steamboats, and unsafe conveyances and places of all kinds. And I cannot help thinking that instead of railing, and attributing savage motives to a people naturally well disposed and humane, it is better to teach them, and lead them argumentatively and reasonably – for they are very reasonable, if you will discuss a matter with them – to more considerate and wise conclusions.

This is a disagreeable intrusion! Here is a man with his throat cut, dashing towards me as I lie awake! A recollection of an old story of a kinsman of mine, who, going home one foggy winter night to Hampstead, when London was much smaller and the road lonesome, suddenly encountered such a figure rushing past him, and presently two keepers from a madhouse in pursuit. A very unpleasant creature indeed, to come into my mind unbidden, as I lie awake.

– The balloon ascents of last season. I must return to the balloons. Why did the bleeding man start out of them? Never mind; if I inquire, he will be back again. The balloons. This particular public have inherently a great pleasure in the contemplation of physical difficulties overcome; mainly, as I take it, because the lives of a large majority of them are exceedingly monotonous and real, and further, are a struggle against continual difficulties, and further still, because anything in the form of accidental injury, or any kind of illness or disability is so very serious in their own sphere. I will explain this seeming paradox of mine. Take the case of a Christmas Pantomime. Surely nobody supposes that the young mother in the pit who falls into fits of laughter when the baby is boiled or sat upon, would be at all diverted by such an occurrence off the stage. Nor is the decent workman in the gallery, who is transported beyond the ignorant present by the delight with which he sees a stout gentleman pushed out of a two pair of stairs window, to be slandered by the suspicion that he would be in the least entertained by such a spectacle in any street in London, Paris, or New York. It always appears to me that the secret of this enjoyment lies in the temporary superiority to the common hazards and mischances of life; in seeing casualties, attended when they really occur with bodily and mental suffering, tears, and poverty, happen through a very rough sort of poetry without the least harm being done to any one – the pretence of distress in a pantomime being so broadly humorous as to be no pretence at all. Much as in the comic fiction I can understand the mother with a very vulnerable baby at home, greatly relishing the invulnerable baby on the stage, so in the Cremorne reality[6] I can understand the mason who is always liable to fall off a scaffold in his working jacket and to be carried to the hospital, having an infinite admiration of the radiant personage in spangles who goes into the clouds upon a bull, or upside down, and who, he takes it for granted – not reflecting upon the thing – has, by uncommon skill and dexterity, conquered such mischances as those to which he and his acquaintance are continually exposed.

I wish the Morgue in Paris would not come here as I lie awake, with its ghastly beds, and the swollen saturated clothes hanging up, and the water dripping, dripping all day long, upon that other swollen saturated something in the corner, like a heap of crushed over-ripe figs that I have seen in Italy! And this detestable Morgue comes back again at the head of a procession of forgotten ghost stories. This will never do. I must think of something else as I lie awake; or, like that sagacious animal in the United States who recognized the colonel who was such a dead shot, I am a gone

'Coon.[7] What shall I think of? The late brutal assaults. Very good subject. The late brutal assaults.

(Though whether, supposing I should see, here before me as I lie awake, the awful phantom described in one of those ghost stories, who, with a head-dress of shroud, was always seen looking in through a certain glass door at a certain dead hour – whether, in such a case it would be the least consolation to me to know on philosophical grounds that it was merely my imagination, is a question I can't help asking myself by the way.)

The late brutal assaults. I strongly question the expediency of advocating the revival of whipping for those crimes. It is a natural and generous impulse to be indignant at the perpetration of inconceivable brutality, but I doubt the whipping panacea gravely. Not in the least regard or pity for the criminal, whom I hold in far lower estimation than a mad wolf, but in consideration for the general tone and feeling, which is very much improved since the whipping times. It is bad for a people to be familiarized with such punishments. When the whip went out of Bridewell, and ceased to be flourished at the cart's tail and at the whipping-post, it began to fade out of madhouses, and workhouses, and schools and families, and to give place to a better system everywhere, than cruel driving. It would be hasty, because a few brutes may be inadequately punished, to revive, in any aspect, what, in so many aspects, society is hardly yet happily rid of. The whip is a very contagious kind of thing, and difficult to confine within one set of bounds. Utterly abolish punishment by fine – a barbarous device, quite as much out of date as wager by battle, but particularly connected in the vulgar mind with this class of offence – at least quadruple the term of imprisonment for aggravated assaults – and above all let us, in such cases, have no Pet Prisoning,[8] vain glorifying, strong soup, and roasted meats, but hard work, and one unchanging and uncompromising dietary of bread and water, well or ill; and we shall do much better than by going down into the dark to grope for the whip among the rusty fragments of the rack, and the branding iron, and the chains and gibbet from the public roads, and the weights that pressed men to death in the cells of Newgate.

I had proceeded thus far, when I found I had been lying awake so long that the very dead began to wake too, and to crowd into my thoughts most sorrowfully. Therefore, I resolved to lie awake no more, but to get up and go out for a night walk – which resolution was an acceptable relief to me, as I dare say it may prove now to a great many more.

THE UNCOMMERCIAL TRAVELLER

His General Line of Business

ALLOW me to introduce myself – first negatively.

No landlord is my friend and brother, no chambermaid loves me, no waiter worships me, no boots admires and envies me. No round of beef or tongue or ham is expressly cooked for me, no pigeon-pie is especially made for me, no hotel-advertisement is personally addressed to me, no hotel-room tapestried with great-coats and railway wrappers is set apart for me, no house of public entertainment in the United Kingdom greatly cares for my opinion of its brandy or sherry. When I go upon my journeys, I am not usually rated at a low figure in the bill; when I come home from my journeys, I never get any commission. I know nothing about prices, and should have no idea, if I were put to it, how to weedle a man into ordering something he doesn't want. As a town traveller, I am never to be seen driving a vehicle externally like a young and volatile pianoforte van, and internally like an oven in which a number of flat boxes are baking in layers. As a country traveller, I am rarely to be found in a gig, and am never to be encountered by a pleasure train, waiting on the platform of a branch station, quite a Druid in the midst of a light Stonehenge of samples.

And yet – proceeding now, to introduce myself positively – I am both a town traveller and a country traveller, and am always on the road. Figuratively speaking, I travel for the great house of Human Interest Brothers, and have rather a large connection in the fancy goods way. Literally speaking, I am always wandering here and there from my rooms in Covent-garden, London – now about the city streets: now, about the country by-roads – seeing many little things, and some great things, which, because they interest me, I think may interest others.

These are my brief credentials as the Uncommercial Traveller.

167

Refreshments for Travellers

In the late high winds I was blown to a great many places – and indeed, wind or no wind, I generally have extensive transactions on hand in the article of Air – but I have not been blown to any English place lately, and I very seldom have blown to any English place in my life, where I could get anything good to eat and drink in five minutes, or where, if I sought it, I was received with a welcome.

This is a curious thing to consider. But before (stimulated by my own experiences and the representations of many fellow-travellers of every uncommercial and commercial degree) I consider it further, I must utter a passing word of wonder concerning high winds.

I wonder why metropolitan gales always blow so hard at Walworth. I cannot imagine what Walworth has done, to bring such windy punishment upon itself, as I never fail to find recorded in the newspapers when the wind has blown at all hard. Brixton seems to have something on its conscience; Peckham suffers more than a virtuous Peckham might be supposed to deserve; the howling neighbourhood of Deptford figures largely in the accounts of the ingenious gentlemen who are out in every wind that blows, and to whom it is an ill high wind that blows no good; but, there can hardly be any Walworth left by this time. It must surely be blown away. I have read of more chimney-stacks and house-copings coming down with terrific smashes at Walworth, and of more sacred edifices being nearly (not quite) blown out to sea from the same accursed locality, than I have read of practised thieves with the appearance and manners of gentlemen[1] – a popular phenomenon which never existed on earth out of fiction and a police report. Again: I wonder why people are always blown into the Surrey Canal, and into no other piece of water! Why do people get up early and go out in groups, to be blown into the Surrey Canal? Do they say to one another, 'Welcome death, so that we get into the newspapers?' Even that would be an insufficient explanation, because even then they might sometimes put themselves in the way of being blown into the Regent's Canal, instead of always saddling

Surrey for the field. Some nameless policeman, too, is constantly, on the slightest provocation, getting himself blown into this same Surrey Canal. Will SIR RICHARD MAYNE[2] see to it, and restrain that weak-minded and feeble-bodied constable?

To resume the consideration of the curious question of Refreshment. I am a Briton, and, as such, I am aware that I never will be a slave – and yet I have latent suspicion that there must be some slavery of wrong custom in this matter.

I travel by railroad. I start from home at seven or eight in the morning, after breakfasting hurriedly. What with skimming over the open landscape, what with mining in the damp bowels of the earth, what with banging, booming and shrieking the scores of miles away, I am hungry when I arrive at the 'Refreshment' station where I am expected. Please to observe, expected. I have said, I am hungry; perhaps I might say, with greater point and force, that I am to some extent exhausted, and that I need – in the expressive French sense of the word – to be restored. What is provided for my restoration? The apartment that is to restore me is a wind-trap, cunningly set to inveigle all the draughts in that countryside, and to communicate a special intensity and velocity to them as they rotate in two hurricanes: one, about my wretched head: one, about my wretched legs. The training of the young ladies behind the counter who are to restore me, has been from their infancy directed to the assumption of a defiant dramatic show that I am *not* expected. It is in vain for me to represent to them by my humble and conciliatory manners, that I wish to be liberal. It is in vain for me to represent to myself, for the encouragement of my sinking soul, that the young ladies have a pecuniary interest in my arrival. Neither my reason nor my feelings can make head against the cold glazed glare of eye with which I am assured that I am not expected, and not wanted. The solitary man among the bottles would sometimes take pity on me, if he dared, but he is powerless against the rights and mights of Woman. (Of the page I make no account, for, he is a boy, and therefore the natural enemy of Creation.) Chilling fast, in the deadly tornadoes to which my upper and lower extremities are exposed, and subdued by the moral disadvantage at which I stand, I turn my disconsolate eyes on the refreshments that are to restore me. I find that I must either scald my throat by insanely ladling into it, against time and for no wager, brown hot water stiffened with flour; or I must make myself flaky and sick with Banbury cake; or, I must stuff into my delicate organization, a currant pincushion which I know will swell into immeasurable dimensions when it has got there; or, I must extort from an iron-bound quarry, with a fork, as if I were farming an inhospitable soil, some glutinous lumps of gristle and grease, called pork-pie. While thus forlornly occupied, I find that the depressing banquet on the table is, in every phase of its profoundly unsatisfactory character, so like the banquet at the meanest and shabbiest of evening parties, that I begin to think I must have 'brought down' to supper, the old lady unknown, blue with cold, who is setting her teeth on edge with a cool orange at my elbow – that the pastrycook who has compounded for the company on the lowest terms per head, is a fraudulent bankrupt, redeeming his contract with the stale stock from his window – that, for some unexplained reason, the family giving the party have become my mortal foes, and have given it on purpose to affront me. Or, I fancy that I am 'breaking up' again, at the evening conversazione at school, charged two-and-sixpence in the half-year's bill; or breaking down again at that celebrated evening party given at Mrs Bogles's boarding-house when I was a boarder there, on which occasion Mrs Bogles was taken in execution by a branch of the legal profession who got in as the harp, and was removed (with the keys and subscribed capital) to a place of durance, half an hour prior to the commencement of the festivities.

Take another case.

Mr Grazinglands, of the Midland Counties, came to London by railroad one morning last week, accompanied by the amiable and fascinating Mrs Grazinglands. Mr G. is a gentleman of a comfortable property, and had a little business to transact at the Bank of England, which required the concurrence and signature of Mrs G. Their business disposed of, Mr and Mrs Grazinglands viewed the Royal Exchange, and the exterior of St Paul's Cathedral. The spirits of Mrs Grazinglands then gradually beginning to flag, Mr Grazinglands (who is the tenderest of husbands) remarked with sympathy, 'Arabella, my dear, I fear you are faint.' Mrs Grazinglands replied, 'Alexander, I am rather faint; but don't mind me, I shall be better presently.' Touched by the feminine meekness of this answer, Mr Grazinglands looked in at a pastrycook's window, hesitating as to the expediency of lunching at that establishment. He beheld nothing to eat, but butter in various forms, slightly charged with jam, and languidly frizzling over tepid water. Two ancient turtle-shells, on which was inscribed the legend, 'SOUPS', decorated a glass partition within, enclosing a stuffy alcove, from which a ghastly mockery of a marriage-breakfast spread on a rickety table, warned the terrified traveller. An oblong box of stale and broken pastry at reduced prices, mounted on a stool, ornamented the doorway; and two high chairs that looked as if they were performing on stilts, embellished the counter. Over the whole, a young lady presided, whose gloomy haughtiness as she surveyed the street, announced a deep-seated grievance against society, and an implacable determination to be avenged. From a beetle-haunted kitchen below this institution, fumes arose, suggestive of a class of soup which Mr Grazinglands knew, from painful experience, enfeebles the mind, distends the stomach, forces itself into the complexion, and tries to ooze out at the eyes. As he decided against entering, and turned away, Mrs Grazinglands becoming perceptibly weaker, repeated, 'I am rather faint, Alexander, but don't mind me.' Urged to new efforts by these words of resignation, Mr Grazinglands looked in at a cold and floury baker's shop, where utilitarian buns unrelieved by a currant, consorted with hard biscuits, a stone filter of cold water, a hard pale clock, and a hard little old woman with flaxen hair, of an undeveloped-farinaceous aspect, as if she had been fed upon seeds. He might have entered even here, but for the timely remembrance coming upon him that Jairing's was but round the corner.

Now, Jairing's being an hotel for families and gentlemen, in high repute among the midland counties, Mr Grazinglands plucked up a great spirit when he told Mrs Grazinglands she should have a chop there. That lady, likewise felt that she was going to see Life. Arriving on that gay and festive scene, they found the second waiter, in a flabby undress, cleaning the windows of the empty coffee-room; and the first waiter, denuded of his white tie, making up his cruets behind the Post-Office Directory. The latter (who took them in hand) was greatly put out by their patronage, and showed his mind to be troubled by a sense of the pressing necessity of instantly smuggling Mrs Grazinglands into the obscurest corner of the building. This slighted lady (who is the pride of her division of the county) was immediately conveyed, by several dark passages, and up and down several steps, into a penitential apartment at the back of the house, where five invalided old plate-warmers leaned up against one another under a discarded old melancholy sideboard, and where the wintry leaves of all the dining-tables in the house lay thick. Also, a sofa, of incomprehensible form regarded from any sofane point of view, murmured 'Bed'; while an air of mingled fluffiness and heeltaps, added, 'Second Waiter's'. Secreted in this dismal hold, objects of a mysterious distrust and suspicion, Mr Grazinglands and his charming partner waited twenty minutes for the smoke (for it never came to a fire), twenty-five minutes for the sherry, half an hour for the tablecloth, forty minutes for the knives and forks, three-quarters of an hour for the chops, and an hour for the potatoes. On settling the little bill – which was not much more than the day's pay of a Lieutenant in the navy – Mr Grazinglands took heart to remonstrate against the general quality and cost of his reception. To whom the waiter replied, substantially, that Jairing's made it a merit to have accepted him on any terms: 'for', added the waiter (unmistakably coughing at Mrs Grazinglands, the pride of her division of the county), 'when indiwiduals is not staying in the 'Ouse, their favours is not as a rule looked upon as making it worth Mr Jairing's while; nor is it, indeed, a style of business Mr Jairing wishes'. Finally, Mr and Mrs Grazinglands passed out of Jairing's hotel for Families and Gentlemen, in a state of the greatest depression, scorned by the bar; and did not recover their self-respect for several days.

Or take another case. Take your own case.

You are going off by railway, from any Terminus. You have twenty minutes for dinner, before you go. You want your dinner, and like Dr Johnson, Sir, you like to dine.[3] You present to your mind, a picture of the refreshment-table at that terminus. The conventional shabby evening-party supper – accepted as the model for all termini and all refreshment stations, because it is the last repast known to this state of existence of which any human creature would partake, but in the direst extremity – sickens your contemplation, and your words are these: 'I cannot dine on stale sponge-cakes that turn to sand in the mouth. I cannot dine on shining brown patties, composed of unknown animals within, and offering to my view the device of an indigestible star-fish in leaden pie-crust without. I cannot dine on a sandwich that has long been pining under an exhausted receiver. I cannot dine on barley-sugar. I cannot dine on Toffee.' You repair to the nearest hotel, and arrive, agitated in the coffee-room.

It is a most astonishing fact that the waiter is very cold to you. Account for it how you may, smooth it over how you will, you cannot deny that he is cold to you. He is not glad to see you, he does not want you, he would much rather you hadn't come. He opposes to your flushed condition, an immovable composure. As if this were not enough, another waiter, born, as it would seem, expressly to look at you in this passage of your life, stands at a little distance, with his napkin under his arm and his hands folded, looking at you with all his might. You impress on your waiter that you have ten minutes for dinner, and he proposes that you shall begin with a bit of fish which will be ready in twenty. That proposal declined, he suggests – as a neat originality – 'a weal or mutton cutlet'. You close with either cutlet, any cutlet, anything. He goes, leisurely, behind a door and calls down some unseen shaft. A ventriloquial dialogue ensues, tending finally to the effect that weal only, is available on the spur of the moment. You anxiously call out, 'Veal, then!' Your waiter having settled that point, returns to array your tablecloth, with a table napkin folded cocked-hat-wise (slowly, for something out of window engages his eye), a white wine-glass, a green wine-glass, a blue finger-glass, a tumbler, and a powerful field battery of fourteen castors with nothing in them; or at all events – which is enough for your purpose – with nothing in them that will come out. All this time, the other waiter looks at you – with an air of mental comparison and curiosity, now, as if it had occurred to him that you are rather like his brother. Half your time gone, and nothing come but the jug of ale and the bread, you implore your waiter to 'See after that cutlet, waiter; pray do!' He cannot go at once, for he is carrying in seventeen pounds of American cheese for you to finish with, and a small Landed Estate of celery and watercresses. The other waiter changes his leg, and takes a new view of you, doubtfully, now, as if he had rejected the resemblance to his brother, and had begun to think you more like his aunt or his grandmother. Again you beseech your waiter with pathetic indignation, to 'see after that cutlet!' He steps out to see after it, and by-and-by, when you are going away without it, comes back with it. Even then, he will not take the sham silver-cover off, without a pause for a flourish, and a look at the musty cutlet as if he were surprised to see it – which cannot possibly be the case, he must have seen it so often before. A sort of fur has been produced upon its surface by the cook's art, and in a sham silver vessel staggering on two feet instead of three, is a cutaneous kind of sauce, of brown pimples and pickled cucumber. You order the bill, but your waiter cannot bring your bill yet, because he is bringing, instead, three flinty-hearted potatoes and two grim head of brocoli, like the occasional ornaments on area railings, badly boiled. You know that you will never come to this pass, any more than to the cheese and celery, and you imperatively demand your bill; but, it takes time to get, even when gone for, because your waiter has to communicate with a lady who lives behind a sash-window in a corner, and who appears to have to refer to several Ledgers before she can make it out – as if you had been staying there a year. You become distracted to get away, and the other waiter, once more changing his leg, still looks at you – but sus-piciously, now, as if you had begun to remind him of the party who took the great-coats last winter. Your bill at last brought and paid, at the rate of sixpence a mouthful, your waiter reproachfully reminds you that 'attendance is not charged for a single meal', and you have to search in all your pockets for sixpence more. He has a worse opinion of you than ever, when you have given it to him, and lets you out into the street with the air of one saying to him-self, as you cannot doubt he is, 'I hope we shall never see *you* here again!'

Or, take any other of the numerous travelling instances in which, with more time at your disposal, you are, have been, or may be, equally ill served. Take the old-established Bull's Head with its old-established knife-boxes on its old-established side-boards, its old-established flue under its old-established four-post bedsteads in its old-established airless rooms, its old-established frouziness up-stairs and down-stairs, its old-established cookery, and its old-established principles of plunder. Count up your injuries, in its side-dishes of ailing sweetbreads in white poultices, of apothecaries' powders in rice for curry, of pale stewed bits of calf ineffectually relying for an adventitious interest on forcemeat balls. You have had experience of the old-established Bull's Head stringy fowls, with lower extremities like wooden legs, sticking up out of the dish; of its cannibalic boiled mutton, gushing horribly among its capers, when carved; of its little dishes of pastry — roofs of spermaceti ointment, erected over half an apple or four gooseberries. Well for you if you have yet forgotten the old-established Bull's Head fruity port: whose reputation was gained solely by the old-established price the Bull's Head put upon it, and by the old-established air with which the Bull's Head set the glasses and D'Oyleys on, and held that Liquid Gout to the three-and-sixpenny wax-candle, as if its old-established colour hadn't come from the dyer's.

Or lastly, take to finish with, two cases that we all know, every day.

We all know the new hotel near the station, where it is always gusty, going up the lane which is always muddy, where we are sure to arrive at night, and where we make the gas start awfully when we open the front door. We all know the flooring of the passages and staircases that is too new, and the walls that are too new, and the house that is haunted by the ghost of mortar. We all know the doors that have cracked, and the cracked shutters through which we get a glimpse of the disconsolate moon. We all know the new people, who have come to keep the new hotel, and who wish they had never come, and who (inevitable result) wish *we* had never come. We all know how much too scant and smooth and bright the new furniture is, and how it has never settled down, and cannot fit itself into right places, and will get into wrong places. We all know how the gas, being lighted, shows maps of Damp upon the walls. We all know how the ghost of mortar passes into our sandwich, stirs our negus, goes up to bed with us, ascends the pale bedroom chimney, and prevents the smoke from following. We all know how a leg of our chair comes off at breakfast in the morning, and how the dejected waiter attributes the accident to a general greenness pervading the establishment, and informs us, in reply to a local inquiry, that he is thankful to say he is an entire stranger in that part of the country, and is going back to his own connexion on Saturday.

We all know, on the other hand, the great station hotel belonging to the company of proprietors, which has suddenly sprung up in the back outskirts of any place we like to name, and where we look out of our palatial windows, at little back yards and gardens, old summer-houses, fowl-houses, pigeon-traps, and pigsties. We all know this hotel in which we can get anything we want, after its kind, for money; but where nobody is glad to see us, or sorry to see us, or minds (our bill paid) whether we come or go, or how, or when, or why, or cares about us. We all know this hotel, where we have no individuality, but put ourselves into the general post, as it were, and are sorted and disposed of according to our division. We all know that we can get on very well indeed at such a place, but still not perfectly well; and this may be, because the place is largely wholesale, and there is a lingering personal retail interest within us that asks to be satisfied.

To sum up. My uncommercial travelling has not yet brought me to the conclusion that we are close to perfection in these matters. And just as I do not believe that the end of the world will ever be near at hand, so long as any of the very tiresome and arrogant people who constantly predict that catastrophe are left in it, so, I shall have small faith in the Hotel Millennium, while any of the uncomfortable superstitions I have glanced at remain in existence.

Travelling Abroad

I GOT into the travelling chariot – it was of German make, roomy, heavy, and unvarnished – I got into the travelling chariot, pulled up the steps after me, shut myself in with a smart bang of the door, and gave the word, 'Go on!'

Immediately, all that W. and S.W. division of London began to slide away at a pace so lively, that I was over the river, and past the

Old Kent Road, and out on Blackheath, and even ascending Shooter's Hill, before I had had time to look about me in the carriage, like a collected traveller.

I had two ample Imperials on the roof, other fitted storage for luggage in front, and other up behind; I had a net for books overhead, great pockets to all the windows, a leathern pouch or two hung up for odds and ends, and a reading lamp fixed in the back of the chariot, in case I should be benighted. I was amply provided in all respects, and had no idea where I was going (which was delightful), except that I was going abroad.

So smooth was the old high road, and so fresh were the horses, and so fast went I, that it was midway between Gravesend and Rochester, and the widening river was bearing the ships, white sailed or black-smoked, out to sea, when I noticed by the wayside a very queer small boy.

'Holloa!' said I, to the very queer small boy, 'where do you live?'

'At Chatham,' says he.

'What do you do there?' says I.

'I go to school,' says he.

I took him up in a moment, and we went on. Presently, the very queer small boy says, 'This is Gads-hill we are coming to, where Falstaff went out to rob those travellers, and ran away.'

'You know something about Falstaff, eh?' said I.

'All about him,' said the very queer small boy. 'I am old (I am nine), and I read all sorts of books. But *do* let us stop at the top of the hill, and look at the house there, if you please!'

'You admire that house?' said I.

'Bless you, sir,' said the very queer small boy, 'when I was not more than half as old as nine, it used to be a treat for me to be brought to look at it. And now, I am nine, I come by myself to look at it. And ever since I can recollect, my father, seeing me so fond of it, has often said to me, "If you were to be very persevering and were to work hard, you might some day come to live in it." Though that's impossible!' said the very queer small boy, drawing a low breath, and now staring at the house out of window with all his might.

I was rather amazed to be told this by the very queer small boy;

for that house happens to be *my* house, and I have reason to believe that what he said was true.

Well! I made no halt there, and I soon dropped the very queer small boy and went on. Over the road where the old Romans used to march, over the road where the old Canterbury pilgrims used to go, over the road where the travelling trains of the old imperious priests and princes used to jingle on horseback between the continent and this Island through the mud and water, over the road where Shakespeare hummed to himself, 'Blow, blow, thou winter wind,'[1] as he sat in the saddle at the gate of the inn yard noticing the carriers; all among the cherry orchards, apple orchards, cornfields and hop-gardens; so went I, by Canterbury to Dover. There, the sea was tumbling in, with deep sounds, after dark, and the revolving French light on Cape Grinez was seen regularly bursting out and becoming obscured, as if the head of a gigantic light-keeper in an anxious state of mind were interposed every half minute, to look how it was burning.

Early in the morning I was on the deck of the steam-packet, and we were aiming at the bar in the usual intolerable manner, and the bar was aiming at us in the usual intolerable manner, and the bar got by far the best of it, and we got by far the worst – all in the usual intolerable manner.

But, when I was clear of the Custom House on the other side, and when I began to make the dust fly on the thirsty French roads, and when the twigsome trees by the wayside (which, I suppose, never will grow leafy, for they never did) guarded here and there a dusty soldier, or field labourer, baking on a heap of broken stones, sound asleep in a fiction of shade, I began to recover my travelling spirits. Coming upon the breaker of the broken stones, in a hard hot shining hat, on which the sun played at a distance as on a burning-glass, I felt that now, indeed, I was in the dear old France of my affections. I should have known it, without the well-remembered bottle of rough ordinary wine, the cold roast fowl, the loaf, and the pinch of salt, on which I lunched with unspeakable satisfaction, from one of the stuffed pockets of the chariot.

I must have fallen asleep after lunch, for when a bright face looked in at the window, I started, and said:

'Good God, Louis, I dreamed you were dead!'

My cheerful servant laughed, and answered:

'Me? Not at all, sir.'

'How glad I am to wake! What are we doing, Louis?'

'We go to take relay of horses. Will you walk up the hill?'

'Certainly.'

Welcome the old French hill, with the old French lunatic (not in the most distant degree related to Sterne's Maria)[2] living in a thatched dog-kennel half way up, and flying out with his crutch and his big head and extended nightcap, to be beforehand with the old men and women exhibiting crippled children, and with the children exhibiting old men and women, ugly and blind, who always seemed by resurrectionary process to be recalled out of the elements for the sudden peopling of the solitude!

'It is well,' said I, scattering among them what small coin I had; 'here comes Louis, and I am quite roused from my nap.'

We journeyed on again, and I welcomed every new assurance that France stood where I had left it. There were the posting-houses, with their archways, dirty stableyards, and clean postmasters' wives, bright women of business, looking on at the putting-to of the horses; there were the postilions counting what money they got, into their hats, and never making enough of it; there were the standard population of grey horses of Flanders descent, invariably biting one another when they got a chance; there were the fleecy sheepskins, looped on over their uniforms by the postilions, like bibbed aprons when it blew and rained; there were their jack-boots, and their cracking whips; there were the cathedrals that I got out to see, as under some cruel bondage, in no wise desiring to see them; there were the little towns that appeared to have no reason for being towns, since most of their houses were to let and nobody could be induced to look at them, except the people who couldn't let them and had nothing else to do but look at them all day. I lay a night upon the road and enjoyed delectable cookery of potatoes, and some other sensible things, adoption of which at home would inevitably be shown to be fraught with ruin, somehow or other, to that rickety national blessing, the British farmer; and at last I was rattled, like a single pill in a box, over leagues of stones, until – madly cracking, plunging, and flourishing two grey tails about – I made my triumphal entry into Paris.

At Paris, I took an upper apartment for a few days in one of the hotels of the Rue de Rivoli; my front windows looking into the garden of the Tuileries (where the principal difference between the nursemaids and the flowers seemed to be that the former were locomotive and the latter not): my back windows looking at all the other back windows in the hotel, and deep down into a paved yard, where my German chariot had retired under a tight-fitting archway, to all appearance for life, and where bells rang all day without anybody's minding them but certain chamberlains with feather brooms and green baize caps, who here and there leaned out of some high window placidly looking down, and where neat waiters with trays on their left shoulders passed and repassed from morning to night.

Whenever I am at Paris, I am dragged by invisible force into the Morgue. I never want to go there, but am always pulled there. One Christmas Day, when I would rather have been anywhere else, I was attracted in, to see an old grey man lying all alone on his cold bed, with a tap of water turned on over his grey hair, and running, drip, drip, drip, down his wretched face until it got to the corner of his mouth, where it took a turn, and made him look sly. One New Year's Morning (by the same token, the sun was shining outside, and there was a mountebank balancing a feather on his nose, within a yard of the gate), I was pulled in again to look at a flaxen-haired boy of eighteen, with a heart hanging on his breast – 'from his mother', was engraven on it – who had come into the net across the river, with a bullet wound in his fair forehead and his hands cut with a knife, but whence or how was a blank mystery. This time, I was forced into the same dread place, to see a large dark man whose disfigurement by water was in a frightful manner, comic, and whose expression was that of a prize-fighter who had closed his eyelids under a heavy blow, but was going immediately to open them, shake his head, and 'come up smiling'. Oh what this large dark man cost me in that bright city!

It was very hot weather, and he was none the better for that, and I was much the worse. Indeed, a very neat and pleasant little woman with the key of her lodging on her forefinger, who had been showing him to her little girl while she and the child ate sweetmeats, observed monsieur looking poorly as we came out together, and asked monsieur, with her wondering little eyebrows prettily raised, if there were anything the matter? Faintly replying in the negative, monsieur crossed the road to a wine-shop, got some brandy, and resolved to freshen himself with a dip in the great floating bath on the river.

The bath was crowded in the usual airy manner, by a male population in striped drawers of various gay colours, who walked up and down arm in arm, drank coffee, smoked cigars, sat at little tables, conversed politely with the damsels who dispensed the towels, and every now and then pitched themselves into the river head foremost, and came out again to repeat this social routine. I made haste to participate in the water part of the entertainments, and was in the full enjoyment of a delightful bath, when all in a moment I was seized with an unreasonable idea that the large dark body was floating straight at me.

I was out of the river, and dressing instantly. In the shock I had taken some water into my mouth, and it turned me sick, for I fancied that the contamination of the creature was in it. I had got back to my cool darkened room in the hotel, and was lying on a sofa there, before I began to reason with myself.

Of course, I knew perfectly well that the large dark creature was stone dead, and that I should no more come upon him out of the place where I had seen him dead, than I should come upon the cathedral of Notre-Dame in an entirely new situation. What troubled me was the picture of the creature; and that had so curiously and strongly painted itself upon my brain, that I could not get rid of it until it was worn out.

I noticed the peculiarities of this possession, while it was a real discomfort to me. That very day, at dinner, some morsel on my plate looked like a piece of him, and I was glad to get up and go out. Later in the evening, I was walking along the Rue St Honoré, when I saw a bill at a public room there, announcing small-sword exercise, broad-sword exercise, wrestling, and other such feats. I went in, and some of the sword-play being very skilful, remained. A specimen of our own national sport, The British Boaxe, was announced to be given at the close of the evening. In an evil hour, I determined to wait for this Boaxe, as became a Briton. It was a clumsy specimen (executed by two English grooms out of place), but one of the combatants, receiving a straight right-hander with the glove between his eyes, did exactly what the large dark creature in the Morgue had seemed going to do – and finished me for that night.

There was rather a sickly smell (not at all an unusual fragrance in Paris) in the little ante-room of my apartment at the hotel. The large dark creature in the Morgue was by no direct experience associated with my sense of smell, because, when I came to the knowledge of him, he lay behind a wall of thick plate-glass as good as a wall of steel or marble for that matter. Yet the whiff of the room never failed to reproduce him. What was more curious, was the capriciousness with which his portrait seemed to light itself up in my mind, elsewhere. I might be walking in the Palais Royal, lazily enjoying the shop windows, and might be regaling myself with one of the ready-made clothes shops that are set out there. My eyes, wandering over impossible-waisted dressing-gowns and luminous waistcoats, would fall upon the master, or the shopman, or even the very dummy at the door, and would suggest to me, 'Something like him!' – and instantly I was sickened again.

This would happen at the theatre, in the same manner. Often it would happen in the street, when I certainly was not looking for the likeness, and when probably there was no likeness there. It was not because the creature was dead that I was so haunted, because I know that I might have been (and I know it because I have been) equally attended by the image of a living aversion. This lasted about a week. The picture did not fade by degrees, in the sense that it became a whit less forcible and distinct, but in the sense that it obtruded itself less and less frequently. The experience may be worth considering by some who have the care of children. It would be difficult to overstate the intensity and accuracy of an intelligent child's observation. At that impressible time of life, it must sometimes produce a fixed impression. If the fixed impression be of an object terrible to the child, it will be (for want of reasoning upon) inseparable from great fear. Force the child at such a time, be Spartan with it, send it into the dark against its will, leave it in a lonely bedroom against its will, and you had better murder it.

On a bright morning I rattled away from Paris, in the German chariot, and left the large dark creature behind me for good. I ought to confess, though, that I had been drawn back to the Morgue, after he was put underground, to look at his clothes, and that I found them frightfully like him – particularly his boots. However, I rattled away for Switzerland, looking forward and not backward, and so we parted company.

Welcome again, the long long spell of France, with the queer country inns, full of vases of flowers and clocks, in the dull little towns, and with the little population not at all dull on the little Boulevard in the evening, under the little trees. Welcome Monsieur the Curé walking alone in the early morning a short way out of the town, reading that eternal Breviary of yours, which surely might be almost read, without book, by this time! Welcome Monsieur the Curé, later in the day, jolting through the highway dust (as if you had already ascended to the cloudy region), in a very big-headed cabriolet, with the dried mud of a dozen winters on it. Welcome again Monsieur the Curé, as we exchange salutations; you, straightening your back to look at the German chariot, while picking in your little village garden a vegetable or two for the day's soup: I, looking out of the German chariot window in that delicious traveller's trance which knows no cares, no yesterdays, no tomorrows, nothing but the passing objects and the passing scents and sounds! And so I came, in due course of delight, to Strasbourg, where I passed a wet Sunday evening at a window, while an idle trifle of a vaudeville was played for me at the opposite house.

How such a large house came to have only three people living in it, was its own affair. There were at least a score of windows in its high roof alone; how many in its grotesque front, I soon gave up counting. The owner was a shopkeeper, by name Straudenheim; by trade – I couldn't make out what by trade, for he had forborne to write that up, and his shop was shut.

At first, as I looked at Straudenheim's, through the steadily falling rain, I set him up in business in the goose-liver line. But, inspection of Straudenheim, who became visible at a window on the second floor, convinced me that there was something more precious than liver in the case. He wore a black velvet skull-cap, and looked usurious and rich. A large-lipped, pear-nosed old man, with white hair, and keen eyes, though near-sighted. He was writing at a desk, was Straudenheim, and ever and again left off writing, put his pen in his mouth, and went through actions with his right hand, like a man steadying piles of cash. Five-franc pieces,

Straudenheim, or golden Napoleons? A jeweller, Straudenheim, a dealer in money, a diamond merchant, or what?

Below Straudenheim, at a window on the first floor, sat his housekeeper – far from young, but of a comely presence, suggestive of a well-matured foot and ankle. She was cheerily dressed, had a fan in her hand, and wore large gold earrings and a large gold cross. She would have been out holiday-making (as I settled it) but for the pestilent rain. Strasbourg had given up holiday-making for that once, as a bad job, because the rain was jerking in gushes out of the old roof-spouts, and running in a brook down the middle of the street. The housekeeper, her arms folded on her bosom and her fan tapping her chin, was bright and smiling at her open window, but otherwise Straudenheim's house front was very dreary. The housekeeper's was the only open window in it; Straudenheim kept himself close, though it was a sultry evening when air is pleasant, and though the rain had brought into the town that vague refreshing smell of grass which rain does bring in the summer-time.

The dim appearance of a man at Straudenheim's shoulder, inspired me with a misgiving that somebody had come to murder that flourishing merchant for the wealth with which I had handsomely endowed him: the rather, as it was an excited man, lean and long of figure, and evidently stealthy of foot. But, he conferred with Straudenheim instead of doing him a mortal injury, and then they both softly opened the other window of that room – which was immediately over the housekeeper's – and tried to see her by looking down. And my opinion of Straudenheim was much lowered when I saw that eminent citizen spit out of window, clearly with the hope of spitting on the housekeeper.

The unconscious housekeeper fanned herself, tossed her head, and laughed. Though unconscious of Straudenheim, she was conscious of somebody else – of me? – there was nobody else.

After leaning so far out of the window, that I confidently expected to see their heels tilt up, Straudenheim and the lean man drew their heads in and shut the window. Presently, the house door secretly opened, and they slowly and spitefully crept forth into the pouring rain. They were coming over to me (I thought) to demand satisfaction for my looking at the housekeeper, when they plunged into a recess in the architecture under my window and dragged out the puniest of little soldiers, begirt with the most innocent of little swords. The tall glazed head-dress of this warrior, Straudenheim instantly knocked off, and out of it fell two sugar-sticks, and three or four large lumps of sugar.

The warrior made no effort to recover his property or to pick up his shako, but looked with an expression of attention at Straudenheim when he kicked him five times, and also at the lean man when *he* kicked him five times, and again at Straudenheim when he tore the breast of his (the warrior's) little coat open, and shook all his ten fingers in his face, as if they were ten thousand. When these outrages had been committed, Straudenheim and his man went into the house again and barred the door. A wonderful circumstance was, that the housekeeper who saw it all (and who could have taken six such warriors to her buxom bosom at once), only fanned herself and laughed as she had laughed before, and seemed to have no opinion about it, one way or other.

But, the chief effect of the drama was the remarkable vengeance taken by the little warrior. Left alone in the rain, he picked up his shako; put it on, all wet and dirty as it was; retired into a court, of which Straudenheim's house formed the corner; wheeled about; and bringing his two forefingers close to the top of his nose, rubbed them over one another, cross-wise, in derision, defiance, and contempt of Straudenheim. Although Straudenheim could not possibly be supposed to be conscious of this strange proceeding, it so inflated and comforted the little warrior's soul, that twice he went away, and twice came back into the court to repeat it, as though it must goad his enemy to madness. Not only that, but he afterwards came back with two other small warriors, and they all three did it together. Not only that – as I live to tell the tale! – but just as it was falling quite dark, the three came back, bringing with them a huge bearded Sapper, whom they moved, by recital of the original wrong, to go through the same performance, with the same complete absence of all possible knowledge of it on the part of Straudenheim. And then they all went away, arm in arm, singing.

I went away too, in the German chariot at sunrise, and rattled on, day after day, like one in a sweet dream; with so many clear little bells on the harness of the horses, that the nursery rhyme about Banbury Cross and the venerable lady who rode in state there,[3] was always in my ears. And now I came to the land of wooden houses, innocent cakes, thin butter soup, and spotless little inn bedrooms with a family likeness to Dairies. And now the Swiss marksmen were for ever rifle-shooting at marks across gorges, so exceedingly near my ear, that I felt like a new Gesler in a Canton of Tells, and went in highly-deserved danger of my tyrannical life.[4] The prizes at these shootings, were watches, smart handkerchiefs, hats, spoons, and (above all) tea-trays; and at these contests I came upon a more than usually accomplished and amiable countryman of my own, who had shot himself deaf in whole years of competition, and had won so many tea-trays that he went about the country with his carriage full of them, like a glorified Cheap-Jack.

In the mountain-country into which I had now travelled, a yoke of oxen were sometimes hooked on before the post-horses, and I went lumbering up, up, up, through mist and rain, with the roar of falling water for change of music. Of a sudden, mist and rain would clear away, and I would come down into picturesque little towns with gleaming spires and odd towers; and would stroll afoot into market-places in steep winding streets, where a hundred women in bodices, sold eggs and honey, butter and fruit, and suckled their children as they sat by their clean baskets, and had such enormous goîtres (or glandular swellings in the throat) that it became a science to know where the nurse ended and the child began. About this time, I deserted my German chariot for the back of a mule (in colour and consistency so very like a dusty old hair trunk I once had at school, that I half-expected to see my initials in brass-headed nails on his backbone), and went up a thousand rugged ways, and looked down at a thousand woods of fir and pine, and would on the whole have preferred my mule's keeping a little nearer to the inside, and not usually travelling with a hoof or two over the precipice – though much consoled by explanation that this was to be attributed to his great sagacity, by reason of his carrying broad loads of wood at other times, and not being clear but that I myself belonged to that station of life, and required as much room as they. He brought me safely, in his own wise way, among the passes of the Alps, and here I enjoyed a dozen climates a day; being now (like Don Quixote on the back of the wooden horse)[5] in the region of wind, now in the region of fire, now in the region of unmelting ice and snow. Here, I passed over trembling domes of ice, beneath which the cataract was roaring; and here was received under arches of icicles, of unspeakable beauty; and here the sweet air was so bracing and so light, that at halting-times I rolled in the snow when I saw my mule do it, thinking that he must know best. At this part of the journey we would come, at mid-day, into half an hour's thaw: when the rough mountain inn would be found on an island of deep mud in a sea of snow, while the baiting strings of mules, and the carts full of casks and bales, which had been in an Arctic condition a mile off, would steam again. By such ways and means, I would come to the cluster of châlets where I had to turn out of the track to see the waterfall; and then, uttering a howl like a young giant, on espying a traveller – in other words, something to eat – coming up the steep, the idiot lying on the wood-pile who sunned himself and nursed his goître, would rouse the woman-guide within the hut, who would stream out hastily, throwing her child over one of her shoulders and her goître over the other, as she came along. I slept at religious houses, and bleak refuges of many kinds, on this journey, and by the stove at night heard stories of travellers who had perished within call, in wreaths and drifts of snow. One night the stove within, and the cold outside, awakened childish associations long forgotten, and I dreamed I was in Russia – the identical serf out of a picture-book I had, before I could read it for myself – and that I was going to be knouted by a noble personage in a fur cap, boots, and earrings, who, I think, must have come out of some melodrama.

Commend me to the beautiful waters among these mountains! Though I was not of their mind: they, being inveterately bent on getting down into the level country, and I ardently desiring to linger where I was. What desperate leaps they took, what dark abysses they plunged into, what rocks they wore away, what echoes they invoked! In one part where I went, they were pressed into the service of carrying wood down, to be burnt next winter, as costly fuel, in Italy. But, their fierce savage nature was not to be easily constrained, and they fought with every limb of the wood; whirling it round and round, stripping its bark away, dashing it against pointed corners, driving it out of the course, and roaring and flying at the peasants who steered it back again from the bank with long stout poles. Alas! concurrent streams of time and water carried *me* down fast, and I came, on an exquisitely clear day, to the Lausanne shore of the Lake of Geneva, where I stood looking at the bright blue water, the flushed white mountains opposite, and the boats at my feet with their furled Mediterranean sails, showing like enormous magnifications of this goose-quill pen that is now in my hand.

– The sky became overcast without any notice; a wind very like the March east wind of England, blew across me; and a voice said, 'How do you like it? Will it do?'

I had merely shut myself, for half a minute, in a German travelling chariot that stood for sale in the Carriage Department of the London Pantechnicon. I had a commission to buy it, for a friend who was going abroad; and the look and manner of the chariot, as I tried the cushions and the springs, brought all these hints of travelling remembrance before me.

'It will do very well,' said I, rather sorrowfully, as I got out at the other door, and shut the carriage up.

City of London Churches

IF the confession that I have often travelled from this Covent Garden lodging of mine on Sundays, should give offence to those who never travel on Sundays, they will be satisfied (I hope) by my adding that the journeys in question were made to churches.

Not that I have any curiosity to hear powerful preachers. Time was, when I was dragged by the hair of my head, as one may say, to hear too many. On summer evenings, when every flower, and tree, and bird, might have better addressed my soft young heart, I have in my day been caught in the palm of a female hand by the crown, have been violently scrubbed from the neck to the roots of the hair as a purification for the Temple, and have then been carried off highly charged with saponaceous electricity, to be steamed like a potato in the unventilated breath of the powerful Boanerges Boiler and his congregation, until what small mind I had, was quite steamed out of me. In which pitiable plight I have been haled out of the place of meeting, at the conclusion of the exercises, and catechized respecting Boanerges Boiler, his fifthly, his sixthly, and his seventhly, until I have regarded that reverend person in the light of a most dismal and oppressive Charade. Time was, when I was carried off to platform assemblages at which no human child, whether of wrath or grace, could possibly keep its eyes open, and when I felt the fatal sleep stealing, stealing over me, and when I gradually heard the orator in possession, spinning and humming like a great top, until he rolled, collapsed, and tumbled over, and I discovered to my burning shame and fear, that as to that last stage it was not he, but I. I have sat under Boanerges when he has specifically addressed himself to us – us, the infants – and at this present writing I hear his lumbering jocularity (which never amused us, though we basely pretended that it did), and I behold his big round face, and I look up the inside of his outstretched coat-sleeve as if it were a telescope with the stopper on, and I hate him with an unwholesome hatred for two hours. Through such means did it come to pass that I knew the powerful preacher from beginning to end, all over and all through, while I was very young, and that I left him behind at an early period of life. Peace be with him! More peace than he brought to me!

Now, I have heard many preachers since that time – not powerful; merely Christian, unaffected, and reverential – and I have had many such preachers on my roll of friends. But, it was not to hear these, any more than the powerful class, that I made my Sunday journeys. They were journeys of curiosity to the numerous churches in the City of London. It came into my head one day, here had I been cultivating a familiarity with all the churches of Rome, and I knew nothing of the insides of the old churches of London! This befell on a Sunday morning. I began my expeditions that very same day, and they lasted me a year.

I never wanted to know the names of the churches to which I went, and to this hour I am profoundly ignorant in that particular of at least nine-tenths of them. Indeed, saving that I know the church of old GOWER's tomb (he lies in effigy with his head upon his books) to be the church of Saint Saviour's, Southwark; and the church of MILTON's tomb to be the church of Cripplegate; and the church on Cornhill with the great golden keys to be the church of Saint Peter; I doubt if I could pass a competitive examination in any of the names. No question did I ever ask of living creature concerning these churches, and no answer to any antiquarian question on the subject that I ever put to books, shall harass the reader's soul. A full half of my pleasure in them arose out of their mystery; mysterious I found them; mysterious they shall remain for me.

Where shall I begin my round of hidden and forgotten old churches in the City of London?

It is twenty minutes short of eleven on a Sunday morning, when I stroll down one of the many narrow hilly streets in the City that tend due south to the Thames. It is my first experiment, and I have come to the region of Whittington in an omnibus, and we have put down a fierce-eyed spare old woman, whose slate coloured gown smells of herbs, and who walked up Aldersgate-street to some chapel where she comforts herself with brimstone doctrine, I warrant. We have also put down a stouter and sweeter old lady, with a pretty large prayer-book in an unfolded pocket-handkerchief, who got out at a corner of a court near Stationers' Hall, and who I think must go to church there, because she is the widow of some deceased old Company's Beadle. The rest of our freight were mere chance pleasure-seekers and rural walkers, and went on to the Blackwall railway. So many bells are ringing, when I stand undecided at a street corner, that every sheep in the ecclesiastical fold might be a bell-wether. The discordance is fearful. My state of indecision is referable to, and about equally divisible among, four great churches, which are all within sight and sound, all within the space of a few square yards.

As I stand at the street corner, I don't see as many as four people at once going to church, though I see as many as four churches with their steeples clamouring for people. I choose my church, and go up the flight of steps to the great entrance in the tower. A mouldy tower within, and like a neglected washhouse. A rope comes through the beamed roof, and a man in the corner pulls it and clashes the bell – a whity-brown man, whose clothes were once black – a man with flue on him, and cobweb. He stares at me, wondering how I come there, and I stare at him, wondering how he comes there. Through a screen of wood and glass, I peep into the dim church. About twenty people are discernible, waiting to begin. Christening would seem to have faded out of this church long ago, for the font has the dust of desuetude thick upon it, and its wooden cover (shaped like an old-fashioned tureen-cover) looks as if it wouldn't come off, upon requirement. I perceive the altar to be rickety and the Commandments damp. Entering after this survey, I jostle the clergyman in his canonicals, who is entering too from a dark lane behind a pew of state with curtains, where nobody sits. The pew is ornamented with four blue wands, once carried by four somebodys, I suppose, before somebody else, but which there is nobody now to hold or receive honour from. I open the door of a family pew, and shut myself in; if I could occupy twenty family pews at once I might have them. The clerk, a brisk young man (how does *he* come here?), glances at me knowingly, as who should say, 'You have done it now; you must stop.' Organ plays. Organ-loft is in a small gallery across the church; gallery congregation, two girls. I wonder within myself what will happen when we are required to sing.

There is a pale heap of books in the corner of my pew, and while the organ which is hoarse and sleepy, plays in such fashion that I can hear more of the rusty working of the stops than of any music, I look at the books, which are mostly bound in faded baize and stuff. They belonged in 1754, to the Dowgate family; and who were they? Jane Comport must have married Young Dowgate, and come into the family that way; Young Dowgate was courting Jane Comport when he gave her her prayer-book, and recorded the presentation in the fly-leaf; if Jane were fond of Young Dowgate, why did she die and leave the book here? Perhaps at the rickety altar, and before the damp Commandments, she, Comport, had taken him, Dowgate, in a flush of youthful hope and joy, and perhaps it had not turned out in the long run as great a success as was expected?

The opening of the service recalls my wandering thoughts. I then find, to my astonishment, that I have been, and still am, taking a strong kind of invisible snuff, up my nose, into my eyes, and down my throat. I wink, sneeze, and cough. The clerk sneezes; the clergyman winks; the unseen organist sneezes and coughs (and probably winks); all our little party wink, sneeze, and cough. The snuff seems to be made of the decay of matting, wood, cloth, stone, iron, earth, and something else. Is the something else, the decay of dead citizens in the vaults below? As sure as Death it is! Not only in the cold damp February day, do we cough and sneeze dead citizens, all through the service, but dead citizens have got into the very bellows of the organ, and half choked the same. We stamp our feet to warm them, and dead citizens arise in heavy clouds. Dead citizens stick upon the walls, and lie pulverized on the sounding-board over the clergyman's head, and, when a gust of air comes, tumble down upon him.

In this first experience I was so nauseated by too much snuff, made of the Dowgate family, the Comport branch, and other families and branches, that I gave but little heed to our dull manner of ambling through the service; to the brisk clerk's manner of encouraging us to try a note or two at psalm time; to the gallery-congregation's manner of enjoying a shrill duet, without a notion of time or tune; to the whity-brown man's manner of shutting the minister into the pulpit, and being very particular with the lock of the door, as if he were a dangerous animal. But, I tried again next Sunday, and soon accustomed myself to the dead citizens when I found that I could not possibly get on without them among the City churches.

Another Sunday.

After being again rung for by conflicting bells, like a leg of mutton or a laced hat a hundred years ago, I make selection of a church oddly put away in a corner among a number of lanes – a smaller church than the last, and an ugly: of about the date of Queen Anne. As a congregation, we are fourteen strong: not counting an exhausted charity school in a gallery, which has dwindled away to four boys, and two girls. In the porch, is a benefaction of loaves of bread, which there would seem to be nobody left in the exhausted congregation to claim, and which I saw an exhausted beadle, long faded out of uniform, eating with his eyes for self and family when I passed in. There is also an exhausted clerk in a brown wig, and two or three exhausted doors and windows have been bricked up, and the service books are musty, and the pulpit cushions are threadbare, and the whole of the church furniture is in a very advanced stage of exhaustion. We are three old women (habitual), two young lovers (accidental), two tradesmen, one with a wife and one alone, an aunt and nephew, again two girls (these two girls dressed out for church with everything about them limp that should be stiff, and *vice versa*, are an invariable experience), and three sniggering boys. The clergyman is, perhaps, the chaplain of a civic company; he has the moist and vinous look, and eke the bulbous boots, of one acquainted with 'Twenty port, and comet vintages.[1]

We are so quiet in our dulness that the three sniggering boys, who have got away into a corner by the altar-railing, give us a start, like crackers, whenever they laugh. And this reminds me of my own village church where, during sermon-time on bright Sundays when the birds are very musical indeed, farmers' boys patter out over the stone pavement, and the clerk steps out from his desk after them, and is distinctly heard in the summer repose to pursue and punch them in the churchyard, and is seen to return with a meditative countenance, making believe that nothing of the sort has happened. The aunt and nephew in this City church are much disturbed by the sniggering boys. The nephew is himself a boy, and the sniggerers tempt him to secular thoughts of marbles and string, by secretly offering such commodities to his distant contemplation. This young Saint Anthony[2] for a while resists, but presently becomes a backslider, and in dumb show defies the sniggerers to 'heave' a marble or two in his direction. Herein he is detected by the aunt (a rigorous reduced gentlewoman who has the charge of offices), and I perceive that worthy relative to poke him in the side, with the corrugated hooked handle of an ancient umbrella. The nephew revenges himself for this, by holding his breath and terrifying his kinswoman with the dread belief that he has made up his mind to burst. Regardless of whispers and shakes, he swells and becomes discoloured, and yet again swells and becomes discoloured, until the aunt can bear it no longer, but leads him out, with no visible neck, and with his eyes going before him like a prawn's. This causes the sniggerers to regard flight as an eligible move, and I know which of them will go out first, because of the over-devout attention that he suddenly concentrates on the clergyman. In a little while, this hypocrite, with an elaborate demonstration of hushing his footsteps, and with a face generally expressive of having until now forgotten a religious appointment elsewhere, is gone. Number two gets out in the same way, but rather quicker. Number three getting safely to the door, there turns reckless, and banging it open, flies forth with a Whoop! that vibrates to the top of the tower above us.

The clergyman, who is of a prandial presence and a muffled voice, may be scant of hearing as well as of breath, but he only glances up, as having an idea that somebody has said Amen in a wrong place, and continues his steady jog-trot, like a farmer's wife going to market. He does all he has to do, in the same easy way, and gives us a concise sermon, still like the jog-trot of the farmer's wife on a level road. Its drowsy cadence soon lulls the three old women asleep, and the unmarried tradesman sits looking out at window, and the married tradesman sits looking at his wife's bonnet, and the lovers sit looking at one another, so superlatively happy, that I mind when I, turned of eighteen, went with my Angelica to a City church on account of a shower (by this special coincidence that it was in Hugginlane), and when I said to my Angelica, 'Let the blessed event, Angelica, occur at no altar but this!' and when my Angelica consented that it should occur at no other – which it certainly never did, for it never occurred anywhere. And O, Angelica, what has become of you, this present Sunday morning when I can't attend to the sermon; and, more difficult question than that, what has become of Me as I was when I sat by your side!

But, we receive the signal to make that unanimous dive which surely is a little conventional – like the strange rustlings and settlings and clearings of throats and noses, which are never dispensed with, at certain points of the Church service, and are never held to be necessary under any other circumstances. In a minute more it is all over, and the organ expresses itself to be as glad of it as it can be of anything in its rheumatic state, and in another minute we are all of us out of the church, and Whity-brown has locked it up. Another minute or little more, and, in the neighbouring churchyard – not the yard of that church, but of another – a churchyard like a great shabby old mignonette box, with two trees in it and one tomb – I meet Whity-brown, in his private capacity, fetching a pint of beer for his dinner from the public-house in the corner, where the keys of the rotting fire-ladders are kept and were never asked for, and where there is a ragged, white-seamed, out-at-elbowed bagatelle board on the first floor.

In one of these City churches, and only in one, I found an individual who might have been claimed as expressly a City personage. I remember the church, by the feature that the clergyman couldn't get to his own desk without going through the clerk's, or couldn't get to the pulpit without going through the reading-desk – I forget which, and it is no matter – and by the presence of this personage among the exceedingly sparse congregation. I doubt if we were a dozen, and we had no exhausted charity school to help us out. The personage was dressed in black of square cut, and was stricken in years, and wore a black velvet cap, and cloth shoes. He was of a staid, wealthy, and dissatisfied aspect. In his hand, he conducted to church a mysterious child: a child of the feminine gender. The child had a beaver hat, with a stiff drab plume that surely never belonged to any bird of the air. The child was further attired in a nankeen frock and spencer,[3] brown boxing-gloves,[4] and a veil. It had a blemish, in the nature of currant jelly, on its chin; and was a thirsty child. Insomuch that the personage carried in his pocket a green bottle, from which, when the first psalm was given out, the child was openly refreshed. At all other times throughout the service it was motionless, and stood on the seat of the large pew, closely fitted into the corner, like a rain-water pipe.

The personage never opened his book, and never looked at the clergyman. *He* never sat down either, but stood with his arms leaning on the top of the pew, and his forehead sometimes shaded with his right hand, always looking at the church door. It was a long church for a church of its size, and he was at the upper end, but he always looked at the door. That he was an old bookkeeper, or an old trader who had kept his own books, and that he might be seen at the Bank of England about Dividend times, no doubt. That he had lived in the City all his life and was disdainful of other localities, no doubt. Why he looked at the door, I never absolutely proved, but it is my belief that he lived in expectation of the time when the citizens would come back to live in the City, and its ancient glories would be renewed. He appeared to expect that this would occur on a Sunday, and that the wanderers would first appear, in the deserted churches, penitent and humbled. Hence, he looked at the door which they never darkened. Whose child the child was, whether the child of a disinherited daughter, or some parish orphan whom the personage had adopted, there was nothing to lead up to. It never played, or skipped, or smiled. Once, the idea occurred to me that it was an automaton, and that the personage had made it; but following the strange couple out one Sunday, I heard the personage say to it, 'Thirteen thousand pounds'; to which it added in a weak human voice, 'Seventeen and fourpence'. Four Sundays I followed them out, and this is all I ever heard or saw them say. One Sunday, I followed them home. They lived behind a pump, and the personage opened their abode with an exceeding large key. The one solitary inscription on their house related to a fire-plug. The house was partly undermined by a deserted and closed gateway; its windows were blind with dirt; and it stood with its face disconsolately turned to a wall. Five great churches and two small ones rang their Sunday bells between this house and the church the couple frequented, so they must have had some special reason for going a quarter of a mile to it. The last time I saw them, was on this wise. I had been to explore another church at a distance, and happened to pass the church they frequented, at about two of the afternoon when that edifice was closed. But, a little side-door, which I had never observed before, stood open, and disclosed certain cellarous steps. Methought 'They are airing the vaults today', when the personage and the child silently arrived at the steps, and silently descended. Of course, I came to the conclusion that the personage had at last despaired of the looked-for return of the penitent citizens, and that he and the child went down to get themselves buried.

In the course of my pilgrimages I came upon one obscure church which had broken out in the melodramatic style, and was got up with various tawdry decorations, much after the manner of the extinct London may-poles. These attractions had induced several young priests or deacons in black bibs for waistcoats, and several young ladies interested in that holy order (the proportion being, as I estimated, seventeen young ladies to a deacon), to come into the City as a new and odd excitement. It was wonderful to see how these young people played out their little play in the heart of the City, all among themselves, without the deserted City's knowing anything about it. It was as if you should take an empty counting-house on a Sunday, and act one of the old Mysteries there. They had impressed a small school (from what neighbourhood I don't know) to assist in the performances, and it was pleasant to notice frantic garlands of inscription on the walls, especially addressing those poor innocents in characters impossible for them to decipher. There was a remarkably agreeable smell of pomatum in this congregation.

But, in other cases, rot and mildew and dead citizens formed the uppermost scent, while, infused into it in a dreamy way not at all displeasing, was the staple character of the neighbourhood. In the churches about Mark-lane, for example, there was a dry whiff of wheat; and I accidentally struck an airy sample of barley out of an aged hassock in one of them. From Rood-lane to Tower-street, and thereabouts, there was often a subtle flavour of wine: sometimes, of tea. One church near Mincing-lane smelt like a druggist's drawer. Behind the Monument the service had a flavour of damaged oranges, which, a little further down towards the river, tempered into herrings, and gradually toned into a cosmopolitan blast of fish. In one church, the exact counterpart of the church in the Rake's Progress where the hero is being married to the horrible old lady,⁵ there was no speciality of atmosphere, until the organ shook a perfume of hides all over us from some adjacent warehouse.

Be the scent what it would, however, there was no speciality in the people. There were never enough of them to represent any calling or neighbourhood. They had all gone elsewhere over-night, and the few stragglers in the many churches languished there inexpressively.

Among the Uncommercial travels in which I have engaged, this year of Sunday travel occupies its own place, apart from all the rest. Whether I think of the church where the sails of the oyster-boats in the river almost flapped against the windows, or of the church where the railroad made the bells hum as the train rushed by above the roof, I recall a curious experience. On summer Sundays, in the gentle rain or the bright sunshine – either, deepening the idleness of the idle City – I have sat, in that singular silence which belongs to resting-places usually astir, in scores of buildings at the heart of the world's metropolis, unknown to far greater numbers of people speaking the English tongue, than the ancient edifices of the Eternal City, or the Pyramids of Egypt. The dark vestries and registries into which I have peeped, and the little hemmed-in churchyards that have echoed to my feet, have left impressions on my memory as distinct and quaint as any it has in that way received. In all those dusty registers that the worms are eating, there is not a line but made some hearts leap, or some tears flow, in their day. Still and dry now, still and dry! and the old tree at the window with no room for its branches, has seen them all out. So with the tomb of the old Master of the old Company, on which it drips. His son restored it and died, his daughter restored it and died, and then he had been remembered long enough, and the tree took possession of him, and his name cracked out.

There are few more striking indications of the changes of manners and customs that two or three hundred years have brought about, than these deserted churches. Many of them are handsome and costly structures, several of them were designed by WREN,[6] many of them arose from the ashes of the great fire, others of them outlived the plague and the fire too, to die a slow death in these later days. No one can be sure of the coming time; but it is not too much to say of it that it has no sign in its outsetting tides, of the reflux to these churches of their congregations and uses. They remain like the tombs of the old citizens who lie beneath them and around them, Monuments of another age. They are worth a Sunday-exploration, now and then, for they yet echo, not unharmoniously, to the time when the City of London really was London; when the 'Prentices and Trained Bands were of mark in the state; when even the Lord Mayor himself was a Reality – not a Fiction conventionally be-puffed on one day in the year by illustrious friends, who no less conventionally laugh at him on the remaining three hundred and sixty-four days.

Shy Neighbourhoods

So much of my travelling is done on foot, that if I cherished betting propensities, I should probably be found registered in sporting newspapers under some such title as the Elastic Novice, challenging all eleven stone mankind to competition in walking. My last special feat was turning out of bed at two, after a hard day, pedestrian and otherwise, and walking thirty miles into the country to breakfast. The road was so lonely in the night, that I fell asleep to the monotonous sound of my own feet, doing their regular four miles an hour. Mile after mile I walked, without the slightest sense of exertion, dozing heavily and dreaming constantly. It was only when I made a stumble like a drunken man, or struck out into the road to avoid a horseman close upon me on the path – who had no existence – that I came to myself and looked about. The day broke mistily (it was autumn time), and I could not disembarrass myself of the idea that I had to climb those heights and banks of cloud, and that there was an Alpine Convent somewhere behind the sun, where I was going to breakfast. This sleepy notion was so much stronger than such substantial objects as villages and haystacks, that, after the sun was up and bright, and when I was sufficiently awake to have a sense of pleasure in the prospect, I still occasionally caught myself looking about for wooden arms to point the right track up the mountain, and wondering there was no snow yet. It is a curiosity of broken sleep that I made immense quantities of verses on that pedestrian occasion (of course I never make any when I am in my right senses), and that I spoke a certain language once pretty familiar to me, but which I have nearly forgotten from disuse, with fluency. Of both these phenomena I have such frequent experience in the state between sleeping and waking, that I sometimes argue with myself that I know I cannot be awake, for, if I were, I should not be half so ready. The readiness is not imaginary, because I often recall long strings of the verses, and many turns of the fluent speech, after I am broad awake.

My walking is of two kinds: one, straight on end to a definite goal at a round pace; one, objectless, loitering, and purely vagabond. In the latter state, no gipsy on earth is a greater vagabond than myself; it is so natural to me, and strong with me, that I think I must be the descendant, at no great distance, of some irreclaimable tramp.

One of the pleasantest things I have lately met with, in a vagabond course of shy metropolitan neighbourhoods and small shops, is the fancy of a humble artist, as exemplified in two portraits representing Mr Thomas Sayers, of Great Britain, and Mr John Heenan,[1] of the United States of America. These illustrious men are highly coloured in fighting trim, and fighting attitude. To suggest the pastoral and meditative nature of their peaceful calling, Mr Heenan is represented on emerald sward, with primroses and other modest flowers springing up under the heels of his half-boots; while Mr Sayers is impelled to the administration of his favourite blow, the Auctioneer, by the silent eloquence of a village church. The humble homes of England, with their domestic virtues and honeysuckle porches, urge both heroes to go in and win; and the lark and other singing birds are observable in the upper air, ecstatically carolling their thanks to Heaven for a fight. On the whole, the associations entwined with the pugilistic art by this artist are much in the manner of Izaak Walton.[2]

But, it is with the lower animals of back streets and by-ways that my present purpose rests. For human notes we may return to such neighbourhoods when leisure and opportunity serve.

Nothing in shy neighbourhoods perplexes my mind more, than the bad company birds keep. Foreign birds often get into good society, but British birds are inseparable from low associates. There is a whole street of them in St Giles's; and I always find them in poor and immoral neighbourhoods, convenient to the public-house and the pawnbroker's. They seem to lead people into drinking, and even the man who makes their cages usually gets into a chronic state of black eye. Why is this? Also, they will do things for people in short-skirted velveteen coats with bone buttons, or in sleeved waistcoats and fur caps, which they cannot be persuaded by the respectable orders of society to undertake. In a dirty court in Spitalfields, once, I found a goldfinch drawing his own water, and drawing as much of it as if he were in a consuming fever. That goldfinch lived at a bird-shop, and offered, in writing, to barter himself against old clothes, empty bottles, or even kitchen stuff. Surely a low thing and a depraved taste in any finch! I bought that goldfinch for money. He was sent home, and hung upon a nail over against my table. He lived outside a counterfeit dwelling-house, supposed (as I argued) to be a dyer's; otherwise it would have been impossible to account for his perch sticking out of the garret window. From the time of his appearance in my room, either he left off being thirsty – which was not in the bond – or he could not make up his mind to hear his little bucket drop back into his well when he let it go: a shock which in the best of times had made him tremble. He drew no water but by stealth and under the cloak of night. After an interval of futile and at length hopeless expectation, the merchant who had educated him was appealed to. The merchant was a bow-legged character, with a flat and cushiony nose, like the last new strawberry. He wore a fur cap, and shorts, and was of the velveteen race, velveteeny. He sent word that he would 'look round'. He looked round, appeared in the doorway of the room, and slightly cocked up his evil eye at the goldfinch. Instantly a raging thirst beset that bird; when it was appeased, he still drew several unnecessary buckets of water; and finally, leaped about his perch and sharpened his bill, as if he had been to the nearest wine vaults and got drunk.

Donkeys again. I know shy neighbourhoods where the Donkey goes in at the street door, and appears to live up-stairs, for I have examined the back-yard from over the palings, and have been unable to make him out. Gentility, nobility, Royalty, would appeal to that donkey in vain to do what he does for a costermonger. Feed him with oats at the highest price, put an infant prince and princess in a pair of panniers on his back, adjust his delicate trappings to a nicety, take him to the softest slopes at Windsor, and try what pace you can get out of him. Then, starve him, harness him anyhow to a truck with a flat tray on it, and see him bowl from Whitechapel to Bayswater. There appears to be no particular private understanding between birds and donkeys, in a state of nature; but in the shy neighbourhood state, you shall see them always in the same hands and always developing their very best energies for the very worst company. I have known a donkey – by sight; we were not on speaking terms – who lived over on the Surrey side of London-bridge, among the fastnesses of Jacob's Island and Dockhead. It was the habit of that animal, when his services were not in immediate requisition, to go out alone, idling. I have met him a mile from his place of residence, loitering about the streets; and the expression of his countenance at such times was most degraded. He was attached to the establishment of an elderly lady who sold peri-winkles, and he used to stand on Saturday nights with a cartful of those delicacies outside a gin-shop, pricking up his ears when a customer came to the cart, and too evidently deriving satisfaction from the knowledge that they got bad measure. His mistress was sometimes overtaken by inebriety. The last time I ever saw him (about five years ago) he was in circumstances of difficulty, caused by this failing. Having been left alone with the cart of periwinkles, and forgotten, he went off idling. He prowled among his usual low haunts for some time, gratifying his depraved tastes, until, not taking the cart into his calculations, he endeavoured to turn up a narrow alley, and became greatly involved. He was taken into custody by the police, and, the Green Yard³ of the district being near at hand, was backed into that place of durance. At that crisis, I encountered him; the stubborn sense he evinced of being – not to compromise the expression – a blackguard, I never saw exceeded in the human subject. A flaring candle in a paper shade, stuck in among his periwinkles, showed him, with his ragged harness broken and his cart extensively shattered, twitching his mouth and shaking his hanging head, a picture of disgrace and obduracy. I have seen boys being taken to station-houses, who were as like him as his own brother.

The dogs of shy neighbourhoods, I observe to avoid play, and to be conscious of poverty. They avoid work, too, if they can, of course; that is in the nature of all animals. I have the pleasure to know a dog in a back street in the neighbourhood of Walworth, who has greatly distinguished himself in the minor drama, and who takes his portrait with him when he makes an engagement, for the illustration of the play-bill. His portrait (which is not at all like him) represents him in the act of dragging to the earth a recreant Indian, who is supposed to have tomahawked, or essayed to tomahawk, a British officer. The design is pure poetry, for there is no such Indian in the piece, and no such incident. He is a dog of the Newfoundland breed, for whose honesty I would be bail to any amount; but whose intellectual qualities in association with dramatic fiction, I cannot rate high. Indeed, he is too honest for the profession he has entered. Being at a town in Yorkshire last summer, and seeing him posted in the bill of the night, I attended the performance. His first scene was eminently successful; but, as it occupied a second in its representation (and five lines in the bill), it scarcely afforded ground for a cool and deliberate judgment of his powers. He had merely to bark, run on, and jump through an inn window, after a comic fugitive. The next scene of importance to the fable was a little marred in its interest by his over-anxiety; forasmuch as while his master (a belated soldier in a den of robbers on a tempestuous night) was feelingly lamenting the absence of his faithful dog, and laying great stress on the fact that he was thirty leagues away, the faithful dog was barking furiously in the prompter's box, and clearly choking himself against his collar. But it was in his greatest scene of all, that his honesty got the better of him. He had to enter a dense and trackless forest, on the trail of the murderer, and there to fly at the murderer when he found him resting at the foot of a tree, with his victim bound ready for slaughter. It was a hot night, and he came into the forest from an altogether unexpected direction, in the sweetest temper, at a very deliberate trot, not in the least excited; trotted to the foot-lights with his tongue out; and there sat down, panting, and amiably surveying the audience, with his tail beating on the boards, like a Dutch clock. Meanwhile the murderer, impatient to receive his doom, was audibly calling to him 'Co-o-ome here!' while the victim, struggling with his bonds, assailed him with the most injurious expressions. It happened through these means, that when he was in course of time persuaded to trot up and rend the murderer limb from limb, he made it (for dramatic purposes) a little too obvious that he worked out that awful retribution by licking butter off his blood-stained hands.

In a shy street, behind Long-acre, two honest dogs live, who perform in Punch's shows.[4] I may venture to say that I am on terms of intimacy with both, and that I never saw either guilty of the falsehood of failing to look down at the man inside the show, during the whole performance. The difficulty other dogs have in satisfying their minds about these dogs, appears to be never overcome by time. The same dogs must encounter them over and over again, as they trudge along in their off-minutes behind the legs of the show and beside the drum; but all dogs seem to suspect their frills and jackets, and to sniff at them as if they thought those articles of personal adornment, an eruption – a something in the nature of mange, perhaps. From this Covent-garden window of mine I noticed a country dog, only the other day, who had come up to Covent-garden Market under a cart, and had broken his cord, an end of which he still trailed along with him. He loitered about the corners of the four streets commanded by my window; and bad London dogs came up, and told him lies that he didn't believe; and worse London dogs came up, and made proposals to him to go and steal in the market, which his principles rejected; and the ways of the town confused him, and he crept aside and lay down in a doorway. He had scarcely got a wink of sleep, when up comes Punch with Toby. He was darting to Toby for consolation and advice, when he saw the frill, and stopped, in the middle of the street, appalled. The show was pitched, Toby retired behind the drapery, the audience formed, the drum and pipes struck up. My country dog remained immovable, intently staring at these strange appearances, until Toby opened the drama by appearing on his ledge, and to him entered Punch, who put a tobacco-pipe into Toby's mouth. At this spectacle, the country dog threw up his head, gave one terrible howl, and fled due west.

We talk of men keeping dogs, but we might often talk more expressively of dogs keeping men. I know a bull-dog in a shy corner of Hammersmith who keeps a man. He keeps him up a yard and makes him go to public-houses and lay wagers on him, and obliges him to lean against posts and look at him, and forces him to neglect work for him, and keeps him under rigid coercion. I once knew a fancy terrier who kept a gentleman – a gentleman who had been brought up at Oxford, too. The dog kept the gentleman entirely for his glorification, and the gentleman never talked about anything but the terrier. This, however, was not in a shy neighbourhood, and is a digression consequently.

There are a great many dogs in shy neighbourhoods, who keep boys. I have my eye on a mongrel in Somerstown who keeps three boys. He feigns that he can bring down sparrows, and unburrow rats (he can do neither), and he takes the boys out on sporting pretences into all sorts of suburban fields. He has likewise made them believe that he possesses some mysterious knowledge of the art of fishing, and they consider themselves incompletely equipped for the Hampstead ponds, with a pickle-jar and a wide-mouthed bottle, unless he is with them and barking tremendously. There is a dog residing in the Borough of Southwark who keeps a blind man. He may be seen, most days, in Oxford-street, haling the blind man away on expeditions wholly uncontemplated by, and unintelligible to, the man: wholly of the dog's conception and execution. Contrariwise, when the man has projects, the dog will sit down in a crowded thoroughfare and meditate. I saw him yesterday, wearing the money-tray like an easy collar, instead of offering it to the public, taking the man against his will, on the invitation of a disreputable cur, apparently to visit a dog at Harrow – he was so intent on that direction. The north wall of Burlington House Gardens, between the Arcade and the Albany, offers a shy spot for appointments among blind men at about two or three o'clock in the afternoon. They sit (very uncomfortably) on a sloping stone there, and compare notes. Their dogs may always be observed at the same time, openly disparaging the men they keep, to one another, and settling where they shall respectively take their men when they begin to move again. At a small butcher's, in a shy neighbourhood (there is no reason for suppressing the name; it is by Notting-hill, and gives upon the district called the Potteries), I know a shaggy black and white dog who keeps a drover. He is a dog of an easy disposition, and too frequently allows this drover to get drunk. On these occasions, it is the dog's custom to sit outside the public-house, keeping his eye on a few sheep, and thinking. I have seen him with six sheep, plainly casting up in his mind how many he began with when he left the market, and at what places he has left the rest. I have seen him perplexed by not being able to account to himself for certain particular sheep. A light has gradually broken on him, he has remembered at what butcher's he left them, and in a burst of grave satisfaction has caught a fly off his nose, and shown himself much relieved. If I could at any time have doubted the fact that it was he who kept the drover, and not the drover who kept him, it would have been abundantly proved by his way of taking undivided charge of the six sheep, when the drover came out besmeared with red ochre and beer, and gave him wrong directions, which he calmly disregarded. He has taken the sheep entirely into his own hands, has merely remarked with respectful firmness, 'That instruction would place them under an omnibus; you had better confine your attention to yourself – you will want it all'; and has driven his charge away, with an intelligence of ears and tail, and a knowledge of business, that has left his lout of a man very, very far behind.

As the dogs of shy neighbourhoods usually betray a slinking consciousness of being in poor circumstances – for the most part manifested in an aspect of anxiety, an awkwardness in their play, and a misgiving that somebody is going to harness them to something, to pick up a living – so the cats of shy neighbourhoods exhibit a strong tendency to relapse into barbarism. Not only are they made selfishly ferocious by ruminating on the surplus population around them, and on the densely crowded state of all the avenues to cat's meat; not only is there a moral and politico-economical haggardness in them, traceable to these reflections; but they evince a physical deterioration. Their linen is not clean, and is wretchedly got up; their black turns rusty, like old mourning; they wear very indifferent fur; and take to the shabbiest cotton velvet, instead of silk velvet. I am on terms of recognition with several small streets of cats, about the Obelisk in Saint George's Fields, and also in the vicinity of Clerkenwell-green, and also in the back settlements of Drury-lane. In appearance, they are very like the women among whom they live. They seem to turn out of their un-wholesome beds into the street, without any preparation. They leave their young families to stagger about the gutters, unassisted, while they frouzily quarrel and swear and scratch and spit, at street corners. In particular, I remark that when they are about to increase their families (an event of frequent recurrence) the resemblance is strongly expressed in a certain dusty dowdiness, down-at-heel self-neglect, and general giving up of things. I cannot honestly report that I have ever seen a feline matron of this class washing her face when in an interesting condition.

Not to prolong these notes of uncommercial travel among the lower animals of shy neighbourhoods, by dwelling at length upon the exasperated moodiness of the tom-cats, and their resemblance in many respects to a man and a brother, I will come to a close with a word on the fowls of the same localities.

That anything born of an egg and invested with wings, should have got to the pass that it hops contentedly down a ladder into a cellar, and calls *that* going home, is a circumstance so amazing as to leave one nothing more in this connexion to wonder at. Otherwise I might wonder at the completeness with which these fowls have become separated from all the birds of the air – have taken to grovelling in bricks and mortar and mud – have forgotten all about live trees, and make roosting-places of shop-boards, barrows, oyster-tubs, bulk-heads, and door-scrapers. I wonder at nothing concerning them, and take them as they are. I accept as products of Nature and things of course, a reduced Bantam family of my acquaintance in the Hackney-road, who are incessantly at the pawnbroker's. I cannot say that they enjoy themselves, for they are of a melancholy temperament; but what enjoyment they are capable of, they derive from crowding together in the pawn-broker's side-entry. Here, they are always to be found in a feeble flutter, as if they were newly come down in the world, and were afraid of being identified. I know a low fellow, originally of a good family from Dorking, who takes his whole establishment of wives, in single file, in at the door of the Jug Department of a disorderly tavern near the Haymarket, manoeuvres them among the company's legs, emerges with them at the Bottle Entrance, and so passes his life: seldom, in the season, going to bed before two in the morning. Over Waterloo-bridge, there is a shabby old speckled couple (they belong to the wooden French-bedstead, washing-stand, and towel-horsemaking trade), who are always trying to get in at the door of a chapel. Whether the old lady, under a delusion reminding one of Mrs Southcott,[6] has an idea of entrusting an egg to that particular denomination, or merely understands that she has no business in the building and is consequently frantic to enter it, I cannot deter-mine; but she is constantly endeavouring to undermine the principal door: while her partner, who is infirm upon his legs, walks up and down, encouraging her and defying the Universe. But, the family I have been best acquainted with, since the removal from this trying sphere of a Chinese circle[7] at Brentford, reside in the densest part of Bethnal-green. Their abstraction from the objects among which they live, or rather their conviction that those objects have all come into existence in express subserviency to fowls, has so enchanted me, that I have made them the subject of many journeys at divers hours. After careful observation of the two lords and the ten ladies of whom this family consists, I have come to the conclusion that their opinions are represented by the leading lord and leading lady: the latter, as I judge, an aged personage, afflicted with a paucity of feather and visibility of quill, that gives her the appearance of a bundle of office pens. When a railway goods van that would crush an elephant comes round the corner, tearing over these fowls, they emerge unharmed from under the horses, perfectly satisfied that the whole rush was a passing property in the air, which may have left something to eat behind it. They look upon old shoes, wrecks of kettles and saucepans, and fragments of bonnets, as a kind of meteoric discharge, for fowls to peck at. Peg-tops and hoops they account, I think, as a sort of hail; shuttlecocks, as rain, or dew. Gaslight comes quite as natural to them as any other light; and I have more than a suspicion that, in the minds of the two lords, the early public-house at the corner has superseded the sun. I have established it as a certain fact, that they always begin to crow when the public-house shutters begin to be taken down, and that they salute the potboy, the instant he appears to perform that duty, as if he were Phoebus in person.

Dullborough Town

It lately happened that I found myself rambling about the scenes among which my earliest days were passed; scenes from which I departed when I was a child, and which I did not revisit until I was a man. This is no uncommon chance, but one that befalls some of us any day; perhaps it may not be quite uninteresting to compare notes with the reader respecting an experience so familiar and a journey so uncommercial.

I call my boyhood's home (and I feel like a Tenor in an English Opera when I mention it) Dullborough. Most of us come from Dullborough who come from a country town.

As I left Dullborough in the days when there were no railroads in the land, I left it in a stage-coach. Through all the years that have since passed, have I ever lost the smell of the damp straw in which I was packed – like game – and forwarded, carriage paid, to the Cross Keys, Wood-street, Cheapside, London? There was no other inside passenger, and I consumed my sandwiches in solitude and dreariness, and it rained hard all the way, and I thought life sloppier than I had expected to find it.

With this tender remembrance upon me, I was cavalierly shunted back into Dullborough the other day, by train. My ticket had been previously collected, like my taxes, and my shining new port-manteau had had a great plaster stuck upon it, and I had been defied by Act of Parliament to offer an objection to anything that was done to it, or me, under a penalty of not less than forty shillings or more than five pounds, compoundable for a term of imprison-ment. When I had sent my disfigured property on to the hotel, I began to look about me; and the first discovery I made, was, that the Station had swallowed up the playing-field.

It was gone. The two beautiful hawthorn-treés, the hedge, the turf, and all those buttercups and daisies, had given place to the stoniest of jolting roads: while, beyond the Station, an ugly dark monster of a tunnel kept its jaws open, as if it had swallowed them and were ravenous for more destruction. The coach that had carried me away, was melodiously called Timpson's Blue-Eyed Maid, and belonged to Timpson, at the coach-office up-street; the locomotive engine that had brought me back, was called severely No. 97, and belonged to S.E.R.,[1] and was spitting ashes and hot-water over the blighted ground.

When I had been let out at the platform-door, like a prisoner whom his turnkey grudgingly released, I looked in again over the low wall, at the scene of departed glories. Here, in the haymaking time, had I been delivered from the dungeons of Seringapatam,[2] an immense pile (of haycock), by my countrymen, the victorious British (boy next door and his two cousins), and had been recog-nized with ecstasy by my affianced one (Miss Green), who had come all the way from England (second house in the terrace) to ransom me, and marry me. Here, had I first heard in confidence, from one whose father was greatly connected, being under Govern-ment, of the existence of a terrible banditti, called 'The Radicals', whose principles were, that the Prince Regent wore stays, and that nobody had a right to any salary, and that the army and navy ought to be put down – horrors at which I trembled in my bed, after supplicating that the Radicals might be speedily taken and hanged. Here, too, had we, the small boys of Boles's, had that cricket match against the small boys of Coles's, when Boles and Coles had actually met upon the ground, and when, instead of instantly hitting out at one another with the utmost fury, as we had all hoped and expected, those sneaks had said respectively, 'I hope Mrs Boles is well,' and 'I hope Mrs Coles and the baby are doing charmingly.' Could it be that, after all this, and much more, the Playing-field was a Station, and No. 97 expectorated boiling-water and redhot cinders on it, and the whole belonged by Act of Parliament to S.E.R.?

As it could be, and was, I left the place with a heavy heart for a walk all over the town. And first of Timpson's up-street. When I departed from Dullborough in the strawy arms of Timpson's Blue-Eyed Maid, Timpson's was a moderate-sized coach-office (in fact, a little coach-office), with an oval transparency in the window, which looked beautiful by night, representing one of Timpson's coaches in the act of passing a milestone on the London road with great velocity, completely full inside and out, and all the passengers dressed in the first style of fashion, and enjoying themselves tremendously. I found no such place as Timpson's now – no such bricks and rafters, not to mention the name – no such edifice on the teeming earth. Pickford had come and knocked Timpson's down. Pickford had not only knocked Timpson's down, but had knocked two or three houses down on each side of Timpson's, and then had knocked the whole into one great establishment with a pair of big gates, in and out of which, his (Pickford's) waggons are, in these days, always rattling, with their drivers sitting up so high, that they look in at the second-floor windows of the old-fashioned houses in the High-street as they shake the town. I have not the honour of Pickford's acquaintance, but I felt that he had done me an injury, not to say committed an act of boyslaughter, in running over my childhood in this rough manner; and if ever I meet Pickford driving one of his own monsters, and smoking a pipe the while (which is the custom of his men), he shall know by the expression of my eye, if it catches his, that there is something wrong between us.

Moreover, I felt that Pickford had no right to come rushing into Dullborough and deprive the town of a public picture. He is not Napoleon Bonaparte. When he took down the transparent stage-coach, he ought to have given the town a transparent van. With a gloomy conviction that Pickford is wholly utilitarian and un-imaginative, I proceeded on my way.

It is a mercy I have not a red and green lamp and a night-bell at my door, for in my very young days I was taken to so many lyings-in that I wonder I escaped becoming a professional martyr to them in after-life. I suppose I had a very sympathetic nurse, with a large circle of married acquaintance. However that was, as I continued my walk through Dullborough, I found many houses to be solely associated in my mind with this particular interest. At one little greengrocer's shop, down certain steps from the street, I remember to have waited on a lady who had had four children (I am afraid to write five, though I fully believe it was five) at a birth. This meritorious woman held quite a reception in her room on the morning when I was introduced there, and the sight of the house brought vividly to my mind how the four (five) deceased young people lay, side by side, on a clean cloth on a chest of drawers; reminding me by a homely association, which I suspect their complexion to have assisted, of pigs' feet as they are usually displayed at a neat tripe-shop. Hot caudle was handed round on the occasion, and I further remembered as I stood contemplating the greengrocer's, that a subscription was entered into among the company, which became extremely alarming to my consciousness of having pocket-money on my person. This fact being known to my conductress, whoever she was, I was earnestly exhorted to contribute, but resolutely declined: therein disgusting the company, who gave me to understand that I must dismiss all expectations of going to Heaven.

How does it happen that when all else is change wherever one goes, there yet seem, in every place, to be some few people who never alter? As the sight of the greengrocer's house recalled these trivial incidents of long ago, the identical greengrocer appeared on the steps, with his hands in his pockets, and leaning his shoulder against the door-post, as my childish eyes had seen him many a time; indeed, there was his old mark on the door-post yet, as if his shadow had become a fixture there. It was he himself; he might formerly have been an old-looking young man, or he might now be a young-looking old man, but there he was. In walking along the street, I had as yet looked in vain for a familiar face, or even a transmitted face; here was the very greengrocer who had been weighing and handling baskets on the morning of the reception. As he brought with him a dawning remembrance that he had had no proprietary interest in those babies, I crossed the road, and accosted him on the subject. He was not in the least excited or gratified, or in any way roused, by the accuracy of my recollection, but said, Yes, summut out of the common – he didn't remember how many it was (as if half-a-dozen babes either way made no difference) – had happened to a Mrs What's-her-name, as once lodged there – but he didn't call it to mind, particular. Nettled by this phlegmatic conduct, I informed him that I had left the town when I was a child. He slowly returned, quite unsoftened, and not without a sarcastic kind of complacency, *Had* I? Ah! And did I find it had got on tolerably well without me? Such is the difference (I thought, when I had left him a few hundred yards behind, and was by so much in a better temper) between going away from a place and remaining in it. I had no right, I reflected, to be angry with the greengrocer for his want of interest, I was nothing to him: whereas he was the town, the cathedral, the bridge, the river, my childhood, and a large slice of my life, to me.

Of course the town had shrunk fearfully, since I was a child there. I had entertained the impression that the High-street was at least as wide as Regent-street, London, or the Italian Boulevard at Paris. I found it little better than a lane. There was a public clock in it, which I had supposed to be the finest clock in the world: whereas it now turned out to be as inexpressive, moon-faced, and weak a clock as ever I saw. It belonged to a Town Hall, where I had seen an Indian (who I now suppose wasn't an Indian) swallow a sword (which I now suppose he didn't). The edifice had appeared to me in those days so glorious a structure, that I had set it up in my mind as the model on which the Genie of the Lamp built the palace for Aladdin.[3] A mean little brick heap, like a demented chapel, with a few yawning persons in leather gaiters, and in the last extremity for something to do, lounging at the door with their hands in their pockets, and calling themselves a Corn Exchange!

The Theatre was in existence, I found, on asking the fishmonger, who had a compact show of stock in his window, consisting of a sole and a quart of shrimps – and I resolved to comfort my mind by going to look at it. Richard the Third, in a very uncomfortable cloak, had first appeared to me there, and had made my heart leap with terror by backing up against the stage-box in which I was posted, while struggling for life against the virtuous Richmond.[4]

It was within those walls that I had learnt as from a page of English history, how that wicked King slept in war-time on a sofa much too short for him, and how fearfully his conscience troubled his boots. There, too, had I first seen the funny countryman, but countryman of noble principles, in a flowered waistcoat, crunch up his little hat and throw it on the ground, and pull off his coat, saying, 'Dom thee, squire, coom on with thy fistes then!' At which the lovely young woman who kept company with him (and who went out gleaning, in a narrow white muslin apron with five beautiful bars of five different coloured ribbons across it) was so frightened for his sake, that she fainted away. Many wondrous secrets of Nature had I come to the knowledge of in that sanctuary: of which not the least terrific were, that the witches in Macbeth bore an awful resemblance to the Thanes and other proper inhabitants of Scotland; and that the good King Duncan couldn't rest in his grave, but was constantly coming out of it and calling himself somebody else.[5] To the Theatre, therefore, I repaired for consolation. But I found very little, for it was in a bad and declining way. A dealer in wine and bottled beer had already squeezed his trade into the box-office, and the theatrical money was taken – when it came – in a kind of meat-safe in the passage. The dealer in wine and bottled beer must have insinuated himself under the stage too; for he announced that he had various descriptions of alcoholic drinks 'in the wood', and there was no possible stowage for the wood anywhere else. Evidently, he was by degrees eating the establishment away to the core, and would soon have sole possession of it. It was To Let, and hopelessly so, for its old purposes; and there had been no entertainment within its walls for a long time except a Panorama; and even that had been announced as 'pleasingly instructive', and I know too well the fatal meaning and the leaden import of those terrible expressions. No, there was no comfort in the Theatre. It was mysteriously gone, like my own youth. Unlike my own youth, it might be coming back some day; but there was little promise of it.

As the town was placarded with references to the Dullborough Mechanics' Institution, I thought I would go and look at that establishment next. There had been no such thing in the town, in my young day, and it occurred to me that its extreme prosperity might have brought adversity upon the Drama. I found the Institution with some difficulty, and should scarcely have known that I had found it if I had judged from its external appearance only; but this was attributable to its never having been finished, and having no front: consequently, it led a modest and retired existence up a stable-yard. It was (as I learnt, on inquiry) a most flourishing Institution, and of the highest benefit to the town: two triumphs which I was glad to understand were not at all impaired by the seeming drawbacks that no mechanics belonged to it, and that it was steeped in debt to the chimney-pots. It had a large room, which was approached by an infirm step-ladder: the builder having declined to construct the intended staircase, without a present payment in cash, which Dullborough (though profoundly appreciative of the Institution) seemed unaccountably bashful about subscribing. The large room had cost – or would, when paid for – five hundred pounds; and it had more mortar in it and more echoes, than one might have expected to get for the money. It was fitted up with a platform, and the usual lecturing tools, including a large black board of a menacing appearance. On referring to lists of the courses of lectures that had been given in this thriving Hall, I fancied I detected a shyness in admitting that human nature when at leisure has any desire whatever to be relieved and diverted; and a furtive sliding in of any poor make-weight piece of amusement, shamefacedly and edgewise. Thus, I observed that it was necessary for the members to be knocked on the head with Gas, Air, Water, Food, the Solar System, the Geological periods, Criticism on Milton, the Steam-engine, John Bunyan, and Arrow-Headed Inscriptions, before they might be tickled by those unaccountable choristers, the negro singers in the court costume of the reign of George the Second. Likewise, that they must be stunned by a weighty inquiry whether there was internal evidence in Shakespeare's works, to prove that his uncle by the mother's side lived for some years at Stoke Newington, before they were brought to by a Miscellaneous Concert. But, indeed the masking of entertainment, and pretending it was something else – as people mask bedsteads when they are obliged to have them in sitting-rooms, and make believe that they are book-cases, sofas, chests of drawers, anything rather than bedsteads – was manifest even in the pretence of dreariness that the unfortunate entertainers themselves felt obliged in decency to put forth when they came here. One very agreeable professional singer who travelled with two professional ladies, knew better than to introduce either of those ladies to sing the ballad 'Comin' through the Rye' without prefacing it himself, with some general remarks on wheat and clover; and even then, he dared not for his life call the song, a song, but disguised it in the bill as an 'Illustration'. In the library, also – fitted with shelves for three thousand books, and containing upwards of one hundred and seventy (presented copies mostly), seething their edges in damp plaster – there was such a painfully apologetic return of 62 offenders who had read Travels, Popular Biography, and mere Fiction descriptive of the aspirations of the hearts and souls of mere human creatures like themselves; and such an elaborate parade of 2 bright examples who had had down Euclid after the day's occupation and confinement; and 3 who had had down Metaphysics after ditto; and 1 who had had down Theology after ditto; and 4 who had worried Grammar, Political Economy, Botany, and Logarithms all at once after ditto; that I suspected the boasted class to be one man, who had been hired to do it.

Emerging from the Mechanics' Institution and continuing my walk about the town, I still noticed everywhere the prevalence, to an extraordinary degree, of this custom of putting the natural demand for amusement out of sight, as some untidy housekeepers put dust, and pretending that it was swept away. And yet it was ministered to, in a dull and abortive manner, by all who made this feint. Looking in at what is called in Dullborough 'the serious bookseller's', where, in my childhood, I had studied the faces of numbers of gentlemen depicted in rostrums with a gaslight on each side of them, and casting my eyes over the open pages of certain printed discourses there, I found a vast deal of aiming at jocosity and dramatic effect, even in them – yes, verily, even on the part of one very wrathful expounder who bitterly anathematised a poor little Circus. Similarly, in the reading provided for the young people enrolled in the Lasso of Love, and other excellent unions, I found the writers generally under a distressing sense that they must start (at all events) like story-tellers, and delude the young persons into the belief that they were going to be interesting. As I looked in at this window for twenty minutes by the clock, I am in a position to offer a friendly remonstrance – not bearing on this particular point – to the designers and engravers of the pictures in those publications. Have they considered the awful consequences likely to flow from their representations of Virtue? Have they asked themselves the question, whether the terrific prospect of acquiring that fearful chubbiness of head, unwieldiness of arm, feeble dislocation of leg, crispiness of hair, and enormity of shirt-collar, which they represent as inseparable from Goodness, may not tend to confirm sensitive waverers, in Evil? A most impressive example (if I had believed it) of what a Dustman and a Sailor may come to, when they mend their ways, was presented to me in this same shop-window. When they were leaning (they were intimate friends) against a post, drunk and reckless, with surpassingly bad hats on, and their hair over their foreheads, they were rather picturesque, and looked as if they might be agreeable men, if they would not be beasts. But, when they had got over their bad propensities, and when, as a consequence, their heads had swelled alarmingly, their hair had got so curly that it lifted their blown-out cheeks up, their coat-cuffs were so long that they never could do any work, and their eyes were so wide open that they never could do any sleep, they presented a spectacle calculated to plunge a timid nature into the depths of Infamy.

But, the clock that had so degenerated since I saw it last, admonished me that I had stayed here long enough; and I resumed my walk.

I had not gone fifty paces along the street when I was suddenly brought up by the sight of a man who got out of a little phaeton at the doctor's door, and went into the doctor's house. Immediately, the air was filled with the scent of trodden grass, and the perspective of years opened, and at the end of it was a little likeness of this man keeping a wicket, and I said, 'God bless my soul! Joe Specks!'

Through many changes and much work, I had preserved a tenderness for the memory of Joe, forasmuch as we had made the acquaintance of Roderick Random together, and had believed him to be no ruffian, but an ingenuous and engaging hero. Scorning to ask the boy left in the phaeton whether it was really Joe, and scorning even to read the brass plate on the door – so sure was I – I rang the bell and informed the servant maid that a stranger sought audience of Mr Specks. Into a room, half surgery, half study, I was shown to await his coming, and I found it, by a series of elaborate accidents, bestrewn with testimonies to Joe. Portrait of Mr Specks, bust of Mr Specks, silver cup from grateful patient to Mr Specks, presentation sermon from local clergyman, dedication poem from local poet, dinner-card from local nobleman, tract on balance of power from local refugee, inscribed *Hommage de l'auteur à Specks.*

When my old schoolfellow came in, and I informed him with a smile that I was not a patient, he seemed rather at a loss to perceive any reason for smiling in connexion with that fact, and inquired to what was he to attribute the honour? I asked him, with another smile, could he remember me at all? He had not (he said) that pleasure. I was beginning to have but a poor opinion of Mr Specks, when he said reflectively, 'And yet there's a something too'. Upon that, I saw a boyish light in his eyes that looked well, and I asked him if he could inform me, as a stranger who desired to know and had not the means of reference at hand, what the name of the young lady was, who married Mr Random?[6] Upon that, he said 'Narcissa', and, after staring for a moment, called me by my name, shook me by the hand, and melted into a roar of laughter. 'Why, of course, you'll remember Lucy Green,' he said, after we had talked a little. 'Of course,' said I. 'Whom do you think she married?' said he. 'You?' I hazarded. 'Me,' said Specks, 'and you shall see her.' So I saw her, and she was fat, and if all the hay in the world had been heaped upon her, it could scarcely have altered her face more than Time had altered it from my remembrance of the face that had once looked down upon me into the fragrant dungeons of Seringapatam. But when her youngest child came in after dinner (for I dined with them, and we had no other company than Specks, Junior, Barrister-at-law, who went away as soon as the cloth was removed, to look after the young lady to whom he was going to be married next week), I saw again, in that little daughter, the little face of the hayfield, unchanged, and it quite touched my foolish heart. We talked immensely, Specks and Mrs Specks, and I, and we spoke of our old selves as though our old selves were dead and gone, and indeed indeed they were – dead and gone as the playing field that had become a wilderness of rusty iron, and the property of S. E. R.

Specks, however, illuminated Dullborough with the rays of interest that I wanted and should otherwise have missed in it, and linked its present to its past, with a highly agreeable chain. And in Specks's society I had new occasion to observe what I had before noticed in similar communications among other men. All the school fellows and others of old, whom I inquired about, had either done superlatively well or superlatively ill – had either become uncertificated bankrupts, or been felonious and got themselves transported; or had made great hits in life, and done wonders. And this is so commonly the case, that I never can imagine what becomes of all the mediocre people of people's youth – especially considering that we find no lack of the species in our maturity. But, I did not propound this difficulty to Specks, for no pause in the conversation gave me an occasion. Nor, could I discover one single flaw in the good doctor – when he reads this, he will receive in a friendly spirit the pleasantly meant record – except that he had forgotten his Roderick Random, and that he confounded Strap with Lieutenant Hatchway; who never knew Random, howsoever intimate with Pickle.[7]

When I went alone to the Railway to catch my train at night (Specks had meant to go with me, but was inopportunely called out), I was in a more charitable mood with Dullborough than I had been all day; and yet in my heart I had loved it all day too. Ah! who was I that I should quarrel with the town for being changed to me, when I myself had come back, so changed, to it! All my early readings and early imaginations dated from this place, and I took them away so full of innocent construction and guileless belief, and I brought them back so worn and torn, so much the wiser and so much the worse!

Nurse's Stories

THERE are not many places that I find it more agreeable to revisit when I am in an idle mood, than some places to which I have never been. For, my acquaintance with those spots is of such long standing, and has ripened into an intimacy of so affectionate a nature, that I take a particular interest in assuring myself that they are unchanged.

I never was in Robinson Crusoe's Island, yet I frequently return there. The colony he established on it soon faded away, and it is uninhabited by any descendants of the grave and courteous Spaniards, or of Will Atkins and the other mutineers, and has relapsed into its original condition. Not a twig of its wicker houses remains, its goats have long run wild again, its screaming parrots would darken the sun with a cloud of many flaming colours if a gun were fired there, no face is ever reflected in the waters of the little creek which Friday swam across when pursued by his two brother cannibals with sharpened stomachs. After comparing notes with other travellers who have similarly revisited the Island and conscientiously inspected it, I have satisfied myself that it contains no vestige of Mr Atkins's domesticity or theology, though his track on the memorable evening of his landing to set his captain ashore, when he was decoyed about and round about until it was dark, and his boat was stove, and his strength and spirits failed him, is yet plainly to be traced. So is the hill-top on which Robinson was struck dumb with joy when the reinstated captain pointed to the ship, riding within half a mile of the shore, that was to bear him away, in the nine-and-twentieth year of his seclusion in that lonely place. So is the sandy beach on which the memorable footstep was impressed, and where the savages hauled up their canoes when they came ashore for those dreadful public dinners, which led to a dancing worse than speech-making. So is the cave where the flaring eyes of the old goat made such a goblin appearance in the dark. So is the site of the hut where Robinson lived with the dog and the parrot and the cat, and where he endured those first agonies of solitude, which – strange to say – never involved any ghostly fancies; a circumstance so very remarkable, that perhaps he left out something in writing his record? Round hundreds of such objects, hidden in the dense tropical foliage, the tropical sea breaks evermore; and over them the tropical sky, saving in the short rainy season, shines bright and cloudless.

Neither, was I ever belated among wolves, on the borders of France and Spain;[1] nor, did I ever, when night was closing in and the ground was covered with snow, draw up my little company among some felled trees which served as a breastwork, and there fire a train of gunpowder so dexterously that suddenly we had three or four score blazing wolves illuminating the darkness around us. Nevertheless, I occasionally go back to that dismal region and perform the feat again; when indeed to smell the singeing and the frying of the wolves afire, and to see them setting one another alight as they rush and tumble, and to behold them rolling in the snow vainly attempting to put themselves out, and to hear their howlings taken up by all the echoes as well as by all the unseen wolves within the woods, makes me tremble.

I was never in the robbers' cave, where Gil Blas lived, but I often go back there and find the trap-door just as heavy to raise as it used to be, while that wicked old disabled Black lies everlastingly cursing in bed.[2] I was never in Don Quixote's study, where he read his books of chivalry until he rose and hacked at imaginary giants, and then refreshed himself with great draughts of water,[3] yet you couldn't move a book in it without my knowledge, or with my consent. I was never (thank Heaven) in company with the little old woman who hobbled out of the chest and told the merchant Abudah to go in search of the Talisman of Oromanes,[4] yet I make it my business to know that she is well preserved and as intolerable as ever. I was never at the school where the boy Horatio Nelson got out of bed to steal the pears: not because he wanted any, but because every other boy was afraid: yet I have several times been back to this Academy, to see him let down out of window with a sheet.[5] So with Damascus, and Bagdad, and Brobingnag[6] (which has the curious fate of being usually misspelt when written), and Lilliput, and Laputa, and the Nile, and Abyssinia, and the Ganges, and the North Pole, and many hundreds of places – I was never at them, yet it is an affair of my life to keep them intact, and I am always going back to them.

But, when I was in Dullborough one day, revisiting the associations of my childhood as recorded in previous pages of these notes, my experience in this wise was made quite inconsiderable and of no account, by the quantity of places and people – utterly impossible places and people, but none the less alarmingly real – that I found I had been introduced to by my nurse before I was six years old, and used to be forced to go back to at night without at all wanting to go. If we all knew our own minds (in a more enlarged sense than the popular acceptation of that phrase), I suspect we should find our nurses responsible for most of the dark corners we are forced to go back to, against our wills.

The first diabolical character who intruded himself on my peaceful youth (as I called to mind that day at Dullborough), was a certain Captain Murderer. This wretch must have been an offshoot of the Blue Beard[7] family, but I had no suspicion of the consanguinity in those times. His warning name would seem to have awakened no general prejudice against him, for he was admitted into the best society and possessed immense wealth. Captain Murderer's mission was matrimony, and the gratification of a cannibal appetite with tender brides. On his marriage morning, he always caused both sides of the way to church to be planted with curious flowers; and when his bride said, 'Dear Captain Murderer, I never saw flowers like these before: what are they called?' he answered, 'They are called Garnish for house-lamb,' and laughed at his ferocious practical joke in a horrid manner, disquieting the minds of the noble bridal company, with a very sharp show of teeth, then displayed for the first time. He made love in a coach and six, and married in a coach and twelve, and all his horses were milk-white horses with one red spot on the back which he caused to be hidden by the harness. For, the spot *would* come there, though every horse was milk-white when Captain Murderer bought him. And the spot was young bride's blood. (To this terrific point I am indebted for my first personal experience of a shudder and cold beads on the forehead.) When Captain Murderer had made an end of feasting and revelry, and had dismissed the noble guests, and was alone with his wife on the day month after their marriage, it was his whimsical custom to produce a golden rolling-pin and a silver pie-board. Now, there was this special feature in the Captain's courtships, that he always asked if the young lady could make pie-crust; and if she couldn't by nature or education, she was taught. Well. When the bride saw Captain Murderer produce the golden rolling-pin and silver pie-board, she remembered this, and turned up her lace-silk sleeves to make a pie. The Captain brought out a silver pie-dish of immense capacity, and the Captain brought out flour and butter and eggs and all things needful, except the inside of the pie; of materials for the staple of the pie itself, the Captain brought out none. Then said the lovely bride, 'Dear Captain Murderer, what pie is this to be?' He replied, 'A meat pie.' Then said the lovely bride, 'Dear Captain Murderer, I see no meat.' The Captain humorously retorted, 'Look in the glass.' She looked in the glass, but still she saw no meat, and then the Captain roared with laughter, and suddenly frowning and drawing his sword, bade her roll out the crust. So she rolled out the crust, dropping large tears upon it all the time because he was so cross, and when she had lined the dish with crust and had cut the crust all ready to fit the top, the Captain called out, '*I* see the meat in the glass!' And the bride looked up at the glass, just in time to see the Captain cutting her head off; and he chopped her in pieces, and peppered her, and salted her, and put her in the pie, and sent it to the baker's, and ate it all, and picked the bones.

Captain Murderer went on in this way, prospering exceedingly, until he came to choose a bride from two twin sisters, and at first didn't know which to choose. For, though one was fair and the other dark, they were both equally beautiful. But the fair twin loved him, and the dark twin hated him, so he chose the fair one. The dark twin would have prevented the marriage if she could, but she couldn't; however, on the night before it, much suspecting Captain Murderer, she stole out and climbed his garden wall, and looked in at his window through a chink in the shutter, and saw him having his teeth filed sharp. Next day she listened all day, and heard him make his joke about the house-lamb. And that day month, he had the paste rolled out, and cut the fair twin's head off, and chopped her in pieces, and peppered her, and salted her, and put her in the pie, and sent it to the baker's, and ate it all, and picked the bones.

Now, the dark twin had had her suspicions much increased by the filing of the Captain's teeth, and again by the house-lamb joke. Putting all things together when he gave out that her sister was dead, she divined the truth, and determined to be revenged. So, she went up to Captain Murderer's house, and knocked at the knocker and pulled at the bell, and when the Captain came to the door, said: 'Dear Captain Murderer, marry me next, for I always loved you and was jealous of my sister.' The Captain took it as a compliment, and made a polite answer, and the marriage was quickly arranged.

On the night before it, the bride again climbed to his window, and again saw him having his teeth filed sharp. At this sight she laughed such a terrible laugh at the chink in the shutter, that the Captain's blood curdled, and he said: 'I hope nothing has disagreed with me!' At that, she laughed again, a still more terrible laugh, and the shutter was opened and search made, but she was nimbly gone, and there was no one. Next day they went to church in a coach and twelve, and were married. And that day month, she rolled the pie-crust out, and Captain Murderer cut her head off, and chopped her in pieces, and peppered her, and salted her, and put her in the pie, and sent it to the baker's, and ate it all, and picked the bones.

But before she began to roll out the paste she had taken a deadly poison of a most awful character, distilled from toads' eyes and spiders' knees; and Captain Murderer had hardly picked her last bone, when he began to swell, and to turn blue, and to be all over spots, and to scream. And he went on swelling and turning bluer, and being more all over spots and screaming, until he reached from floor to ceiling and from wall to wall; and then, at one o'clock in the morning, he blew up with a loud explosion. At the sound of it, all the milk-white horses in the stables broke their halters and went mad, and then they galloped over everybody in Captain Murderer's house (beginning with the family blacksmith who had filed his teeth) until the whole were dead, and then they galloped away.

Hundreds of times did I hear this legend of Captain Murderer, in my early youth, and added hundreds of times was there a mental compulsion upon me in bed, to peep in at his window as the dark twin peeped, and to revisit his horrible house, and look at him in his blue and spotty and screaming stage, as he reached from floor to ceiling and from wall to wall. The young woman who brought me acquainted with Captain Murderer had a fiendish enjoyment of my terrors, and used to begin, I remember – as a sort of introductory overture – by clawing the air with both hands, and uttering a long low hollow groan. So acutely did I suffer from this ceremony in combination with this infernal Captain, that I sometimes used to plead I thought I was hardly strong enough and old enough to hear the story again just yet. But, she never spared me one word of it, and indeed commended the awful chalice to my lips as the only preservative known to science against 'The Black Cat' – a weird and glaring-eyed supernatural Tom, who was reputed to prowl about the world by night, sucking the breath of infancy, and who was endowed with a special thirst (as I was given to understand) for mine.[8]

This female bard – may she have been repaid my debt of obligation to her in the matter of nightmares and perspirations! – reappears in my memory as the daughter of a shipwright. Her name was Mercy, though she had none on me. There was something of a shipbuilding flavour in the following story. As it always recurs to me in a vague association with calomel pills, I believe it to have been reserved for dull nights when I was low with medicine.

There was once a shipwright, and he wrought in a Government Yard, and his name was Chips. And his father's name before him was Chips, and *his* father's name before *him* was Chips, and they were all Chipses. And Chips the father had sold himself to the Devil for an iron pot and a bushel of tenpenny nails and half a ton of copper and a rat that could speak; and Chips the grandfather had sold himself to the Devil for an iron pot and a bushel of tenpenny nails and half a ton of copper and a rat that could speak; and Chips the great-grandfather had disposed of himself in the same direction on the same terms; and the bargain had run in the family for a long long time. So, one day, when young Chips was at work in the Dock Slip all alone, down in the dark hold of an old Seventy-four that was haled up for repairs, the Devil presented himself, and remarked:

'A Lemon has pips,
And a Yard has ships,
And *I*'ll have Chips!'

(I don't know why, but this fact of the Devil's expressing himself in rhyme was peculiarly trying to me.) Chips looked up when he heard the words, and there he saw the Devil with saucer eyes that squinted on a terrible great scale, and that struck out sparks of blue fire continually. And whenever he winked his eyes, showers of blue sparks came out, and his eyelashes made a clattering like flints and steels striking lights. And hanging over one of his arms by the handle was an iron pot, and under that arm was a bushel of tenpenny nails, and under his other arm was half a ton of copper, and sitting on one of his shoulders was a rat that could speak. So, the Devil said again:

'A Lemon has pips,
And a Yard has ships,
And *I*'ll have Chips!'

(The invariable effect of this alarming tautology on the part of
the Evil Spirit was to deprive me of my senses for some moments.)
So, Chips answered never a word, but went on with his work.
'What are you doing, Chips?' said the rat that could speak. 'I am
putting in new planks where you and your gang have eaten old
away,' said Chips. 'But we'll eat them too,' said the rat that could
speak; 'and we'll let in the water and drown the crew, and we'll eat
them too.' Chips, being only a shipwright, and not a Man-of-war's
man, said, 'You are welcome to it.' But he couldn't keep his eyes
off the half a ton of copper or the bushel of tenpenny nails; for
nails and copper are a shipwright's sweethearts, and shipwrights
will run away with them whenever they can. So, the Devil said,
'I see what you are looking at, Chips. You had better strike the
bargain. You know the terms. Your father before you was well
acquainted with them, and so were your grandfather and great-
grandfather before him.' Says Chips, 'I like the copper, and I like
the nails, and I don't mind the pot, but I don't like the rat.' Says the
Devil, fiercely, 'You can't have the metal without him – and *he's*
a curiosity. I'm going.' Chips, afraid of losing the half a ton of
copper and the bushel of nails, then said, 'Give us hold!' So, he
got the copper and the nails and the pot and the rat that could speak,
and the Devil vanished. Chips sold the copper, and he sold the
nails, and he would have sold the pot; but whenever he offered it
for sale, the rat was in it, and the dealers dropped it, and would have
nothing to say to the bargain. So, Chips resolved to kill the rat, and,
being at work in the Yard one day with a great kettle of hot pitch
on one side of him and the iron pot with the rat in it on the other,
he turned the scalding pitch into the pot, and filled it full. Then, he
kept his eye upon it till it cooled and hardened, and then he let it
stand for twenty days, and then he heated the pitch again and
turned it back into the kettle, and then he sank the pot in water for
twenty days more, and then he got the smelters to put it in the
furnace for twenty days more, and then they gave it him out, red
hot, and looking like red-hot glass instead of iron – yet there was
the rat in it, just the same as ever! And the moment it caught his
eye, it said with a jeer:

'A Lemon has pips,
And a Yard has ships,
And *I*'ll have Chips!'

(For this Refrain I had waited since its last appearance, with inexpressible horror, which now culminated.) Chips now felt certain in his own mind that the rat would stick to him; the rat, answering his thought, said, 'I will – like pitch!'

Now, as the rat leaped out of the pot when it had spoken, and made off, Chips began to hope that it wouldn't keep its word. But, a terrible thing happened next day. For, when dinner-time came, and the Dock-bell rang to strike work, he put his rule into the long pocket at the side of his trousers, and there he found a rat – not that rat, but another rat. And in his hat, he found another; and in his pocket-handkerchief, another; and in the sleeves of his coat, when he pulled it on to go to dinner, two more. And from that time he found himself so frightfully intimate with all the rats in the Yard, that they climbed up his legs when he was at work, and sat on his tools while he used them. And they could all speak to one another, and he understood what they said. And they got into his lodging, and into his bed, and into his teapot, and into his beer, and into his boots. And he was going to be married to a corn-chandler's daughter; and when he gave her a workbox he had himself made for her, a rat jumped out of it; and when he put his arm round her waist, a rat clung about her; so the marriage was broken off, though the banns were already twice put up – which the parish clerk well remembers, for, as he handed the book to the clergyman for the second time of asking, a large fat rat ran over the leaf. (By this time a special cascade of rats was rolling down my back, and the whole of my small listening person was overrun with them. At intervals ever since, I have been morbidly afraid of my own pocket, lest my exploring hand should find a specimen or two of those vermin in it.)

You may believe that all this was very terrible to Chips; but even all this was not the worst. He knew besides, what the rats were doing, wherever they were. So, sometimes he would cry aloud, when he was at his club at night, 'Oh! Keep the rats out of the convicts' burying-ground! Don't let them do that!' Or, 'There's one of them at the cheese down-stairs!', 'Or There's two of them smelling at the baby in the garret!' Or, other things of that sort. At last, he was voted mad, and lost his work in the Yard, and could get no other work. But, King George wanted men, so before very long he got pressed for a sailor. And so he was taken off in a boat one evening to his ship, lying at Spithead, ready to sail. And so the first thing he made out in her as he got near her, was the figure-head of the old Seventy-four, where he had seen the Devil. She was called the Argonaut, and they rowed right under the bowsprit where the figure-head of the Argonaut, with a sheepskin in his hand and a blue gown on, was looking out to sea; and sitting staring on his forehead was the rat who could speak, and his exact words were these: 'Chips ahoy! Old boy! We've pretty well eat them too, and we'll drown the crew, and will eat them too!' (Here I always became exceedingly faint, and would have asked for water, but that I was speechless.)

The ship was bound for the Indies; and if you don't know where that is, you ought to it, and angels will never love you. (Here I felt myself an outcast from a future state.) The ship set sail that very night, and she sailed, and sailed, and sailed. Chips's feelings were dreadful. Nothing ever equalled his terrors. No wonder. At last, one day he asked leave to speak to the Admiral. The Admiral giv' leave. Chips went down on his knees in the Great State Cabin. 'Your Honour, unless your Honour, without a moment's loss of time make sail for the nearest shore, this is a doomed ship, and her name is the Coffin!' 'Young man, your words are a madman's words.' 'Your Honour no; they are nibbling us away.' 'They?' 'Your Honour, them dreadful rats. Dust and hollowness where solid oak ought to be! Rats nibbling a grave for every man on board! Oh! Does your Honour love your Lady and your pretty children?' 'Yes, my man, to be sure.' 'Then, for God's sake, make for the nearest shore, for at this present moment the rats are all stopping in their work, and are all looking straight towards you with bare teeth, and are all saying to one another that you shall never, never, never, never, see your Lady and your children more.' 'My poor fellow, you are a case for the doctor. Sentry, take care of this man!'

So, he was bled and he was blistered, and he was this and that, for six whole days and nights. So, then he again asked leave to speak to the Admiral. The Admiral giv' leave. He went down on his knees in the Great State Cabin. 'Now, Admiral, you must die! You took no warning; you must die! The rats are never wrong in their calculations, and they make out that they'll be through, at twelve tonight. So, you must die! – With me and all the rest!' And so at twelve o'clock there was a great leak reported in the ship, and a torrent of water rushed in and nothing could stop it, and they all went down, every living soul. And what the rats – being water-rats – left of Chips, at last floated to shore, and sitting on him was an immense overgrown rat, laughing, that dived when the corpse touched the beach and never came up. And there was a deal of sea-weed on the remains. And if you get thirteen bits of seaweed, and dry them and burn them in the fire, they will go off like in these thirteen words as plain can be:

> 'A Lemon has pips,
> And a Yard has ships,
> And *I*'ve got Chips!'

The same female bard – descended, possibly, from those terrible old Scalds who seem to have existed for the express purpose of addling the brains of mankind when they begin to investigate languages – made a standing pretence which greatly assisted in forcing me back to a number of hideous places that I would by all means have avoided. This pretence was, that all her ghost stories had occurred to her own relations. Politeness towards a meritorious family, therefore forbade my doubting them, and they acquired an air of authentication that impaired my digestive powers for life. There was a narrative concerning an unearthly animal foreboding death, which appeared in the open street to a parlour-maid who 'went to fetch the beer' for supper: first (as I now recall it) assuming the likeness of a black dog, and gradually rising on its hind-legs and swelling into the semblance of some quadruped greatly surpassing a hippopotamus: which apparition – not because I deemed it in the least improbable, but because I felt it to be really too large to bear – I feebly endeavoured to explain away. But, on Mercy's retorting with wounded dignity that the parlour-maid was her own sister-in-law, I perceived there was no hope, and resigned myself to this zoological phenomenon as one of my many pursuers. There was another narrative describing the apparition of a young woman who came out of a glass-case and haunted another young woman until the other young woman questioned it and elicited that its bones (Lord! To think of its being so particular about its bones!) were buried under the glass-case, whereas she required them to be interred, with every Undertaking solemnity up to twenty-four pound ten, in another particular place. This narrative I considered I had a personal interest in disproving, because we had glass-cases at home, and how, otherwise, was I to be guaranteed from the intrusion of young women requiring *me* to bury them up to twenty-four pound ten, when I had only twopence a week? But my remorseless nurse cut the ground from under my tender feet, by informing me that She was the other young woman; and I couldn't say 'I don't believe you'; it was not possible.

Such are a few of the uncommercial journeys that I was forced to make, against my will, when I was very young and unreasoning. And really, as to the latter part of them, it is not so very long ago – now I come to think of it – that I was asked to undertake them once again, with a steady countenance.

Arcadian London

BEING in a humour for complete solitude and uninterrupted meditation this autumn, I have taken a lodging for six weeks in the most unfrequented part of England – in a word, in London.

The retreat into which I have withdrawn myself, is Bond-street. From this lonely spot I make pilgrimages into the surrounding wilderness, and traverse extensive tracts of the Great Desert. The first solemn feeling of isolation overcome, the first oppressive consciousness of profound retirement conquered, I enjoy that sense of freedom, and feel reviving within me that latent wildness of the original savage, which has been (upon the whole somewhat frequently) noticed by Travellers.

My lodgings are at a hatter's – my own hatter's. After exhibiting no articles in his window for some weeks, but sea-side wide-awakes, shooting-caps, and a choice of rough waterproof head-gear for the moors and mountains, he has put upon the heads of his family as much of this stock as they could carry, and has taken them off to the Isle of Thanet. His young man alone remains – and remains alone – in the shop. The young man has let out the fire at which the irons are heated, and, saving his strong sense of duty, I see no reason why he should take the shutters down.

Happily for himself and for his country, the young man is a Volunteer;[1] most happily for himself, or I think he would become the prey of a settled melancholy. For, to live surrounded by human hats, and alienated from human heads to fit them on, is surely a great endurance. But, the young man, sustained by practising his exercise, and by constantly furbishing up his regulation plume (it is unnecessary to observe that, as a hatter, he is in a cock's-feather corps), is resigned, and uncomplaining. On a Saturday, when he closes early and gets his Knickerbockers on, he is even cheerful. I am gratefully particular in this reference to him, because he is my companion through many peaceful hours. My hatter has a desk up certain steps behind his counter, enclosed like the clerk's desk at Church. I shut myself into this place of seclusion, after breakfast, and meditate. At such times, I observe the young man loading an imaginary rifle with the greatest precision, and maintaining a most galling and destructive fire upon the national enemy. I thank him publicly for his companionship and his patriotism.

The simple character of my life, and the calm nature of the scenes by which I am surrounded, occasion me to rise early. I go forth in my slippers, and promenade the pavement. It is pastoral to feel the freshness of the air in the uninhabited town, and to appreciate the shepherdess character of the few milkwomen who purvey so little milk that it would be worth nobody's while to adulterate it, if anybody were left to undertake the task. On the crowded sea-shore, the great demand for milk, combined with the strong local temptation of chalk, would betray itself in the lowered quality of the article. In Arcadian London I derive it from the cow.

The Arcadian simplicity of the metropolis altogether, and the primitive ways into which it has fallen in this autumnal Golden Age, make it entirely new to me. Within a few hundred yards of my retreat, is the house of a friend who maintains a most sumptuous butler. I never, until yesterday, saw that butler out of superfine black broadcloth. Until yesterday, I never saw him off duty, never saw him (he is the best of butlers) with the appearance of having any mind for anything but the glory of his master and his master's friends. Yesterday morning, walking in my slippers near the house of which he is the prop and ornament – a house now a waste of shutters – I encountered that butler, also in his slippers, and in a shooting suit of one colour, and in a low-crowned straw-hat, smoking an early cigar. He felt that we had formerly met in another state of existence, and that we were translated into a new sphere. Wisely and well, he passed me without recognition. Under his arm he carried the morning paper, and shortly afterwards I saw him sitting on a rail in the pleasant open landscape of Regent-street, perusing it at his ease under the ripening sun.

My landlord having taken his whole establishment to be salted down, I am waited on by an elderly woman labouring under a chronic sniff, who, at the shadowy hour of half-past nine o'clock of every evening, gives admittance at the street door to a meagre and mouldy old man whom I have never yet seen detached from a flat pint of beer in a pewter pot. The meagre and mouldy old man is her husband, and the pair have a dejected consciousness that they are not justified in appearing on the surface of the earth. They come out of some hole when London empties itself, and go in again when it fills. I saw them arrive on the evening when I myself took possession, and they arrived with the flat pint of beer, and their bed in a bundle. The old man is a weak old man, and appeared to me to get the bed down the kitchen stairs by tumbling down with and upon it. They make their bed in the lowest and remotest corner of the basement, and they smell of bed, and have no possession but bed: unless it be (which I rather infer from an under-current of flavour in them) cheese. I know their name, through the chance of having called the wife's attention, at half-past nine on the second evening of our acquaintance, to the circumstance of there being some one at the house door; when she apologetically explained, 'It's only Mr Klem.' What becomes of Mr Klem all day, or when he goes out, or why, is a mystery I cannot penetrate; but at half-past nine he never fails to turn up on the door-step with the flat pint of beer. And the pint of beer, flat as it is, is so much more important than himself, that it always seems to my fancy as if it had found him drivelling in the street and had humanely brought him home. In making his way below, Mr Klem never goes down the middle of the passage, like another Christian, but shuffles against the wall as if entreating me to take notice that he is occupying as little space as possible in the house; and whenever I come upon him face to face, he backs from me in fascinated confusion. The most extraordinary circumstance I have traced in connexion with this aged couple, is, that there is a Miss Klem, their daughter, apparently ten years older than either of them, who has also a bed and smells of it, and carries it about the earth at dusk and hides it in deserted houses. I came into this piece of knowledge through Mrs Klem's beseeching me to sanction the sheltering of Miss Klem under that roof for a single night, 'between her takin' care of the upper part in Pall Mall which the family of his back, and a 'ouse in Serjameses-street, which the family of leaves towng ter-morrer.' I gave my gracious consent (having nothing that I know of to do with it), and in the shadowy hours Miss Klem became perceptible on the door-step, wrestling with a bed in a bundle. Where she made it up for the night I cannot positively state, but, I think, in a sink. I know that with the instinct of a reptile or an insect, she stowed it and herself away in deep obscurity. In the Klem family, I have noticed another remarkable gift of nature, and that is a power they possess of converting everything into flue. Such broken victuals as they take by stealth, appear (whatever the nature of the viands) invariably to generate flue; and even the nightly pint of beer, instead of assimilating naturally, strikes me as breaking out in that form, equally on the shabby gown of Mrs Klem, and the threadbare coat of her husband.

Mrs Klem has no idea of my name – as to Mr Klem he has no idea of anything – and only knows me as her good gentleman. Thus, if doubtful whether I am in my room or no, Mrs Klem taps at the door and says, 'Is my good gentleman here?' Or, if a messenger desiring to see me were consistent with my solitude, she would show him in with 'Here is my good gentleman.' I find this to be a generic custom. For, I meant to have observed now, that in its Arcadian time all my part of London is indistinctly pervaded by the Klem species. They creep about with beds, and go to bed in miles of deserted houses. They hold no companionship except that sometimes, after dark, two of them will emerge from opposite houses, and meet in the middle of the road as on neutral ground, or will peep from adjoining houses over an interposing barrier of area railings, and compare a few reserved mistrustful notes respecting their good ladies or good gentlemen. This I have discovered in the course of various solitary rambles I have taken Northward from my retirement, along the awful perspectives of Wimpole-street, Harley-street, and similar frowning regions. Their effect would be scarcely distinguishable from that of the primeval forests, but for the Klem stragglers; these may be dimly observed, when the heavy shadows fall, flitting to and fro, putting up the door-chain, taking in the pint of beer, lowering like phantoms at the dark parlour windows, or secretly consorting underground with the dust-bin and the water-cistern.

In the Burlington Arcade, I observe, with peculiar pleasure, a primitive state of manners to have superseded the baneful influences of ultra civilization. Nothing can surpass the innocence of the ladies' shoe-shops, the artificial-flower repositories, and the head-dress depôts. They are in strange hands at this time of year – hands of unaccustomed persons, who are imperfectly acquainted with the prices of the goods, and contemplate them with unsophisticated delight and wonder. The children of these virtuous people exchange familiarities in the Arcade, and temper the asperity of the two tall beadles. Their youthful prattle blends in an unwonted manner with the harmonious shade of the scene, and the general effect is, as of the voices of birds in a grove. In this happy restoration of the golden time, it has been my privilege even to see the bigger beadle's wife. She brought him his dinner in a basin, and he ate it in his arm-chair, and afterwards fell asleep like a satiated child. At Mr Truefitt's, the excellent hairdresser's, they are learning French to beguile the time; and even the few solitaries left on guard at Mr Atkinson's, the perfumer's round the corner (generally the most inexorable gentleman in London, and the most scornful of three-and-sixpence), condescend a little, as they drowsily bide or recall their turn for chasing the ebbing Neptune on the ribbed sea-sand.[2] From Messrs Hunt and Roskell's, the jewellers, all things are absent but the precious stones, and the gold and silver, and the soldierly pensioner at the door with his decorated breast. I might stand night and day for a month to come, in Saville-row, with my tongue out, yet not find a doctor to look at it for love or money. The dentists' instruments are rusting in their drawers, and their horrible cool parlours, where people pretend to read the Every-Day Book[3] and not to be afraid, are doing penance for their grimness in white sheets. The light-weight of shrewd appearance, with one eye always shut up, as if he were eating a sharp gooseberry in all seasons, who usually stands at the gateway of the livery-stables on very little legs under a very large waistcoat, has gone to Doncaster. Of such undesigning aspect is his guileless yard now, with its gravel and scarlet beans, and the yellow Break[4] housed under a glass roof in a corner, that I almost believe I could not be taken in there, if I tried. In the places of business of the great tailors, the cheval-glasses are dim and dusty for lack of being looked into. Ranges of brown paper coat and waistcoat bodies look as funereal as if they were the hatchments of the customers with whose names they are inscribed; the measuring tapes hang idle on the wall; the order-taker, left on the hopeless chance of some one looking in, yawns in the last extremity over the book of patterns, as if he were trying to read that entertaining library. The hotels in Brook-street have no one in them, and the staffs of servants stare disconsolately for next season out of all the windows. The very man who goes about like an erect Turtle, between two boards recommendatory of the Sixteen Shilling Trousers, is aware of himself as a hollow mockery, and eats filberts while he leans his hinder shell against a wall.

Among these tranquillizing objects, it is my delight to walk and meditate. Soothed by the repose around me, I wander insensibly to considerable distances, and guide myself back by the stars. Thus, I enjoy the contrast of a few still partially inhabited and busy spots where all the lights are not fled, where all the garlands are not dead, whence all but I have not departed. Then, does it appear to me that in this age three things are clamorously required of Man in the miscellaneous thoroughfares of the metropolis. Firstly, that he have his boots cleaned. Secondly, that he eat a penny ice. Thirdly, that he get himself photographed. Then do I speculate, What have those seam-worn artists been who stand at the photograph doors in Greek caps, sample in hand, and mysteriously salute the public – the female public with a pressing tenderness – to come in and be 'took'? What did they do with their greasy blandishments, before the era of cheap photography? Of what class were their previous victims, and how victimised? And how did they get, and how did they pay for, that large collection of likenesses, all purporting to have been taken inside, with the taking of none of which had that establishment any more to do than with the taking of Delhi?[5]

But, these are small oases, and I am soon back again in metropolitan Arcadia. It is my impression that much of its serene and peaceful character is attributable to the absence of customary Talk. How do I know but there may be subtle influences in Talk, to vex the souls of men who don't hear it? How do I know but that Talk, five, ten, twenty miles off, may get into the air and disagree with me? If I rise from my bed, vaguely troubled and wearied and sick of my life, in the session of Parliament, who shall say that my noble friend, my right reverend friend, my right honourable friend, my honourable friend, my honourable and learned friend, or my honourable and gallant friend, may not be responsible for that effect upon my nervous system. Too much Ozone in the air, I am informed and fully believe (though I have no idea what it is), would affect me in a marvellously disagreeable way; why may not too much Talk? I don't see or hear the Ozone; I don't see or hear the Talk. And there is so much Talk; so much too much; such loud cry, and such scant supply of wool; such a deal of fleecing, and so little fleece! Hence, in the Arcadian season, I find it a delicious triumph to walk down to deserted Westminster, and see the Courts shut up; to walk a little further and see the Two Houses shut up; to stand in the Abbey Yard, like the New Zealander of the grand English History[6] (concerning which unfortunate man, a whole rookery of mares' nests is generally being discovered), and gloat upon the ruins of Talk. Returning to my primitive solitude and lying down to sleep, my grateful heart expands with the consciousness that there is no adjourned Debate, no ministerial explanation, nobody to give notice of intention to ask the noble Lord at the head of her Majesty's Government five-and-twenty bootless questions in one, no term time with legal argument, no Nisi Prius with eloquent appeal to British Jury; that the air will tomorrow, and tomorrow, and tomorrow,[7] remain untroubled by this superabundant generating of Talk. In a minor degree it is a delicious triumph to me to go into the club, and see the carpets up, and the Bores and the other dust dispersed to the four winds. Again New Zealander-like, I stand on the cold hearth, and say in the solitude, 'Here I watched Bore A 1, with voice always mysteriously low and head always mysteriously drooped, whispering political secrets into the ears of Adam's confiding children. Accursed be his memory for ever and a day!'

But, I have all this time been coming to the point, that the happy nature of my retirement is most sweetly expressed in its being the abode of Love. It is, as it were, an inexpensive Agapemone:[8] nobody's speculation; everybody's profit. The one great result of the resumption of primitive habits, and (convertible terms) the not having much to do, is, the abounding of Love.

The Klem species are incapable of the softer emotions; probably, in that low nomadic race, the softer emotions have all degenerated into flue. But, with this exception, all the sharers of my retreat make love.

I have mentioned Saville-row. We all know the Doctor's servant. We all know what a respectable man he is, what a hard dry man, what a firm man, what a confidential man: how he lets us into the waiting-room, like a man who knows minutely what is the matter with us, but from whom the rack should not wring the secret. In the prosaic 'season', he has distinctly the appearance of a man conscious of money in the savings bank, and taking his stand on his respectability with both feet. At that time it is as impossible to associate him with relaxation, or any human weakness, as it is to meet his eye without feeling guilty of indisposition. In the blest Arcadian time, how changed! I have seen him, in a pepper-and-salt jacket – jacket – and drab trousers, with his arm round the waist of a bootmaker's housemaid, smiling in open day. I have seen him at the pump by the Albany, unsolicitedly pumping for two fair young creatures, whose figures as they bent over their cans, were – if I may be allowed an original expression – a model for the sculptor. I have seen him trying the piano in the Doctor's drawing-room with his forefinger, and have heard him humming tunes in praise of lovely woman. I have seen him seated on a fire-engine, and going (obviously in search of excitement) to a fire. I saw him, one moonlight evening when the peace and purity of our Arcadian west were at their height, polk with the lovely daughter of a cleaner of gloves, from the door-steps of his own residence, across Saville-row, round by Clifford-street and Old Burlington-street, back to Burlington-gardens. Is this the Golden Age revived, or Iron London?

The Dentist's servant. Is that man no mystery to us, no type of invisible power? The tremendous individual knows (who else does?) what is done with the extracted teeth; he knows what goes on in the little room where something is always being washed or filed; he knows what warm spicy infusion is put into the comfortable tumbler from which we rinse our wounded mouth, with a gap in it that feels a foot wide; he knows whether the thing we spit into is a fixture communicating with the Thames, or could be cleared away for a dance; he sees the horrible parlour when there are no-patients in it, and he could reveal, if he would, what becomes of the Every-Day Book then. The conviction of my coward conscience when I see that man in a professional light, is, that he knows all the statistics of my teeth and gums, my double teeth, my single teeth, my stopped teeth, and my sound. In this Arcadian rest, I am fearless of him as of a harmless, powerless creature in a Scotch cap, who adores a young lady in a voluminous crinoline, at a neighbouring billiard-room, and whose passion would be uninfluenced if every one of her teeth were false. They may be. He takes them all on trust.

In secluded corners of the place of my seclusion, there are little shops withdrawn from public curiosity, and never two together, where servants' perquisites are bought. The cook may dispose of grease at these modest and convenient marts; the butler, of bottles; the valet and lady's maid, of clothes; most servants, indeed, of most things they may happen to lay hold of. I have been told that in sterner times loving correspondence, otherwise interdicted, may be maintained by letter through the agency of some of these useful establishments. In the Arcadian autumn, no such device is necessary. Everybody loves, and openly and blamelessly loves. My landlord's young man loves the whole of one side of the way of Old Bond-street, and is beloved several doors up New Bond-street besides. I never look out of window but I see kissing of hands going on all around me. It is the morning custom to glide from shop to shop and exchange tender sentiments; it is the evening custom for couples to stand hand in hand at house doors, or roam, linked in that flowery manner, through the unpeopled streets. There is nothing else to do but love; and what there is to do, is done.

In unison with this pursuit, a chaste simplicity obtains in the domestic habits of Arcadia. Its few scattered people dine early, live moderately, sup socially, and sleep soundly. It is rumoured that the Beadles of the Arcade, from being the mortal enemies of boys, have signed with tears, an address to Lord Shaftesbury,[9] and subscribed to a ragged school. No wonder! For, they might turn their heavy maces into crooks and tend sheep in the Arcade, to the purling of the water-carts as they give the thirsty streets much more to drink than they can carry.

A happy Golden Age, and a serene tranquillity. Charming picture, but it will fade. The iron age will return, London will come back to town, if I show my tongue then in Saville-row for half a minute I shall be prescribed for, the Doctor's man and the Dentist's man will then pretend that these days of unprofessional innocence never existed. Where Mr and Mrs Klem and their bed will be at that time, passes human knowledge; but my hatter hermitage will then know them no more, nor will it then know me. The desk at which I have written these meditations will retributively assist at the making out of my account, and the wheels of gorgeous carriages and the hoofs of high-stepping horses will crush the silence out of Bond-street – will grind Arcadia away, and give it to the elements in granite powder.

The Calais Night-Mail

IT is an unsettled question with me whether I shall leave Calais something handsome in my will, or whether I shall leave it my malediction. I hate it so much, and yet I am always so very glad to see it, that I am in a state of constant indecision on this subject.

When I first made acquaintance with Calais, it was as a maundering young wretch in a clammy perspiration and dripping saline particles, who was conscious of no extremities but the one great extremity, sea-sickness – who was a mere bilious torso, with a mislaid headache somewhere in its stomach – who had been put into a horrible swing in Dover Harbour, and had tumbled giddily out of it on the French coast, or the Isle of Man, or anywhere. Times have changed, and now I enter Calais self-reliant and rational. I know where it is before-hand, I keep a look out for it, I recognize its landmarks when I see any of them, I am acquainted with its ways, and I know – and I can bear – its worst behaviour.

Malignant Calais! Low-lying alligator, evading the eyesight and discouraging hope! Dodging flat streak, now on this bow, now on that, now anywhere, now everywhere, now nowhere! In vain Cape Grinez, coming frankly forth into the sea, exhorts the failing to be stout of heart and stomach: sneaking Calais, prone behind its bar, invites emetically to despair. Even when it can no longer quite conceal itself in its muddy dock, it has an evil way of falling off, has Calais, which is more hopeless than its invisibility. The pier is all but on the bowsprit, and you think you are there – roll, roar, wash! – Calais has retired miles inland, and Dover has burst out to look for it. It has a last dip and slide in its character, has Calais, to be especially commended to the infernal gods. Thrice accursed be that garrison-town, when it dives under the boat's keel, and comes up a league or two to the right, with the packet shivering and spluttering and staring about for it!

Not but what I have my animosities towards Dover. I particularly detest Dover for the self-complacency with which it goes to bed. It always goes to bed (when I am going to Calais) with a more brilliant display of lamp and candle than any other town. Mr and Mrs Birmingham, host and hostess of the Lord Warden Hotel, are my much esteemed friends, but they are too conceited about the comforts of that establishment when the Night Mail is starting. I know it is a good house to stay at, and I don't want the fact insisted upon in all its warm bright windows at such an hour. I know the Warden is a stationary edifice that never rolls or pitches, and I object to its big outline seeming to insist upon that circumstance, and, as it were, to come over me with it, when I am reeling on the deck of the boat. Beshrew the Warden likewise, for obstructing that corner, and making the wind so angry as it rushes round. Shall I not know that it blows quite soon enough, without the officious Warden's interference?

As I wait here on board the night packet, for the South Eastern Train to come down with the Mail, Dover appears to me to be illuminated for some intensely aggravating festivity in my personal dishonour. All its noises smack of taunting praises of the land, and dispraises of the gloomy sea, and of me for going on it. The drums upon the heights have gone to bed, or I know they would rattle taunts against me for having my unsteady footing on this slippery deck. The many gas eyes of the Marine Parade twinkle in an offensive manner, as if with derision. The distant dogs of Dover bark at me in my mis-shapen wrappers, as if I were Richard the Third.[1]

A screech, a bell, and two red eyes come gliding down the Admiralty Pier with a smoothness of motion rendered more smooth by the heaving of the boat. The sea makes noises against the pier, as if several hippopotami were lapping at it, and were prevented by circumstances over which they had no control from drinking peaceably. We, the boat, become violently agitated – rumble, hum, scream, roar, and establish an immense family washing-day at each paddle-box. Bright patches break out in the train as the doors of the post-office vans are opened, and instantly stooping figures with sacks upon their backs begin to be beheld among the piles, descending as it would seem in ghostly procession to Davy Jones's Locker. The passengers come on board; a few shadowy Frenchmen, with hatboxes shaped like the stopper of gigantic case-bottles; a few shadowy Germans in immense fur coats and boots; a few shadowy Englishmen prepared for the worst and pretending not to expect it. I cannot disguise from my uncommercial mind the miserable fact that we are a body of outcasts; that the attendants on us are as scant in number as may serve to get rid of us with the least possible delay; that there are no night-loungers interested in us; that the unwilling lamps shiver and shudder at us; that the sole object is to commit us to the deep and abandon us. Lo, the two red eyes glaring in increasing distance, and then the very train itself has gone to bed before we are off!

What is the moral support derived by some sea-going amateurs from an umbrella? Why do certain voyagers across the Channel always put up that article, and hold it up with a grim and fierce tenacity? A fellow-creature near me – whom I only know to *be* a fellow-creature, because of his umbrella: without which he might be a dark bit of cliff, pier, or bulkhead – clutches that instrument with a desperate grasp, that will not relax until he lands at Calais. Is there any analogy, in certain constitutions, between keeping an umbrella up, and keeping the spirits up? A hawser thrown on board with a flop replies 'Stand by!' 'Stand by, below.' 'Half a turn a head!' 'Half a turn a head!' 'Half speed!' 'Half speed!' 'Port!' 'Port!' 'Steady!' 'Steady!' 'Go on!' 'Go on!'

A stout wooden wedge driven in at my right temple and out at my left, a floating deposit of lukewarm oil in my throat, and a compression of the bridge of my nose in a blunt pair of pincers, – these are the personal sensations by which I know we are off, and by which I shall continue to know it until I am on the soil of France. My symptoms have scarcely established themselves comfortably, when two or three skating shadows that have been trying to walk or stand, get flung together, and other two or three shadows in tarpauling slide with them into corners and cover them up. Then the South Foreland lights begin to hiccup at us in a way that bodes no good.

It is at about this period that my detestation of Calais knows no bounds. Inwardly I resolve afresh that I never will forgive that hated town. I have done so before, many times, but that is past. Let me register a vow. Implacable animosity to Calais everm – that was an awkward sea, and the funnel seems of my opinion, for it gives a complaining roar.

The wind blows stiffly from the Nor'-East, the sea runs high, we ship a deal of water, the night is dark and cold, and the shapeless passengers lie about in melancholy bundles, as if they were sorted out for the laundress; but for my own uncommercial part I cannot pretend that I am much inconvenienced by any of these things. A general howling whistling flopping gurgling and scooping, I am aware of, and a general knocking about of Nature; but the impressions I receive are very vague. In a sweet faint temper, something like the smell of damaged oranges, I think I should feel languidly benevolent if I had time. I have not time, because I am under a curious compulsion to occupy myself with the Irish melodies. 'Rich and rare were the gems she wore,'[2] is the particular melody to which I find myself devoted. I sing it to myself in the most charming manner and with the greatest expression. Now and then, I raise

my head (I am sitting on the hardest of wet seats, in the most uncomfortable of wet attitudes, but I don't mind it,) and notice that I
am a whirling shuttlecock between a fiery battledore of a lighthouse
on the French coast and a fiery battledore of a lighthouse on the
English coast; but I don't notice it particularly, except to feel en-
venomed in my hatred of Calais. Then I go on again, 'Rich and
rare were the ge-ems she-e-e-e wore. And a bright gold ring on her
wa-and she bo-ore, But O her beauty was fa-a-a-a-r beyond' – I
am particularly proud of my execution here, when I become aware
of another awkward shock from the sea, and another protest from
the funnel, and a fellow-creature at the paddle-box more audibly
indisposed than I think he need be – 'Her sparkling gems, or snow-
white wand, But O her beauty was fa-a-a-a-r beyond' – another
awkward one here, and the fellow-creature with the umbrella down
and picked up, 'Her spa-a-rkling ge-ems, or her Port! port! steady!
steady! snow-white fellow-creature at the paddle-box very selfishly
audible, bump roar wash white wand.'

As my execution of the Irish melodies partakes of my imperfect
perceptions of what is going on around me, so what is going on
around me becomes something else than what it is. The stokers
open the furnace doors below, to feed the fires, and I am again on
the box of the old Exeter Telegraph fast coach, and that is the light
of the for ever extinguished coach-lamps, and the gleam on the
hatches and paddle-box is *their* gleam on cottages and haystacks,
and the monotonous noise of the engines is the steady jingle of the
splendid team. Anon, the intermittent funnel roar of protest at
every violent roll, becomes the regular blast of a high pressure
engine, and I recognize the exceedingly explosive steamer in which
I ascended the Mississippi when the American civil war was not,
and when only its causes were. A fragment of mast on which the
light of a lantern falls, an end of rope, and a jerking block or so,
become suggestive of Franconi's Circus at Paris where I shall be
this very night mayhap (for it must be morning now), and they
dance to the self-same time and tune as the trained steed, Black
Raven. What may be the speciality of these waves as they come
rushing on, I cannot desert the pressing demands made upon me by
the gems she wore, to inquire, but they are charged with something about Robinson Crusoe, and I think it was in Yarmouth

Roads that he first went a seafaring and was near foundering (what a terrific sound that word had for me when I was a boy!) in his first gale of wind.[3] Still, through all this, I must ask her (who *was* she I wonder!) for the fiftieth time, and without ever stopping, Does she not fear to stray, So lone and lovely through this bleak way, And are Erin's sons so good or so cold, As not to be tempted by more fellow-creatures at the paddle-box or gold? Sir Knight I feel not the least alarm, No son of Erin will offer me harm, For though they love fellow-creature with umbrella down again and golden store, Sir Knight they what a tremendous one love honour and virtue more: For though they love Stewards with a bull's eye bright,[4] they'll trouble you for your ticket, sir – rough passage to-night!

I freely admit it to be a miserable piece of human weakness and inconsistency, but I no sooner become conscious of those last words from the steward than I begin to soften towards Calais. Whereas I have been vindictively wishing that those Calais burghers who came out of their town by a short cut into the History of England, with those fatal ropes round their necks[5] by which they have since been towed into so many cartoons, had all been hanged on the spot, I now begin to regard them as highly respectable and virtuous tradesmen. Looking about me, I see the light of Cape Grinez well astern of the boat on the davits to leeward, and the light of Calais Harbour undeniably at its old tricks, but still ahead and shining. Sentiments of forgiveness of Calais, not to say of attachment to Calais, begin to expand my bosom. I have weak notions that I will stay there a day or two on my way back. A faded and recumbent stranger pausing in a profound reverie over the rim of a basin, asks me what kind of place Calais is? I tell him (Heaven forgive me!) a very agreeable place indeed – rather hilly than otherwise.

So strangely goes the time, and on the whole so quickly – though still I seem to have been on board a week – that I am bumped rolled gurgled washed and pitched into Calais Harbour before her maiden smile has finally lighted her through the Green Isle, When blest for ever is she who relied, On entering Calais at the top of the tide. For we have not to land to-night down among those slimy timbers – covered with green hair as if it were the mermaids' favourite combing-place – where one crawls to the surface of the jetty, like a stranded shrimp, but we go steaming up the harbour to the Railway Station Quay. And as we go, the sea washes in and out among piles and planks, with dead heavy beats and in quite a furious manner (whereof we are proud), and the lamps shake in the wind, and the bells of Calais striking One seem to send their vibrations struggling against troubled air, as we have come struggling against troubled water. And now, in the sudden relief and wiping of faces, every-body on board seems to have had a prodigious double-tooth out, and to be this very instant free of the Dentist's hands. And now we all know for the first time how wet and cold we are, and how salt we are; and now I love Calais with my heart of hearts!

'Hôtel Dessin!' (but in this one case it is not a vocal cry; it is but a bright lustre in the eyes of the cheery representative of that best of inns). 'Hôtel Meurice!' 'Hôtel de France!' 'Hôtel de Calais!' 'The Royal Hôtel, Sir, Angaishe ouse!' 'You going to Parry, Sir?' 'Your baggage, registair froo, Sir?' Bless ye, my Touters, bless ye, my commissionaires, bless ye, my hungry-eyed mysteries in caps of a military form, who are always here, day or night, fair weather or foul, seeking inscrutable jobs which I never see you get! Bless ye, my Custom House officers in green and grey; permit me to grasp the welcome hands that descend into my travelling-bag, one on each side, and meet at the bottom to give my change of linen a peculiar shake up, as if it were a measure of chaff or grain! I have nothing to declare, Monsieur le Douanier, except that when I cease to breathe, Calais will be found written on my heart.[6] No article liable to local duty have I with me, Monsieur l'Officier de l'Octroi, unless the overflowing of a breast devoted to your charm-ing town should be in that wise chargeable. Ah! see at the gangway by the twinkling lantern, my dearest brother and friend, he once of the Passport Office, he who collects the names! May he be for ever changeless in his buttoned black surtout, with his note-book in his hand, and his tall black hat, surmounting his round smiling patient face! Let us embrace, my dearest brother. I am yours à tout jamais – for the whole of ever.

Calais up and doing at the railway station, and Calais down and dreaming in its bed; Calais with something of 'an ancient and fish-like smell'[7] about it, and Calais blown and sea-washed pure; Calais represented at the Buffet by savoury roast fowls, hot coffee, cognac, and Bordeaux; and Calais represented everywhere by flitting persons with a monomania for changing money – though I never shall be able to understand in my present state of existence how they live by it, but I suppose I should, if I understood the currency question – Calais *en gros*, and Calais *en détail*, forgive one who has deeply wronged you. – I was not fully aware of it on the other side, but I meant Dover.

Ding, ding! To the carriages, gentlemen the travellers. Ascend then, gentlemen the travellers, for Hazebroucke, Lille, Douai, Bruxelles, Arras, Amiens, and Paris! I, humble representative of the uncommercial interest, ascend with the rest. The train is light to-night, and I share my compartment with but two fellow-travellers; one, a compatriot in an obsolete cravat, who thinks it a quite unaccountable thing that they don't keep 'London time' on a French railway, and who is made angry by my modestly suggesting the possibility of Paris time being more in their way; the other, a young priest, with a very small bird in a very small cage, who feeds the small bird with a quill, and then puts him up in the network above his head, where he advances twittering, to his front wires, and seems to address me in an electioneering manner. The compatriot (who crossed in the boat, and whom I judge to be some person of distinction, as he was shut up, like a stately species of rabbit, in a private hutch on deck) and the young priest (who joined us at Calais) are soon asleep, and then the bird and I have it all to ourselves.

A stormy night still; a night that sweeps the wires of the electric telegraph with a wild and fitful hand; a night so very stormy, with the added storm of the train-progress through it, that when the Guard comes clambering round to mark the tickets while we are at full speed (a really horrible performance in an express train, though he holds on to the open window by his elbows in the most deliberate manner), he stands in such a whirlwind that I grip him fast by the collar, and feel it next to manslaughter to let him go. Still, when he is gone, the small small bird remains at his front wires feebly twittering to me – twittering and twittering, until, leaning back in my place and looking at him in drowsy fascination, I find that he seems to jog my memory as we rush along.

Uncommercial travels (thus the small small bird) have lain in their idle thriftless way through all this range of swamp and dyke, as through many other odd places; and about here, as you very well know, are the queer old stone farm-houses, approached by draw-bridges, and the windmills that you get at by boats. Here, are the lands where the women hoe and dig, paddling canoe-wise from field to field, and here are the cabarets and other peasant-houses where the stone dove-cotes in the littered yards are as strong as warders' towers in old castles. Here, are the long monotonous miles of canal, with the great Dutch-built barges garishly painted, and the towing girls, sometimes harnessed by the forehead, sometimes by the girdle and the shoulders, not a pleasant sight to see. Scattered through this country are mighty works of VAUBAN,[8] whom you know about, and regiments of such corporals as you heard of once upon a time, and many a blue-eyed Bebelle.[9] Through these flat districts, in the shining summer days, walk those long grotesque files of young novices in enormous shovel hats, whom you re-member blackening the ground checkered by the avenues of leafy trees. And now that Hazebroucke slumbers certain kilometres ahead, recall the summer evening when your dusty feet strolling up from the station tended hap-hazard to a Fair there, where the oldest inhabitants were circling round and round a barrel-organ on hobby-horses, with the greatest gravity, and where the principal show in the Fair was a Religious Richardson's[10] – literally, on its own announcement in great letters, THEATRE RELIGIEUX. In which improving Temple, the dramatic representation was of 'all the interesting events in the life of our Lord, from the Manger to the Tomb'; the principal female character, without any reservation or exception, being at the moment of your arrival, engaged in trimming the external Moderators (as it was growing dusk), while the next principal female character took the money, and the Young Saint John disported himself upside down on the platform.

Looking up at this point to confirm the small small bird in every particular he has mentioned, I find he has ceased to twitter, and has put his head under his wing. Therefore, in my different way I follow the good example.

DRAMATIC MONOLOGUES

SOMEBODY'S LUGGAGE

His Leaving it till called for

THE writer of these humble lines being a Waiter, and having come of a family of Waiters, and owning at the present time five brothers who are all Waiters, and likewise an only sister who is a Waitress, would wish to offer a few words respecting his calling; first having the pleasure of hereby in a friendly manner offering the Dedication of the same unto JOSEPH, much respected Head Waiter at the Slamjam Coffee-house, London, E.C., than which an individual more eminently deserving of the name of man, or a more amenable honour to his own head and heart, whether considered in the light of a Waiter or regarded as a human being, do not exist.

In case confusion should arise in the public mind (which it is open to confusion on many subjects) respecting what is meant or implied by the term Waiter, the present humble lines would wish to offer an explanation. It may not be generally known that the person as goes out to wait, is *not* a Waiter. It may not be generally known that the hand as is called in extra, at the Freemasons' Tavern, or the London, or the Albion, or otherwise, is *not* a Waiter. Such hands may be took on for Public Dinners by the bushel (and you may know them by their breathing with difficulty when in attendance, and taking away the bottle 'ere yet it is half out), but such are *not* Waiters. For, you cannot lay down the tailoring, or the shoemaking, or the brokering, or the green-grocering, or the pictorial periodicalling, or the second-hand wardrobe, or the small fancy, businesses – you cannot lay down those lines of life at your will and pleasure by the half-day or evening, and take up Waitering. You may suppose you can, but you cannot; or you may go so far as to say you do, but you do not. Nor yet can you lay down the gentleman's-service when stimulated by prolonged incompatibility on the part of Cooks (and here it may be remarked that Cooking and Incompatibility will be mostly found united), and take up

Waitering. It has been ascertained that what a gentleman will sit meek under, at home, he will not bear out of doors, at the Slamjam or any similar establishment. Then, what is the inference to be drawn respecting true Waitering? You must be bred to it. You must be born to it.

Would you know how born to it, Fair Reader – if of the adorable female sex? Then learn from the biographical experience of one that is a Waiter in the sixty-first year of his age.

You were conveyed, ere yet your dawning powers were otherwise developed than to harbour vacancy in your inside – you were conveyed, by surreptitious means, into a pantry adjoining the Admiral Nelson, Civic and General Dining Rooms, there to receive by stealth that healthful sustenance which is the pride and boast of the British female constitution. Your mother was married to your father (himself a distant Waiter) in the profoundest secresy; for a Waitress known to be married would ruin the best of businesses – it is the same as on the stage. Hence your being smuggled into the pantry, and that – to add to the infliction – by an unwilling grandmother. Under the combined influence of the smells of roast and boiled, and soup, and gas, and malt liquors, you partook of your earliest nourishment; your unwilling grandmother sitting prepared to catch you when your mother was called and dropped you; your grandmother's shawl ever ready to stifle your natural complainings; your innocent mind surrounded by uncongenial cruets, dirty plates, dish-covers, and cold gravy; your mother calling down the pipe for veals and porks, instead of soothing you with nursery rhymes. Under these untoward circumstances you were early weaned. Your unwilling grandmother, ever growing more unwilling as your food assimilated less, then contracted habits of shaking you till your system curdled, and your food would not assimilate at all. At length she was no longer spared, and could have been thankfully spared much sooner. When your brothers began to appear in succession, your mother retired, left off her smart dressing (she had previously been a smart dresser), and her dark ringlets (which had previously been flowing), and haunted your father late of nights, lying in wait for him, through all weathers, up the shabby court which led to the back door of the Royal Old Dust-Binn (said to have been so named by George the

Fourth), where your father was Head. But the Dust-Binn was going down then, and your father took but little – excepting from a liquid point of view. Your mother's object in those visits was of a housekeeping character, and you was set on to whistle your father out. Sometimes he came out, but generally not. Come or not come, however, all that part of his existence which was unconnected with open Waitering, was kept a close secret, and was acknowledged by your mother to be a close secret, and you and your mother flitted about the court, close secrets both of you, and would scarcely have confessed under torture that you knew your father, or that your father had any name than Dick (which wasn't his name, though he was never known by any other), or that he had kith or kin or chick or child. Perhaps the attraction of this mystery, combined with your father's having a damp compartment to himself, behind a leaky cistern, at the Dust-Binn – a sort of a cellar compartment, with a sink in it, and a smell, and a plate-rack and a bottle-rack, and three windows that didn't match each other or anything else, and no daylight – caused your young mind to feel convinced that you must grow up to be a Waiter too; but you did feel convinced of it, and so did all your brothers, down to your sister. Every one of you felt convinced that you was born to the Waitering. At this stage of your career, what was your feelings one day when your father came home to your mother in open broad daylight – of itself an act of Madness on the part of a Waiter – and took to his bed (leastwise, your mother and family's bed), with the statement that his eyes were devilled kidneys. Physicians being in vain, your father expired, after repeating at intervals for a day and a night, when gleams of reason and old business fitfully illuminated his being, 'Two and two is five. And three is sixpence.' Interred in the parochial department of the neighbouring churchyard, and accompanied to the grave by as many Waiters of long standing as could spare the morning time from their soiled glasses (namely, one), your bereaved form was attired in a white neckankecher, and you was took on from motives of benevolence at The George and Gridiron, theatrical and supper. Here, supporting nature on what you found in the plates (which was as it happened, and but too often thoughtlessly immersed in mustard), and on what you found in the glasses (which rarely went beyond driblets and lemon), by night you dropped asleep standing, till you was cuffed awake, and by day was set to polishing every individual article in the coffee-room. Your couch being sawdust; your counterpane being ashes of cigars. Here, frequently hiding a heavy heart under the smart tie of your white neckankecher (or correctly speaking lower down and more to the left), you picked up the rudiments of knowledge from an extra, by the name of Bishops, and by calling plate-washer, and gradually elevating your mind with chalk on the back of the corner-box-partition, until such time as you used the inkstand when it was out of hand, attained to manhood and to be the Waiter that you find yourself.

I could wish here to offer a few respectful words on behalf of the calling so long the calling of myself and family, and the public interest in which is but too often very limited. We are not generally understood. No, we are not. Allowance enough is not made for us. For, say that we ever show a little drooping listlessness of spirits, or what might be termed indifference or apathy. Put it to yourself what would your own state of mind be, if you was one of an enormous family every member of which except you was always greedy, and in a hurry. Put it to yourself that you was regularly replete with animal food at the slack hours of one in the day and again at nine P.M., and that the repleter you was, the more voracious all your fellow-creatures came in. Put it to yourself that it was your business when your digestion was well on, to take a personal interest and sympathy in a hundred gentlemen fresh and fresh (say, for the sake of argument, only a hundred), whose imaginations was given up to grease and fat and gravy and melted butter, and abandoned to questioning you about cuts of this, and dishes of that – each of 'em going on as if him and you and the bill of fare was alone in the world. Then look what you are expected to know. You are never out, but they seem to think you regularly attend everywhere. 'What's this, Christopher, that I hear about the smashed Excursion Train?' – 'How are they doing at the Italian Opera, Christopher?' – 'Christopher, what are the real particulars of this business at the Yorkshire Bank?' Similarly a ministry gives me more trouble than it gives the Queen. As to Lord Palmerston,[1] the constant and wearing connexion into which I have been brought with his lordship during the last few years, is deserving of a pension. Then look at the Hypocrites we are made, and the lies (white, I hope) that are forced upon us! Why must a sedentary-pursuited Waiter be considered to be a judge of horseflesh, and to have a most tremenjous interest in horse-training and racing? Yet it would be half our little incomes out of our pockets if we didn't take on to have those sporting tastes. It is the same (inconceivable why!) with Farming. Shooting, equally so. I am sure that so regular as the months of August, September, and October come round, I am ashamed of myself in my own private bosom for the way in which I make believe to care whether or not the grouse is strong on the wing (much their wings or drumsticks either signifies to me, uncooked!), and whether the partridges is plentiful among the turnips, and whether the pheasants is shy or bold, or anything else you please to mention. Yet you may see me, or any other Waiter of my standing, holding on by the back of the box and leaning over a gentleman with his purse out and his bill before him, discussing these points in a confidential tone of voice, as if my happiness in life entirely depended on 'em.

I have mentioned our little incomes. Look at the most unreasonable point of all, and the point on which the greatest injustice is done us! Whether it is owing to our always carrying so much change in our right-hand trousers-pocket, and so many halfpence in our coat-tails, or whether it is human nature (which I were loathe to believe), what is meant by the everlasting fable that Head Waiters is rich? How did that fable get into circulation? Who first put it about, and what are the facts to establish the unblushing statement? Come forth, thou slanderer, and refer the public to the Waiter's will in Doctors' Commons supporting thy malignant hiss! Yet this is so commonly dwelt upon – especially by the screws[2] who give Waiters the least – that denial is vain, and we are obliged, for our credit's sake, to carry our heads as if we were going into a business, when of the two we are much more likely to go into a union.[3] There was formerly a screw as frequented the Slamjam ere yet the present writer had quitted that establishment on a question of tea-ing his assistant staff out of his own pocket, which screw carried the taunt to its bitterest heighth. Never soaring above three-pence, and as often as not grovelling on the earth a penny lower, he yet represented the present writer as a large holder of Consols,[4] a lender of money on mortgage, a Capitalist. He has been overheard to dilate to other customers on the allegation that the present writer put out thousands of pounds at interest, in Distilleries and Breweries. 'Well, Christopher,' he would say (having grovelled his lowest on the earth, half a moment before), 'looking out for a House to open, eh? Can't find a business to be disposed of, on a scale as is up to your resources, humph?' To such a dizzy precipice of falsehood has this misrepresentation taken wing, that the well-known and highly-respected OLD CHARLES, long eminent at the West Country Hotel, and by some considered the Father of the Waitering, found himself under the obligation to fall into it through so many years that his own wife (for he had an unbeknown old lady in that capacity towards himself) believed it! And what was the consequence? When he was borne to his grave on the shoulders of six picked Waiters, with six more for change, six more acting as pall-bearers, all keeping step in a pouring shower without a dry eye visible, and a concourse only inferior to Royalty, his pantry and lodgings was equally ransacked high and low for property and none was found! How could it be found, when, beyond his last monthly collection of walking-sticks, umbrellas, and pocket-handkerchiefs (which happened to have been not yet disposed of, though he had ever been through life punctual in clearing off his collections by the month), there was no property existing? Such, however, is the force of this universal libel, that the widow of Old Charles, at the present hour an inmate of the Almshouses of the Cork-Cutters' Company, in Blue Anchor-road (identified sitting at the door of one of 'em, in a clean cap and a Windsor armchair, only last Monday), expects John's hoarded wealth to be found hourly! Nay, ere yet he had succumbed to the grisly dart, and when his portrait was painted in oils, life-size, by subscription of the frequenters of the West Country, to hang over the coffee-room chimney-piece, there were not wanting those who contended that what is termed the accessories of such portrait ought to be the Bank of England out of window, and a strong-box on the table. And but for better-regulated minds contending for a bottle and screw and the attitude of drawing — and carrying their point — it would have been so handed down to posterity.

I am now brought to the title of the present remarks. Having, I hope without offence to any quarter, offered such observations as I felt it my duty to offer, in a free country which has ever dominated the seas, on the general subject, I will now proceed to wait on the particular question.

At a momentous period of my life, when I was off, so far as concerned notice given, with a House that shall be nameless – for the question on which I took my departing stand was a fixed charge for Waiters, and no House as commits itself to that eminently Un-English act of more than foolishness and baseness shall be advertised by me – I repeat, at a momentous crisis when I was off with a House too mean for mention, and not yet on with that to which I have ever since had the honour of being attached in the capacity of Head,* I was casting about what to do next. Then it were that proposals were made to me on behalf of my present establishment. Stipulations were necessary on my part, emendations were necessary on my part; in the end, ratifications ensued on both sides, and I entered on a new career.

We are a bed business, and a coffee-room business. We are not a general dining business, nor do we wish it. In consequence, when diners drop in, we know what to give 'em as will keep 'em away another time. We are a Private Room or Family business also; but Coffee Room principal. Me and the Directory and the Writing Materials and cetrer occupy a place to ourselves: a place fended off up a step or two at the end of the Coffee Room, in what I call the good old-fashioned style. The good old-fashioned style is, that whatever you want, down to a wafer, you must be olely and solely dependent on the Head Waiter for. You must put yourself a new-born Child into his hands. There is no other way in which a business untinged with Continental Vice can be conducted. (It were bootless to add that if languages is required to be jabbered and English is not good enough, both families and gentlemen had better go somewhere else.)

When I began to settle down in this right-principled and well-conducted House, I noticed under the bed in No. 24 B (which it is up a angle off the staircase, and usually put off upon the lowly-minded), a heap of things in a corner. I asked our Head Chambermaid in the course of the day:

*Its name and address at length, with other full particulars, all editorially struck out.

'What are them things in 24 B?'

To which she answered with a careless air:

'Somebody's Luggage.'

Regarding her with a eye not free from severity, I says:

'Whose Luggage?'

Evading my eye, she replied:

'Lor! How should *I* know!'

– Being, it may be right to mention, a female of some pertness, though acquainted with her business.

A Head Waiter must be either Head or Tail. He must be at one extremity or the other of the social scale. He cannot be at the waist of it, or anywhere else but the extremities. It is for him to decide which of the extremities.

On the eventful occasion under consideration, I give Mrs Pratchett so distinctly to understand my decision that I broke her spirit as towards myself, then and there, and for good. Let not inconsistency be suspected on account of my mentioning Mrs Pratchett as 'Mrs', and having formerly remarked that a waitress must not be married. Readers are respectfully requested to notice that Mrs Pratchett was not a waitress, but a chambermaid. Now, a chambermaid *may* be married: if Head, generally is married – or says so. It comes to the same thing as expressing what is customary. (N.B. Mr Pratchett is in Australia, and his address there is 'the Bush'.)

Having took Mrs Pratchett down as many pegs as was essential to the future happiness of all parties, I requested her to explain herself.

'For instance,' I says, to give her a little encouragement, 'who is Somebody?'

'I give you my sacred honour, Mr Christopher,' answers Pratchett, 'that I haven't the faintest notion.'

But for the manner in which she settled her cap-strings, I should have doubted this; but in respect of positiveness it was hardly to be discriminated from an affidavit.

'Then you never saw him?' I followed her up with.

'Nor yet,' said Mrs Pratchett, shutting her eyes and making as if she had just took a pill of unusual circumference – which gave a remarkable force to her denial – 'nor yet any servant in this house. All have been changed, Mr Christopher, within five year, and Somebody left his Luggage here before then.'

Inquiry of Miss Martin yielded (in the language of the Bard of
A 1) 'confirmation strong'. So it had really and truly happened.
Miss Martin is the young lady at the bar as makes out our bills; and
though higher than I could wish, considering her station, is
perfectly well behaved.

Further investigations led to the disclosure that there was a bill
against this Luggage to the amount of two sixteen six. The Luggage
had been lying under the bedstead in 24 B, over six year. The bedstead is a four-poster, with a deal of old hanging and valance, and
is, as I once said, probably connected with more than 24 Bs – which
I remember my hearers was pleased to laugh at, at the time.

I don't know why – when DO we know why? – but this Luggage
laid heavy on my mind. I fell a wondering about Somebody, and
what he had got and been up to. I couldn't satisfy my thoughts why
he should leave so much Luggage against so small a bill. For I had
the Luggage out within a day or two and turned it over, and the
following were the items: – A black portmanteau, a black bag, a
desk, a dressing-case, a brown-paper parcel, a hat-box, and an
umbrella strapped to a walking-stick. It was all very dusty and fluey. I
had our porter up to get under the bed and fetch it out; and though
he habitually wallows in dust – swims in it from morning to night, and
wears a close-fitting waistcoat with black calimanco sleeves for the
purpose – it made him sneeze again, and the throat was that hot with
it, that it was obliged to be cooled with a drink of Allsopp's draft.

The Luggage so got the better of me, that instead of having it
put back when it was well dusted and washed with a wet cloth –
previous to which it was so covered with feathers, that you might
have thought it was turning into poultry, and would by-and-by
begin to Lay – I say, instead of having it put back, I had it carried
into one of my places down stairs. There from time to time I stared
at it and stared at it, till it seemed to grow big and grow little, and
come forward at me and retreat again, and go through all manner
of performances resembling intoxication. When this had lasted
weeks – I may say, months, and not be far out – I one day thought
of asking Miss Martin for the particulars of the Two sixteen six
total. She was so obliging as to extract from it the books – it dating
before her time – and here follows a true copy:

Coffee Room
1856.   No. 4.

		£		
February 2nd.	Pen and paper	£0	0	6
	Port Negus	0	2	0
	Ditto	0	2	0
	Pen and paper	0	0	6
	Tumbler broken.........	0	2	6
	Brandy	0	2	0
	Pen and paper	0	0	6
	Anchovy toast	0	2	6
	Pen and paper	0	0	6
	Bed........................	0	3	0
February 3rd.	Pen and paper	0	0	6
	Breakfast	0	2	6
	„ Broiled ham...	0	2	0
	„ Eggs	0	1	0
	„ Watercresses	0	1	0
	„ Shrimps	0	1	0[6]
	Pen and paper	0	0	6
	Blotting-paper	0	0	6
	Messenger to Paternoster-row and back ...	0	1	6
	Again, when No Answer	0	1	6
	Brandy 2s., Devilled Pork chop 2s.	0	4	0
	Pens and paper	0	1	0
	Messenger to Albemarle-street and back	0	1	0
	Again (detained), when No Answer	0	1	6
	Saltcellar broken..........	0	3	6
	Large Liqueur - glass Orange Brandy	0	1	6
	Dinner, Soup Fish Joint and bird	0	7	6
	Bottle old East India Brown	0	8	0
	Pen and paper	0	0	6
		£2	16	6

Mem.: January 1st, 1857. He went out after dinner, directing Luggage to be ready when he called for it. Never called.

So far from throwing a light upon the subject, this bill appeared to me, if I may so express my doubts, to involve it in a yet more lurid halo. Speculating it over with the Mistress, she informed me that the luggage had been advertised in the Master's time as being to be sold after such and such a day to pay expenses, but no further steps had been taken. (I may here remark that the Mistress is a widow in her fourth year. The Master was possessed of one of those unfortunate constitutions in which Spirits turns to Water, and rises in the ill-starred Victim.)

My speculating it over, not then only but repeatedly, sometimes with the Mistress, sometimes with one, sometimes with another, led up to the Mistress's saying to me – whether at first in joke or in earnest, or half joke and half earnest, it matters not:

'Christopher, I am going to make you a handsome offer.'

(If this should meet her eye – a lovely blue – may she not take it ill my mentioning that if I had been eight or ten year younger, I would have done as much by her! That is, I would have made her *a* offer. It is for others than me to denominate it a handsome one.)

'Christopher, I am going to make you a handsome offer.'

'Put a name to it, ma'am.'

'Look here, Christopher. Run over the articles of Somebody's Luggage. You've got it all by heart, I know.'

'A black portmanteau, ma'am, a black bag, a desk, a dressing-case, a brown-paper parcel, a hat-box, and an umbrella strapped to a walking-stick.'

'All just as they were left. Nothing opened, nothing tampered with.'

'You are right, ma'am. All locked but the brown-paper parcel, and that sealed.'

The Mistress was leaning on Miss Martin's desk at the bar-window, and she taps the open book that lays upon the desk – she has a pretty-made hand, to be sure – and bobs her head over it, and laughs.

'Come,' says she, 'Christopher. Pay me Somebody's bill, and you shall have Somebody's luggage.'

I rather took to the idea from the first moment; but,

'It mayn't be worth the money,' I objected, seeming to hold back.

'That's a Lottery,' says the Mistress, folding her arms upon the book – it ain't her hands alone that's pretty made: the observation extends right up her arms – 'Won't you venture two pound sixteen shillings and sixpence in the Lottery? Why, there's no blanks!' says the Mistress, laughing and bobbing her head again, 'you *must* win. If you lose, you must win! All prizes in this Lottery! Draw a blank, and remember, Gentlemen-Sportsmen, you'll still be entitled to a black portmanteau, a black bag, a desk, a dressing-case, a sheet of brown paper, a hat-box, and an umbrella strapped to a walking-stick!'

To make short of it, Miss Martin come round me, and Mrs Pratchett come round me, and the Mistress she was completely round me already, and all the women in the house come round me, and if it had been Sixteen two instead of Two sixteen, I should have thought myself well out of it. For what can you do when they do come round you?

So I paid the money – down – and such a laughing as there was among 'em! But I turned the tables on 'em regularly, when I said:

'My family name is Blue Beard.[7] I'm going to open Somebody's Luggage all alone in the Secret Chamber, and not a female eye catches sight of the contents!'

Whether I thought proper to have the firmness to keep to this, don't signify, or whether any female eye, and if any how many, was really present when the opening of the Luggage came off. Somebody's Luggage is the question at present: Nobody's eyes, nor yet noses.

What I still look at most, in connexion with that Luggage, is the extraordinary quantity of writing-paper, and all written on! And not our paper neither – not the paper charged in the bill, for we know our paper – so he must have been always at it. And he had crumpled up this writing of his, everywhere, in every part and parcel of his luggage. There was writing in his dressing-case, writing in his boots, writing among his shaving-tackle, writing in his hat-box, writing folded away down among the very whalebones of his umbrella.

His clothes wasn't bad, what there was of 'em. His dressing-case was poor – not a particle of silver stopper – bottle apertures with nothing in 'em, like empty little dog-kennels – and a most searching description of tooth-powder diffusing itself around, as under a deluded mistake that all the chinks in the fittings was divisions in teeth. His clothes I parted with, well enough, to a second-hand dealer not far from St Clement's Danes, in the Strand – him as the officers in the Army mostly dispose of their uniforms to, when hard pressed with debts of honour, if I may judge from their coats and epaulettes diversifying the window, with their backs towards the public. The same party bought in one lot, the portmanteau, the bag, the desk, the dressing-case, the hat-box, the umbrella, strap, and walking-stick. On my remarking that I should have thought those articles not quite in his line, he said: 'No more ith a man'th grandmother, Mithter Chrithtopher; but if any man will bring hith grandmother here, and offer her at a fair trifle below what the'll feth with good luck when the'th thcoured and turned – I'll buy her!'

These transactions brought me home, and, indeed, more than home, for they left a goodish profit on the original investment. And now there remained the writings; and the writings I particular wish to bring under the candid attention of the reader.

I wish to do so without postponement, for this reason. That is to say, namely, viz., i.e., as follows, thus: – Before I proceed to recount the mental sufferings of which I became the prey in consequence of the writings, and before following up that harrowing tale with a statement of the wonderful and impressive catastrophe, as thrilling in its nature as unlooked for in any other capacity, which crowned the ole and filled the cup of unexpectedness to overflowing, the writings themselves ought to stand forth to view. Therefore it is that they now come next. One word to introduce them, and I lay down my pen (I hope, my unassuming pen), until I take it up to trace the gloomy sequel of a mind with something on it.

He was a smeary writer, and wrote a dreadful bad hand. Utterly regardless of ink, he lavished it on every undeserving object – on his clothes, his desk, his hat, the handle of his tooth-brush, his umbrella. Ink was found freely on the coffee-room carpet by No. 4 table, and two blots was on his restless couch. A reference to the document I have given entire, will show that on the morning of the third of February, eighteen 'fifty-six, he procured his no less than fifth pen and paper. To whatever deplorable act of ungovernable composition he immolated those materials obtained from the bar, there is no doubt that the fatal deed was committed in bed, and that it left its evidences but too plainly, long afterwards, upon the pillow-case.

He had put no Heading to any of his writings. Alas! Was he likely to have a Heading without a Head, and where was *his* Head when he took such things into it! The writings are consequently called, here, by the names of the articles of Luggage to which they was found attached. In some cases, such as his Boots, he would appear to have hid the writings: thereby involving his style in greater obscurity. But his Boots was at least pairs – and no two of his writings can put in any claim to be so regarded.

With a low-spirited anticipation of the gloomy state of mind in which it will be my lot to describe myself as having drooped, when I next resume my artless narrative, I will now withdraw. If there should be any flaw in the writings, or anything missing in the writings, it is Him as is responsible – not me. With that observation in justice to myself, I for the present conclude.

His Brown-Paper Parcel

MY works are well known. I am a young man in the Art line. You have seen my works many a time, though it's fifty thousand to one if you have seen me. You say you don't want to see me? You say your interest is in my works and not in me? Don't be too sure about that. Stop a bit.

Let us have it down in black and white at the first go off, so that there may be no unpleasantness or wrangling afterwards. And this is looked over by a friend of mine, a ticket-writer, that is up to literature. I am a young man in the Art line – in the Fine Art line. You have seen my works over and over again, and you have been curious about me, and you think you have seen me. Now, as a safe rule, you never have seen me, and you never do see me, and you never will see me. I think that's plainly put – and it's what knocks me over.

If there's a blighted public character going, I am the party.

It has been remarked by a certain (or an uncertain) philosopher, that the world knows nothing of its greatest men. He might have put it plainer if he had thrown his eye in my direction. He might have put it, that while the world knows something of them that apparently go in and win, it knows nothing of them that really go in and don't win. There it is again in another form – and that's what knocks me over.

Not that it's only myself that suffers from injustice, but that I am more alive to my own injuries than to any other man's. Being, as I have mentioned, in the Fine Art line, and not the Philanthropic line, I openly admit it. As to company in injury, I have company enough. Who are you passing every day at your Competitive Excruciations? The fortunate candidates whose heads and livers you have turned upside-down for life? Not you. You are really passing the Crammers and Coaches. If your principle is right, why don't you turn out tomorrow morning with the keys of your cities on velvet cushions, your musicians playing, and your flags flying, and read addresses to the Crammers and Coaches on your bended knees, beseeching them to come out and govern you? Then, again, as to your public business of all sorts, your Financial statements and your Budgets; the Public knows much, truly, about the real doers of all that! Your Nobles and Right Honourables are first-rate men? Yes, and so is a goose a first-rate bird. But I'll tell you this about the goose; – you'll find his natural flavour disappointing, without stuffing.

Perhaps I am soured by not being popular? But suppose I AM popular. Suppose my works never fail to attract. Suppose that whether they are exhibited by natural light or by artificial, they invariably draw the public. Then no doubt they are preserved in some Collection? No they are not; they are not preserved in any Collection. Copyright? No, nor yet copyright. Anyhow they must be somewhere? Wrong again, for they are often nowhere.

Says you, 'at all events you are in a moody state of mind, my friend.' My answer is, I have described myself as a public character with a blight upon him – which fully accounts for the curdling of the milk in *that* cocoa-nut.

Those that are acquainted with London, are aware of a locality on the Surrey side of the river Thames, called the Obelisk, or more generally, the Obstacle. Those that are not acquainted with London, will also be aware of it, now that I have named it. My lodging is not far from that locality. I am a young man of that easy disposition, that I lie abed till it's absolutely necessary to get up and earn something, and then I lie abed again till I have spent it.

It was on an occasion when I had had to turn to with a view to victuals, that I found myself walking along the Waterloo-road, one evening after dark, accompanied by an acquaintance and fellow-lodger in the gas-fitting way of life. He is very good company, having worked at the theatres, and indeed he has a theatrical turn himself and wishes to be brought out in the character of Othello; but whether on account of his regular work always blacking his face and hands more or less, I cannot say.

'Tom,' he says, 'what a mystery hangs over you!'

'Yes, Mr Click' – the rest of the house generally give him his name, as being first, front, carpeted all over, his own furniture, and if not mahogany, an out-and-out imitation – 'Yes, Mr Click, a mystery does hang over me.'

'Makes you low, you see, don't it?' says he, eyeing me sideways.

'Why yes, Mr Click, there are circumstances connected with it that have,' I yielded to a sigh, 'a lowering effect.'

'Gives you a touch of the misanthrope too, don't it?' says he. 'Well, I'll tell you what. If I was you, I'd shake it off.'

'If I was you, I would, Mr Click; but if you was me, you wouldn't.'

'Ah!' says he, 'there's something in that.'

When we had walked a little further, he took it up again by touching me on the chest.

'You see, Tom, it seems to me as if, in the words of the poet who wrote the domestic drama of the Stranger, you had a silent sorrow there.'[1]

'I have, Mr Click.'

'I hope, Tom,' lowering his voice in a friendly way, 'it isn't coining, or smashing?'[2]

'No, Mr Click. Don't be uneasy.'

'Nor yet forg –' Mr Click checked himself, and added, 'counterfeiting anything, for instance?'

'No, Mr Click. I am lawfully in the Art line – Fine Art line – but I can say no more.'

'Ah! Under a species of star? A kind of a malignant spell? A sort of a gloomy destiny? A cankerworm pegging away at your vitals in secret, as well as I make it out?' said Mr Click, eyeing me with some admiration.

I told Mr Click that was about it, if we came to particulars; and I thought he appeared rather proud of me.

Our conversation had brought us to a crowd of people, the greater part struggling for a front place from which to see something on the pavement, which proved to be various designs executed in coloured chalks on the pavement-stones, lighted by two candles stuck in mud sconces. The subjects consisted of a fine fresh salmon's head and shoulders, supposed to have been recently sent home from the fishmonger's; a moonlight night at sea (in a circle); dead game; scroll-work; the head of a hoary hermit engaged in devout contemplation; the head of a pointer smoking a pipe; and a cherubim, his flesh creased as in infancy, going on a horizontal errand against the wind. All these subjects appeared to me to be exquisitely done.

On his knees on one side of this gallery, a shabby person of modest appearance who shivered dreadfully (though it wasn't at all cold), was engaged in blowing the chalk-dust off the moon, toning the outline of the back of the hermit's head with a bit of leather, and fattening the down-stroke of a letter or two in the writing. I have forgotten to mention that writing formed a part of the composition, and that it also – as it appeared to me – was exquisitely done. It ran as follows, in fine round characters: 'An honest man is the noblest work of God.³ 1 2 3 4 5 6 7 8 9 0. £, s. d. Employment in an office is humbly requested. Honour the Queen. Hunger is a o 9 8 7 6 5 4 3 2 1 sharp thorn.⁴ Chip chop, cherry chop, fol de rol de ri do. Astronomy and mathematics. I do this to support my family.'

Murmurs of admiration at the exceeding beauty of this performance went about among the crowd. The artist having finished his touching (and having spoilt those places), took his seat on the pavement with his knees crouched up very nigh his chin; and halfpence began to rattle in.

'A pity to see a man of that talent brought so low; ain't it?' said one of the crowd to me.

'What he might have done in the coach-painting, or house-decorating!' said another man, who took up the first speaker because I did not.

'Why he writes – alone – like the Lord Chancellor!' said another man.

'Better,' said another. 'I know *his* writing. *He* couldn't support his family this way.'

Then, a woman noticed the natural fluffiness of the hermit's hair, and another woman, her friend, mentioned of the salmon's gills that you could almost see him gasp. Then, an elderly country gentleman stepped forward and asked the modest man how he executed his work? And the modest man took some scraps of brown paper with colours in 'em out of his pockets and showed them. Then a fair-complexioned donkey with sandy hair and spectacles, asked if the hermit was a portrait? To which the modest man, casting a sorrowful glance upon it, replied that it was, to a certain extent, a recollection of his father. This caused a boy to yelp out, 'Is the Pinter a smoking the pipe, your mother?' who was immediately shoved out of view by a sympathetic carpenter with his basket of tools at his back.

At every fresh question or remark, the crowd leaned forward more eagerly, and dropped the halfpence more freely, and the modest man gathered them up more meekly. At last, another elderly gentleman came to the front, and gave the artist his card, to come to his office tomorrow and get some copying to do. The card was accompanied by sixpence, and the artist was profoundly grateful, and, before he put the card in his hat, read it several times by the light of his candles to fix the address well in his mind, in case he should lose it. The crowd was deeply interested by this last incident, and a man in the second row with a gruff voice, growled to the artist, 'You've got a chance in life now, ain't you?' The artist answered (sniffing in a very low-spirited way, however), 'I'm thankful to hope so.' Upon which there was a general chorus of '*You* are all right,' and the halfpence slackened very decidedly.

I felt myself pulled away by the arm, and Mr Click and I stood alone at the corner of the next crossing.

'Why, Tom,' said Mr Click, 'what a horrid expression of face you've got!'

'Have I?' says I.

'Have you?' says Mr Click. 'Why you looked as if you would have his blood.'

'Whose blood?'

'The artist's.'

'The artist's!' I repeated. And I laughed, frantically, wildly, gloomily, incoherently, disagreeably. I am sensible that I did. I know I did.

Mr Click stared at me in a scared sort of a way, but said nothing until we had walked a street's length. He then stopped short, and said, with excitement on the part of his fore-finger:

'Thomas, I find it necessary to be plain with you. I don't like the envious man. I have identified the cankerworm that's pegging away at *your* vitals, and it's envy, Thomas.'

'Is it?' says I.

'Yes, it is,' says he. 'Thomas, beware of envy. It is the green-eyed monster[5] which never did and never will improve each shining hour,[6] but quite the reverse. I dread the envious man, Thomas. I confess that I am afraid of the envious man, when he is so envious as you are. Whilst you contemplated the works of a gifted rival, and whilst you heard that rival's praises, and especially whilst you met his humble glance as he put that card away, your countenance was so malevolent as to be terrific. Thomas, I have heard of the envy of them that follows the Fine Art line, but I never believed it could be what yours is. I wish you well, but I take my leave of you. And if you should ever get into trouble through knifeing – or say, garotting – a brother artist, as I believe you will, don't call me to character, Thomas, or I shall be forced to injure your case.'

Mr Click parted from me with those words, and we broke off our acquaintance.

I became enamoured. Her name was Henerietta. Contending with my easy disposition, I frequently got up to go after her. She also dwelt in the neighbourhood of the Obstacle, and I did fondly hope that no other would interpose in the way of our union.

To say that Henerietta was volatile, is but to say that she was woman. To say that she was in the bonnet-trimming, is feebly to express the taste which reigned predominant in her own.

She consented to walk with me. Let me do her justice to say

that she did so upon trial. 'I am not,' said Henerietta, 'as yet prepared to regard you, Thomas, in any other light than as a friend; but as a friend I am willing to walk with you, on the understanding that softer sentiments may flow.'

We walked.

Under the influence of Henerietta's beguilements, I now got out of bed daily. I pursued my calling with an industry before unknown, and it cannot fail to have been observed at that period, by those most familiar with the streets of London, that there was a larger supply – but hold! The time is not yet come!

One evening in October, I was walking with Henerietta, enjoying the cool breezes wafted over Vauxhall Bridge. After several slow turns, Henerietta gaped frequently (so inseparable from woman is the love of excitement), and said, 'Let's go home by Grosvenor place, Piccadilly, and Waterloo' – localities, I may state for the information of the stranger and the foreigner, well known in London, and the last a Bridge.

'No. Not by Piccadilly, Henerietta,' said I.

'And why not Piccadilly, for goodness' sake?' said Henerietta.

Could I tell her? Could I confess to the gloomy presentiment that overshadowed me? Could I make myself intelligible to her? No.

'I don't like Piccadilly, Henerietta.'

'But I do,' said she. 'It's dark now, and the long rows of lamps in Piccadilly after dark are beautiful. I *will* go to Piccadilly!'

Of course we went. It was a pleasant night, and there were numbers of people in the streets. It was a brisk night, but not too cold, and not damp. Let me darkly observe, it was the best of all nights – FOR THE PURPOSE.

As we passed the garden-wall of the Royal Palace, going up Grosvenor-place, Henerietta murmured,

'I wish I was a Queen!'

'Why so, Henerietta?'

'I would make *you* Something,' said she, and crossed her two hands on my arm, and turned away her head.

Judging from this that the softer sentiments alluded to above had begun to flow, I adapted my conduct to that belief. Thus happily we passed on into the detested thoroughfare of Piccadilly. On the right of that thoroughfare is a row of trees, the railing of the Green Park, and a fine broad eligible piece of pavement.

'O my!' cried Henerietta, presently. 'There's been an accident!'
I looked to the left, and said, 'Where, Henerietta?'

'Not there, stupid,' said she. 'Over by the Park railings. Where the crowd is! O no, it's not an accident, it's something else to look at! What's them lights?'

She referred to two lights twinkling low amongst the legs of the assemblage: two candles on the pavement.

'O do come along!' cried Henerietta, skipping across the road with me; – I hung back, but in vain. 'Do let's look!'

Again, designs upon the pavement. Centre compartment, Mount Vesuvius going it (in a circle), supported by four oval compartments, severally representing a ship in heavy weather, a shoulder of mutton attended by two cucumbers, a golden harvest with distant cottage of proprietor, and a knife and fork after nature; above the centre compartment a bunch of grapes, and over the whole a rainbow. The whole, as it appeared to me, exquisitely done.

The person in attendance on these works of art was in all respects, shabbiness excepted, unlike the former person. His whole appearance and manner denoted briskness. Though threadbare, he expressed to the crowd that poverty had not subdued his spirit or tinged with any sense of shame this honest effort to turn his talents to some account. The writing which formed a part of his composition was conceived in a similarly cheerful tone. It breathed the following sentiments: 'The writer is poor but not despondent. To a British 1 2 3 4 5 6 7 8 9 0 Public he £ s. d. appeals. Honour to our brave Army! And also 0 9 8 7 6 5 4 3 2 1 to our gallant Navy. BRITONS STRIKE the A B C D E F G writer in common chalks would be grateful for any suitable employment HOME![7] HURRAH!' The whole of this writing appeared to me to be exquisitely done.

But this man, in one respect like the last, though seemingly hard at it with a great show of brown paper and rubbers, was only really fattening the down-stroke of a letter here and there, or blowing the loose chalk off the rainbow, or toning the outside edge of the shoulder of mutton. Though he did this with the greatest confidence, he did it (as it struck me) in so ignorant a manner, and so spoilt everything he touched, that when he began upon the purple smoke from the chimney of the distant cottage of the proprietor of the golden harvest (which smoke was beautifully soft), I found myself saying aloud, without considering of it:

'Let that alone, will you?'

'Halloa!' said the man next me in the crowd, jerking me roughly from him with his elbow, 'why didn't you send a telegram? If we had known you was coming, we'd have provided something better for you. You understand the man's work better than he does himself, don't you? Have you made your will? You're too clever to live long.'

'Don't be hard upon the gentleman, sir,' said the person in attendance on the works of art, with a twinkle in his eye as he looked at me, 'he may chance to be an artist himself. If so, sir, he will have a fellow-feeling with me, sir, when I' – he adapted his action to his words as he went on, and gave a smart slap of his hands between each touch, working himself all the time about and about the composition – 'when I lighten the bloom of my grapes – shade off the orange in my rainbow – dot the i of my Britons – throw a yellow-light into my cow-cum-*ber* – insinuate another morsel of fat into my shoulder of mutton – dart another zig-zag flash of lightning at my ship in distress!'

He seemed to do this so neatly, and was so nimble about it, that the halfpence came flying in.

'Thanks, generous public, thanks!' said the professor. 'You will stimulate me to further exertions. My name will be found in the list of British Painters yet. I shall do better than this, with encouragement. I shall indeed.'

'You never can do better than that bunch of grapes,' said Henerietta. 'O, Thomas, them grapes!'

'Not better than *that*, lady? I hope for the time when I shall paint anything but your own bright eyes and lips, equal to life.'

'(Thomas, did you ever?) But it must take a long time, sir,' said Henerietta, blushing, 'to paint equal to that.'

'I was prenticed to it, Miss,' said the young man, smartly touching up the composition – 'prenticed to it in the caves of Spain and Portingale, ever so long and two year over.'

There was a laugh from the crowd; and a new man who had worked himself in next me, said, 'He's a smart chap, too; ain't he?'

'And what a eye!' exclaimed Henerietta, softly.

'Ah! He need have a eye,' said the man.

'Ah! He just need,' was murmured among the crowd.

'He couldn't come that 'ere burning mountain without a eye,' said the man. He had got himself accepted as an authority, somehow, and everybody looked at his finger as it pointed out Vesuvius. 'To come that effect in a general illumination, would require a eye; but to come it with two dips – why it's enough to blind him!'

That impostor pretending not to have heard what was said, now winked to any extent with both eyes at once, as if the strain upon his sight was too much, and threw back his long hair – it was very long – as if to cool his fevered brow. I was watching him doing it, when Henerietta suddenly whispered, 'Oh, Thomas, how horrid you look!' and pulled me out by the arm.

Remembering Mr Click's words, I was confused when I retorted, 'What do you mean by horrid?'

'Oh gracious! Why, you looked,' said Henerietta, 'as if you would have his blood.'

I was going to answer, 'So I would, for twopence – from his nose,' when I checked myself and remained silent.

We returned home in silence. Every step of the way, the softer sentiments that had flowed, ebbed twenty mile an hour. Adapting my conduct to the ebbing, as I had done to the flowing, I let my arm drop limp, so as she could scarcely keep hold of it, and I wished her such a cold good night at parting, that I keep within the bounds of truth when I characterize it as a Rasper.

In the course of the next day, I received the following document:

Henerietta informs Thomas that my eyes are open to you. I must ever wish you well, but walking and us is separated by an unfarmable abyss. One so malignant to superiority – Oh that look at him! – can never never conduct

HENERIETTA.

P.S.—To the altar

Yielding to the easiness of my disposition, I went to bed for a week, after receiving this letter. During the whole of such time, London was bereft of the usual fruits of my labour. When I resumed it, I found that Henerietta was married to the artist of Piccadilly.

Did I say to the artist? What fell words were those, expressive of what a galling hollowness, of what a bitter mockery! I – I – I – am the artist. I was the real artist of Piccadilly, I was the real artist of the Waterloo-road, I am the only artist of all those pavement-subjects which daily and nightly arouse your admiration. I do 'em, and I let 'em out. The man you behold with the papers of chalks and the rubbers, touching up the down-strokes of the writing and shading off the salmon, the man you give the credit to, the man you give the money to, hires – yes! and I live to tell it! – hires those works of art of me, and brings nothing to 'em but the candles.

Such is genius in a commercial country. I am not up to the shivering, I am not up to the liveliness, I am not up to the-wanting-employment-in-an-office move; I am only up to originating and executing the work. In consequence of which you never see me, you think you see me when you see somebody else, and that somebody else is a mere Commercial character. The one seen by self and Mr Click in the Waterloo-road, can only write a single word, and that I taught him, and it's MULTIPLICATION – which you may see him execute upside down, because he can't do it the natural way. The one seen by self and Henerietta by the Green Park railings, can just smear into existence the two ends of a rainbow, with his cuff and a rubber – if very hard put upon making a show – but he could no more come the arch of the rainbow, to save his life, than he could come the moonlight, fish, volcano, shipwreck, mutton, hermit, or any of my most celebrated effects.

To conclude as I began; if there's a blighted public character going, I am the party. And often as you have seen, do see, and will see, my Works, it's fifty thousand to one if you'll ever see me, unless, when the candles are burnt down and the Commercial character is gone, you should happen to notice a neglected young man perseveringly rubbing out the last traces of the pictures, so that nobody can renew the same. That's me.

His Wonderful End

It will have been, 'ere now, perceived that I sold the foregoing writings. From the fact of their being printed in these pages, the inference will, 'ere now, have been drawn by the reader (may I add the gentle reader?) that I sold them to One who never yet.*

Having parted with the writings on most satisfactory terms – for in opening negotiations with the present Journal, was I not placing myself in the hands of One of whom it may be said, in the words of Another† – I resumed my usual functions. But I too soon discovered that peace of mind had fled from a brow which, up to that time, Time had merely took the hair off, leaving an unruffled expanse within.

It were superfluous to veil it, – the brow to which I allude, is my own.

Yes, over that brow, uneasiness gathered like the sable wing of the fabled bird, as – as no doubt will be easily identified by all right-minded individuals. If not, I am unable, on the spur of the moment, to enter into particulars of him. The reflection that the writings must now inevitably get into print, and that He might yet live and meet with them, sat like the Hag of Night upon my jaded form. The elasticity of my spirits departed. Fruitless was the Bottle, whether Wine or Medicine. I had recourse to both, and the effect of both upon my system was witheringly lowering.

In this state of depression, into which I subsided when I first began to revolve what could I ever say if He – the unknown – was to appear in the Coffee Room and demand reparation, I one forenoon in this last November received a turn that appeared to be given me by the finger of Fate and Conscience, hand in hand. I was alone in the Coffee Room and had just poked the fire into a blaze, and was standing with my back to it, trying whether heat would penetrate with soothing influence to the Voice within, when a

---

*The remainder of this complimentary sentence editorially struck out.
†The remainder of this complimentary parenthesis editorially struck out.

young man in a cap, of an intelligent countenance though requiring his hair cut, stood before me.

'Mr Christopher, the Head Waiter?'

'The same.'

The young man shook his hair out of his vision – which it impeded – took a packet from his breast, and, handing it over to me, said, with his eye (or did I dream?) fixed with a lambent meaning on me, 'THE PROOFS.'

Although I smelt my coat-tails singeing at the fire, I had not the power to withdraw them. The young man put the packet in my faltering grasp, and repeated – let me do him the justice to add, with civility:

'THE PROOFS. A. Y. R.'

With those words he departed.

A. Y. R.? And You Remember. Was that his meaning? At Your Risk. Were the letters short for *that* reminder? Anticipate Your Retribution. Did they stand for *that* warning? Outdacious Youth Repent? But no; for that, a O was happily wanting, and the vowel here was a A.

I opened the packet and found that its contents were the foregoing writings printed, just as the reader (may I add the discerning reader?) peruses them. In vain was the reassuring whisper – A. Y. R., All the Year Round – it could not cancel the Proofs. Too appropriate name. The Proofs of my having sold the Writings.

My wretchedness daily increased. I had not thought of the risk I ran, and the defying publicity I put my head into, until all was done, and all was in print. Give up the money to be off the bargain and prevent the publication, I could not. My family was down in the world, Christmas was coming on, a brother in the hospital and a sister in the rheumatics could not be entirely neglected. And it was not only ins in the family that had told on the resources of one unaided Waitering; outs were not wanting. A brother out of a situation, and another brother out of money to meet an acceptance, and another brother out of his mind, and another brother out at New York (not the same, though it might appear so), had really and truly brought me to a stand till I could turn myself round. I got worse and worse in my meditations, constantly reflecting 'The Proofs', and reflecting that when Christmas drew nearer, and the

Proofs were published, there could be no safety from hour to hour but that He might confront me in the Coffee Room, and in the face of day and his country demand his rights.

The impressive and unlooked-for catastrophe towards which I dimly pointed the reader (shall I add, the highly intellectual reader?) in my first remarks, now rapidly approaches.

It was November still, but the last echoes of the Guy-Foxes[2] had long ceased to reverberate. We was slack – several joints under our average mark, and wine of course proportionate. So slack had we become at last, that Beds Nos. 26, 27, 28, and 31 having took their six o'clock dinners and dozed over their respective pints, had drove away in their respective Hansoms for their respective Night Mail-Trains, and left us empty.

I had took the evening paper to No. 6 table – which is warm and most to be preferred – and lost in the all-absorbing topics of the day, had dropped into a slumber. I was recalled to consciousness by the well-known intimation, 'Waiter!' and replying 'Sir!' found a gentleman standing at No. 4 table. The reader (shall I add, the observant reader?) will please to notice the locality of the gentleman – *at No. 4 table.*

He had one of the new-fangled uncollapsable bags in his hand (which I am against, for I don't see why you shouldn't collapse, while you are about it, as your fathers collapsed before you), and he said:

'I want to dine, waiter. I shall sleep here tonight.'

'Very good, sir. What will you take for dinner, sir?'

'Soup, bit of codfish, oyster sauce, and the joint.'

'Thank you, sir.'

I rang the chambermaid's bell; and Mrs Pratchett marched in, according to custom, demurely carrying a lighted flat candle before her, as if she was one of a long, public procession, all the other members of which was invisible.

In the mean while the gentleman had gone up to the mantelpiece, right in front of the fire, and had laid his forehead against the mantelpiece (which is a low one, and brought him into the attitude of leap-frog), and had heaved a tremenjous sigh. His hair was long and lightish; and when he laid his forehead against the mantelpiece, his hair all fell in a dusty fluff together, over his eyes; and when he now turned round and lifted up his head again, it all fell in a dusty fluff together, over his ears. This give him a wild appearance, similar to a blasted heath.

'Oh! The chambermaid, Ah!' He was turning something in his mind. 'To be sure. Yes. I won't go upstairs now, if you will take my bag. It will be enough for the present to know my number. – Can you give me 24 B?'

(O Conscience, what a Adder art thou!)

Mrs Pratchett allotted him the room, and took his bag to it. He then went back before the fire, and fell a biting his nails.

'Waiter!' biting between the words, 'give me,' bite, 'pen and paper; and in five minutes,' bite, 'let me have, if you please,' bite, 'a', bite, 'Messenger.'

Unmindful of his waning soup, he wrote and sent off six notes before he touched his dinner. Three were City; three West-End. The City letters were to Cornhill, Ludgate-hill, and Farringdon-street. The West-End letters were to Great Marlborough-street, New Burlington-street, and Piccadilly. Everybody was systematically denied at every one of the six places, and there was not a vestige of any answer. Our light porter whispered to me when he came back with that report, 'All Booksellers.'

But before then, he had cleared off his dinner, and his bottle of wine. He now – mark the concurrence with the document formerly given in full! – knocked a plate of biscuits off the table with his agitated elber (but without breakage), and demanded boiling brandy-and-water.

Now fully convinced that it was Himself, I perspired with the utmost freedom. When he become flushed with the heated stimulant referred to, he again demanded pen and paper, and passed the succeeding two hours in producing a manuscript, which he put in the fire when completed. He then went up to bed, attended by Mrs Pratchett. Mrs Pratchett (who was aware of my emotions) told me on coming down that she had noticed his eye rolling into every corner of the passages and staircase, as if in search of his Luggage, and that, looking back as she shut the door of 24 B, she perceived him with his coat already thrown off immersing himself bodily under the bedstead, like a chimley-sweep before the application of machinery.

The next day – I forbear the horrors of that night – was a very foggy day in our part of London, insomuch that it was necessary to light the Coffee Room gas. We were still alone, and no feverish words of mine can do justice to the fitfulness of his appearance as he sat at No. 4 table, increased by there being something wrong with the meter.

Having again ordered his dinner he went out, and was out for the best part of two hours. Inquiring on his return whether any of the answers had arrived, and receiving an unqualified negative, his instant call was for mulligatawny, the cayenne pepper, and orange brandy.

Feeling that the mortal struggle was now at hand, I also felt that I must be equal to him, and with that view resolved that whatever he took, I would take. Behind my partition, but keeping my eye on him over the curtain, I therefore operated on Mulligatawny, Cayenne Pepper, and Orange Brandy. And at a later period of the day, when he again said 'Orange Brandy,' I said so too, in a lower tone, to George, my Second Lieutenant (my First was absent on leave), who acts between me and the bar.

Throughout that awful day, he walked about the Coffee Room continually. Often he came close up to my partition, and then his eye rolled within, too evidently in search of any signs of his Luggage. Half-past six came, and I laid his cloth. He ordered a bottle of old Brown. I likewise ordered a bottle of old Brown. He drank his. I drank mine (as nearly as my duties would permit) glass for glass against his. He topped with coffee and a small glass. I topped with coffee and a small glass. He dozed. I dozed. At last, 'Waiter!' – and he ordered his bill. The moment was now at hand when we two must be locked in the deadly grapple.

Swift as the arrow from the bow, I had formed my resolution; in other words, I had hammered it out between nine and nine. It was, that I would be the first to open up the subject with a full acknowledgement, and would offer any gradual settlement within my power. He paid his bill (doing what was right by attendance) with his eye rolling about him to the last, for any tokens of his Luggage. One only time our gaze then met, with the lustrous fixedness (I believe I am correct in imputing that character to it?) of the well-known Basilisk.[3] The decisive moment had arrived.

With a tolerable steady hand, though with humility, I laid The Proofs before him.

'Gracious Heavens!' he cries out, leaping up and catching hold of his hair. 'What's this! Print!'

'Sir,' I replied, in a calming voice, and bending forward, 'I humbly acknowledge to being the unfortunate cause of it. But I hope, sir, that when you have heard the circumstances explained, and the innocence of my intentions—'

To my amazement, I was stopped short by his catching me in both his arms, and pressing me to his breast-bone; where I must confess to my face (and particular nose) having undergone some temporary vexation from his wearing his coat buttoned high up, and his buttons being uncommon hard.

'Ha, ha, ha!' he cries, releasing me with a wild laugh, and grasping my hand. 'What is your name, my Benefactor?'

'My name, sir?' (I was crumpled, and puzzled to make him out), 'is Christopher; and I hope, sir, that as such when you've heard my ex—'

'In print!' he exclaims again, dashing the proofs over and over as if he was bathing in them. 'In print!! Oh, Christopher! Philanthropist! Nothing can recompense you – but what sum of money would be acceptable to you?'

I had drawn a step back from him, or I should have suffered from his buttons again.

'Sir, I assure you I have been already well paid, and—'

'No, no, Christopher! Don't talk like that! What sum of money would be acceptable to you, Christopher? Would you find twenty pounds acceptable, Christopher?'

However great my surprise, I naturally found words to say, 'Sir, I am not aware that the man was ever yet born without more than the average amount of water on the brain, as would *not* find twenty pound acceptable. But – extremely obliged to you, sir, I'm sure;' for he had tumbled it out of his purse and crammed it in my hand in two bank-notes; 'but I could wish to know, sir, if not intruding, how I have merited this liberality?'

'Know then, my Christopher,' he says, 'that from boyhood's hour, I have unremittingly and unavailingly endeavoured to get into print. Know, Christopher, that all the Booksellers alive – and several dead – have refused to put me into print. Know, Christopher, that I have written unprinted Reams. But they shall be read to you, my friend and brother. You sometimes have a holiday?'

Seeing the great danger I was in, I had the presence of mind to answer, 'Never!' To make it more final, I added, 'Never! Not from the cradle to the grave.'

'Well,' says he, thinking no more about that, and chuckling at his proofs again. 'But I am in print! The first flight of ambition emanating from my father's lowly cot, is realized at length! The golden bowl' – he was getting on – 'struck by the magic hand, has emitted a complete and perfect sound! When did this happen, my Christopher?'

'Which happen, sir?'

'This,' he held it out at arm's length to admire it, 'this Per-rint.'

When I had given him my detailed account of it, he grasped me by the hand again, and said:

'Dear Christopher, it should be gratifying to you to know that you are an instrument in the hands of Destiny. Because you *are*.'

A passing Something of a melancholy cast put it into my head to shake it, and to say: 'Perhaps we all are.'

'I don't mean that,' he answered; 'I don't take that wide range; I confine myself to the special case. Observe me well, my Christopher! Hopeless of getting rid, through any effort of my own, of any of the manuscripts among my Luggage – all of which, send them where I would, were always coming back to me – it is now some seven years since I left that Luggage here, on the desperate chance, either that the too too faithful manuscripts would come back to me no more, or that some one less accursed than I might give them to the world. You follow me, my Christopher?'

'Pretty well, sir.' I followed him so far as to judge that he had a weak head, and that the Orange the Boiling and Old Brown combined was beginning to tell. (The old Brown being heady, is best adapted to seasoned cases.)

'Years elapsed, and those compositions slumbered in dust. At length, Destiny, choosing her agent from all mankind, sent You here, Christopher, and lo! the Casket was burst asunder, and the Giant was free!'

He made hay of his hair after he said this, and he stood a tiptoe.

'But,' he reminded himself in a state of great excitement, 'we must sit up all night, my Christopher. I must correct these Proofs for the press. Fill all the inkstands and bring me several new pens.'

He smeared himself and he smeared the Proofs, the night through, to that degree, that when Sol give him warning to depart (in a four-wheeler[4]), few could have said which was them, and which was him, and which was blots. His last instructions was, that I should instantly run and take his corrections to the office of the present Journal. I did so. They most likely will not appear in print, for I noticed a message being brought round from Beaufort Printing House[5] while I was a throwing this concluding statement on paper, that the ole resources of that establishment was unable to make out what they meant. Upon which a certain gentleman in company, as I will not more particularly name – but of whom it will be sufficient to remark, standing on the broad basis of a wave-girt isle, that whether we regard him in the light of – * laughed, and put the corrections in the fire.

*The remainder of this complimentary parenthesis editorially struck out.

MRS LIRRIPER'S LODGINGS

How Mrs Lirriper carried on the Business

WHOEVER would begin to be worried with letting Lodgings that wasn't a lone woman with a living to get is a thing inconceivable to me my dear, excuse the familiarity but it comes natural to me in my own little room when wishing to open my mind to those that I can trust and I should be truly thankful if they were all mankind but such is not so, for have but a Furnished bill in the window and your watch on the mantelpiece and farewell to it if you turn your back for but a second however gentlemanly the manners, nor is being of your own sex any safeguard as I have reason in the form of sugar-tongs to know, for that lady (and a fine woman she was) got me to run for a glass of water on the plea of going to be confined, which certainly turned out true but it was in the Station-House.

Number Eighty-one Norfolk Street Strand – situated midway between the City and St James's and within five minutes' walk of the principal places of public amusement – is my address. I have rented this house many years as the parish rate-books will testify and I could wish my landlord was as alive to the fact as I am myself, but no bless you not a half a pound of paint to save his life nor so much my dear as a tile upon the roof though on your bended knees.

My dear you never have found Number Eighty-one Norfolk Street Strand advertised in Bradshaw's Railway Guide and with the blessing of Heaven you never will or shall so find it. Some there are who do not think it lowering themselves to make their names that cheap and even going the lengths of a portrait of the house not like it with a blot in every window and a coach and four at the door, but what will suit Wozenham's lower down on the other side of the way will not suit me, Miss Wozenham having her opinions and me having mine, though when it comes to systematic underbidding capable of being proved on oath in a court of justice and taking the form of 'If Mrs Lirriper names eighteen shillings a week, I name fifteen and six' it then comes to a settlement between yourself and your conscience supposing for the sake of argument your name to be Wozenham which I am well aware it is not or my opinion of you would be greatly lowered, and as to airy bedrooms and a night-porter in constant attendance the less said the better, the bedrooms being stuffy and the porter stuff.

It is forty years ago since me and my poor Lirriper got married at St Clement's Danes where I now have a sitting in a very pleasant pew with genteel company and my own hassock and being partial to evening service not too crowded. My poor Lirriper was a hand-some figure of a man with a beaming eye and a voice as mellow as a musical instrument made of honey and steel, but he had ever been a free liver being in the commercial travelling line and travelling what he called a limekiln road – 'a dry road, Emma my dear,' my poor Lirriper says to me 'where I have to lay the dust with one drink or another all day long and half the night, and it wears me Emma' – and this led to his running through a good deal and might have run through the turnpike too when that dreadful horse that never would stand still for a single instant set off, but for its being night and the gate shut and consequently took his wheel my poor Lirriper and the gig smashed to atoms and never spoke afterwards. He was a handsome figure of a man and a man with a jovial heart and a sweet temper, but if they had come up then they never could have given you the mellowness of his voice, and indeed I consider photographs wanting in mellowness as a general rule and making you look like a new-ploughed field.

My poor Lirriper being behindhand with the world and being buried at Hatfield church in Hertfordshire, not that it was his native place but that he had a liking for the Salisbury Arms where we went upon our wedding-day and passed as happy a fortnight as ever happy was, I went round to the creditors and I says 'Gentle-men I am acquainted with the fact that I am not answerable for my late husband's debts but I wish to pay them for I am his lawful wife and his good name is dear to me. I am going into the Lodgings gentlemen as a business and if I prosper every farthing that my late husband owed shall be paid for the sake of the love I bore him, by this right hand.' It took a long time to do but it was done, and the silver cream-jug which is between ourselves and the bed and the mattress in my room up-stairs (or it would have found legs so sure as ever the Furnished bill was up) being presented by the gentlemen engraved 'To Mrs Lirriper a mark of grateful respect for her honourable conduct' gave me a turn which was too much for my feelings, till Mr Betley which at that time had the parlours and loved his joke says 'Cheer up Mrs Lirriper, you should feel as if it was only your christening and they were your godfathers and godmothers which did promise for you.' And it brought me round, and I don't mind confessing to you my dear that I then put a sandwich and a drop of sherry in a little basket and went down to Hatfield churchyard outside the coach and kissed my hand and laid it with a kind of a proud and swelling love on my husband's grave, though bless you it had taken me so long to clear his name that my wedding ring was worn quite fine and smooth when I laid it on the green green waving grass.

I am an old woman now and my good looks are gone but that's me my dear over the plate-warmer and considered like in the times when you used to pay two guineas on ivory and took your chance pretty much how you came out, which made you very careful how you left it about afterwards because people were turned so red and uncomfortable by mostly guessing it was somebody else quite different, and there was once a certain person that had put his money in a hop business that came in one morning to pay his rent and his respects being the second floor that would have taken it down from its hook and put it in his breast pocket – you understand my dear – for the L, he says, of the original – only there was no mellowness in *his* voice and I wouldn't let him, but his opinion of it you may gather from his saying to it 'Speak to me Emma!' which was far from a rational observation no doubt but still a tribute to its being a likeness, and I think myself it *was* like me when I was young and wore that sort of stays.

But it was about the Lodgings that I was intending to hold forth and certainly I ought to know something of the business having been in it so long, for it was early in the second year of my married life that I lost my poor Lirriper and I set up at Islington directly afterwards and afterwards came here, being two houses and eight and thirty years and some losses and a deal of experience.

Girls are your first trial after fixtures and they try you even worse than what I call the Wandering Christians, though why *they* should roam the earth looking for bills and then coming in and viewing the apartments and stickling about terms and never at all wanting them or dreaming of taking them being already provided, is a mystery I should be thankful to have explained if by any miracle it could be. It's wonderful they live so long and thrive so on it but I suppose the exercise makes it healthy, knocking so much and going from house to house and up and down stairs all day, and then their pretending to be so particular and punctual is a most astonishing thing, looking at their watches and saying 'Could you give me the refusal of the rooms till twenty minutes past eleven the day after tomorrow in the forenoon, and supposing it to be considered essential by my friend from the country could there be a small iron bedstead put in the little room upon the stairs?' Why when I was new to it my dear I used to consider before I promised and to make my mind anxious with calculations and to get quite wearied out with disappointments, but now I says 'Certainly by all means' well knowing it's a Wandering Christian and I shall hear no more about it, indeed by this time I know most of the Wandering Christians by sight as well as they know me, it being the habit of each individual revolving round London in that capacity to come back about twice a year, and it's very remarkable that it runs in families and the children grow up to it, but even were it otherwise I should no sooner hear of the friend from the country which is a certain sign than I should nod and say to myself You're a Wandering Christian, though whether they are (as I *have* heard) persons of small property with a taste for regular employment and frequent change of scene I cannot undertake to tell you.

Girls as I was beginning to remark are one of your first and your lasting troubles, being like your teeth which begin with convulsions and never cease tormenting you from the time you cut them till they cut you, and then you don't want to part with them which seems hard but we must all succumb or buy artificial, and even where you get a will nine times out of ten you'll get a dirty face with it and naturally lodgers do not like good society to be shown in with a smear of black across the nose or a smudgy eyebrow. Where they pick the black up is a mystery I cannot solve, as in the case of the willingest girl that ever came into a house half starved poor thing, a girl so willing that I called her Willing Sophy down upon her knees scrubbing early and late and ever cheerful but always smiling with a black face. And I says to Sophy 'Now Sophy my good girl have a regular day for your stoves and keep the width of the Airy[1] between yourself and the blacking and do not brush your hair with the bottoms of the saucepans and do not meddle with the snuffs of the candles and it stands to reason that it can no longer be' yet there it was and always on her nose, which turning up and being broad at the end seemed to boast of it and caused warning from a steady gentleman and excellent lodger with break-fast by the week but a little irritable and use of a sitting-room when required, his words being 'Mrs Lirriper I have arrived at the point of admitting that the Black is a man and a brother,[2] but only in a natural form and when it can't be got off.' Well consequently I put poor Sophy on to other work and forbid her answering the door or answering a bell on any account but she was so unfortunately willing that nothing would stop her flying up the kitchen stairs whenever a bell was heard to tingle. I put it to her 'Oh Sophy Sophy for goodness goodness sake where does it come from?' To which that poor unlucky willing mortal bursting out crying to see me so vexed replied 'I took a deal of black into me ma'am when I was a small child, being much neglected and I think it must be, that it works out,' so it continuing to work out of that poor thing and not having another fault to find with her I says Sophy 'what do you seriously think of my helping you away to New South Wales where it might not be noticed?' Nor did I ever repent the money which was well spent, for she married the ship's cook on the voyage (himself a Mulotter) and did well and lived happy, and so far as ever I heard it was *not* noticed in a new state of society to her dying day.

In what way Miss Wozenham lower down on the other side of the way reconciled it to her feelings as a lady (which she is not) to entice Mary Anne Perkinsop from my service is best known to herself, I do not know and I do not wish to know how opinions are formed at Wozenham's on any point. But Mary Anne Perkinsop although I behaved handsomely to her and she behaved un-handsomely to me was worth her weight in gold as overawing lodgers without driving them away, for lodgers would be far more sparing of their bells with Mary Anne than I ever knew them be with Maid or Mistress, which is a great triumph especially when accompanied with a cast in the eye and a bag of bones, but it was the steadiness of her way with them through her father's having failed in Pork. It was Mary Anne's looking so respectable in her person and being so strict in her spirits that conquered the tea-and-sugarest gentleman (for he weighed them both in a pair of scales every morning) that I have ever had to deal with and no lamb grew meeker, still it afterwards came round to me that Miss Wozenham happening to pass and seeing Mary Anne take in the milk of a milkman that made free in a rosy-faced way (I think no worse of him) with every girl in the street but was quite frozen up like the statue at Charing Cross by her, saw Mary Anne's value in the lodging business and went as high as one pound per quarter more, consequently Mary Anne with not a word betwixt us says 'If *you* will provide yourself Mrs Lirriper in a month from this day *I* have already done the same,' which hurt me and I said so, and she then hurt me more by insinuating that her father having failed in Pork had laid her open to it.

My dear I do assure you it's a harassing thing to know what kind of girls to give the preference to, for if they are lively they get bell'd off their legs and if they are sluggish you suffer from it yourself in complaints and if they are sparkling-eyed they get made love to and if they are smart in their persons they try on your Lodger's bonnets and if they are musical I defy you to keep them away from bands and organs, and allowing for any difference you like in their heads their heads will be always out of window just the same. And then what the gentlemen like in girls the ladies don't, which is fruitful hot water for all parties, and then there's temper though such a temper as Caroline Maxey's I hope not often. A good-looking black-eyed girl was Caroline and a comely-made girl to your cost when she did break out and laid about her, as took place first and last through a new-married couple come to see London in the first floor and the lady very high and it *was* supposed not liking the good looks of Caroline having none of her own to spare, but anyhow she did try Caroline though that was no excuse. So one afternoon Caroline comes down into the kitchen flushed and flashing, and she says to me 'Mrs Lirriper that woman in the first has aggravated me past bearing', I says 'Caroline keep your temper', Caroline says with a curdling laugh 'Keep my temper? You're right Mrs Lirriper, so I will. Capital D her!' bursts out Caroline (you might have struck me into the centre of the earth with a feather when she said it) 'I'll give her a touch of the temper that *I* keep!' Caroline downs with her hair my dear, screeches and rushes upstairs, I following as fast as my trembling legs could bear me, but before I got into the room the dinner cloth and pink and white service all dragged off upon the floor with a crash and the new married couple on their backs in the firegrate, him with the shovel and tongs and a dish of cucumber across him and a mercy it was summer-time. 'Caroline' I says 'be calm', but she catches off my cap and tears it in her teeth as she passes me, then pounces on the new married lady makes her a bundle of ribbons takes her by the two ears and knocks the back of her head upon the carpet Murder screaming all the time Policemen running down the street and Wozenham's windows (judge of my feelings when I came to know it) thrown up and Miss Wozenham calling out from the balcony with crocodile's tears 'It's Mrs Lirriper been overcharging some-body to madness – she'll be murdered – I always thought so – Pleeseman save her!' My dear four of them and Caroline behind the chiffoniere attacking with the poker and when disarmed prize fighting with her double fists, and down and up and up and down and dreadful! But I couldn't bear to see the poor young creature roughly handled and her hair torn when they got the better of her, and I says 'Gentlemen Policemen pray remember that her sex is the sex of your mothers and sisters and your sweethearts, and God bless them and you!' And there she was sitting down on the ground handcuffed, taking breath against the skirting-board and them cool with their coats in strips, and all she says was 'Mrs Lirriper I am sorry as ever I touched *you*, for you're a kind motherly old thing,' and it made me think that I had often wished I had been a mother indeed and how would my heart have felt if I had been the mother of that girl! Well you know it turned out at the Police-office that she had done it before, and she had her clothes away and was sent to prison, and when she was to come out I trotted off to the gate in the evening with just a morsel of jelly in that little basket of mine to give her a mite of strength to face the world again, and there I met with a very decent mother waiting for her son through bad company and a stubborn one he was with his half boots not laced. So out came Caroline and I says 'Caroline come along with me and sit down under the wall where it's retired and eat a little trifle that I have brought with me to do you good' and she throws her arms round my neck and says sobbing 'O why were you never a mother when there are such mothers as there are!' she says, and in half a minute more she begins to laugh and says 'Did I really tear your cap to shreds?' and when I told her 'You certainly did so Caroline' she laughed again and said while she patted my face 'Then why do you wear such queer old caps you dear old thing? If you hadn't worn such queer old caps I don't think I should have done it even then.' Fancy the girl! Nothing could get out of her what she was going to do except O she would do well enough, and we parted she being very thankful and kissing my hands, and I never more saw or heard of that girl, except that I shall always believe that a very genteel cap which was brought anonymous to me one Saturday night in an oilskin basket by a most impertinent young sparrow of a monkey whistling with dirty shoes on the clean steps and playing the harp on the Airy railings with a hoop-stick came from Caroline.

What you lay yourself open to my dear in the way of being the object of uncharitable suspicions when you go into the Lodging business I have not the words to tell you, but never was I so dishonourable as to have two keys nor would I willingly think it even of Miss Wozenham lower down on the other side of the way sincerely hoping that it may not be, though doubtless at the same time money cannot come from nowhere and it is not reason to suppose that Bradshaws put it in for love be it blotty as it may. It *is* a hardship hurting to the feelings that Lodgers open their minds so wide to the idea that you are trying to get the better of them and shut their minds so close to the idea that they are trying to get the betters of you, but as Major Jackman says to me 'I know the ways of this circular world Mrs Lirriper, and that's one of 'em all round it' and many is the little ruffle in my mind that the Major has smoothed, for he is a clever man who has seen much. Dear dear, thirteen years have passed though it seems but yesterday since I was sitting with my glasses on at the open front parlour window one evening in

August (the parlours being then vacant) reading yesterday's paper my eyes for print being poor though still I am thankful to say a long sight at a distance, when I hear a gentleman come posting across the road and up the street in a dreadful rage talking to himself in a fury and d'ing and c'ing somebody. 'By George!' says he out loud and clutching his walking-stick, 'I'll go to Mrs Lirriper's. Which is Mrs Lirriper's?' Then looking round and seeing me he flourishes his hat right off his head as if I had been the queen and he says 'Excuse the intrusion Madam, but pray Madam can you tell me at what number in this street there resides a well-known and much-respected lady by the name of Lirriper?' A little flustered though I must say gratified I took off my glasses and curtseyed and said 'Sir, Mrs Lirriper is your humble servant.' 'As-tonishing!' says he. 'A million pardons! Madam, may I ask you to have the kindness to direct one of your domestics to open the door to a gentleman in search of apartments, by the name of Jackman?' I had never heard the name but a politer gentleman I never hoped to see, for says he 'Madam I am shocked at your opening the door yourself to no worthier a fellow than Jemmy Jackman. After you Madam. I never precede a lady.' Then he comes into the parlours and he sniffs and he says 'Hah! These are parlours! Not musty cupboards' he says 'but parlours, and no smell of coal-sacks.' Now my dear it having been remarked by some inimical to the whole neighbourhood that it always smells of coal-sacks which might prove a drawback to Lodgers if encouraged, I says to the Major gently though firmly that I think he is referring to Arundel or Surrey or Howard but not Norfolk. 'Madam' says he 'I refer to Wozenham's lower down over the way – Madam you can form no notion what Wozenham's is – Madam it is a vast coal-sack, and Miss Wozenham has the principles and manners of a female heaver – Madam from the manner in which I have heard her mention you I know she has no appreciation of a lady, and from the manner in which she has conducted herself towards me I know she has no appreciation of a gentleman – Madam my name is Jackman – should you require any other reference than what I have already said, I name the Bank of England – perhaps you know it!' Such was the beginning of the Major's occupying the parlours and from that hour to this the same and a most obliging Lodger and punctual in all respects except one irregular which I need not particularly specify, but made up for by his being a protection and at all times ready to fill in the papers of the Assessed Taxes and Juries and that, and once collared a young man with the drawing-room clock under his cloak, and once on the parapets with his own hands and blankets put out the kitchen chimney and afterwards attending the summons made a most eloquent speech against the Parish before the magistrates and saved the engine,[3] and ever quite the gentleman though passionate. And certainly Miss Wozenham's detaining the trunks and umbrella was not in a liberal spirit though it may have been according to her rights in law or an act I would myself have stooped to, the Major being so much the gentleman that though he is far from tall he seems almost so when he has his shirt frill out and his frock-coat on and his hat with the curly brims, and in what service he was I cannot truly tell you my dear whether Militia or Foreign, for I never heard him even name himself as Major but always simple 'Jemmy Jackman' and once soon after he came when I felt it my duty to let him know that Miss Wozenham had put it about that he was no Major and I took the liberty of adding 'which you are sir' his words were 'Madam at any rate I am not a Minor, and sufficient for the day is the evil thereof'[4] which cannot be denied to be the sacred truth, nor yet his military ways of having his boots with only the dirt brushed off taken to him in the front parlour every morning on a clean plate and varnishing them himself with a little sponge and a saucer and a whistle in a whisper so sure as ever his breakfast is ended, and so neat his ways that it never soils his linen which is scrupulous though more in quality than quantity, neither that nor his moustachios which to the best of my belief are done at the same time and which are as black and shining as his boots, his head of hair being a lovely white.

It was the third year nearly up of the Major's being in the parlours that early one morning in the month of February when Parliament was coming on and you may therefore suppose a number of impostors were about ready to take hold of anything they could get, a gentleman and lady from the country came in to view the Second, and I well remember that I had been looking out of window and had watched them and the heavy sleet driving down the street together looking for bills. I did not quite take to the face of the gentleman though he was good-looking too but the lady was a very pretty young thing and delicate, and it seemed too rough for her to be out at all though she had only come from the Adelphi Hotel which would not have been much above a quarter of a mile if the weather had been less severe. Now it did so happen my dear that I had been forced to put five shillings weekly additional on the second in consequence of a loss from running away full-dressed as if going out to a dinner-party, which was very artful and had made me rather suspicious taking it along with Parliament, so when the gentleman proposed three months certain and the money in advance and leave then reserved to renew on the same terms for six months more, I says I was not quite certain but that I might have engaged myself to another party but would step down stairs and look into it if they would take a seat. They took a seat and I went down to the handle of the Major's door that I had already began to consult finding it a great blessing, and I knew by his whistling in a whisper that he was varnishing his boots which was generally considered private, however he kindly calls out 'If it's you, Madam, come in,' and I went in and told him.

'Well, Madam,' says the Major rubbing his nose – as I did fear at the moment with the black sponge but it was only his knuckle, he being always neat and dexterous with his fingers – 'well, Madam, I suppose you would be glad of the money?'

I was delicate of saying 'Yes' too out, for a little extra colour rose into the Major's cheeks and there was irregularity which I will not particularly specify in a quarter which I will not name.

'I am of the opinion, Madam,' says the Major 'that when money is ready for you – when it is ready for you Mrs Lirriper – you ought to take it. What is there against it, Madam, in this case up-stairs?'

'I really cannot say there is anything against it sir, still I thought I would consult you.'

'You said a newly-married couple, I think, Madam?' says the Major.

I says 'Ye-es. Evidently. And indeed the young lady mentioned to me in a casual way that she had not been married many months.'

The Major rubbed his nose again and stirred the varnish round and round in its little saucer with his piece of sponge and took to his whistling in a whisper for a few moments. Then he says 'You would call it a Good Let, Madam?'

'Oh certainly a Good Let sir.'

'Say they renew for the additional six months. Would it put you about very much Madam if – if the worst was to come to the worst?' said the Major.

'Well I hardly know,' I says to the Major. 'It depends upon circumstances. Would *you* object Sir for instance?'

'I?' says the Major. 'Object? Jemmy Jackman? Mrs Lirriper close with the proposal.'

So I went up-stairs and accepted, and they came in next day which was Saturday and the Major was so good as to draw up a Memorandum of an agreement in a beautiful round hand and expressions that sounded to me equally legal and military, and Mr Edson signed it on the Monday morning and the Major called upon Mr Edson on the Tuesday and Mr Edson called upon the Major on the Wednesday and the Second and the parlours were as friendly as could be wished.

The three months paid for had run out and we had got without any fresh overtures as to payment into May my dear, when there came an obligation upon Mr Edson to go a business expedition right across the Isle of Man, which fell quite unexpected on that pretty little thing and is not a place that according to my views is particularly in the way to anywhere at any time but that may be a matter of opinion. So short a notice was it that he was to go next day, and dreadfully she cried poor pretty and I am sure I cried too when I saw her on the cold pavement in the sharp east wind – it being a very backward spring that year – taking a last leave of him with her pretty bright hair blowing this way and that and her arms clinging round his neck and him saying 'There there there! Now let me go Peggy.' And by that time it was plain that what the Major had been so accommodating as to say he would not object to happening in the house, would happen in it, and I told her as much,when he was gone while I comforted her with my arm up the staircase, for I says 'You will soon have others to keep up for my pretty and you must think of that.'

His letter never came when it ought to have come and what she went through morning after morning when the postman brought none for her the very postman himself compassionated when she ran down to the door, and yet we cannot wonder at its being calculated to blunt the feelings to have all the trouble of other people's letters and none of the pleasure and doing it oftener in the mud and mizzle than not and at a rate of wages more resembling Little Britain than Great. But at last one morning when she was too poorly to come running down stairs he says to me with a pleased look in his face that made me next to love the man in his uniform coat though he was dripping wet 'I have taken you first in the street this morning Mrs Lirriper, for here's the one for Mrs Edson.' I went up to her bedroom with it fast as ever I could go, and she sat up in bed when she saw it and kissed it and tore it open and then a blank stare came upon her. 'It's very short!' she says lifting her large eyes to my face. 'O Mrs Lirriper it's very short!' I says 'My dear Mrs Edson no doubt that's because your husband hadn't time to write more just at that time.' 'No doubt, no doubt,' says she, and puts her two hands on her face and turns round in her bed.

I shut her softly in and I crept down stairs and I tapped at the Major's door, and when the Major having his thin slices of bacon in his own Dutch oven saw me he came out of his chair and put me down on the sofa. 'Hush!' says he, 'I see something's the matter. Don't speak – take time.' I says 'O Major I am afraid there's cruel work up-stairs.' 'Yes yes' says he 'I had begun to be afraid of it – take time.' And then in opposition to his own words he rages out frightfully, and says 'I shall never forgive myself Madam, that I, Jemmy Jackman, didn't see it all that morning – didn't go straight up-stairs when my boot-sponge was in my hand – didn't force it down his throat – and choke him dead with it on the spot!'

The Major and me agreed when we came to ourselves that just at present we could do no more than take on to suspect nothing and use our best endeavours to keep that poor young creature quiet, and what I ever should have done without the Major when it got about among the organ-men that quiet was our object is unknown, for he made lion and tiger war upon them to that degree that without seeing it I could not have believed it was in any gentleman to have such a power of bursting out with fire-irons walking-sticks water-jugs coals potatoes off his table the very hat off his head, and at the same time so furious in foreign languages that they would stand with their handles half turned fixed like the Sleeping Ugly – for I cannot say Beauty.[5]

Ever to see the postman come near the house now gave me such a fear that it was a reprieve when he went by, but in about another ten days or a fortnight he says again 'Here's one for Mrs Edson. – Is she pretty well?' 'She is pretty well postman, but not well enough to rise so early as she used' which was so far gospel-truth.

I carried the letter in to the Major at his breakfast and I says tottering 'Major I have not the courage to take it up to her.'

'It's an ill-looking villain of a letter,' says the Major.

'I have not the courage Major' I says again in a tremble 'to take it up to her.'

After seeming lost in consideration for some moments the Major says, raising his head as if something new and useful had occurred to his mind 'Mrs Lirriper, I shall never forgive myself that I, Jemmy Jackman, didn't go straight up-stairs that morning when my boot-sponge was in my hand – and force it down his throat – and choke him dead with it.'

'Major' I says a little hasty 'you didn't do it which is a blessing, for it would have done no good and I think your sponge was better employed on your own honourable boots.'

So we got to be rational, and planned that I should tap at her bedroom door and lay the letter on the mat outside and wait on the upper landing for what might happen, and never was gunpowder cannon-balls or shells or rockets more dreaded than that dreadful letter was by me as I took it to the second floor.

A terrible loud scream sounded through the house the minute after she had opened it, and I found her on the floor lying as if her life was gone. My dear I never looked at the face of the letter which was lying open by her, for there was no occasion.

Everything I needed to bring her round the Major brought up with his own hands, besides running out to the chemist's for what was not in the house and likewise having the fiercest of all his many skirmishes with a musical instrument representing a ball-room I do not know in what particular country and company waltzing in and out at folding-doors with rolling eyes. When after a long time I saw her coming to, I slipped on the landing till I heard her cry, and then I went in and says cheerily 'Mrs Edson you're not well my dear and it's not to be wondered at,' as if I had not been in before. Whether she believed or disbelieved I cannot say and it would signify nothing if I could, but I stayed by her for hours and then she God ever blesses me! and says she will try to rest for her head is bad.

'Major,' I whispers, looking in at the parlours, 'I beg and pray of you don't go out.'

The Major whispers 'Madam, trust me I will do no such a thing. How is she?'

I says 'Major the good Lord above us only knows what burns and rages in her poor mind. I left her sitting at her window. I am going to sit at mine.'

It came on afternoon and it came on evening. Norfolk is a delightful street to lodge in – provided you don't go lower down – but of a summer evening when the dust and waste paper lie in it and stray children play in it and a kind of a gritty calm and bake settles on it and a peal of church-bells is practising in the neighbourhood it is a trifle dull, and never have I seen it since at such a time and never shall I see it ever more at such a time without seeing the dull June evening when that forlorn young creature sat at her open corner window on the second and me at my open corner window (the other corner) on the third. Something merciful, something wiser and better far than my own self, had moved me while it was yet light to sit in my bonnet and shawl, and as the shadows fell and the tide rose I could sometimes – when I put out my head and looked at her window below – see that she leaned out a little looking down the street. It was just settling dark when I saw *her* in the street.

So fearful of losing sight of her that it almost stops my breath while I tell it, I went down stairs faster than I ever moved in all my life and only tapped with my hand at the Major's door in passing it and slipping out. She was gone already. I made the same speed down the street and when I came to the corner of Howard-street I saw that she had turned it and was there plain before me going towards the west. O with what a thankful heart I saw her going along!

She was quite unacquainted with London and had very seldom been out for more than an airing in our own street where she knew two or three little children belonging to neighbours and had sometimes stood among them at the end of the street looking at the water. She must be going at hazard I knew, still she kept the by-streets quite correctly as long as they would serve her, and then turned up into the Strand. But at every corner I could see her head turned one way, and that way was always the river way.

It may have been only the darkness and quiet of the Adelphi that caused her to strike into it but she struck into it much as readily as if she had set out to go there, which perhaps was the case. She went straight down to the Terrace and along it and looked over the iron rail, and I often woke afterwards in my own bed with the horror of seeing her doing it. The desertion of the wharf below and the flowing of the high water there seemed to settle her purpose. She looked about as if to make out the way down, and she struck out the right way or the wrong way – I don't know which, for I don't know the place before or since – and I followed her the way she went.

It was noticeable that all this time she never once looked back. But there was now a great change in the manner of her going, and instead of going at a steady quick walk with her arms folded before her, – among the dark dismal arches she went in a wild way with her arms opened wide, as if they were wings and she was flying to her death.

We were on the wharf and she stopped. I stopped. I saw her hands at her bonnet-strings, and I rushed between her and the brink and took her round the waist with both my arms. She might have drowned me, I felt then, but she could never have got quit of me.

Down to that moment my mind had been all in a maze and not half an idea had I had in it what I should say to her, but the instant I touched her it came to me like magic and I had my natural voice and my senses and even almost my breath.

'Mrs Edson!' I says 'My dear! Take care. How ever did you lose your way and stumble on a dangerous place like this? Why you must have come here by the most perplexing streets in all London. No wonder you are lost, I am sure. And this place too! Why I thought nobody ever got here, except me to order my coals and the Major in the parlours to smoke his cigar!' – for I saw that blessed man close by, pretending to it.

'Hah – Hah – Hum!' coughs the Major.

'And good gracious me' I says, 'why here he is!'

'Halloa! who goes there!' says the Major in a military manner.

'Well!' I says, 'if this don't beat everything! Don't you know us Major Jackman?'

'Halloa!' says the Major. 'Who calls on Jemmy Jackman?' (and more out of breath he was, and did it less like life, than I should have expected).

'Why here's Mrs Edson Major' I says, 'strolling out to cool her poor head which has been very bad, has missed her way and got lost, and Goodness knows where she might have got to but for me coming here to drop an order into my coal merchant's letter-box and you coming here to smoke your cigar! – And you really are not well enough my dear' I says to her 'to be half so far from home without me. – And your arm will be very acceptable I am sure Major' I says to him 'and I know she may lean upon it as heavy as she likes.' And now we had both got her – thanks be Above! – one on each side.

She was all in a cold shiver and she so continued till I laid her on her own bed, and up to the early morning she held me by the hand and moaned and moaned 'O wicked, wicked, wicked!' But when at last I made believe to droop my head and be overpowered with a dead sleep, I heard that poor young creature give such touching and such humble thanks for being preserved from taking her own life in her madness that I thought I should have cried my eyes out on the counterpane and I knew she was safe.

Being well enough to do and able to afford it, me and the Major laid our little plans next day while she was asleep worn out, and so I says to her as soon as I could do it nicely:

'Mrs Edson my dear, when Mr Edson paid me the rent for these further six months – '

She gave a start and I felt her large eyes look at me, but I went on with it and with my needlework.

'– I can't say that I am quite sure I dated the receipt right. Could you let me look at it?'

She laid her frozen cold hand upon mine and she looked through me when I was forced to look up from my needlework, but I had taken the precaution of having on my spectacles.

'I have no receipt' says she.

'Ah! Then he has got it' I says in a careless way. 'It's of no great consequence. A receipt's a receipt.'

From that time she always had hold of my hand when I could spare it which was generally only when I read to her, for of course she and me had our bits of needlework to plod at and neither of us was very handy at those little things, though I am still rather proud of my share in them too considering. And though she took to all I read to her, I used to fancy that next to what was taught upon the Mount she took most of all to His gentle compassion for us poor women and to His young life and to how His mother was proud of him and treasured His sayings in her heart.[6] She had a grateful look in her eyes that never never never will be out of mine until they are closed in my last sleep, and when I chanced to look at her without thinking of it I would always meet that look, and she would often offer me her trembling lip to kiss, much more like a little affectionate half-broken-hearted child than ever I can imagine any grown person.

One time the trembling of this poor lip was so strong and her tears ran down so fast that I thought she was going to tell me all her woe, so I takes her two hands in mine and I says:

'No my dear not now, you had best not try to do it now. Wait for better times when you have got over this and are strong, and then you shall tell me whatever you will. Shall it be agreed?'

With our hands still joined she nodded her head many times, and she lifted my hands and put them to her lips and to her bosom.

'Only one word now my dear' I says. 'Is there any one?'

She looked inquiringly 'Any one?'

'That I can go to?'

She shook her head.

'No one that I can bring?'

She shook her head.

'No one is wanted by *me* my dear. Now that may be considered past and gone.'

Not much more than a week afterwards – for this was far on in the time of our being so together – I was bending over at her bedside with my ear down to her lips, by turns listening for her breath and looking for a sign of life in her face. At last it came in a solemn way – not in a flash but like a kind of pale faint light brought very slow to the face.

She said something to me that had no sound in it, but I saw she asked me:

'Is this death?'

And I says 'Poor dear poor dear, I think it is.'

Knowing somehow that she wanted me to move her weak right hand, I took it and laid it on her breast and then folded her other hand upon it, and she prayed a good good prayer and I joined in it poor me though there were no words spoke. Then I brought the baby in its wrappers from where it lay, and I says:

'My dear this is sent to a childless old woman. This is for me to take care of.'

The trembling lip was put up towards my face for the last time, and I dearly kissed it.

'Yes my dear' I says. 'Please God! Me and the Major.'

I don't know how to tell it right, but I saw her soul brighten and leap up, and get free and fly away in the grateful look.

* * *

So this is the why and wherefore of its coming to pass my dear that we called him Jemmy, being after the Major his own godfather with Lirriper for a surname being after myself, and never was a dear child such a brightening thing in a Lodgings or such a playmate to his grandmother as Jemmy to this house and me, and always good and minding what he was told (upon the whole) and soothing for the temper and making everything pleasanter except when he grew old enough to drop his cap down Wozenham's Airy and they wouldn't hand it up to him, and being worked into a state I put on my best bonnet and gloves and parasol with the child in my hand and I says 'Miss Wozenham I little thought ever to have entered *your* house but unless my grandson's cap is instantly restored, the laws of this country regulating the property of the Subject shall at length decide betwixt yourself and me, cost what it may.' With a sneer upon her face which did strike me I must say as being expressive of two keys but it may have been a mistake and if there is any doubt let Miss Wozenham have the full benefit of it as is but right, she rang the bell and she says 'Jane, is there a street-child's old cap down our Airy?' I says 'Miss Wozenham before your housemaid answers that question you must allow me to inform you to your face that my grandson is *not* a street-child and is *not* in the habit of wearing old caps. In fact' I says 'Miss Wozenham I am far from sure that my grandson's cap may not be newer than your own' which was perfectly savage in me, her lace being the commonest machine-make washed and torn besides, but I had been put into a state to begin with fomented by impertinence. Miss Wozenham says red in the face 'Jane you heard my question, is there any child's cap down our Airy?' 'Yes Ma'am' says Jane 'I think I did see some such rubbish a lying there.' 'Then' says Miss Wozenham 'let these visitors out, and then throw up that worthless article out of my premises.' But here the child who had been staring at Miss Wozenham with all his eyes and more, frowns down his little eyebrows purses up his little mouth puts his chubby legs far apart turns his little dimpled fists round and round slowly over one another like a little coffee-mill, and says to her 'Oo impdent to mi Gran, me tut oor hi!' 'Oh!' says Miss Wozenham looking down scornfully at the Mite 'this is not a street-child is it not! Really!' I bursts out laughing and I says 'Miss Wozenham if this an't a pretty sight to you I don't envy your feelings and I wish you good day. Jemmy come along with Gran.' And I was still in the best of humours though his cap came flying up into the street as if it had been just turned on out of the water-plug, and I went home laughing all the way, all owing to that dear boy.

The miles and miles that me and the Major have travelled with Jemmy in the dusk between the lights are not to be calculated, Jemmy driving on the coach-box which is the Major's brass-bound writing-desk on the table, me inside in the easy-chair and the Major Guard up behind with a brown-paper horn doing it really wonderful. I do assure you my dear that sometimes when I have taken a few winks in my place inside the coach and have come half awake by the flashing light of the fire and have heard that precious pet driving and the Major blowing up behind to have the change of horses ready when we got to the Inn, I have half believed we were on the old North Road that my poor Lirriper knew so well. Then to see that child and the Major both wrapped up getting down to warm their feet and going stamping about and having glasses of ale out of the paper match-boxes on the chimney-piece is to see the Major enjoying it fully as much as the child I am very sure, and it's equal to any play when Coachee opens the coach-door to look in at me inside and say 'Wery 'past that 'tage. – 'Prightened old lady?'

But what my inexpressible feelings were when we lost that child can only be compared to the Major's which were not a shade better, through his straying out at five years old and eleven o'clock in the forenoon and never heard of by word or sign or deed till half-past nine at night, when the Major had gone to the Editor of the Times newspaper to put in an advertisement, which came out next day four and twenty hours after he was found, and which I mean always carefully to keep in my lavender drawer as the first printed account of him. The more the day got on, the more I got distracted and the Major too and both of us made worse by the composed ways of the police though very civil and obliging and what I must call their obstinacy in not entertaining the idea that he was stolen. 'We mostly find Mum' says the sergeant who came round to comfort me, which he didn't at all and he had been one of the private constables in Caroline's time to which he referred in his opening words when he said 'Don't give way to uneasiness in your mind Mum, it'll all come as right as my nose did when I got the same barked by that young woman in your second floor' – says this sergeant 'we mostly find Mum as people ain't over anxious to have what I may call second-hand children. *You'll* get him back Mum.' 'O but my dear good sir' I says clasping my hands and wringing them and clasping them again 'he is such an uncommon child!' 'Yes Mum' says the sergeant, 'we mostly find that too Mum. The question is what his clothes were worth.' 'His clothes' I says 'were not worth much sir for he had only got his playing-dress on, but the dear child! – ' 'All right Mum' says the sergeant. '*You'll* get him back, Mum. And even if he'd had his best clothes on, it wouldn't come to worse than his being found wrapped up in a cabbage-leaf, a shivering in a lane.' His words pierced my heart like daggers and daggers, and me and the Major ran in and out like wild things all day long till the Major returning from his interview with the Editor of the Times at night rushes into my little room hysterical and squeezes my hand and wipes his eyes and says 'Joy joy – officer in plain clothes came up on the steps as I was letting myself in – compose your feelings – Jemmy's found.' Consequently I fainted away and when I came to, embraced the legs of the officer

in plain clothes who seemed to be taking a kind of a quiet inventory
in his mind of the property in my little room with brown whiskers,
and I says 'Blessings on you sir where is the Darling!' and he says
'In Kennington Station House.' I was dropping at his feet Stone at
the image of that Innocence in cells with murderers when he adds
'He followed the Monkey.' I says deeming it slang language 'Oh
sir explain for a loving grandmother what Monkey!' He says 'him
in the spangled cap with the strap under the chin, as won't keep on
– him as sweeps the crossings[7] on a round table and don't want to
draw his sabre more than he can help.' Then I understood it all and
most thankfully thanked him, and me and the Major and him drove
over to Kennington and there we found our boy lying quite comfortable before a blazing fire having sweetly played himself to sleep
upon a small accordion nothing like so big as a flat iron which they
had been so kind as to lend him for the purpose and which it appeared had been stopped upon a very young person.

My dear the system upon which the Major commenced and as I
may say perfected Jemmy's learning when he was so small that if
the dear was on the other side of the table you had to look under it
instead of over it to see him with his mother's own bright hair in
beautiful curls, is a thing that ought to be known to the Throne and
Lords and Commons and then might obtain some promotion for
the Major which he well deserves and would be none the worse for
(speaking between friends) L. S. D.-ically.[8] When the Major first
undertook his learning he says to me:

'I'm going Madam' he says 'to make our child a Calculating Boy.'

'Major' I says, 'you terrify me and may do the pet a permanent
injury you would never forgive yourself.'

'Madam,' says the Major, 'next to my regret that when I had my
boot-sponge in my hand, I didn't choke that scoundrel with it – on
the spot – '

'There! For Gracious sake,' I interrupts, 'let his conscience find
him without sponges.'

' – I say next to that regret, Madam,' says the Major 'would be
the regret with which my breast', which he tapped, 'would be sur-
charged if this fine mind was not early cultivated. But mark me
Madam', says the Major holding up his forefinger 'cultivated on a
principle that will make it a delight.'

'Major' I says 'I will be candid with you and tell you openly that if ever I find the dear child fall off in his appetite I shall know it is his calculations and shall put a stop to them at two minutes' notice. Or if I find them mounting to his head' I says, 'or striking any ways cold to his stomach or leading to anything approaching flabbiness in his legs, the result will be the same, but Major you are a clever man and have seen much and you love the child and are his own godfather, and if you feel a confidence in trying try.'

'Spoken Madam' says the Major 'like Emma Lirriper. All I have to ask Madam, is, that you will leave my godson and myself to make a week or two's preparations for surprising you, and that you will give me leave to have up and down any small articles not actually in use that I may require from the kitchen.'

'From the kitchen Major?' I says half feeling as if he had a mind to cook the child.

'From the kitchen' says the Major, and smiles and swells, and at the same time looks taller.

So I passed my word and the Major and the dear boy were shut up together for half an hour at a time through a certain while, and never could I hear anything going on betwixt them but talking and laughing and Jemmy clapping his hands and screaming out numbers, so I says to myself 'it has not harmed him yet' nor could I on examining the dear find any signs of it anywhere about him which was likewise a great relief. At last one day Jemmy brings me a card in joke in the Major's neat writing 'The Messrs Jemmy Jackman' for we had given him the Major's other name too 'request the honour of Mrs Lirriper's company at the Jackman Institution in the front parlour this evening at five, military time, to witness a few slight feats of elementary arithmetic.' And if you'll believe me there in the front parlour at five punctual to the moment was the Major behind the Pembroke table with both leaves up and a lot of things from the kitchen tidily set out on old newspapers spread atop of it, and there was the Mite stood up on a chair with his rosy cheeks flushing and his eyes sparkling clusters of diamonds.

'Now Gran' says he, 'oo tit down and don't oo touch ler poople' – for he saw with every one of those diamonds of his that I was going to give him a squeeze.

'Very well sir' I says 'I am obedient in this good company I am

303

sure.' And I sits down in the easy-chair that was put for me, shaking my sides.

But picture my admiration when the Major going on almost as quick as if he was conjuring sets out all the articles he names, and says, 'Three saucepans, an Italian iron,⁹ a hand-bell, a toasting-fork, a nutmeg-grater, four pot-lids, a spice-box, two egg-cups, and a chopping-board – how many?' and when that Mite instantly cries 'Fifteen, tut down tive and carry ler 'toppin-board' and then claps his hands draws up his legs and dances on his chair!

My dear with the same astonishing ease and correctness him and the Major added up the tables chairs and sofy, the picters fender and fire-irons their own selves me and the cat and the eyes in Miss Wozenham's head, and whenever the sum was done Young Roses and Diamonds claps his hands and draws up his legs and dances on his chair.

The pride of the Major! ('*Here's* a mind Ma'am!' he says to me behind his hand.)

Then he says aloud, 'We now come to the next elementary rule: which is called – '

'Umtraction!' cries Jemmy.

'Right' says the Major. 'We have here a toasting-fork, a potato in its natural state, two pot-lids, one egg-cup, a wooden spoon, and two skewers, from which it is necessary for commercial purposes to subtract a sprat-gridiron, a small pickle-jar, two lemons, one pepper-castor, a blackbeetle-trap, and a knob of the dresser-drawer – what remains?'

'Toatin-fork!' cries Jemmy.

'In numbers how many?' says the Major.

'One!' cries Jemmy.

('*Here's* a boy, Ma'am?' says the Major to me, behind his hand.)

Then the Major goes on:

'We now approach the next elementary rule: which is entitled – '

'Tickleication' cries Jemmy.

'Correct' says the Major.

But my dear to relate to you in detail the way in which they multiplied fourteen sticks of firewood by two bits of ginger and a larding-needle,¹⁰ or divided pretty well everything else there was on the table by the heater of the Italian iron and a chamber candle-stick, and got a lemon over, would make my head spin round and round and round as it did at the time. So I says 'if you'll excuse my addressing the chair Professor Jackman I think the period of the lecture has now arrived when it becomes necessary that I should take a good hug of this young scholar.' Upon which Jemmy calls out from his station on the chair 'Gran oo open oor arms and me'll make a 'pring into 'em.' So I opened my arms to him as I had opened my sorrowful heart when his poor young mother lay a dying, and he had his jump and we had a good long hug together and the Major prouder than any peacock says to me behind his hand, 'You need not let him know it Madam' (which I certainly need not for the Major was quite audible) 'but he is a boy!'·

In this way Jemmy grew and grew and went to day-school and continued under the Major too, and in summer we were as happy as the days were lor.g and in winter we were as happy as the days were short and there seemed to rest a Blessing on the Lodgings for they as good as Let themselves and would have done it if there had been twice the accommodation, when sore and hard against my will I one day says to the Major.

'Major you know what I am going to break to you. Our boy must go to boarding-school.'

It was a sad sight to see the Major's countenance drop, and I pitied the good soul with all my heart.

'Yes Major' I says 'though he is as popular with the Lodgers as you are yourself and though he is to you and me what only you and me know, still it is in the course of things and Life is made of partings and we must part with our Pet.'

Bold as I spoke, I saw two Majors and half a dozen fireplaces, and when the poor Major put one of his neat bright-varnished boots upon the fender and his elbow on his knee and his head upon his hand and rocked himself a little to and fro, I was dreadfully cut up.

'But' says I clearing my throat 'you have so well prepared him Major – he has had such a Tutor in you – that he will have none of the first drudgery to go through. And he is so clever besides that he'll soon make his way to the front rank.'

'He is a boy' says the Major – having sniffed – 'that has not his like on the face of the earth.'

'True as you say Major, and it is not for us merely for our own sakes to do anything to keep him back from being a credit and an ornament wherever he goes and perhaps even rising to be a great man, is it Major? He will have all my little savings when my work is done (being all the world to me) and we must try to make him a wise man and a good man, mustn't we Major?'

'Madam' says the Major rising 'Jemmy Jackman is becoming an older file than I was aware of, and you put him to shame. You are thoroughly right Madam. You are simply and undeniably right. – And if you'll excuse me, I'll take a walk.'

So the Major being gone out and Jemmy being at home, I got the child into my little room here and I took his mother's own curls in my hand and I spoke to him loving and serious. And when I had reminded the darling how that he was now in his tenth year and when I had said to him about his getting on in life pretty much what I had said to the Major I broke to him how that we must have this same parting, and there I was forced to stop for there I saw of a sudden the well remembered lip with its tremble, and it so brought back that time! But with the spirit that was in him he controlled it soon and he says gravely nodding through his tears, 'I understand Gran – I know it *must* be, Gran – go on Gran, don't be afraid of *me*.' And when I had said all that ever I could think of, he turned his bright steady face to mine and he says just a little broken here and there 'You shall see Gran that I can be a man and that I can do anything that is grateful and loving to you – and if I don't grow up to be what you would like to have me – I hope it will be – because I shall die.' And with that he sat down by me and I went on to tell him of the school of which I had excellent recommendations and where it was and how many scholars and what games they played as I had heard and what length of holidays, to all of which he listened bright and clear. And so it came that at last he says 'And now dear Gran let me kneel down here where I have been used to say my prayers and let me fold my face for just a minute in your gown and let me cry, for you have been more than father – more than mother – more than brothers sisters friends – to me!' And so he did cry and I too and we were both much the better for it.

From that time forth he was true to his word and ever blithe and ready, and even when me and the Major took him down into Lincolnshire he was far the gayest of the party though for sure and certain he might easily have been that, but he really was and put life into us only when it came to the last Good-by, he says with a wistful look 'You wouldn't have me not really sorry would you Gran?' and when I says 'No dear, Lord forbid!' he says 'I am glad of that!' and ran in out of sight.

But now that the child was gone out of the Lodgings the Major fell into a regularly moping state. It was taken notice of by all the Lodgers that the Major moped. He hadn't even the same air of being rather tall that he used to have, and if he varnished his boots with a single gleam of interest it was as much as he did.

One evening the Major came into my little room to take a cup of tea and a morsel of buttered toast and to read Jemmy's newest letter which had arrived that afternoon (by the very same postman more than middle-aged upon the Beat now), and the letter raising him up a little I says to the Major:

'Major you mustn't get into a moping way.'

The Major shook his head. 'Jemmy Jackman Madam,' he says with a deep sigh, 'is an older file than I thought him'.

'Moping is not the way to grow younger Major.'

'My dear Madam,' says the Major, 'is there *any* way of growing younger?'

Feeling that the Major was getting rather the best of that point I made a diversion to another.

'Thirteen years! Thir-teen years! Many Lodgers have come and gone, in the thirteen years that you have lived in the parlours Major.'

'Hah!' says the Major warming. 'Many Madam, many.'

'And I should say you have been familiar with them all?'

'As a rule (with its exceptions like all rules) my dear Madam' says the Major, 'they have honoured me with their acquaintance, and not unfrequently with their confidence.'

Watching the Major as he drooped his white head and stroked his black moustachios and moped again, a thought which I think must have been going about looking for an owner somewhere dropped into my old noddle if you will excuse the expression.

'The walls of my Lodgings' I says in a casual way – for my dear it is of no use going straight at a man who mopes – 'might have something to tell, if they could tell it.'

The Major neither moved nor said anything but I saw he was attending with his shoulders my dear – attending with his shoulders to what I said. In fact I saw that his shoulders were struck by it.

'The dear boy was always fond of story-books' I went on, like as if I was talking to myself. 'I am sure this house – his own home – might write a story or two for his reading one day or another.'

The Major's shoulders gave a dip and a curve and his head came up in his shirt-collar. The Major's head came up in his shirt-collar as I hadn't seen it come up since Jemmy went to school.

'It is unquestionable that in intervals of cribbage and a friendly rubber, my dear Madam,' says the Major, 'and also over what used to be called in my young times – in the salad days[11] of Jemmy Jackman – the social glass, I have exchanged many a reminiscence with your Lodgers.'

My remark was – I confess I made it with the deepest and artfullest of intentions – 'I wish our dear boy had heard them!'

'Are you serious Madam?' asks the Major starting and turning full round.

'Why not Major?'

'Madam' says the Major, turning up one of his cuffs, 'they shall be written for him.'

'Ah! Now you speak' I says giving my hands a pleased clap. 'Now you are in a way out of moping Major!'

'Between this and my holidays – I mean the dear boy's' says the Major turning up his other cuff, 'a good deal may be done towards it.'

'Major you are a clever man and you have seen much and not a doubt of it.'

'I'll begin,' says the Major looking as tall as ever he did, 'to-morrow.'

My dear the Major was another man in three days and he was himself again in a week and he wrote and wrote and wrote with his pen scratching like rats behind the wainscot, and whether he had many grounds to go upon or whether he did at all romance I cannot tell you, but what he has written is in the left-hand glass closet of the little bookcase close behind you, and if you'll put your hand in you'll find it come out heavy in lumps sewn together and being beautifully plain and unknown Greek and Hebrew to myself and me quite wakeful, I shall take it as a favour if you'll read out loud and read on.

How the Parlours added a few words

I have the honour of presenting myself by the name of Jackman. I esteem it a proud privilege to go down to posterity through the instrumentality of the most remarkable boy that ever lived – by the name of JEMMY JACKMAN LIRRIPER – and of my most worthy and most highly respected friend, Mrs Emma Lirriper, of Eighty-one, Norfolk-street, Strand, in the County of Middlesex, in the United Kingdom of Great Britain and Ireland.

It is not for me to express the rapture with which we received that dear and eminently remarkable boy, on the occurrence of his first Christmas holidays. Suffice it to observe that when he came flying into the house with two splendid prizes (Arithmetic, and Exemplary Conduct), Mrs Lirriper and myself embraced with emotion, and instantly took him to the Play, where we were all three admirably entertained.

Nor, is it to render homage to the virtues of the best of her good and honoured sex – whom, in deference to her unassuming worth, I will only here designate by the initials E. L. – that I add this record to the bundle of papers with which our, in a most distinguished degree, remarkable boy has expressed himself delighted, before re-consigning the same to the left-hand glass closet of Mrs Lirriper's little bookcase.

Neither, is it to obtrude the name of the old original super-annuated obscure Jemmy Jackman, once (to his degradation) of Wozenham's, long (to his elevation) of Lirriper's. If I could be consciously guilty of that piece of bad taste, it would indeed be a work of supererogation, now that the name is borne by JEMMY JACKMAN LIRRIPER.

No. I take up my humble pen to register a little record of our strikingly remarkable boy, which my poor capacity regards as presenting a pleasant little picture of the dear boy's mind. The picture may be interesting to himself when he is a man.

Our first re-united Christmas-day was the most delightful one we have ever passed together. Jemmy was never silent for five minutes, except in church-time. He talked as we sat by the fire, he talked when we were out walking, he talked as we sat by the fire again, he talked incessantly at dinner, though he made a dinner almost as remarkable as himself. It was the spring of happiness in his fresh young heart flowing and flowing, and it fertilized (if I may be allowed so bold a figure) my much-esteemed friend, and J – J – the present writer.

There were only we three. We dined in my esteemed friend's little room, and our entertainment was perfect. But everything in the establishment is, in neatness, order, and comfort, always perfect. After dinner, our boy slipt away to his old stool at my esteemed friend's knee, and there, with his hot chesnuts and his glass of brown sherry (really, a most excellent wine!) on a chair for a table, his face outshone the apples in the dish.

We talked of these jottings of mine, which Jemmy had read through and through by that time; and so it came about that my esteemed friend remarked, as she sat smoothing Jemmy's curls:

'And as you belong to the house too, Jemmy, – and so much more than the Lodgers, having been born in it – why, your story ought to be added to the rest, I think, one of these days.'

Jemmy's eyes sparkled at this, and he said, 'So *I* think, Gran.'

Then, he sat looking at the fire, and then he began to laugh, in a sort of confidence with the fire, and then he said, folding his arms across my esteemed friend's lap and raising his bright face to hers:

'Would you like to hear a boy's story, Gran?'

'Of all things,' replied my esteemed friend.

'Would you, godfather?'

'Of all things,' I too replied.

'Well then,' said Jemmy, 'I'll tell you one.'

Here, our indisputably remarkable boy gave himself a hug, and laughed again, musically, at the idea of his coming out in that new line. Then, he once more took the fire into the same sort of confidence as before, and began:

'Once upon a time, When pigs drank wine, And monkeys chewed tobaccer, 'Twas neither in your time nor mine, But that's no macker –'

'Bless the child!' cried my esteemed friend, 'what's amiss with his brain!'

'It's poetry, Gran,' returned Jemmy, shouting with laughter. 'We always begin stories that way, at school.'

'Gave me quite a turn, Major,' said my esteemed friend, fanning herself with a plate. 'Thought he was light-headed!'

'In those remarkable times, Gran and Godfather, there was once a boy; – not me, you know.'

'No, no,' says my respected friend, 'not you. Not him, Major, you understand?'

'No, no,' says I.

'And he went to school in Rutlandshire –'

'Why not Lincolnshire?' says my respected friend.

'Why not, you dear old Gran? Because *I* go to school in Lincolnshire, don't I?'

'Ah, to be sure!' says my respected friend. 'And it's not Jemmy, you understand, Major?'

'No, no,' says I.

'Well!' our boy proceeded, hugging himself comfortably, and laughing merrily (again in confidence with the fire), before he again looked up in Mrs Lirriper's face, 'and so he was tremendously in love with his schoolmaster's daughter, and she was the most beautiful creature that ever was seen, and she had brown eyes, and she had brown hair all curling beautifully, and she had a delicious voice, and she was delicious altogether, and her name was Seraphina.'

'What's the name of *your* schoolmaster's daughter Jemmy?' asks my respected friend.

'Polly!' replied Jemmy, pointing his forefinger at her. 'There now! Caught you! Ha! ha! ha!'

When he and my respected friend had had a laugh and a hug together, our admittedly remarkable boy resumed with a great relish:

'Well! And so he loved her. And so he thought about her, and dreamed about her, and made her presents of oranges and nuts, and would have made her presents of pearls and diamonds if he could have afforded it out of his pocket-money, but he couldn't. And so her father – O, he WAS a Tartar! Keeping the boys up to the mark, holding examinations once a month, lecturing upon all sorts of subjects at all sorts of times, and knowing everything in the world out of book. And so this boy –'

'Had he any name?' asks my respected friend.

'No he hadn't, Gran. Ha! ha! There now! Caught you again!'

After this, they had another laugh and another hug, and then our boy went on.

'Well! And so this boy he had a friend about as old as himself, at the same school, and his name (for He *had* a name, as it happened) was – let me remember – was Bobbo.'

'Not Bob,' says my respected friend.

'Of course not,' says Jemmy. 'What made you think it was, Gran? Well! And so this friend was the cleverest and bravest and best looking and most generous of all the friends that ever were, and so he was in love with Seraphina's sister, and so Seraphina's sister was in love with him, and so they all grew up.'

'Bless us!' says my respected friend. 'They were very sudden about it.'

'So they all grew up,' our boy repeated, laughing heartily, 'and Bobbo and this boy went away together on horseback to seek their fortunes, and they partly got their horses by favour, and partly in a bargain; that is to say, they had saved up between them seven-and-fourpence, and the two horses, being Arabs, were worth more, only the man said he would take that, to favour them. Well! And so they made their fortunes and came prancing back to the school, with their pockets full of gold enough to last for ever. And so they rang at the parents' and visitors' bell (not the back gate), and when the bell was answered they proclaimed, "The same as if it was scarlet fever! Every boy goes home for an indefinite period!" And then there was great hurrahing, and then they kissed Seraphina and her sister – each his own love and not the other's on any account – and then they ordered the Tartar into instant confinement.'

'Poor man!' said my respected friend.

'Into instant confinement, Gran,' repeated Jemmy, trying to look severe and roaring with laughter, 'and he was to have nothing to eat but the boys' dinners, and was to drink half a cask of their beer, every day. And so then the preparations were made for the two weddings, and there were hampers, and potted things, and sweet things, and nuts, and postage-stamps, and all manner of things. And so they were so jolly, that they let the Tartar out, and he was jolly too.'

'I am glad they let him out,' says my respected friend, 'because he had only done his duty.'

'Oh but hadn't he overdone it though!' cried Jemmy. 'Well! And so then this boy mounted his horse, with his bride in his arms and cantered away, and cantered on and on till he came to a certain place where he had a certain Gran and a certain godfather – not you two, you know.'

'No, no,' we both said.

'And there he was received with great rejoicings, and he filled the cupboard and the bookcase with gold, and he showered it out on his Gran and his godfather because they were the two kindest and dearest people that ever lived in this world. And so while they were sitting up to their knees in gold, a knocking was heard at the street door, and who should it be but Bobbo, also on horseback with his bride in his arms, and what had he come to say but that he would take (at double rent) all the Lodgings for ever, that were not wanted by this boy and this Gran and this godfather, and that they would all live together, and all be happy! And so they were, and so it never ended!'

'And was there no quarrelling?' asked my respected friend, as Jemmy sat upon her lap, and hugged her.

'No! Nobody ever quarrelled.'

'And did the money never melt away?'

'No! Nobody could ever spend it all.'

'And did none of them ever grow older?'

'No! Nobody ever grew older after that.'

'And did none of them ever die?'

'O no, no, no, Gran!' exclaimed our dear boy, laying his cheek upon her breast, and drawing her closer to him. 'Nobody ever died.'

'Ah Major, Major,' says my respected friend, smiling benignly upon me. 'This beats our stories. Let us end with the Boy's story, Major, for the Boy's story is the best that is ever told!'

In submission to which request on the part of the best of women, I have here noted it down as faithfully as my best abilities, coupled with my best intentions, would admit, subscribing it with my name,

J. JACKMAN.

The Parlours.
Mrs Lirriper's Lodgings.

MRS LIRRIPER'S LEGACY

Mrs Lirriper Relates how She Went On, and Went Over

AH! It's pleasant to drop into my own easy-chair my dear though
a little palpitating what with trotting up-stairs and what with trotting down, and why kitchen-stairs should all be corner stairs is for
the builders to justify though I do not think they fully understand
their trade and never did, else why the sameness and why not more
conveniences and fewer draughts and likewise making a practice of
laying the plaster on too thick I am well convinced which holds
the damp, and as to chimney-pots putting them on by guess-work
like hats at a party and no more knowing what their effect will be
upon the smoke bless you than I do if so much, except that it will
mostly be either to send it down your throat in a straight form or
give it a twist before it goes there. And what I says speaking as I
find of those new metal chimneys all manner of shapes (there's a
row of 'em at Miss Wozenham's lodging-house lower down on the
other side of the way) is that they only work your smoke into
artificial patterns for you before you swallow it and that I'd quite as
soon swallow mine plain, the flavour being the same, not to mention the conceit of putting up signs on the top of your house to
show the forms in which you take your smoke into your inside.

Being here before your eyes my dear in my own easy-chair in my
own quiet room in my own Lodging House Number Eighty-one
Norfolk-street Strand London situated midway between the City
and St James's – if anything is where it used to be with these hotels
calling themselves Limited but called Unlimited by Major Jackman
rising up everywhere and rising up into flagstaffs where they can't
go any higher, but my mind of those monsters is give me a landlord's or landlady's wholesome face when I come off a journey and
not a brass plate with an electrified number clicking out of it which
it's not in nature can be glad to see me and to which I don't want to
be hoisted like molasses at the Docks and left there telegraphing

for help with the most ingenious instruments but quite in vain – being here my dear I have no call to mention that I am still in the Lodgings as a business hoping to die in the same and if agreeable to the clergy party read over at Saint Clement's Danes and concluded in Hatfield churchyard when lying once again by my poor Lirriper ashes to ashes and dust to dust.[1]

Neither should I tell you any news my dear in telling you that the Major is still a fixture in the Parlours quite as much so as the roof of the house, and that Jemmy is of boys the best and brightest and has ever had kept from him the cruel story of his poor pretty young mother Mrs Edson being deserted in the second floor and dying in my arms, fully believing that I am his born Gran and him an orphan, though what with engineering since he took a taste for it and him and the Major making Locomotives out of parasols broken iron pots and cotton-reels and them absolutely a getting off the line and falling over the table and injuring the passengers almost equal to the originals it really is quite wonderful. And when I says to the Major, 'Major can't you by *any* means give us a communication with the guard?' the Major says quite huffy, 'No madam it's not to be done,' and when I says 'Why not?' the Major says, 'That is between us who are in the Railway Interest madam and our friend the Right Honourable Vice-President of the Board of Trade and if you'll believe me my dear the Major wrote to Jemmy at school to consult him on the answer I should have before I could get even that amount of unsatisfactoriness out of the man, the reason being that when we first began with the little model and the working signals beautiful and perfect (being in general as wrong as the real) and when I says laughing 'What appointment am I to hold in this undertaking gentlemen?' Jemmy hugs me round the neck and tells me dancing, 'You shall be the Public Gran' and consequently they put upon me just as much as ever they like and I sit a growling in my easy-chair.

My dear whether it is that a grown man as clever as the Major cannot give half his heart and mind to anything – even a plaything – but must get into right down earnest with it, whether it is so or whether it is not so I do not undertake to say, but Jemmy is far outdone by the serious and believing ways of the Major in the management of the United Grand Junction Lirriper and Jackman Great

Norfolk Parlour Line, 'For' says my Jemmy with the sparkling eyes when it was christened, 'we must have a whole mouthful of name Gran or our dear old Public' and there the young rogue kissed me, 'won't stump up.'² So the Public took the shares – ten at ninepence, and immediately when that was spent twelve Preferences at one-and-sixpence – and they were all signed by Jemmy and countersigned by the Major, and between ourselves much better worth the money than some shares I have paid for in my time. In the same holidays the line was made and worked and opened and ran excursions and had collisions and burst its boilers and all sorts of accidents and offences all most regular correct and pretty. The sense of responsibility entertained by the Major as a military style of station-master my dear starting the down train behind time and ringing one of those little bells that you buy with the little coal-scuttles off the tray round the man's neck in the street did him honour, but noticing the Major of a night when he is writing out his monthly report to Jemmy at school of the state of the Rolling Stock and the Permanent Way and all the rest of it (the whole kept upon the Major's sideboard and dusted with his own hands every morning before varnishing his boots) I notice him as full of thought and care as full can be and frowning in a fearful manner, but indeed the Major does nothing by halves as witness his great delight in going out surveying with Jemmy when he has Jemmy to go with, carrying a chain and a measuring tape and driving I don't know what improvements right through Westminster Abbey and fully believed in the streets to be knocking everything upside down by Act of Parliament. As please Heaven will come to pass when Jemmy takes to that as a profession!

Mentioning my poor Lirriper brings into my head his own youngest brother the Doctor though Doctor of what I am sure it would be hard to say unless Liquor, for neither Physic nor Music nor yet Law does Joshua Lirriper know a morsel of except continually being summoned to the County Court and having orders made upon him which he runs away from, and once was taken in the passage of this very house with an umbrella up and the Major's hat on, giving his name with the door-mat round him as Sir Johnson Jones K.C.B. in spectacles residing at the Horse Guards. On which occasion he had got into the house not a minute before, through the girl letting him on to the mat when he sent in a piece of paper twisted more like one of those spills for lighting candles than a note, offering me the choice between thirty shillings in hand and his brains on the premises marked immediate and waiting for an answer. My dear it gave me such a dreadful turn to think of the brains of my poor dear Lirriper's own flesh and blood flying about the new oilcloth however unworthy to be so assisted, that I went out of my room here to ask him what he would take once for all not to do it for life when I found him in the custody of two gentlemen that I should have judged to be in the feather-bed trade if they had not announced the law, so fluffy were their personal appearance. 'Bring your chains sir,' says Joshua to the littlest of the two in the biggest hat, 'rivet on my fetters'! Imagine my feelings when I pictered him clanking up Norfolk-street in irons and Miss Wozenham looking out of window! 'Gentlemen' I says all of a tremble and ready to drop 'please to bring him into Major Jackman's apartments'. So they brought him into the Parlours, and when the Major spies his own curly-brimmed hat on him which Joshua Lirriper had whipped off its peg in the passage for a military disguise he goes into such a tearing passion that he tips it off his head with his hand and kicks it up to the ceiling with his foot, where it grazed long afterwards. 'Major' I says 'be cool and advise me what to do with Joshua my dead and gone Lirriper's own youngest brother'. 'Madam' says the Major 'my advice is that you board and lodge him in a Powder Mill, with a handsome gratuity to the proprietor when exploded.' 'Major' I says 'as a Christian you cannot mean your words.' 'Madam' says the Major 'by the Lord I do!' and indeed the Major beside being with all his merits a very passionate man for his size had a bad opinion of Joshua on account of former troubles even unattended by liberties taken with his apparel. When Joshua Lirriper hears this conversation betwixt us he turns upon the littlest one with the biggest hat and says 'Come sir! Remove me to my vile dungeon. Where is my mouldy straw!' My dear at the picter of him rising in my mind dressed almost entirely in padlocks like Baron Trenck[3] in Jemmy's book I was so overcome that I burst into tears and I says to the Major, 'Major take my keys and settle with these gentlemen or I shall never know a happy minute more,' which was done several times both before and since, but still I must remember that Joshua Lirriper has his good feelings and shows them in being always so troubled in his mind when he cannot wear mourning for his brother. Many a long year have I left off my widow's mourning not being wishful to intrude, but the tender point in Joshua that I cannot help a little yielding to is when he writes 'One single sovereign would enable me to wear a decent suit of mourning for my much-loved brother. I vowed at the time of his lamented death that I would ever wear sables in memory of him but Alas how short-sighted is man, How keep that vow when penniless!' It says a good deal for the strength of his feelings that he couldn't have been seven year old when my poor Lirriper died and to have kept to it ever since is highly creditable. But we know there's good in all of us – if we only knew where it was in some of us – and though it was far from delicate in Joshua to work upon the dear child's feelings when first sent to school and write down into Lincolnshire for his pocket-money by return of post and got it, still he is my poor Lirriper's own youngest brother and mightn't have meant not paying his bill at the Salisbury Arms when his affection took him down to stay a fortnight at Hatfield churchyard and might have meant to keep sober but for bad company. Consequently if the Major *had* played on him with the garden-engine[4] which he got privately into his room without my knowing of it, I think that much as I should have regretted it there would have been words betwixt the Major and me. Therefore my dear though he played on Mr Buffle by mistake being hot in his head, and though it might have been misrepresented down at Wozenham's into not being ready for Mr Buffle in other respects he being the Assessed Taxes, still I do not so much regret it as perhaps I ought. And whether Joshua Lirriper will yet do well in life I cannot say, but I did hear of his coming out at a Private Theatre in the character of a Bandit without receiving any offers afterwards from the regular managers.

Mentioning Mr Buffle gives an instance of there being good in persons where good is not expected, for it cannot be denied that Mr Buffle's manners when engaged in his business were not agreeable. To collect is one thing and to look about as if suspicious of the goods being gradually removing in the dead of the night by a back door is another, over taxing you have no control but suspecting is voluntary. Allowances too must ever be made for a gentleman of the Major's warmth not relishing being spoke to with a pen in the mouth; and while I do not know that it is more irritable to my own feelings to have a low-crowned hat with a broad brim kept on indoors than any other hat still I can appreciate the Major's, besides which without bearing malice or vengeance the Major is a man that scores up arrears as his habit always was with Joshua Lirriper. So at last my dear the Major lay in wait for Mr Buffle and it worrited me a good deal. Mr Buffle gives his rap of two sharp knocks one day and the Major bounces to the door. 'Collector has called for two quarters' Assessed Taxes' says Mr Buffle. 'They are ready for him' says the Major and brings him in here. But on the way Mr Buffle looks about him in his usual suspicious manner and the Major fires and asks him 'Do you see a Ghost sir?' 'No sir' says Mr Buffle. 'Because I have before noticed you' says the Major 'apparently looking for a spectre very hard beneath the roof of my respected friend. When you find that supernatural agent, be so good as point him out sir.' Mr Buffle stares at the Major and then nods at me. 'Mrs Lirriper sir' says the Major going off into a perfect steam and introducing me with his hand. 'Pleasure of knowing her' says Mr Buffle. 'A – hum! – Jemmy Jackman sir!' says the Major introducing himself. 'Honour of knowing you by sight' says Mr Buffle. 'Jemmy Jackman sir' says the Major wagging his head sideways in a sort of an obstinate fury 'presents to you his esteemed friend that lady Mrs Emma Lirriper of Eighty-one Norfolk-street Strand London in the County of Middlesex in the United Kingdom of Great Britain and Ireland. Upon which occasion sir,' says the Major, 'Jemmy Jackman takes your hat off.' Mr Buffle looks at his hat where the Major drops it on the floor and he picks it up and puts it on again. 'Sir' says the Major very red and looking him full in the face 'there are two quarters of the Gallantry Taxes due and the Collector has called.' Upon which if you can believe my words my dear the Major drops Mr Buffle's hat off again. 'This – ' Mr Buffle begins very angry with his pen in his mouth, when the Major steaming more and more says 'Take your bit out sir! Or by the whole infernal system of Taxation of this country and every individual figure in the National Debt, I'll get upon your back and ride you like a horse!' which it's my belief he would have done and even actually jerking his neat little legs ready for a spring as it was. 'This' says Mr Buffle without his pen 'is an assault and I'll have the law of you,' 'Sir' replies the Major 'if you are a man of honour, your Collector of whatever may be due on the Honourable Assessment by applying to Major Jackman at the Parlours Mrs Lirriper's Lodgings, may obtain what he wants in full at any moment.'

When the Major glared at Mr Buffle with those meaning words my dear I literally gasped for a teaspoonful of sal volatile in a wineglass of water, and I says 'Pray let it go no further gentlemen I beg and beseech of you!' But the Major could be got to do nothing else but snort long after Mr Buffle was gone, and the effect it had upon my whole mass of blood when on the next day of Mr Buffle's rounds the Major spruced himself up and went humming a tune up and down the street with one eye almost obliterated by his hat there are not expressions in Johnson's Dictionary⁵ to state. But I safely put the street door on the jar and got behind the Major's blinds with my shawl on and my mind made up the moment I saw danger to rush out screeching till my voice failed me and catch the Major round the neck till my strength went and have all parties bound. I had not been behind the blinds a quarter of an hour when I saw Mr Buffle approaching with his Collecting-books in his hand. The Major likewise himself approached. They met before the Airy railings. The Major takes off his hat at arm's length and says 'Mr Buffle I believe?' Mr Buffle takes off *his* hat at arm's length and says 'That is my name sir.' Says the Major 'Have you any commands for me, Mr Buffle?' Says Mr Buffle 'Not any sir.' Then my dear both of 'em bowed very low and haughty and parted, and whenever Mr Buffle made his rounds in future him and the Major always met and bowed before the Airy railings, putting me much in mind of Hamlet and the other gentleman in mourning before killing one another,⁶ though I could have wished the other gentleman had done it fairer and even if less polite no poison.

Mr Buffle's family were not liked in this neighbourhood, for when you are a householder my dear you'll find it does not come by nature to like the Assessed, and it was considered besides that a one-horse pheayton ought not to have elevated Mrs Buffle to that heighth especially when purloined from the Taxes which I myself did consider uncharitable. But they were *not* liked and there was that domestic unhappiness in the family in consequence of their both being very hard with Miss Buffle and one another on account of Miss Buffle's favouring Mr Buffle's articled young gentleman, that it *was* whispered that Miss Buffle would go either into a consumption or a convent she being so very thin and off her appetite and two close-shaved gentlemen with white bands round their necks peeping round the corner whenever she went out in waistcoats resembling black pinafores. So things stood towards Mr Buffle when one night I was woke by a frightful noise and a smell of burning, and going to my bedroom window saw the whole street in a glow. Fortunately we had two sets empty just then and before I could hurry on some clothes I heard the Major hammering at the attics' doors and calling out 'Dress yourselves! – Fire! Don't be frightened! – Fire! Collect your presence of mind! – Fire! All right – Fire!' most tremenjously. As I opened my bedroom door the Major came tumbling in over himself and me and caught me in his arms. 'Major' I says breathless 'where is it'? 'I don't know dearest madam' says the Major – 'Fire! Jemmy Jackman will defend you to the last drop of his blood – Fire! If the dear boy was at home what a treat this would be for him – Fire!' and altogether very collected and bold except that he couldn't say a single sentence without shaking me to the very centre with roaring Fire. We ran down to the drawing-room and put our heads out of window, and the Major calls to an unfeeling young monkey scampering by be joyful and ready to split 'Where is it? – Fire!' The monkey answers without stopping 'Oh here's a lark! Old Buffle's been setting his house alight to prevent its being found out that he boned[7] the Taxes. Hurrah! Fire!' And then the sparks came flying up and the smoke came pouring down and the crackling of flames and spatting of water and banging of engines and hacking of axes and breaking of glass and knocking at doors and the shouting and crying and hurrying and the heat and altogether gave me a dreadful palpitation. 'Don't be frightened dearest madam,' says the Major, ' – Fire! There's nothing to be alarmed at – Fire! Don't open the street door till I come back – Fire! You're quite composed and comfortable ain't you? – Fire, Fire, Fire!' It was in vain for me to hold the man and tell him he'd be galloped to death by the engines – pumped to death by his over-exertions – wet-feeted to death by the slop and mess – flattened to death when the roofs fell in – his spirit was up and he went scampering off after the young monkey with all the breath he had and none to spare, and me and the girls huddled together at the parlour windows looking at the dreadful flames above the houses over the way, Mr Buffle's being round the corner. Presently what should we see but some people running down the street straight to our door, and then the Major directing operations in the busiest way, and then some more people and then – carried in a chair similar to Guy Fawkes – Mr Buffle in a blanket!

My dear the Major has Mr Buffle brought up our steps and whisked into the parlour and carted out on the sofy, and then he and all the rest of them without so much as a word burst away again full speed, leaving the impression of a vision except for Mr Buffle awful in his blanket with his eyes a rolling. In a twinkling they all burst back again with Mrs Buffle in another blanket, which whisked in and carted out on the sofy they all burst off again and all burst back again with Miss Buffle in another blanket, which again whisked in and carted out they all burst off again and all burst back again with Mr Buffle's articled young gentleman in another blanket – him a holding round the necks of two men carrying him by the legs, similar to the picter of the disgraceful creetur who has lost the fight (but where the chair I do not know) and his hair having the appearance of newly played upon. When all four of a row, the Major rubs his hands and whispers me with what little hoarseness he can get together, 'If our dear remarkable boy was only at home what a delightful treat this would be for him!'

My dear we made them some hot tea and toast and some hot brandy-and-water with a little comfortable nutmeg in it, and at first they were scared and low in their spirits but being fully insured got sociable. And the first use Mr Buffle made of his tongue was to call the Major his Preserver and his best of friends and to say 'My dearest sir let me make you known to Mrs Buffle' which also addressed him as her Preserver and her best of friends and was fully cordial as the blanket would admit of. Also Miss Buffle. The articled young gentleman's head was a little light and he sat a moaning 'Robina is reduced to cinders, Robina is reduced to cinders!' Which went more to the heart on account of his having got wrapped in his blanket as if he was looking out of a violin-celler-case, until Mr Buffle says 'Robina speak to him!' Miss Buffle says 'Dear George!' and but for the Major's pouring down brandy-and-water on the instant which caused a catching in his throat owing to the nutmeg and a violent fit of coughing it might have proved too much for his strength. When the articled young gentleman got the better of it Mr Buffle leaned up against Mrs Buffle being two bundles, a little while in confidence, and then says with tears in his eyes which the Major noticing wiped, 'We have not been an united family, let us after this danger become so, take her George.' The young gentleman could not put his arm out far to do it, but his spoken expressions were very beautiful though of a wandering class. And I do not know that I ever had a much pleasanter meal than the breakfast we took together after we had all dozed, when Miss Buffle made tea very sweetly in quite the Roman style as depicted formerly at Covent Garden Theatre and when the whole family was most agreeable, as they have ever proved since that night when the Major stood at the foot of the Fire-Escape and claimed them as they came down – the young gentleman headforemost, which accounts. And though I do not say that we should be less liable to think ill of one another if strictly limited to blankets, still I do say that we might most of us come to a better understanding if we kept one another less at a distance.

Why there's Wozenham's lower down on the other side of the street. I had a feeling of much soreness several years respecting what I must still ever call Miss Wozenham's systematic under-bidding and the likeness of the house in Bradshaw having far too many windows and a most umbrageous and outrageous Oak which never yet was seen in Norfolk-street nor yet a carriage and four at Wozenham's door, which it would have been far more to Brad-shaw's credit to have drawn a cab. This frame of mind continued bitter down to the very afternoon in January last when one of my girls, Sally Rairyganoo which I still suspect of Irish extraction though family represented Cambridge, else why abscond with a bricklayer of the Limerick persuasion and be married in patterns not waiting till his black eye was decently got round with all the company fourteen in number and one horse fighting outside on the roof of the vehicle – I repeat my dear my ill-regulated state of mind

towards Miss Wozenham continued down to the very afternoon
of January last past when Sally Rairyganoo came banging (I can use
no milder expression) into my room with a jump which may be
Cambridge and may not, and said 'Hurroo Missis! Miss Wozenham's sold up!' My dear when I had it thrown in my face and conscience that the girl Sally had reason to think I could be glad of the
ruin of a fellow-creeter, I burst into tears and dropped back in my
chair and I says 'I am ashamed of myself!'

Well! I tried to settle to my tea but I could not do it what with
thinking of Miss Wozenham and her distresses. It was a wretched
night and I went up to a front window and looked over at Wozenham's and as well as I could make it out down the street in the fog
it was the dismalest of the dismal and not a light to be seen. So at
last I says to myself 'This will not do', and I puts on my oldest
bonnet and shawl not wishing Miss Wozenham to be reminded of
my best at such a time, and lo and behold you I goes over to
Wozenham's and knocks. 'Miss Wozenham at home?' I says turning my head when I heard the door go. And then I saw it was Miss
Wozenham herself who had opened it and sadly worn she was poor
thing and her eyes all swelled and swelled with crying. 'Miss
Wozenham' I says 'it is several years since there was a little unpleasantness betwixt us on the subject of my grandson's cap being
down your Airy. I have overlooked it and I hope you have done
the same.' 'Yes Mrs Lirriper' she says in surprise 'I have.' 'Then
my dear' I says 'I should be glad to come in and speak a word to
you.' Upon my calling her my dear Miss Wozenham breaks out a
crying most pitiful, and a not unfeeling elderly person that might
have been better shaved in a nightcap with a hat over it offering a
polite apology for the mumps having worked themselves into his
constitution, and also for sending home to his wife on the bellows
which was in his hand as a writing-desk, looks out of the back parlour and says 'The lady wants a word of comfort' and goes in
again. So I was able to say quite natural 'Wants a word of comfort
does she sir? Then please the pigs she shall have it!' And Miss
Wozenham and me we go into the front room with a wretched
light that seemed to have been crying too and was sputtering out,
and I says 'Now my dear, tell me all,' and she wrings her hands and
says 'Oh Mrs Lirriper that man is in possession here, and I have not

a friend in the world who is able to help me with a shilling.'

It doesn't signify a bit what a talkative old body like me said to Miss Wozenham when she said that, and so I'll tell you instead my dear that I'd have given thirty shillings to have taken her over to tea, only I durstn't on account of the Major. Not you see but what I knew I could draw the Major out like thread and wind him round my finger on most subjects and perhaps even on that if I was to set myself to it, but him and me had so often belied Miss Wozenham to one another that I was shamefaced, and I knew she had offended his pride and never mine, and likewise I felt timid that that Rairyganoo girl might make things awkward. So I says 'My dear if you could give me a cup of tea to clear my muddle of a head I should better understand your affairs.' And we had the tea and the affairs too and after all it was but forty pound, and – There! she's as industrious and straight a creeter as ever lived and has paid back half of it already, and where's the use of saying more, particularly when it ain't the point? For the point is that when she was a kissing my hands and holding them in hers and kissing them again and blessing blessing blessing, I cheered up at last and I says 'Why what a waddling old goose I have been my dear to take you for something so very different!' 'Ah but I too' says she 'how have *I* mistaken *you!*' 'Come for goodness' sake tell me' I says 'what you thought of me?' 'Oh' says she 'I thought you had no feeling for such a hard hand-to-mouth life as mine, and were rolling in affluence.' I says shaking my sides (and very glad to do it for I had been a choking quite long enough) 'Only look at my figure my dear and give me your opinion whether if I was in affluence I should be likely to roll in it!' That did it! We got as merry as grigs (whatever *they* are, if you happen to know my dear – *I* don't) and I went home to my blessed home as happy and as thankful as could be. But before I make an end of it, think even of my having misunderstood the Major! Yes! For next forenoon the Major came into my little room with his brushed hat in his hand and he begins 'My dearest madam – and then put his face in his hat as if he had just come into church. As I sat all in a maze he came out of his hat and began again. 'My esteemed and beloved friend – ' and then went into his hat again. 'Major,' I cries out frightened 'has anything happened to our darling boy?' 'No, no, no' says the Major 'but Miss Wozenham has been here this morning to make her excuses to me, and by the Lord I can't get over what she told me.' 'Hoity toity, Major,' I says 'you don't know yet that I was afraid of you last night and didn't think half as well of you as I ought! So come out of church Major and forgive me like a dear old friend and I'll never do so any more.' And I leave you to judge my dear whether I ever did or will. And how affecting to think of Miss Wozenham out of her small income and her losses doing so much for her poor old father, and keeping a brother that had had the misfortune to soften his brain against the hard mathematics as neat as a new pin in the three back represented to lodgers as a lumber-room and consuming a whole shoulder of mutton whenever provided!

And now my dear I really am a going to tell you about my Legacy if you're inclined to favour me with your attention, and I did fully intend to have come straight to it only one thing does so bring up another. It was the month of June and the day before Midsummer Day when my girl Winifred Madgers – she was what is termed a Plymouth Sister[8] and the Plymouth Brother that made away with her was quite right, for a tidier young woman for a wife never came into a house and afterwards called with the beautifullest Plymouth Twins – it was the day before Midsummer Day when Winifred Madgers comes and says to me 'A gentleman from the Consul's wishes particular to speak to Mrs Lirriper.' If you'll believe me my dear the Consols at the bank got into my head, and I says 'Good gracious I hope he ain't had any dreadful fall!' Says Winifred 'He don't look as if he had ma'am.' And I says 'Show him in.'

The gentleman came in dark and with his hair cropped what I should consider too close, and he says very polite 'Madame Lirrwiper!' I says 'Yes sir. Take a chair.' 'I come,' says he 'frrwom the Frrwench Consul's.' So I saw at once that it wasn't the Bank of England. 'We have rrweceived,' says the gentleman turning his r's very curious and skilful, 'frrwom the Mairrwie at Sens, a communication which I will have the honour to rrwead. Madame Lirrwiper understands Frrwench?' 'Oh dear no sir!' says I. 'Madame Lirriper don't understand anything of the sort.' 'It matters not,' says the gentleman, 'I will trrwanslate.'

With that my dear the gentleman after reading something about a Department and a Mairie (which Lord forgive me I supposed till the Major came home was Mary, and never was I more puzzled than to think how that young woman came to have so much to do with it) translated a lot with the most obliging pains, and it came to this: – That in the town of Sens in France, an unknown Englishman lay a dying. That he was speechless and without motion. That in his lodging there was a gold watch and a purse containing such and such money and a trunk containing such and such clothes, but no passport and no papers, except that on his table was a pack of cards and that he had written in pencil on the back of the ace of hearts: 'To the authorities. When I am dead, pray send what is left, as a last Legacy, to Mrs Lirriper Eighty-one Norfolk-street Strand London.' When the gentleman had explained all this, which seemed to be drawn up much more methodical than I should have given the French credit for, not at that time knowing the nation, he put the document into my hand. And much the wiser I was for that you may be sure, except that it had the look of being made out upon grocery-paper and was stamped all over with eagles.

'Does Madame Lirrwiper' says the gentleman 'believe she rrwecognizes her unfortunate compatrrwiot?'

You may imagine the flurry it put me into my dear to be talked to about my compatriots.

I says 'Excuse me. Would you have the kindness sir to make your language as simple as you can?'

'This Englishman unhappy, at the point of death. This compatrrwiot afflicted,' says the gentleman.

'Thank you sir' I says 'I understand you now. No sir I have not the least idea who this can be.'

'Has Madame Lirrwiper no son, no nephew, no godson, no frrwiend, no acquaintance of any kind in Frrwance?'

'To my certain knowledge' says I 'no relation or friend, and to the best of my belief no acquaintance.'

'Pardon me. You take Locataires?' says the gentleman.

My dear fully believing he was offering me something with his obliging foreign manners – snuff for anything I knew – I gave a little bend of my head and I says if you'll credit it, 'No I thank you. I have not contracted the habit.'

The gentleman looks perplexed and says 'Lodgers?'

'Oh!' says I laughing. 'Bless the man! Why yes to be sure!'

'May it not be a former lodger?' says the gentleman. 'Some lodger that you pardoned some rrwent? You have pardoned lodgers some rrwent?'

'Hem! It has happened sir' says I, 'but I assure you I can call to mind no gentleman of that description that this is at all likely to be.'

In short my dear we could make nothing of it, and the gentleman noted down what I said and went away. But he left me the paper of which he had two with him, and when the Major came in I says to the Major as I put it in his hand 'Major here's Old Moore's Almanack with the hieroglyphic complete,[9] for your opinion.'

It took the Major a little longer to read than I should have thought, judging from the copious flow with which he seemed to be gifted when attacking the organ-men, but at last he got through it and stood a gazing at me in amazement.

'Major' I says 'you're paralysed.'

'Madam' says the Major, 'Jemmy Jackman is doubled up.'

Now it did so happen that the Major had been out to get a little information about railroads and steam-boats, as our boy was coming home for his Midsummer holidays next day and we were going to take him somewhere for a treat and a change. So while the Major stood a gazing it came into my head to say to him 'Major I wish you'd go and look at some of your books and maps, and see whereabouts this same town of Sens is in France.'

The Major he roused himself and he went into the Parlours and he poked about a little, and he came back to me and he says: 'Sens my dearest madam is seventy odd miles south of Paris.'

With what I may truly call a desperate effort 'Major' I says 'we'll go there with our blessed boy!'

If ever the Major was beside himself it was at the thoughts of that journey. All day long he was like the wild man of the woods after meeting with an advertisement in the papers telling him something to his advantage, and early next morning hours before Jemmy could possibly come home he was outside in the street ready to call out to him that we was all a going to France. Young Rosy-cheeks you may believe was as wild as the Major, and they did carry on to that degree that I says 'If you two children ain't more orderly I'll pack you both off to bed.' And then they fell to cleaning up the Major's telescope to see France with, and went out and bought a leather bag with a snap to hang round Jemmy, and him to carry the money like a little Fortunatus with his purse.[10]

If I hadn't passed my word and raised their hopes, I doubt if I could have gone through with the undertaking but it was too late to go back now. So on the second day after Midsummer Day we went off by the morning mail. And when we came to the sea which I had never seen but once in my life and that when my poor Lirriper was courting me, the freshness of it and the deepness and the airiness and to think that it had been rolling ever since and that it was always a rolling and so few of us minding, made me feel quite serious. But I felt happy too and so did Jemmy and the Major and not much motion on the whole, though me with a swimming in the head and a sinking but able to take notice that the foreign insides appear to be constructed hollower than the English leading to much more tremenjous noises when bad sailors.

But my dear the blueness and the lightness and the coloured look of everything and the very sentry-boxes striped and the shining rattling drums and the little soldiers with their waists and tidy gaiters, when we got across to the Continent—it made me feel as if I don't know what — as if the atmosphere had been lifted off me. And as to lunch why bless you if I kept a man-cook and two kitchen-maids I couldn't get it done for twice the money, and no injured young women a glaring at you and grudging you and acknowledging your patronage by wishing that your food might choke you, but so civil and so hot and attentive and every way comfortable except Jemmy pouring wine down his throat by tumblers-full and me expecting to see him drop under the table.

And the way in which Jemmy spoke his French was a real charm. It was often wanted of him, for whenever anybody spoke a syllable to me I says 'Noncomprenny, you're very kind but it's no use—Now Jemmy!' and then Jemmy he fires away at 'em lovely, the only thing wanting in Jemmy's French being as it appeared to me that he hardly ever understood a word of what they said to him which made it scarcely of the use it might have been though in other respects a perfect Native, and regarding the Major's fluency I should have been of the opinion judging French by English that there might have been a greater choice of words in the language though still I must admit that if I hadn't known him when he asked a military gentleman in a grey cloak what o'clock it was I should have took him for a Frenchman born.

Before going on to look after my Legacy we were to make one regular day in Paris, and I leave you to judge my dear what a day *that* was with Jemmy and the Major and the telescope and me and the prowling young man at the inn door (but very civil too) that went along with us to show the sights. All along the railway to Paris Jemmy and the Major had been frightening me to death by stooping down on the platforms at stations to inspect the engines underneath their mechanical stomachs, and by creeping in and out I don't know where all, to find improvements for the United Grand Junction Parlour, but when we got out into the brilliant streets on a bright morning they gave up all their London improvements as a bad job and gave their minds to Paris. Says the prowling young man to me 'Will I speak Inglis No?' So I says 'If you can young man I shall take it as a favour,' but after half an hour of it when I fully believed the man had gone mad and me too I says 'Be so good as fall back on your French sir,' knowing that then I shouldn't have the agonies of trying to understand him which was a happy release. Not that I lost much more than the rest either, for I generally noticed that when he had described something very long indeed and I says to Jemmy 'What does he say Jemmy?' Jemmy says looking at him with vengeance in his eye 'He is so jolly indistinct!' and that when he had described it longer all over again and I says to Jemmy 'Well Jemmy what's it all about?' Jemmy says 'He says the building was repaired in seventeen hundred and four, Gran.'

Wherever that prowling young man formed his prowling habits I cannot be expected to know, but the way in which he went round the corner while we had our breakfasts and was there again when we swallowed the last crumb was most marvellous, and just the same at dinner and at night, prowling equally at the theatre and the inn gateway and the shop-doors when we bought a trifle or two and everywhere else but troubled with a tendency to spit. And of Paris I can tell you no more my dear than that it's town and country both in one, and carved stone and long streets of high houses and gardens and fountains and statues and trees and gold, and immensely big soldiers and immensely little soldiers and the pleasantest nurses with the whitest caps a playing at skipping-rope with the bunchiest babies in the flattest caps, and clean tablecloths spread everywhere for dinner and people sitting out of doors smoking and sipping all day long and little plays being acted in the open air for little people and every shop a complete and elegant room, and everybody seeming to play at everything in this world. And as to the sparkling lights my dear after dark, glittering high up and low down and on before and on behind and all round, and the crowd of theatres and the crowd of people and the crowd of all sorts, it's pure enchantment. And pretty well the only thing that grated on me was that whether you pay your fare at the railway or whether you change your money at a money-dealer's or whether you take your ticket at the theatre, the lady or gentleman is caged up (I suppose by Government) behind the strongest iron bars having more of a Zoological appearance than a free country.

Well to be sure when I did after all get my precious bones to bed that night, and my Young Rogue came in to kiss me and asks 'What do you think of this lovely lovely Paris, Gran?' I says 'Jemmy I feel as if it was beautiful fireworks being let off in my head.' And very cool and refreshing the pleasant country was next day when we went on to look after my Legacy, and rested me much and did me a deal of good.

So at length and at last my dear we come to Sens a pretty little town with a great two-towered cathedral and the rooks flying in and out of the loopholes and another tower atop of one of the towers like a sort of a stone pulpit. In which pulpit with the birds skimming below him if you'll believe me, I saw a speck while I was resting at the inn before dinner which they made signs to me was Jemmy and which really was. I had been a fancying as I sat in the balcony of the hotel that an Angel might light there and call down to the people to be good, but I little thought what Jemmy all unknown to himself was a calling down from that high place to some one in the town.

The pleasantest-situated inn my dear! Right under the two towers, with their shadows a changing upon it all day like a kind of a sundial, and country people driving in and out of the court-yard in carts and hooded cabriolets and such-like, and a market outside in front of the cathedral, and all so quaint and like a picter. The Major and me agreed that whatever came of my Legacy this was the place to stay in for our holiday, and we also agreed that our dear boy had best not be checked in his joy that night by the sight of the Englishman if he was still alive, but that we would go together and alone. For you are to understand that the Major not feeling himself quite equal in his wind to the heighth to which Jemmy had climbed, had come back to me and left him with the Guide.

So after dinner when Jemmy had set off to see the river, the Major went down to the Mairie, and presently came back with a military character in a sword and spurs and a cocked-hat and a yellow shoulder-belt and long tags about him that he must have found inconvenient. And the Major says 'The Englishman still lies in the same state dearest madam. This gentleman will conduct us to his lodging.' Upon which the military character pulled off his cocked-hat to me, and I took notice that he had shaved his forehead in imitation of Napoleon Bonaparte but not like.

We went out at the court-yard gate and past the great doors of the cathedral and down a narrow High Street where the people were sitting chatting at their shop-doors and the children were at play. The military character went in front and he stopped at a pork-shop with a little statue of a pig sitting up, in the window, and a private door that a donkey was looking out of.

When the donkey saw the military character he came slipping out on the pavement to turn round and then clattered along the passage into a back-yard. So the coast being clear, the Major and me were conducted up the common stair and into the front room on the second, a bare room with a red tiled floor and the outside lattice blinds close to darken it. As the military character opened the blinds I saw the tower where I had seen Jemmy, darkening as the sun got low, and I turned to the bed by the wall and saw the Englishman.

It was some kind of brain fever he had had, and his hair was all gone, and some wetted folded linen lay upon his head. I looked at him very attentive as he lay there all wasted away with his eyes closed, and I says to the Major

'I never saw this face before.'

The Major looked at him very attentive too, and he says

'*I* never saw this face before.'

332

When the Major explained our words to the military character, that gentleman shrugged his shoulders and showed the Major the card on which it was written about the Legacy for me. It had been written with a weak and trembling hand in bed, and I knew no more of the writing than of the face. Neither did the Major.

Though lying there alone, the poor creetur was as well taken care of as could be hoped, and would have been quite unconscious of any one's sitting by him then. I got the Major to say that we were not going away at present and that I would come back tomorrow and watch a bit by the bedside. But I got him to add – and I shook my head hard to make it stronger – 'We agree that we never saw this face before.'

Our boy was greatly surprised when we told him sitting out in the balcony in the starlight, and he ran over some of those stories of former Lodgers, of the Major's putting down, and asked wasn't it possible that it might be this lodger or that lodger. It was not possible and we went to bed.

In the morning just at breakfast-time the military character came jingling round, and said that the doctor thought from the signs he saw there might be some rally before the end. So I says to the Major and Jemmy, 'You two boys go and enjoy yourselves, and I'll take my Prayer-Book and go sit by the bed.' So I went, and I sat there some hours, reading a prayer for him poor soul now and then, and it was quite on in the day when he moved his hand.

He had been so still, that the moment he moved I knew of it, and I pulled off my spectacles and laid down my book and rose and looked at him. From moving one hand he began to move both, and then his action was the action of a person groping in the dark. Long after his eyes had opened, there was a film over them and he still felt for his way out into light. But by slow degrees his sight cleared and his hands stopped. He saw the ceiling, he saw the wall, he saw me. As his sight cleared, mine cleared too, and when at last we looked in one another's faces, I started back and I cries passionately:

'O you wicked wicked man! Your sin has found you out!'[11]

For I knew him, the moment life looked out of his eyes, to be Mr Edson, Jemmy's father who had so cruelly deserted Jemmy's young unmarried mother who had died in my arms, poor tender creetur, and left Jemmy to me.

'You cruel wicked man! You bad black traitor!'

With the little strength he had, he made an attempt to turn over on his wretched face to hide it. His arm dropped out of the bed and his head with it, and there he lay before me crushed in body and in mind. Surely the miserablest sight under the summer sun!

'Oh blessed Heaven' I says a crying, 'teach me what to say to this broken mortal! I am a poor sinful creetur, and the Judgment is not mine.'

As I lifted my eyes up to the clear bright sky, I saw the high tower where Jemmy had stood above the birds, seeing that very window; and the last look of that poor pretty young mother when her soul brightened and got free, seemed to shine down from it.

'O man, man, man!' I says, and I went on my knees beside the bed; 'if your heart is rent asunder and you are truly penitent for what you did, Our Saviour will have mercy on you yet!'

As I leaned my face against the bed, his feeble hand could just move itself enough to touch me. I hope the touch was penitent. It tried to hold my dress and keep hold, but the fingers were too weak to close.

I lifted him back upon the pillows, and I says to him:

'Can you hear me?'

He looked yes.

'Do you know me?'

He looked yes, even yet more plainly.

'I am not here alone. The Major is with me. You recollect the Major?'

Yes. That is to say he made out yes, in the same way as before.

'And even the Major and I are not alone. My grandson – his godson – is with us. Do you hear? My grandson.'

The fingers made another trial to catch at my sleeve, but could only creep near it and fall.

'Do you know who my grandson is?'

Yes.

'I pitied and loved his lonely mother. When his mother lay a dying I said to her, "My dear this baby is sent to a childless old woman." He has been my pride and joy ever since. I love him as dearly as if he had drunk from my breast. Do you ask to see my grandson before you die?'

Yes.

'Show me, when I leave off speaking, if you correctly understand what I say. He has been kept unacquainted with the story of his birth. He has no knowledge of it. No suspicion of it. If I bring him here to the side of this bed, he will suppose you to be a perfect stranger. It is more than I can do, to keep from him the knowledge that there is such wrong and misery in the world; but that it was ever so near him in his innocent cradle, I have kept from him, and I do keep from him, and I ever will keep from him. For his mother's sake, and for his own.'

He showed me that he distinctly understood, and the tears fell from his eyes.

'Now rest, and you shall see him.'

So I got him a little wine and some brandy and I put things straight about his bed. But I began to be troubled in my mind lest Jemmy and the Major might be too long of coming back. What with this occupation for my thoughts and hands, I didn't hear a foot upon the stairs, and was startled when I saw the Major stopped short in the middle of the room by the eyes of the man upon the bed, and knowing him then, as I had known him a little while ago.

There was anger in the Major's face, and there was horror and repugnance and I don't know what. So I went up to him and I led him to the bedside and when I clasped my hands and lifted of them up, the Major did the like.

'O Lord' I says 'Thou knowest what we two saw together of the sufferings and sorrows of that young creetur now with Thee. If this dying man is truly penitent, we two together humbly pray Thee to have mercy on him!'

The Major says 'Amen!' and then after a little stop I whispers him, 'Dear old friend fetch our beloved boy.' And the Major, so clever as to have got to understand it all without being told a word went away and brought him.

Never never never, shall I forget the fair bright face of our boy when he stood at the foot of the bed, looking at his unknown father. And O so like his dear young mother then!

'Jemmy' I says, 'I have found out all about this poor gentleman who is so ill, and he did lodge in the old house once. And as he wants to see all belonging to it, now that he is passing away, I sent for you.'

'Ah poor man!' says Jemmy stepping forward and touching one of his hands with great gentleness. 'My heart melts for him. Poor, poor, man!'

The eyes that were so soon to close for ever, turned to me, and I was not that strong in the pride of my strength that I could resist them.

'My darling boy, there is a reason in the secret history of this fellow-creetur, lying as the best and worst of us must all lie one day which I think would ease his spirit in his last hour if you would lay your cheek against his forehead and say "May God forgive you!"'

'O Gran,' says Jemmy with a full heart 'I am not worthy!' But he leaned down and did it. Then the faltering fingers made out to catch hold of my sleeve at last, and I believe he was a trying to kiss me when he died.

*   *   *

There my dear! There you have the story of my Legacy in full, and it's worth ten times the trouble I have spent upon it if you are pleased to like it.

You might suppose that it set us against the little French town of Sens, but no we didn't find that. I found myself that I never looked up at the high tower atop of the other tower, but the days came back again when that fair young creetur with her pretty bright hair trusted in me like a mother, and the recollection made the place so peaceful to me as I can't express. And every soul about the hotel down to the pigeons in the court-yard made friends with Jemmy and the Major, and went lumbering away with them on all sorts of expeditions in all sorts of vehicles drawn by rampagious cart-horses – with heads and without – mud for paint and ropes for harness – and every new friend dressed in blue like a butcher,[12] and every new horse standing on his hind legs wanting to devour and consume every other horse, and every man that had a whip to crack crack-crack-crack-crack-cracking it as if it was a schoolboy with his first. As to the Major my dear that man lived the greater part of his time with a little tumbler in one hand and a bottle of small wine in the other, and whenever he saw anybody else with a little tumbler no matter who it was – the military character with the tags, or the inn servants at their supper in the court-yard, or towns-people a chatting on a bench, or country-people a starting home after market – down rushes the Major to clink his glass against their glasses and cry – Hola! Vive Somebody! or Vive Something! as if he was beside himself. And though I could not quite approve of the Major's doing it, still the ways of the world are the ways of the world varying according to different parts of it, and dancing at all in the open Square with a lady that kept a barber's shop my opinion is that the Major was right to dance his best and to lead off with a power that I did not think was in him, though I was a little uneasy at the Barricading[13] sound of the cries that were set up by the other dancers and the rest of the company, until when I says 'What are they ever calling out Jemmy?' Jemmy says 'They're calling out Gran, Bravo the Military English! Bravo the Military English!' which was very gratifying to my feelings as a Briton and became the name the Major was known by.

But every evening at a regular time we all three sat out in the balcony of the hotel at the end of the court-yard, looking up at the golden and rosy light as it changed on the great towers, and looking at the shadows of the towers as they changed on all about us ourselves included, and what do you think we did there? My dear if Jemmy hadn't brought some other of those stories of the Major's taking down from the telling of former lodgers at Eighty-one Norfolk-street, and if he didn't bring 'em out with this speech:

'Here you are Gran! Here you are Godfather! More of 'em! *I'll* read. And though you wrote 'em for me Godfather, I know you won't disapprove of my making 'em over to Gran; will you?'

'No my dear boy,' says the Major. 'Everything we have is hers, and we are hers.'

'Hers ever affectionately and devotedly J. Jackman, and J. Jackman Lirriper,' cries the Young Rogue giving me a close hug. 'Very well then Godfather. Look here. As Gran is in the Legacy way just now. I shall make these stories a part of Gran's Legacy. I'll leave 'em to her. What do you say Godfather?'

'Hip hip Hurrah!' says the Major.

'Very well then' cries Jemmy all in a bustle. 'Vive the Military English! Vive the Lady Lirriper! Vive the Jemmy Jackman Ditto! Vive the Legacy! Now, you look out, Gran. And you look out, Godfather, *I'll* read! And I'll tell you what I'll do besides. On the last night of our holiday here when we are all packed and going away, I'll top up with something of my own.'

'Mind you do sir' says I.

'Don't you be afraid, Gran' cries Young Sparkles. 'Now then! I'm going to read. Once, twice, three and away. Open your mouths and shut your eyes, and see what Fortune sends you. All in to begin. Look out Gran. Look out Godfather!'

So in his lively spirits Jemmy began reading, and he read every evening while we were there, and sometimes we were about it late enough to have a candle burning quite steady out in the balcony in the still air. And so here is the rest of my Legacy my dear that I now hand over to you in this bundle of papers all in the Major's plain round writing. I wish I could hand you the church towers over too, and the pleasant air and the inn yard and the pigeons often coming and perching on the rail by Jemmy and seeming to be critical with their heads on one side, but you'll take as you find.

Mrs Lirriper Relates how Jemmy Topped Up

Well my dear and so the evening readings of these jottings of the Major's brought us round at last to the evening when we were all packed and going away next day, and I do assure you that by that time though it was deliciously comfortable to look forward to the dear old house in Norfolk-street again, I had formed quite a high opinion of the French nation and had noticed them to be much more homely and domestic in their families and far more simple and amiable in their lives than I had ever been led to expect, and it did strike me between ourselves that in one particular they might be imitated to advantage by another nation which I will not mention, and that is in the courage with which they take their little enjoyments on little means and with little things and don't let solemn bigwigs stare them out of countenance or speechify them dull, of which said solemn big-wigs I have ever had the one opinion that I wish they were all made comfortable separately in coppers with the lids on and never let out any more.

'Now young man', I says to Jemmy when we brought our chairs into the balcony that last evening, 'you please to remember who was to "top up."'

'All right Gran' says Jemmy. 'I am the illustrious personage.'

But he looked so serious after he had made me that light answer, that the Major raised his eyebrows at me and I raised mine at the Major.

'Gran and Godfather,' says Jemmy, 'you can hardly think how much my mind has run on Mr Edson's death.'

It gave me a little check. 'Ah! It was a sad scene my love' I says, 'and sad remembrances come back stronger than merry. But this' I says after a little silence, to rouse myself and the Major and Jemmy all together, 'is not topping up. Tell us your story my dear.'

'I will' says Jemmy.

'What is the date sir?' says I. 'Once upon a time when pigs drank wine?'

'No Gran,' says Jemmy, still serious; 'once upon a time when the French drank wine.'

Again I glanced at the Major, and the Major glanced at me.

'In short, Gran and Godfather', says Jemmy looking up, 'the date is this time, and I'm going to tell you Mr Edson's story.'

The flutter that it threw me into. The change of colour on the part of the Major!

'That is to say, you understand', our bright-eyed boy says, 'I am going to give you my version of it. I shall not ask whether it's right or not, firstly because you said you knew very little about it, Gran, and secondly because what little you did know was a secret.'

I folded my hands in my lap and I never took my eyes off Jemmy as he went running on.

'The unfortunate gentleman' Jemmy commences, 'who is the subject of our present narrative was the son of Somebody, and was born Somewhere, and chose a profession Somehow. It is not with those parts of his career that we have to deal; but with his early attachment to a young and beautiful lady.'

I thought I should have dropped. I durstn't look at the Major; but I knew what his state was, without looking at him.

'The father of our ill-starred hero' says Jemmy, copying as it seemed to me the style of some of his story-books, 'was a worldly man who entertained ambitious views for his only son and who firmly set his face against the contemplated alliance with a virtuous but penniless orphan. Indeed he went so far as roundly to assure our hero that unless he weaned his thoughts from the object of his devoted affection, he would disinherit him. At the same time, he proposed as a suitable match, the daughter of a neighbouring gentleman of a good estate, who was neither ill favoured nor unamiable, and whose eligibility in a pecuniary point of view could not be disputed. But young Mr Edson, true to the first and only love that had inflamed his breast, rejected all considerations of self-advancement, and, deprecating his father's anger in a respectful letter, ran away with her.'

My dear I had begun to take a turn for the better, but when it come to running away I began to take another turn for the worse.

'The lovers' says Jemmy 'fled to London and were united at the altar of Saint Clement's Danes. And it is at this period of their simple but touching story, that we find them inmates of the dwelling of a highly respected and beloved lady of the name of Gran, residing within a hundred miles of Norfolk-street.'

I felt that we were almost safe now, I felt that the dear boy had no suspicion of the bitter truth, and I looked at the Major for the first time and drew a long breath. The Major gave me a nod.

'Our hero's father' Jemmy goes on 'proving implacable and carrying his threat into unrelenting execution, the struggles of the young couple in London were severe, and would have been far more so, but for their good angel's having conducted them to the abode of Mrs Gran: who, divining their poverty (in spite of their endeavours to conceal it from her), by a thousand delicate arts smoothed their rough way, and alleviated the sharpness of their first distress.'

Here Jemmy took one of my hands in one of his, and began a marking the turns of his story by making me give a beat from time to time upon his other hand.

'After a while, they left the house of Mrs Gran, and pursued their fortunes through a variety of successes and failures elsewhere. But in all reverses, whether for good or evil, the words of Mr

Edson to the fair young partner of his life, were: "Unchanging Love and Truth will carry us through all!"'

My hand trembled in the dear boy's, those words were so wofully unlike the fact.

'Unchanging Love and Truth' says Jemmy over again, as if he had a proud kind of a noble pleasure in it, 'will carry us through all! Those were his words. And so they fought their way, poor but gallant and happy, until Mrs Edson gave birth to a child.'

'A daughter,' I says.

'No' says Jemmy, 'a son. And the father was so proud of it that he could hardly bear it out of his sight. But a dark cloud overspread the scene. Mrs Edson sickened, drooped, and died.'

'Ah! Sickened, drooped, and died!' I says.

'And so Mr Edson's only comfort, only hope on earth, and only stimulus to action, was his darling boy. As the child grew older, he grew so like his mother that he was her living picture. It used to make him wonder why his father cried when he kissed him. But unhappily he was like his mother in constitution as well as in face, and he died too before he had grown out of childhood. Then Mr Edson, who had good abilities, in his forlornness and despair threw them all to the winds. He became apathetic, reckless, lost. Little by little he sank down, down, down, down, until at last he almost lived (I think) by gaming. And so sickness overtook him in the town of Sens in France, and he lay down to die. But now that he laid him down when all was done, and looked back upon the green Past beyond the time when he had covered it with ashes, he thought gratefully of the good Mrs Gran long lost sight of, who had been so kind to him and his young wife in the early days of their marriage, and he left the little that he had as a last Legacy to her. And she, being brought to see him, at first no more knew him than she would know from seeing the ruin of a Greek or Roman Temple, what it used to be before it fell; but at length she remembered him. And then he told her with tears, of his regret for the misspent part of his life, and besought her to think as mildly of it as she could, because it was the poor fallen Angel of his unchanging Love and Constancy after all. And because she had her grandson with her, and he fancied that his own boy, if he had lived, might have grown to be something like him, he asked her to let him touch his forehead with his cheek and say certain parting words.'

Jemmy's voice sank low when it got to that, and tears filled my eyes, and filled the Major's.

'You little Conjuror' I says, 'how did you ever make it all out? Go in and write it every word down, for it's a wonder.'

Which Jemmy did, and I have repeated it to you my dear from his writing.

Then the Major took my hand and kissed it, and said 'Dearest madam all has prospered with us.'

'Ah Major' I says drying my eyes, 'we needn't have been afraid. We might have known it. Treachery don't come natural to beaming youth; but trust and pity, love and constancy – they do, thank God!'

DOCTOR MARIGOLD'S PRESCRIPTIONS

To Be Taken Immediately

I AM a Cheap Jack, and my own father's name was Willum Marigold. It was in his lifetime supposed by some that his name was William, but my own father always consistently said, No, it was Willum. On which point I content myself with looking at the argument this way:— If a man is not allowed to know his own name in a free country, how much is he allowed to know in a land of slavery? As to looking at the argument through the medium of the Register, Willum Marigold come into the world before Registers come up much — and went out of it too. They wouldn't have been greatly in his line neither, if they had chanced to come up before him.

I was born on the Queen's highway, but it was the King's at that time. A doctor was fetched to my own mother by my own father, when it took place on a common; and in consequence of his being a very kind gentleman, and accepting no fee but a tea-tray, I was named Doctor, out of gratitude and compliment to him. There you have me. Doctor Marigold.

I am at present a middle-aged man of a broadish build, in cords, leggings, and a sleeved waistcoat the strings of which is always gone behind. Repair them how you will, they go like fiddle-strings. You have been to the theatre, and you have seen one of the wiolin-players screw up his wiolin, after listening to it as if it had been whispering the secret to him that it feared it was out of order, and then you have heard it snap. That's as exactly similar to my waistcoat, as a waistcoat and a wiolin can be like one another.

I am partial to a white hat, and I like a shawl round my neck wore loose and easy. Sitting down is my favourite posture. If I have a taste in point of personal jewellery, it is mother-of-pearl buttons. There you have me again, as large as life.

The doctor having accepted a tea-tray, you'll guess that my father was a Cheap Jack before me. You are right. He was. It was a pretty tray. It represented a large lady going along a serpentining up-hill gravel-walk, to attend a little church. Two swans had like-wise come astray with the same intentions. When I call her a large lady, I don't mean in point of breadth, for there she fell below my views, but she more than made it up in heighth; her heighth and slimness was – in short THE heighth of both.

I often saw that tray, after I was the innocently smiling cause (or more likely screeching one) of the doctor's standing it up on a table against the wall in his consulting-room. Whenever my own father and mother were in that part of the country, I used to put my head (I have heard my own mother say it was flaxen curls at that time, though you wouldn't know an old hearth-broom from it now, till you come to the handle and found it wasn't me) in at the doctor's door, and the doctor was always glad to see me, and said, 'Aha, my brother practitioner! Come in, little M.D. How are your inclinations as to sixpence?'

You can't go on for ever, you'll find, nor yet could my father nor yet my mother. If you don't go off as a whole when you are about due, you're liable to go off in part and two to one your head's the part. Gradually my father went off his, and my mother went off hers. It was in a harmless way, but it put out the family where I boarded them. The old couple, though retired, got to be wholly and solely devoted to the Cheap Jack business, and were always selling the family off. Whenever the cloth was laid for dinner, my father began rattling the plates and dishes, as we do in our line when we put up crockery for a bid, only he had lost the trick of it, and mostly let 'em drop and broke 'em. As the old lady had been used to sit in the cart, and hand the articles out one by one to the old gentleman on the footboard to sell, just in the same way she handed him every item of the family's property, and they disposed of it in their own imaginations from morning to night. At last the old gentleman, lying bedridden in the same room with the old lady, cries out in the old patter, fluent, after having been silent for two days and nights: 'Now here, my jolly companions every one – which the Nightingale club in a village was held, At the sign of the Cabbage[1] and Shears, Where the singers no doubt would have greatly excelled, But for want of taste voices and ears – now here, my jolly companions every one, is a working model of a used-up old Cheap Jack, without a tooth in his head, and with a pain in every bone: so like life that it would be just as good if it wasn't better, just as bad if it wasn't worse, and just as new if it wasn't worn out. Bid for the working model of the old Cheap Jack, who has drunk more gunpowder-tea with the ladies in his time than would blow the lid off a washer-woman's copper, and carry it as many thousands of miles higher than the moon as nought nix nought, divided by the national debt, carry nothing to the poor-rates, three under, and two over. Now my hearts of oak[2] and men of straw, what do you say for the lot? Two shillings, a shilling, tenpence, eightpence, sixpence, fourpence. Twopence? Who said twopence? The gentleman in the scare-crow's hat? I am ashamed of the gentleman in the scarecrow's hat. I really am ashamed of him for his want of public spirit. Now I'll tell you what I'll do with you. Come! I'll throw you in a working model of a old woman that was married to the old Cheap Jack so long ago, that upon my word and honour it took place in Noah's Ark, before the Unicorn could get in to forbid the banns by blow-ing a tune upon his horn. There now! Come! What do you say for both? I'll tell you what I'll do with you. I don't bear you malice for being so backward. Here! If you make me a bid that'll only reflect a little credit on your town, I'll throw you in a warming-pan for nothing, and lend you a toasting-fork for life. Now come; what do you say after that splendid offer? Say two pound, say thirty shillings, say a pound, say ten shillings, say five, say two and six. You don't say even two and six? You say two and three? No. You shan't have the lot for two and three. I'd sooner give it you, if you was good looking enough. Here! Missis! Chuck the old man and woman into the cart, put the horse to, and drive 'em away and bury 'em!' Such were the last words of Willum Marigold, my own father, and they were carried out, by him and by his wife my own mother on one and the same day, as I ought to know, having fol-lowed as mourner.

My father had been a lovely one in his time at the Cheap Jack work, as his dying observations went to prove. But I top him. I don't say it because it's myself, but because it has been universally acknowledged by all that has had the means of comparison. I have worked at it. I have measured myself against other public speakers, Members of Parliament, Platforms, Pulpits, Counsel learned in the law – and where I have found 'em good, I have took a bit of imitation from 'em, and where I have found 'em bad, I have let 'em alone. Now I'll tell you what. I mean to go down into my grave declaring that of all the callings ill used in Great Britain, the Cheap Jack calling is the worst used. Why ain't we a profession? Why ain't we endowed with privileges? Why are we forced to take out a hawker's license, when no such thing is expected of the political hawkers? Where's the difference betwixt us? Except that we are Cheap Jacks and they are Dear Jacks. *I* don't see any difference but what's in our favour.

For look here! Say it's election-time. I am on the footboard of my cart in the market-place on a Saturday night. I put up a general miscellaneous lot. I say: 'Now here my free and independent woters, I'm a going to give you such a chance as you never had in all your born days, nor yet the days preceding. Now I'll show you what I am a going to do with you. Here's a pair of razors that'll shave you closer than the Board of Guardians,[3] here's a flat-iron worth its weight in gold, here's a frying-pan artificially flavoured with essence of beefsteaks to that degree that you've only got for the rest of your lives to fry bread and dripping in it and there you are replete with animal food, here's a genuine chronometer watch in such a solid silver case that you may knock at the door with it when you come home late from a social meeting and rouse your wife and family and save up your knocker for the postman, and here's half a dozen dinner plates that you may play the cymbals with to charm the baby when it's fractious. Stop! I'll throw you in another article and I'll give you that, and it's a rolling-pin, and if the baby can only get it well into its mouth when its teeth is coming and rub the gums once with it, they'll come through double, in a fit of laughter equal to being tickled. Stop again! I'll throw you in another article, because I don't like the looks of you, for you haven't the appearance of buyers unless I lose by you, and because I'd rather lose than not take money to-night, and that's a looking-glass in which you may see how ugly you look when you don't bid. What do you say now? Come! Do you say a pound? Not you, for you haven't got it. Do you say ten shillings? Not you, for you owe more to the tallyman. Well then, I'll tell you what I'll do with you. I'll heap 'em all on the footboard of the cart – there they are!

razors, flat-iron, frying-pan, chronometer watch, dinner plates, rolling-pin, and looking-glass – take 'em all away for four shillings, and I'll give you sixpence for your trouble!' This is me, the Cheap Jack. But on the Monday morning, in the same market-place, comes the Dear Jack on the hustings – *his* cart – and what does *he* say? 'Now my free and independent woters, I am going to give you such a chance' (he begins just like me) 'as you never had in all your born days, and that's the chance of sending Myself to Parliament. Now I'll tell you what I am going to do for you. Here's the interests of this magnificent town promoted above all the rest of the civilised and uncivilised earth. Here's your railways carried, and your neighbours' railways jockeyed. Here's all your sons in the Post-office. Here's Britannia smiling on you. Here's the eyes of Europe on you. Here's uniwersal prosperity for you, repletion of animal food, golden cornfields, gladsome homesteads, and rounds of applause from your own hearts, all in one lot and that's myself. Will you take me as I stand? You won't? Well then, I'll tell you what I'll do with you. Come now! I'll throw you in anything you ask for. There! Church-rates, abolition of church-rates, more malt tax, no malt tax, uniwersal education to the highest mark or uniwersal ignorance to the lowest, total abolition of flogging in the army or a dozen for every private once a month all round. Wrongs of Men or Rights of Women, – only say which it shall be, take 'em or leave 'em, and I'm of your opinion altogether, and the lot's your own on your own terms. There! You won't take it yet? Well then, I'll tell you what I'll do with you. Come! You *are* such free and independent woters, and I *am* so proud of you – you *are* such a noble and enlightened constituency, and I *am* so ambitious of the honour and dignity of being your member, which is by far the highest level to which the wings of the human mind can soar – that I'll tell you what I'll do with you. I'll throw you in all the public-houses in your magnificent town for nothing. Will that content you? It won't? You won't take the lot yet? Well then, before I put the horse in and drive away, and make the offer to the next most magnificent town that can be discovered, I'll tell you what I'll do. Take the lot, and I'll drop two thousand pounds in the streets of your magnificent town for them to pick up that can. Not enough? Now look here. This is the very furthest that I'm a going to. I'll make it two thousand five hundred. And still you won't? Here, missis! Put the horse – no, stop half a moment, I shouldn't like to turn my back upon you neither for a trifle, I'll make it two thousand seven hundred and fifty pound. There! Take the lot on your own terms, and I'll count out two thousand seven hundred and fifty pound on the footboard of the cart, to be dropped in the streets of your magnificent town for them to pick up that can. What do you say? Come now! You won't do better, and you may do worse. You take it? Hooray! Sold again, and got the seat!'

These Dear Jacks soap the people shameful, but we Cheap Jacks don't. We tell 'em the truth about themselves to their faces, and scorn to court 'em. As to wenturesomeness in the way of puffing up the lots, the Dear Jacks beat us hollow. It is considered in the Cheap Jack calling that better patter can be made out of a gun than any article we put up from the cart, except a pair of spectacles. I often hold forth about a gun for a quarter of an hour, and feel as if I need never leave off. But when I tell 'em what the gun can do, and what the gun has brought down, I never go half so far as the Dear Jacks do when they make speeches in praise of *their* guns – their great guns that set 'em on to do it. Besides, I'm in business for myself, I ain't sent down into the market-place to order, as they are. Besides again, my guns don't know what I say in their laudation, and their guns do, and the whole concern of 'em have reason to be sick and ashamed all round. These are some of my arguments for declaring that the Cheap Jack calling is treated ill in Great Britain, and for turning warm when I think of the other Jacks in question setting themselves up to pretend to look down upon it.

I courted my wife from the footboard of the cart. I did indeed. She was a Suffolk young woman, and it was in Ipswich market-place right opposite the corn-chandler's shop. I had noticed her up at a window last Saturday that was, appreciating highly. I had took to her, and I had said to myself, 'If not already disposed of, I'll have that lot.' Next Saturday that come, I pitched the cart on the same pitch, and I was in very high feather indeed, keeping 'em laughing the whole of the time and getting off the goods briskly. At last I took out of my waistcoat-pocket, a small lot wrapped in soft paper, and I put it this way (looking up at the window where she was). 'Now here my blooming English maidens is an article, the last article of the present evening's sale, which I offer to only you the lovely Suffolk Dumplings biling over with beauty, and I won't take a bid of a thousand pounds for, from any man alive. Now what is it? Why, I'll tell you what it is. It's made of fine gold, and it's not broke though there's a hole in the middle of it, and it's stronger than any fetter that ever was forged, though it's smaller than any finger in my set of ten. Why ten? Because when my parents made over my property to me, I tell you true, there was twelve sheets, twelve towels, twelve tablecloths, twelve knives, twelve forks, twelve tablespoons, and twelve teaspoons, but my set of fingers was two short of a dozen and could never since be matched. Now what else is it? Come I'll tell you. It's a hoop of solid gold, wrapped in a silver curl-paper that I myself took off the shining locks of the ever beautiful old lady in Threadneedle-street,⁴ London city. I wouldn't tell you so if I hadn't the paper to show, or you mightn't believe it even of me. Now what else is it? It's a man-trap and a handcuff, the parish stocks and a leg-lock, all in gold and all in one. Now what else is it? It's a wedding ring. Now I'll tell you what I'm a-going to do with it. I'm not a-going to offer this lot for money, but I mean to give it to the next of you beauties that laughs, and I'll pay her a visit to-morrow morning at exactly half after nine o'clock as the chimes go, and I'll take her out for a walk to put up the banns.' *She* laughed, and got the ring handed up to her. When I called in the morning, she says, 'Oh dear! It's never you and you never mean it?' 'It's ever me,' said I, 'and I am ever yours, and I ever mean it.' So we got married, after being put up three times – which, by-the-by, is quite in the Cheap Jack way again, and shows once more how the Cheap Jack customs pervade society.

She wasn't a bad wife, but she had a temper. If she could have parted with that one article at a sacrifice, I wouldn't have swopped her away in exchange for any other woman in England. Not that I ever did swop her away, for we lived together till she died, and that was thirteen year. Now my lords and ladies and gentlefolks all, I'll let you into a secret, though you won't believe it. Thirteen year of temper in a Palace would try the worst of you, but thirteen year of temper in a Cart would try the best of you. You are kept so very close to it in a cart, you see. There's thousands of couples among you, getting on like sweet ile upon a whetstone in houses five and six pairs of stairs high, that would go to the Divorce Court in a cart. Whether the jolting makes it worse, I don't undertake to decide, but in a cart it does come home to you and stick to you. Wiolence in a cart, is *so* wiolent, and aggrawation in a cart is *so* aggrawating.

We might have had such a pleasant life! A roomy cart, with the large goods hung outside and the bed slung underneath it when on the road, an iron pot and a kettle, a fireplace for the cold weather, a chimney for the smoke, a hanging shelf and a cupboard, a dog, and a horse. What more do you want? You draw off upon a bit of turf in a green lane or by the roadside, you hobble your old horse and turn him grazing, you light your fire upon the ashes of the last visitors, you cook your stew, and you wouldn't call the Emperor of France your father. But have a temper in the cart, flinging language and the hardest goods in stock at you, and where are you then? Put a name to your feelings.

My dog knew as well when she was on the turn as I did. Before she broke out, he would give a howl, and bolt. How he knew it, was a mystery to me, but the sure and certain knowledge of it would wake him up out of his soundest sleep, and he would give a howl, and bolt. At such times I wished I was him.

The worst of it was, we had a daughter born to us, and I love children with all my heart. When she was in her furies, she beat the child. This got to be so shocking as the child got to be four or five year old, that I have many a time gone on with my whip over my shoulder, at the old horse's head, sobbing and crying worse than ever little Sophy did. For how could I prevent it? Such a thing is not to be tried with such a temper – in a cart – without coming to a fight. It's in the natural size and formation of a cart to bring it to a fight. And then the poor child got worse terrified than before, as well as worse hurt generally, and her mother made complaints to the next people we lighted on, and the word went round, 'Here's a wretch of a Cheap Jack been a beating his wife.'

Little Sophy was such a brave child! She grew to be quite devoted to her poor father, though he could do so little to help her. She had a wonderful quantity of shining dark hair, all curling natural about her. It is quite astonishing to me now, that I didn't go tearing mad when I used to see her run from her mother before the cart, and her mother catch her by this hair, and pull her down by it, and beat her.

Such a brave child I said she was. Ah! with reason.

'Don't you mind next time, father dear,' she would whisper to me, with her little face still flushed, and her bright eyes still wet; 'if I don't cry out, you may know I am not much hurt. And even if I do cry out, it will only be to get mother to let go and leave off.' What I have seen the little spirit bear – for me – without crying out!

Yet in other respects her mother took great care of her. Her clothes were always clean and neat, and her mother was never tired of working at 'em. Such is the inconsistency in things. Our being down in the marsh country in unhealthy weather, I consider the cause of Sophy's taking bad low fever; but however she took it, once she got it she turned away from her mother for evermore, and nothing would persuade her to be touched by her mother's hand. She would shiver and say 'No, no, no,' when it was offered at, and would hide her face on my shoulder, and hold me tighter round the neck.

The Cheap Jack business had been worse than ever I had known it, what with one thing and what with another (and not least what with railroads, which will cut it all to pieces, I expect at last), and I was run dry of money. For which reason, one night at that period of little Sophy's being so bad, either we must have come to a dead-lock for victuals and drink, or I must have pitched the cart as I did.

I couldn't get the dear child to lie down or leave go of me, and indeed I hadn't the heart to try, so I stepped out on the footboard with her holding round my neck. They all set up a laugh when they see us, and one chuckle-headed Joskin⁵ (that I hated for it) made the bidding, 'tuppence for her!'

'Now, you country boobies,' says I, feeling as if my heart was a heavy weight at the end of a broken sash-line, 'I give you notice that I am a going to charm the money out of your pockets, and to give you so much more than your money's worth that you'll only persuade yourselves to draw your Saturday night's wages ever again arterwards, by the hopes of meeting me to lay 'em out with, which you never will, and why not? Because I've made my fortune by selling my goods on a large scale for seventy-five per cent less than I give for 'em, and I am consequently to be elevated to the House of Peers next week, by the title of the Duke of Cheap and Markis Jackaloorul. Now let's know what you want to-night, and you shall have it. But first of all, shall I tell you why I have got this little girl round my neck? You don't want to know? Then you shall. She belongs to the Fairies. She's a fortune-teller. She can tell me all about you in a whisper, and can put me up to whether you're a-going to buy a lot or leave it. Now do you want a saw? No, she says you don't, because you're too clumsy to use one. Else here's a saw which would be a lifelong blessing to a handy man, at four shillings, at three and six, at three, at two and six, at two, at eighteenpence. But none of you shall have it at any price, on account of your well-known awkwardness which would make it manslaughter. The same objection applies to this set of three planes which I won't let you have neither, so don't bid for 'em. Now I am a-going to ask her what you do want. (Then I whispered, 'Your head burns so, that I am afraid it hurts you bad, my pet,' and she answered, without opening her heavy eyes, 'Just a little, father.') Oh! This little fortune-teller says it's a memorandum-book you want. Then why didn't you mention it? Here it is. Look at it. Two hundred super-fine hot-pressed wire-wove pages – if you don't believe me, count 'em – ready ruled for your expenses, an ever-lastingly-pointed pencil to put 'em down with, a double-bladed penknife to scratch 'em out with, a book of printed tables to calculate your income with, and a camp-stool to sit down upon while you give your mind to it! Stop! And an umbrella to keep the moon off when you give your mind to it on a pitch dark night. Now I won't ask you how much for the lot, but how little? How little are you thinking of? Don't be ashamed to mention it, because my fortune-teller knows already. (Then making believe to whisper, I kissed her, and she kissed me.) Why, she says you're thinking of as little as three and threepence! I couldn't have believed it, even of you, unless she told me. Three and threepence! And a set of printed tables in the lot that'll calculate your income up to forty thousand a year! With an income of forty thousand a year, you grudge three and sixpence. Well then, I'll tell you my opinion. I so despise the threepence, that I'd sooner take three shillings. There. For three shilling, three shillings, three shillings! Gone. Hand 'em over to the lucky man.'

As there had been no bid at all, everybody looked about and grinned at everybody, while I touched little Sophy's face and asked her if she felt faint or giddy. 'Not very, father. It will soon be over.' Then turning from the pretty patient eyes, which were opened now, and seeing nothing but grins across my lighted grease-pot, I went on again in my Cheap Jack style. 'Where's the butcher?' (My sorrowful eye had just caught sight of a fat young butcher on the outside of the crowd.) She says the good luck is the butcher's. 'Where is he?' Everybody handed on the blushing butcher to the front, and there was a roar, and the butcher felt himself obliged to put his hand in his pocket and take the lot. The party so picked out, in general does feel obliged to take the lot – good four times out of six. Then we had another lot the counterpart of that one, and sold it sixpence cheaper, which is always very much enjoyed. Then we had the spectacles. It ain't a special profitable lot, but I put 'em on, and I see what the Chancellor of the Exchequer is going to take off the taxes, and I see what the sweetheart of the young woman in the shawl is doing at home, and I see what the Bishops has got for dinner, and a deal more that seldom fails to fetch 'em up in their spirits; and the better their spirits, the better their bids. Then we had the ladies' lot – the teapot, tea-caddy, glass sugar basin, half a dozen spoons, and caudle-cup – and all the time I was making similar excuses to give a look or two and say a word or two to my poor child. It was while the second ladies' lot was holding 'em enchained that I felt her lift herself a little on my shoulder, to look across the dark street. 'What troubles you, darling?' 'Nothing troubles me, father. I am not at all troubled. But don't I see a pretty churchyard over there?' 'Yes, my dear.' 'Kiss me twice, dear father, and lay me down to rest upon that churchyard grass so soft and green.' I staggered back into the cart with her head dropped on my shoulder, and I says to her mother, 'Quick. Shut the door! Don't let those laughing people see!' 'What's the matter?' she cries. 'O, woman, woman,' I tells her, 'you'll never catch my little Sophy by her hair again, for she has flown away from you!'

Maybe those were harder words than I meant 'em, but from that time forth my wife took to brooding, and would sit in the cart or walk beside it, hours at a stretch, with her arms crossed and her eyes looking on the ground. When her furies took her (which was rather seldomer than before) they took her in a new way, and she banged herself about to that extent that I was forced to hold her. She got none the better for a little drink now and then, and through some years I used to wonder as I plodded along at the old horse's head whether there was many carts upon the road that held so much dreariness as mine, for all my being looked up to as the King of the Cheap Jacks. So sad our lives went on till one summer evening, when as we were coming into Exeter out of the further West of England, we saw a woman beating a child in a cruel manner, who screamed, 'Don't beat me! O mother, mother, mother!' Then my wife stopped her ears and ran away like a wild thing, and next day she was found in the river.

Me and my dog were all the company left in the cart now, and the dog learned to give a short bark when they wouldn't bid, and to give another and a nod of his head when I asked him: 'Who said half-a-crown? Are you the gentleman, sir, that offered half-a-crown?' He attained to an immense heighth of popularity, and I shall always believe taught himself entirely out of his own head to growl at any person in the crowd that bid as low as sixpence. But he got to be well on in years, and one night when I was conwulsing York with the spectacles, he took a conwulsion on his own account upon the very footboard by me, and it finished him.

Being naturally of a tender turn, I had dreadful lonely feelings on me arter this. I conquered 'em at selling times, having a reputation to keep (not to mention keeping myself), but they got me down in private and rolled upon me. That's often the way with us public characters. See us on the footboard, and you'd give pretty well anything you possess to be us. See us off the footboard, and you'd add a trifle to be off your bargain. It was under those circumstances that I come acquainted with a giant. I might have been too high to fall into conversation with him, had it not been for my lonely feelings. For the general rule is, going round the country, to draw the line at dressing up. When a man can't trust his getting a living to his undisguised abilities, you consider him below your sort. And this giant when on view figured as a Roman.

He was a languid young man, which I attribute to the distance betwixt his extremities. He had a little head and less in it, he had weak eyes and weak knees, and altogether you couldn't look at him without feeling that there was greatly too much of him both for his joints and his mind. But he was an amiable though timid young man (his mother let him out, and spent the money), and we come acquainted when he was walking to ease the horse betwixt two fairs. He was called Rinaldo di Velasco, his name being Pickleson.

This giant otherwise Pickleson mentioned to me under the seal of confidence, that beyond his being a burden to himself, his life was made a burden to him, by the cruelty of his master towards a step-daughter who was deaf and dumb. Her mother was dead, and she had no living soul to take her part, and was used most hard. She travelled with his master's caravan only because there was no-where to leave her, and this giant otherwise Pickleson did go so far as to believe that his master often tried to lose her. He was such a very languid young man, that I don't know how long it didn't take him to get this story out, but it passed through his defective circulation to his top extremity in course of time.

When I heard this account from the giant otherwise Pickleson, and likewise that the poor girl had beautiful long dark hair, and was often pulled down by it and beaten, I couldn't see the giant through what stood in my eyes. Having wiped 'em, I give him sixpence (for he was kept as short as he was long), and he laid it out in two threepennorths of gin-and-water, which so brisked him up, that he sang the Favourite Comic of Shivery Shakey, ain't it cold.[6] A popular effect which his master had tried every other means to get out of him as a Roman, wholly in vain.

His master's name was Mim, a wery hoarse man and I knew him to speak to. I went to that Fair as a mere civilian, leaving the cart outside the town, and I looked about the back of the Vans while the performing was going on, and at last sitting dozing against a muddy cartwheel, I come upon the poor girl who was deaf and dumb. At the first look I might almost have judged that she had escaped from the Wild Beast Show, but at the second I thought better of her, and thought that if she was more cared for and more kindly used she would be like my child. She was just the same age that my own daughter would have been, if her pretty head had not fell down upon my shoulder that unfortunate night.

To cut it short, I spoke confidential to Mim while he was beating the gong outside betwixt two lots of Pickleson's publics, and I put it to him, 'She lies heavy on your own hands; what'll you take for her?' Mim was a most ferocious swearer. Suppressing that part of his reply, which was much the longest part, his reply was, 'A pair of braces.' 'Now I'll tell you,' says I, 'what I'm a going to do with you. I'm a going to fetch you half a dozen pair of the primest braces in the cart, and then to take her away with me.' Says Mim (again ferocious), 'I'll believe it when I've got the goods, and no sooner.' I made all the haste I could, lest he should think twice of it, and the bargain was completed, which Pickleson he was thereby so relieved in his mind that he come out at his little back door, longways like a serpent, and give us Shivery Shakey in a whisper among the wheels at parting.

It was happy days for both of us when Sophy and me began to travel in the cart. I at once give her the name of Sophy, to put her ever towards me in the attitude of my own daughter. We soon made out to begin to understand one another through the goodness of the Heavens, when she knowed that I meant true and kind by her. In a very little time she was wonderful fond of me. You have no idea what it is to have any body wonderful fond of you, unless you have been got down and rolled upon by the lonely feelings that I have mentioned as having once got the better of me.

You'd have laughed – or the rewerse – it's according to your disposition – if you could have seen me trying to teach Sophy. At first I was helped – you'd never guess by what – milestones. I got large alphabets in a box, all the letters separate on bits of bone, and say we was going to WINDSOR, I give her those letters in that order, and then at every milestone I showed her those same letters in that same order again, and pointed towards the abode of royalty. Another time I give her CART, and then chalked the same upon the cart. Another time I give her DOCTOR MARIGOLD, and hung a corresponding inscription outside my waistcoat. People that met us might stare a bit and laugh, but what did *I* care if she caught the idea? She caught it after long patience and trouble, and then we did begin to get on swimmingly, I believe you! At first she was a little given to consider me the cart, and the cart the abode of royalty, but that soon wore off.

We had our signs, too, and they was hundreds in number. Sometimes, she would sit looking at me and considering hard how to communicate with me about something fresh – how to ask me what she wanted explained – and then she was (or I thought she was; what does it signify?) so like my child with those years added to her, that I half believed it was herself, trying to tell me where she had been to up in the skies, and what she had seen since that unhappy night when she flied away. She had a pretty face, and now that there was no one to drag at her bright dark hair and it was all in order, there was a something touching in her looks that made the cart most peaceful and most quiet, though not at all melancolly. [N.B. In the Cheap Jack patter, we generally sound it, lemonjolly, and it gets a laugh.]

The way she learnt to understand any look of mine was truly surprising. When I sold of a night, she would sit in the cart unseen by them outside, and would give a eager look into my eyes when I looked in, and would hand me straight the precise article or articles I wanted. And then she would clap her hands and laugh for joy. And as for me, seeing her so bright, and remembering what she was when I first lighted on her, starved and beaten and ragged, leaning asleep against the muddy cart-wheel, it give me such heart that I gained a greater heighth of reputation than ever, and I put Pickleson down (by the name of Mim's Travelling Giant otherwise Pickleson) for a fypunnote in my will.

This happiness went on in the cart till she was sixteen year old. By which time I began to feel not satisfied that I had done my whole duty by her, and to consider that she ought to have better teaching than I could give her. It drew a many tears on both sides when I commenced explaining my views to her, but what's right is right and you can't neither by tears nor laughter do away with its character.

So I took her hand in mine, and I went with her one day to the Deaf and Dumb Establishment in London, and when the gentleman come to speak to us, I says to him: 'Now I'll tell you what I'll do with you sir. I am nothing but a Cheap Jack, but of late years I have laid by for a rainy day notwithstanding. This is my only daughter (adopted) and you can't produce a deafer nor a dumber. Teach her the most that can be taught her, in the shortest separation that can

357

be named – state the figure for it – and I am game to put the money down. I won't bate you a single farthing sir but I'll put down the money here and now, and I'll thankfully throw you in a pound to take it. There!' The gentleman smiled, and then, 'Well, well,' says he, 'I must first know what she has learnt already. How do you communicate with her?' Then I showed him, and she wrote in printed writing many names of things and so forth, and we held some sprightly conversation, Sophy and me, about a little story in a book which the gentleman showed her and which she was able to read. 'This is most extraordinary,' says the gentleman; 'is it possible that you have been her only teacher?' 'I have been her only teacher, sir,' I says, 'besides herself.' 'Then,' says the gentleman, and more acceptable words was never spoke to me, 'you're a clever fellow, and a good fellow.' This he makes known to Sophy, who kisses his hands, claps her own, and laughs and cries upon it.

We saw the gentleman four times in all, and when he took down my name and asked how in the world it ever chanced to be Doctor, it come out that he was own nephew by the sister's side, if you'll believe me, to the very Doctor that I was called after. This made our footing still easier, and he says to me:

'Now Marigold, tell me what more do you want your adopted daughter to know?'

'I want her sir to be cut off from the world as little as can be, considering her deprivations, and therefore to be able to read whatever is wrote, with perfect ease and pleasure.'

'My good fellow,' urges the gentleman, opening his eyes wide, 'why *I* can't do that myself!'

I took his joke and give him a laugh (knowing by experience how flat you fall without it) and I mended my words accordingly.

'What do you mean to do with her afterwards?' asks the gentleman, with a sort of a doubtful eye. 'To take her about the country?'

'In the cart sir, but only in the cart. She will live a private life, you understand, in the cart. I should never think of bringing her infirmities before the public. I wouldn't make a show of her, for any money.'

The gentleman nodded and seemed to approve.

'Well,' says he, 'can you part with her for two years?'

'To do her that good – yes, sir.'

'There's another question,' says the gentleman, looking towards her: 'Can she part with you for two years?'

I don't know that it was a harder matter of itself (for the other was hard enough to me), but it was harder to get over. However, she was pacified to it at last, and the separation betwixt us was settled. How it cut up both of us when it took place, and when I left her at the door in the dark of an evening, I don't tell. But I know this: – remembering that night, I shall never pass that same establishment without a heart-ache and a swelling in the throat, and I couldn't put you up the best of lots in sight of it with my usual spirit – no, not even the gun, nor the pair of spectacles – for five hundred pound reward from the Secretary of State for the Home Department, and throw in the honour of putting my legs under his mahogany arterwards.

Still, the loneliness that followed in the cart was not the old loneliness, because there was a term put to it however long to look forward to, and because I could think, when I was anyways down, that she belonged to me and I belonged to her. Always planning for her coming back, I bought in a few months' time another cart, and what do you think I planned to do with it? I'll tell you. I planned to fit it up with shelves, and books for her reading, and to have a seat in it where I could sit and see her read, and think that I had been her first teacher. Not hurrying over the job, I had the fittings knocked together in contriving ways under my own inspection, and here was her bed in a berth with curtains, and there was her reading-table, and here was her writing-desk, and elsewhere was her books in rows upon rows, picters and no picters, bindings and no bindings, gilt-edged and plain, just as I could pick 'em up for her in lots up and down the country, North and South and West and East, Winds liked best and winds liked least, Here and there and gone astray, Over the hills and far away.[7] And when I had got together pretty well as many books as the cart would neatly hold, a new scheme come into my head which, as it turned out, kept my time and attention a good deal employed and helped me over the two years stile.

Without being of an awaricious temper, I like to be the owner of things. I shouldn't wish, for instance, to go partners with yourself in the Cheap Jack cart. It's not that I mistrust you, but that I'd rather know it was mine. Similarly, very likely you'd rather know it was yours. Well! A kind of a jealousy began to creep into my mind when I reflected that all those books would have been read by other people long before they was read by her. It seemed to take away from her being the owner of 'em like. In this way, the question got into my head: – Couldn't I have a book new-made express for her, which she should be the first to read?

It pleased me, that thought did, and as I never was a man to let a thought sleep (you must wake up all the whole family of thoughts you've got and burn their nightcaps, or you won't do in the cheap Jack line), I set to work at it. Considering that I was in the habit of changing so much about the country, and that I should have to find out a literary character here to make a deal with, and another literary character there to make a deal with, as opportunities presented, I hit on the plan that this same book should be a general miscellaneous lot – like the razors, flat-iron, chronometer watch, dinner plates, rolling-pin, and looking-glass – and shouldn't be offered as a single indiwidual article like the spectacles or the gun. When I had come to that conclusion, I come to another, which shall likewise be yours.

Often had I regretted that she never had heard me on the foot-board, and that she never could hear me. It ain't that *I* am vain, but that *you* don't like to put your own light under a bushel.[8] What's the worth of your reputation, if you can't convey the reason for it to the person you most wish to value it? Now I'll put it to you. Is it worth sixpence, fippence, fourpence, threepence, twopence, a penny, a halfpenny, a farthing? No, it ain't. Not worth a farthing. Very well then. My conclusion was, that I would begin her book with some account of myself. So that, through reading a specimen or two of me on the foot-board, she might form an idea of my merits there. I was aware that I couldn't do myself justice. A man can't write his eye (at least *I* don't know how to), nor yet can a man write his voice, nor the rate of his talk, nor the quickness of his action, nor his general spicy way. But he can write his turns of speech, when he is a public speaker – and indeed I have heard that he very often does, before he speaks 'em.

Well! Having formed that resolution, then come the question of a name. How did I hammer that hot iron into shape? This way.

The most difficult explanation I had ever had with her was, how I come to be called Doctor, and yet was no Doctor. After all, I felt that I had failed of getting it correctly into her mind, with my utmost pains. But trusting to her improvement in the two years, I thought that I might trust to her understanding it when she should come to read it as put down by my own hand. Then I thought I would try a joke with her and watch how it took, by which of itself I might fully judge of her understanding it. We had first discovered the mistake we had dropped into, through her having asked me to prescribe for her when she had supposed me to be a Doctor in a medical point of view, so thinks I, 'Now, if I give this book the name of my Prescriptions, and if she catches the idea that my only Prescriptions are for her amusement and interest – to make her laugh in a pleasant way, or to make her cry in a pleasant way – it will be a delightful proof to both of us that we have got over our difficulty.' It fell out to absolute perfection. For when she saw the book, as I had it got up – the printed and pressed book – lying on her desk in her cart, and saw the title, DOCTOR MARIGOLD'S PRESCRIPTIONS, she looked at me for a moment with astonishment, then fluttered the leaves, then broke out a laughing in the charmingest way, then felt her pulse and shook her head, then turned the pages pretending to read them most attentive, then kissed the book to me, and put it to her bosom with both her hands. I never was better pleased in all my life!

But let me not anticipate. (I take that expression out of a lot of romances I bought for her. I never opened a single one of 'em – and I have opened many – but I found the romancer saying 'let me not anticipate.' Which being so, I wonder why he did anticipate, or who asked him to it.) Let me not, I say, anticipate. This same book took up all my spare time. It was no play to get the other articles together in the general miscellaneous lot, but when it come to my own article! There! I couldn't have believed the blotting, nor yet the buckling to at it, nor the patience over it. Which again is like the footboard. The public have no idea.

At last it was done, and the two years' time was gone after all the other time before it, and where it's all gone to, Who knows? The new cart was finished – yellow outside, relieved with wermillion and brass fittings – the old horse was put in it, a new 'un and a boy being laid on for the Cheap Jack cart – and I cleaned myself up to go and fetch her. Bright cold weather it was, cart-chimneys smoking, carts pitched private on a piece of waste ground over at Wandsworth where you may see 'em from the Sou' Western Railway when not upon the road. (Look out of the right-hand window going down.)

'Marigold,' says the gentleman, giving his hand hearty, 'I am very glad to see you.'

'Yet I have my doubts, sir,' says I, 'if you can be half as glad to see me, as I am to see you.'

'The time has appeared so long; has it, Marigold?'

'I won't say that, sir, considering its real length; but – '

'What a start, my good fellow!'

Ah! I should think it was! Grown such a woman, so pretty, so intelligent, so expressive! I knew then that she must be really like my child, or I could never have known her, standing quiet by the door.

'You are affected,' says the gentleman in a kindly manner.

'I feel, sir,' says I, 'that I am but a rough chap in a sleeved waistcoat.'

'*I* feel,' says the gentleman, 'that it was you who raised her from misery and degradation, and brought her into communication with her kind. But why do we converse alone together, when we can converse so well with her? Address her in your own way.'

'I am such a rough chap in a sleeved waistcoat, sir,' says I, 'and she is such a graceful woman, and she stands so quiet at the door!'

'Try if she moves at the old sign,' says the gentleman.

They had got it up together o' purpose to please me! For when I give her the old sign, she rushed to my feet, and dropped upon her knees, holding up her hands to me with pouring tears of love and joy; and when I took her hands and lifted her, she clasped me round the neck and lay there; and I don't know what a fool I didn't make of myself, until we all three settled down into talking without sound, as if there was a something soft and pleasant spread over the whole world for us.

Now I'll tell you what I am a going to do with you. I am a going to offer you the general miscellaneous lot, her own book, never read by anybody else but me, added to and completed by me after her first reading of it, eight-and-forty printed pages, six-and-ninety columns,9 Whiting's own work, Beaufort House to wit, thrown off by the steam-ingine, best of paper, beautiful green wrapper, folded like clean linen come home from the clear-starcher's, and so exquisitely stitched that, regarded as a piece of needlework alone it's better than the sampler of a seamstress undergoing a Competitive Examination for Starvation before the Civil Service Commissioners – and I offer the lot for what? For eight pound? Not so much. For six pound? Less. For four pound? Why, I hardly expect you to believe me, but that's the sum. Four pound! The stitching alone cost half as much again. Here's forty-eight original pages, ninety-six original columns, for four pound. You want more for the money? Take it. Three whole pages of advertisements of thrilling interest thrown in for nothing. Read 'em and believe 'em. More? My best of wishes for your merry Christmases and your happy New Years, your long lives and your true prosperities. Worth twenty pound good if they are delivered as I send them. Remember! Here's a final prescription added, 'To be taken for life,' which will tell you how the cart broke down, and where the journey ended. You think Four Pound too much? And still you think so? Come! I'll tell you what then. Say Four Pence, and keep the secret.

To Be Taken for Life

Sophy read through the whole of the foregoing several times over, and I sat in my seat in the Library Cart (that's the name we give it) seeing her read, and I was as pleased and as proud as a Pug-Dog with his muzzle black-leaded for an evening party and his tail extra curled by machinery. Every item of my plan was crowned with success. Our reunited life was more than all that we had looked forward to. Content and joy went with us as the wheels of the two carts went round, and the same stopped with us when the two carts stopped.

But I had left something out of my calculations. Now, what had I left out? To help you to a guess, I'll say, a figure. Come. Make a guess, and guess right. Nought? No. Nine? No. Eight? No. Seven? No. Six? No. Five? No. Four? No. Three? No. Two? No. One? No. Now I'll tell you what I'll do with you. I'll say it's another sort of figure altogether. There. Why then, says you, it's a mortal figure. No nor yet a mortal figure. By such means you get yourself penned into a corner, and you can't help guessing a *im*mortal figure. That's about it. Why didn't you say so sooner?

Yes. It was a immortal figure that I had altogether left out of my calculations. Neither man's nor woman's, but a child's. Girl's, or boy's? Boy's. 'I says the sparrow, with my bow and arrow.'[1] Now you have got it.

We were down at Lancaster, and I had done two nights' more than fair average business (though I cannot in honour recommend them as a quick audience) in the open square there, near the end of the street where Mr Sly's King's Arms and Royal Hotel stands. Mim's travelling giant otherwise Pickleson happened at the self-same time to be a trying it on in the town. The genteel lay was adopted with him. No hint of a van. Green baize alcove leading up to Pickleson in a Auction Room. Printed poster 'Free list suspended, with the exception of that proud boast of an enlightened country, a free press. Schools admitted by private arrangement. Nothing to raise a blush in the cheek of youth or shock the most fastidious.' Mim swearing most horrible and terrific in a pink calico pay-place, at the slackness of the public. Serious hand-bill in the shops, importing that it was all but impossible to come to a right understanding of the history of David[2], without seeing Pickleson.

I went to the Auction Room in question, and I found it entirely empty of everything but echoes and mouldiness, with the single exception of Pickleson on a piece of red drugget. This suited my purpose, as I wanted a private and confidential word with him, which was: 'Pickleson. Owing much happiness to you, I put you in my will for a fypunnote; but, to save trouble here's fourpunten down, which may equally suit your views, and let us so conclude the transaction.' Pickleson, who up to that remark had had the dejected appearance of a long Roman rushlight that couldn't any-how get lighted, brightened up at his top extremity and made his acknowledgments in a way which (for him) was parliamentary eloquence. He likewise did add, that, having ceased to draw as a Roman, Mim had made proposals for his going in as a converted Indian Giant worked upon by The Dairyman's Daughter.[3] This, Pickleson, having no acquaintance with the tract named after that young woman, and not being willing to couple gag with his serious views, had declined to do, thereby leading to words and the total stoppage of the unfortunate young man's beer. All of which, during the whole of the interview, was confirmed by the ferocious growling of Mim down below in the pay-place, which shook the giant like a leaf.

But what was to the present point in the remarks of the travelling giant otherwise Pickleson, was this: 'Doctor Marigold' – I give his words without a hope of conweying their feebleness – 'who is the strange young man that hangs about your carts?' – 'The strange young *man*?' I gives him back, thinking that he meant her, and his languid circulation had dropped a syllable. 'Doctor,' he returns, with a pathos calculated to draw a tear from even a manly eye, 'I am weak, but not so weak yet as that I don't know my words. I repeat them, Doctor. The strange young man.' It then appeared that Pickleson being forced to stretch his legs (not that they wanted it) only at times when he couldn't be seen for nothing, to wit in the dead of the night and towards daybreak, had twice seen hanging about my carts, in that same town of Lancaster where I had been only two nights, this same unknown young man.

It put me rather out of sorts. What it meant as to particulars I no more foreboded then, than you forebode now, but it put me rather out of sorts. Howsoever, I made light of it to Pickleson, and I took leave of Pickleson advising him to spend his legacy in getting up his stamina, and to continue to stand by his religion. Towards morning I kept a look-out for the strange young man, and what was more – I saw the strange young man. He was well dressed and well looking. He loitered very nigh my carts, watching them like as if he was taking care of them, and soon after daybreak turned and went away. I sent a hail after him, but he never started or looked round, or took the smallest notice.

We left Lancaster within an hour or two, on our way towards Carlisle. Next morning at daybreak, I looked out again for the strange young man. I did not see him. But next morning I looked out again, and there he was once more. I sent another hail after him, but as before he gave not the slightest sign of being anyways disturbed. This put a thought into my head. Acting on it, I watched him in different manners and at different times not necessary to enter into, till I found that this strange young man was deaf and dumb.

The discovery turned me over, because I knew that a part of that establishment where she had been, was allotted to young men (some of them well off), and I thought to myself 'If she favours him, where am I, and where is all that I have worked and planned for?' Hoping – I must confess to the selfishness – that she might *not* favour him, I set myself to find out. At last I was by accident present at a meeting between them in the open air, looking on leaning behind a fir-tree without their knowing of it. It was a moving meeting for all the three parties concerned. I knew every syllable that passed between them, as well as they did. I listened with my eyes, which had come to be as quick and true with deaf and dumb conversation, as my ears with the talk of people that can speak. He was a going out to China as clerk in a merchant's house, which his father had been before him. He was in circumstances to keep a wife, and he wanted her to marry him and go along with him. She persisted, no. He asked if she didn't love him? Yes, she loved him dearly, dearly, but she could never disappoint her beloved good noble generous and I don't-know-what-all father (meaning me, the Cheap Jack in the sleeved waistcoat), and she would stay with him, Heaven bless him, though it was to break her heart! Then she cried most bitterly, and that made up my mind.

While my mind had been in an unsettled state about her favouring this young man, I had felt that unreasonable towards Pickleson, that it was well for him he had got his legacy down. For I often thought 'If it hadn't been for this same weak-minded giant, I might never have come to trouble my head and wex my soul about the young man.' But, once that I knew she loved him – once that I had seen her weep for him – it was a different thing. I made it right in my mind with Pickleson on the spot, and I shook myself together to do what was right by all.

She had left the young man by that time (for it took a few minutes to get me thoroughly well shook together), and the young man was leaning against another of the fir-trees – of which there was a cluster – with his face upon his arm. I touched him on the back. Looking up and seeing me, he says, in our deaf and dumb talk: 'Do not be angry.'

'I am not angry, good boy. I am your friend. Come with me.'

I left him at the foot of the steps of the Library Cart, and I went up alone. She was drying her eyes.

'You have been crying, my dear.'

'Yes, father.'

'Why?'

'A head-ache.'

'Not a heart-ache?'

'I said a head-ache, father.'

'Doctor Marigold must prescribe for that head-ache.'

She took up the book of my Prescriptions, and held it up with a forced smile, but seeing me keep still and look earnest, she softly laid it down again, and her eyes were very attentive.

'The Prescription is not there, Sophy.'

'Where is it?'

'Here, my dear.'

I brought her young husband in, and I put her hand in his, and my only further words to both of them were these: 'Doctor Marigold's last prescription. To be taken for life.' After which I bolted.

When the wedding come off, I mounted a coat (blue, and bright buttons), for the first and last time in all my days, and I give Sophy away with my own hand. There were only us three and the gentleman who had had charge of her for those two years. I give the wedding dinner for four in the Library Cart. Pigeon pie, a leg of pickled pork, a pair of fowls, and suitable garden-stuff. The best of drinks. I give them a speech, and the gentlemen give us a speech, and all our jokes told, and the whole went off like a sky-rocket. In the course of the entertainment I explained to Sophy that I should keep the Library Cart as my living-cart when not upon the road, and that I should keep all her books for her just as they stood, till she come back to claim them. So she went to China with her young husband, and it was a parting sorrowful and heavy, and I got the boy I had another service, and so as of old when my child and wife were gone, I went plodding along alone, with my whip over my shoulder, at the old horse's head.

Sophy wrote me many letters, and I wrote her many letters. About the end of the first year she sent me one in an unsteady hand: 'Dearest father, not a week ago I had a darling little daughter, but I am so well that they let me write these words to you. Dearest and best father, I hope my child may not be deaf and dumb, but I do not yet know.' When I wrote back, I hinted the question; but as Sophy never answered that question, I felt it to be a sad one, and I never repeated it. For a long time our letters were regular, but then they got irregular through Sophy's husband being moved to another station, and through my being always on the move. But we were in one another's thoughts, I was equally sure, letters or no letters.

Five years, odd months, had gone since Sophy went away. I was still the King of the Cheap Jacks, and at a greater heighth of popularity than ever. I had had a first-rate autumn of it, and on the twenty-third of December, one thousand eight hundred and sixty-four, I found myself at Uxbridge, Middlesex, clean sold out. So I jogged up to London with the old horse, light and easy, to have my Christmas-Eve and Christmas Day alone by the fire in the Library Cart, and then to buy a regular new stock of goods all round, to sell 'em again and get the money.

I am a neat hand at cookery, and I'll tell you what I knocked up for my Christmas-Eve dinner in the Library Cart. I knocked up a beefsteak pudding for one, with two kidneys, a dozen oysters, and a couple of mushrooms, thrown in. It's a pudding to put a man in good humour with everything, except the two bottom buttons of his waistcoat. Having relished that pudding and cleared away, I turned the lamp low, and sat down by the light of the fire, watching it as it shone upon the backs of Sophy's books.

Sophy's books so brought up Sophy's self, that I saw her touching face quite plainly, before I dropped off dozing by the fire. This may be a reason why Sophy, with her deaf and dumb child in her arms, seemed to stand silent by me all through my nap. I was on the road, off the road, in all sorts of places, North and South and West and East, Winds liked best and winds liked least, Here and there and gone astray, Over the hills and far away, and still she stood silent by me, with her silent child in her arms. Even when I woke with a start, she seemed to vanish, as if she had stood by me in that very place only a single instant before.

I had started at a real sound, and the sound was on the steps of the cart. It was the light hurried tread of a child, coming clambering up. That tread of a child had once been so familiar to me, that for half a moment I believed I was a going to see a little ghost.

But the touch of a real child was laid upon the outer handle of the door, and the handle turned and the door opened a little way, and a real child peeped in. A bright little comely girl with large dark eyes.

Looking full at me, the tiny creature took off her mite of a straw hat, and a quantity of dark curls fell all about her face. Then she opened her lips, and said in a pretty voice:

'Grandfather!'

'Ah my God!' I cries out. 'She can speak!'

'Yes, dear grandfather. And I am to ask you whether there was ever any one that I remind you of?'

In a moment Sophy was round my neck as well as the child, and her husband was a wringing my hand with his face hid, and we all had to shake ourselves together before we could get over it. And when we did begin to get over it, and I saw the pretty child a talking, pleased and quick and eager and busy, to her mother, in the signs that I had first taught her mother, the happy and yet pitying tears fell rolling down my face.

MUGBY JUNCTION

Main Line. The Boy at Mugby

I AM The Boy at Mugby. That's about what *I* am.

You don't know what I mean? What a pity! But I think you do. I think you must. Look here. I am the Boy at what is called the Refreshment Room at Mugby Junction, and what's proudest boast is, that it never yet refreshed a mortal being.

Up in a corner of the Down Refreshment Room at Mugby Junction, in the height of twenty-seven cross draughts (I've often counted 'em while they brush the First Class hair twenty-seven ways), behind the bottles, among the glasses, bounded on the nor'-west by the beer, stood pretty far to the right of a metallic object that's at times the tea-urn and at times the soup-tureen, according to the nature of the last twang imparted to its contents which are the same groundwork, fended off from the traveller by a barrier of stale sponge-cakes erected atop of the counter, and lastly exposed sideways to the glare of Our Missis's eye – you ask a Boy so siti-wated, next time you stop in a hurry at Mugby, for anything to drink; you take particular notice that he'll try to seem not to hear you, that he'll appear in a absent manner to survey the Line through a transparent medium composed of your head and body, and that he won't serve you as long as you can possibly bear it. That's Me.

What a lark it is! We are the Model Establishment, we are, at Mugby. Other Refreshment Rooms send their imperfect young ladies up to be finished off by our Missis. For some of the young ladies, when they're new to the business, come into it mild! Ah! Our Missis, she soon takes that out of 'em. Why, I originally come into the business meek myself. But Our Missis she soon took that out of *me*.

What a delightful lark it is! I look upon us Refreshmenters as ockipying the only proudly independent footing on the Line. There's Papers for instance – my honourable friend if he will allow me to call him so – him as belongs to Smith's bookstall. Why he no more dares to be up to our Refreshmenting games, than he dares to jump atop of a locomotive with her steam at full pressure, and cut away upon her alone, driving himself, at limited-mail speed. Papers, he'd get his head punched at every compartment, first second and third, the whole length of a train, if he was to ventur to imitate my demeanour. It's the same with the porters, the same with the guards, the same with the ticket clerks, the same the whole way up to the secretary, traffic manager, or very chairman. There ain't a one among 'em on the nobly independent footing we are. Did you ever catch one of *them*, when you wanted anything of him, making a system of surveying the Line through a transparent medium composed of your head and body? I should hope not.

You should see our Bandolining[1] Room at Mugby Junction. It's led to, by the door behind the counter which you'll notice usually stands ajar, and it's the room where Our Missis and our young ladies Bandolines their hair. You should see 'em at it, betwixt trains, Bandolining away, as if they was anointing themselves for the combat. When you're telegraphed, you should see their noses all a going up with scorn, as if it was a part of the working of the same Cooke and Wheatstone electrical machinery.[2] You should hear Our Missis give the word 'Here comes the Beast to be Fed!' and then you should see 'em indignantly skipping across the Line, from the Up to the Down, or Wicer Warsaw, and begin to pitch the stale pastry into the plates, and chuck the sawdust sangwiches under the glass covers, and get out the – ha ha ha! – the Sherry – O my eye, my eye! – for your Refreshment.

It's only in the Isle of the Brave and Land of the Free (by which of course I mean to say Británnia) that Refreshmenting is so effective, so 'olesome, so constitutional, a check upon the public. There was a foreigner, which having politely, with his hat off, beseeched our young ladies and Our Missis for 'a leetel gloss hoff prarndee,' and having had the Line surveyed through him by all and no other acknowledgment, was a proceeding at last to help himself, as seems to be the custom in his own country, when Our Missis with her hair almost a coming un-Bandolined with rage, and her eyes omitting sparks, flew at him, cotched the decanter out of his hand, and said: 'Put it down! I won't allow that!' The foreigner turned pale, stepped back with his arms stretched out in front of him, his hands clasped, and his shoulders riz, and exclaimed: 'Ah! It is possible this! That these disdaineous females and this ferocious

old woman are placed here by the administration, not only to em-
poison the voyagers, but to affront them! Great Heaven! How
arrives it? The English people. Or is he then a slave? Or idiot?'
Another time, a merry wideawake American gent had tried the
sawdust and spit it out, and had tried the Sherry and spit that out,
and had tried in vain to sustain exhausted natur upon Butter-
Scotch, and had been rather extra Bandolined and Line-surveyed
through, when, as the bell was ringing and he paid Our Missis, he
says, very loud and good-tempered: 'I tell Yew what 'tis, ma'arm.
I la'af. Theer! I la'af. I Dew. I oughter ha' seen most things, for I
hail from the Onlimited side of the Atlantic Ocean, and I haive
travelled righ slick over the Limited, head on through Jee-rusalemm
and the East, and likeways France and Italy, Europe Old World, and
am now upon the track to the Chief Europian Village; but such
an Institution as Yew, and Yewer young ladies, and Yewer fixin's
solid and liquid, afore the glorious Tarnal I never did see yet!
And if I hain't found the eighth wonder of monarchical Creation,
in finding Yew, and Yewer young ladies, and Yewer fixin's solid
and liquid, all as aforesaid, established in a country where the people
air not absolute Loo-naticks, I am Extra Double Darned with a
Nip and Frizzle to the innermostest grit! Wheerfur – Theer! – I la'af!
I Dew, ma'arm. I la'af!' And so he went, stamping and shaking
his sides, along the platform all the way to his own compartment.

I think it was her standing up agin the Foreigner, as giv' Our
Missis the idea of going over to France, and droring a comparison
betwixt Refreshmenting as followed among the frog-eaters, and
Refreshmenting as triumphant in the Isle of the Brave and Land of
the Free (by which of course I mean to say agin, Britannia). Our
young ladies, Miss Whiff, Miss Piff, and Mrs Sniff, was unanimous
opposed to her going; for, as they says to Our Missis one and all,
it is well beknown to the hends of the herth as no other nation
except Britain has a idea of anythink, but above all of business. Why
then should you tire yourself to prove what is already proved? Our
Missis however (being a teazer at all pints) stood out grim obstinate,
and got a return pass by South-Eastern Tidal, to go right through,
if such should be her dispositions, to Marseilles.

Sniff is husband to Mrs Sniff, and is a regular insignificant cove.
He looks arter the sawdust department in a back room, and is

sometimes when we are very hard put to it let in behind the counter with a corkscrew; but never when it can be helped, his demeanour towards the public being disgusting servile. How Mrs Sniff ever come so far to lower herself as to marry him, I don't know; but I suppose *he* does, and I should think he wished he didn't, for he leads a awful life. Mrs Sniff couldn't be much harder with him if he was public. Similarly, Miss Whiff and Miss Piff, taking the tone of Mrs Sniff, they shoulder Sniff about when he *is* let in with a cork-screw, and they whisk things out of his hands when in his servility he is a going to let the public have 'em, and they snap him up when in the crawling baseness of his spirit he is a going to answer a public question, and they drore more tears into his eyes than ever the mustard does which he all day long lays on to the sawdust. (But it ain't strong.) Once, when Sniff had the repulsiveness to reach across to get the milk-pot to hand over for a baby, I see Our Missis in her rage catch him by both his shoulders and spin him out into the Bandolining Room.

But Mrs Sniff. How different! She's the one! She's the one as you'll notice to be always looking another way from you, when you look at her. She's the one with the small waist buckled in tight in front, and with the lace cuffs at her wrists, which she puts on the edge of the counter before her, and stands a smoothing while the public foams. This smoothing the cuffs and looking another way while the public foams, is the last accomplishment taught to the young ladies as come to Mugby to be finished by Our Missis; and it's always taught by Mrs Sniff.

When Our Missis went away upon her journey, Mrs Sniff was left in charge. She did hold the public in check most beautiful! In all my time, I never see half so many cups of tea given without milk to people as wanted it with, nor half so many cups of tea with milk given to people as wanted it without. When foaming ensued, Mrs Sniff would say: 'Then you'd better settle it among yourselves, and change with one another.' It was a most highly delicious lark. I enjoyed the Refreshmenting business more than ever, and was so glad I had took to it when young.

Our Missis returned. It got circulated among the young ladies, and it as it might be penetrated to me through the crevices of the Bandolining Room, that she had Orrors to reveal, if revelations so contemptible could be dignified with the name. Agitation become awakened. Excitement was up in the stirrups. Expectation stood a tiptoe. At length it was put forth that on our slackest evening in the week, and at our slackest time of that evening betwixt trains, Our Missis would give her views of foreign Refreshmenting, in the Bandolining Room.

It was arranged tasteful for the purpose. The Bandolining table and glass was hid in a corner, a arm-chair was elevated on a packing-case for Our Missis's ockypation, a table and a tumbler of water (no sherry in it, thankee) was placed beside it. Two of the pupils, the season being autumn, and hollyhocks and daliahs being in, ornamented the wall with three devices in those flowers. On one might be read, 'MAY ALBION NEVER LEARN;' on another, 'KEEP THE PUBLIC DOWN;' on another, 'OUR REFRESH-MENTING CHARTER.' The whole had a beautiful appearance, with which the beauty of the sentiments corresponded.

On Our Missis's brow was wrote Severity, as she ascended the fatal platform. (Not that that was anythink new.) Miss Whiff and Miss Piff sat at her feet. Three chairs from the Waiting Room might have been perceived by a average eye, in front of her, on which the pupils was accommodated. Behind them, a very close observer might have discerned a Boy. Myself.

'Where,' said Our Missis, glancing gloomily around, 'is Sniff?'

'I thought it better,' answered Mrs Sniff, 'that he should not be let to come in. He is such an Ass.'

'No doubt,' assented Our Missis. 'But for that reason is it not desirable to improve his mind?'

'O! Nothing will ever improve *him*,' said Mrs Sniff.

'However,' pursued Our Missis, 'call him in, Ezekiel.'

I called him in. The appearance of the low-minded cove was hailed with disapprobation from all sides, on account of his having brought his corkscrew with him. He pleaded 'the force of habit.'

'The force!' said Mrs Sniff. 'Don't let us have you talking about force, for Gracious sake. There! Do stand still where you are, with your back against the wall.'

He is a smiling piece of vacancy, and he smiled in the mean way in which he will even smile at the public if he gets a chance (language can say no meaner of him), and he stood upright near the door with the back of his head agin the wall, as if he was a waiting for somebody to come and measure his heighth for the Army.

'I should not enter, ladies,' says Our Missis, 'on the revolting disclosures I am about to make, if it was not in the hope that they will cause you to be yet more implacable in the exercise of the power you wield in a constitutional country, and yet more devoted to the constitutional motto which I see before me:' it was behind her, but the words sounded better so; '"May Albion never learn!"'

Here the pupils as had made the motto, admired it, and cried, 'Hear! Hear! Hear!' Sniff, showing an inclination to join in chorus, got himself frowned down by every brow.

'The baseness of the French,' pursued Our Missis, 'as displayed in the fawning nature of their Refreshmenting, equals, if not surpasses, anythink as was ever heard of the baseness of the celebrated Buonaparte.'

Miss Whiff, Miss Piff and me, we drored a heavy breath, equal to saying, 'We thought as much!' Miss Whiff and Miss Piff seeming to object to my droring mine along with theirs, I drored another, to aggravate 'em.

'Shall I be believed,' says Our Missis, with flashing eyes, 'when I tell you that no sooner had I set my foot upon that treacherous shore – '

Here Sniff, either busting out mad, or thinking aloud, says, in a low voice: 'Feet. Plural, you know.'

The cowering that come upon him when he was spurned by all eyes, added to his being beneath contempt, was sufficient punishment for a cove so grovelling. In the midst of a silence rendered more impressive by the turned-up female noses with which it was pervaded, Our Missis went on:

'Shall I be believed when I tell you that no sooner had I landed,' this word with a killing look at Sniff, 'on that treacherous shore, than I was ushered into a Refreshment Room where there were, I do not exaggerate, actually eatable things to eat?'

A groan burst from the ladies. I not only did myself the honour of jining, but also of lengthening it out.

'Where there were,' Our Missis added, 'not only eatable things to eat, but also drinkable things to drink?'

A murmur, swelling almost into a scream, ariz. Miss Piff, trembling with indignation, called out: 'Name!'

'I *will* name,' said Our Missis. 'There was roast fowls, hot and cold; there was smoking roast veal surrounded with browned potatoes; there was hot soup with (again I ask shall I be credited?) nothing bitter in it, and no flour to choke off the consumer; there was a variety of cold dishes set off with jelly; there was salad; there was – mark me! – *fresh* pastry, and that of a light construction; there was a luscious show of fruit. There was bottles and decanters of sound small wine, of every size and adapted to every pocket; the same odious statement will apply to brandy; and these were set out upon the counter so that all could help themselves.'

Our Missis's lips so quivered, that Mrs Sniff, though scarcely less convulsed than she were, got up and held the tumbler to them.

'This,' proceeds Our Missis, 'was my first unconstitutional experience. Well would it have been, if it had been my last and worst. But no. As I proceeded further into that enslaved and ignorant land, its aspect became more hideous. I need not explain to this assembly, the ingredients and formation of the British Refreshment sangwich?'

Universal laughter – except from Sniff, who, as sangwich-cutter, shook his head in a state of the utmost dejection as he stood with it agin the wall.

'Well!' said Our Missis, with dilated nostrils. 'Take a fresh crisp long crusty penny loaf made of the whitest and best flour. Cut it longwise through the middle. Insert a fair and nicely fitting slice of ham. Tie a smart piece of ribbon round the middle of the whole to bind it together. Add at one end a neat wrapper of clean white paper by which to hold it. And the universal French Refreshment sangwich busts on your disgusted vision.'

A cry of 'Shame!' from all – except Sniff, which rubbed his stomach with a soothing hand.

'I need not,' said Our Missis, 'explain to this assembly, the usual formation and fitting of the British Refreshment Room?'

No, no, and laughter. Sniff agin shaking his head in low spirits agin the wall.

'Well,' said Our Missis, 'what would you say to a general decoration of everythink, to hangings (sometimes elegant), to easy velvet furniture, to abundance of little tables, to abundance of little seats, to brisk bright waiters, to great convenience, to a pervading cleanliness and tastefulness positively addressing the public and making the Beast thinking itself worth the pains?'

Contemptuous fury on the part of all the ladies. Mrs Sniff looking as if she wanted somebody to hold her, and everybody else looking as if they'd rayther not.

'Three times,' said Our Missis, working herself into a truly terrimenjious state, 'three times did I see these shameful things, only between the coast and Paris, and not counting either: at Hazebroucke, at Arras, at Amiens. But worse remains. Tell me, what would you call a person who should propose in England that there should be kept, say at our own model Mugby Junction, pretty baskets, each holding an assorted cold lunch and dessert for one, each at a certain fixed price, and each within a passenger's power to take away, to empty in the carriage at perfect leisure, and to return at another station fifty or a hundred miles further on?'

There was disagreement what such a person should be called. Whether revolutionist, atheist, Bright[3] (*I* said him), or Un-English. Miss Piff screeched her shrill opinion last, in the words: 'A malignant maniac!'

'I adopt,' says Our Missis, 'the brand set upon such a person by the righteous indignation of my friend Miss Piff. A malignant maniac. Know then, that that malignant maniac has sprung from the congenial soil of France, and that his malignant madness was in unchecked action on this same part of my journey.'

I noticed that Sniff was a rubbing his hands, and that Mrs Sniff had got her eye upon him. But I did not take more particular notice, owing to the excited state in which the young ladies was, and to feeling myself called upon to keep it up with a howl.

'On my experience south of Paris,' said Our Missis, in a deep tone, 'I will not expatiate. Too loathsome were the task! But fancy this. Fancy a guard coming round, with the train at full speed, to inquire how many for dinner. Fancy his telegraphing forward, the number of diners. Fancy every one expected, and the table elegantly laid for the complete party. Fancy a charming dinner, in a charming room, and the head-cook, concerned for the honour of every dish, superintending in his clean white jacket and cap. Fancy the Beast travelling six hundred miles on end, very fast, and with great punctuality, yet being taught to expect all this to be done for it!'

A spirited chorus of 'The Beast!'

I noticed that Sniff was agin a rubbing his stomach with a sooth-ing hand, and that he had drored up one leg. But agin I didn't take particular notice, looking on myself as called upon to stimilate public feeling. It being a lark besides.

'Putting everything together,' said Our Missis, 'French Re-freshmenting comes to this, and O it comes to a nice total! First: eatable things to eat, and drinkable things to drink.'

A groan from the young ladies, kep' up by me.

'Second: convenience, and even elegance.'

Another groan from the young ladies, kep' up by me.

'Third: moderate charges.'

This time, a groan from me, kep' up by the young ladies.

'Fourth: – and here,' says Our Missis, 'I claim your angriest sympathy – attention, common civility, nay, even politeness!'

Me and the young ladies regularly raging mad all together.

'And I cannot in conclusion,' says Our Missis, with her spite-fullest sneer, 'give you a completer pictur of that despicable nation (after what I have related), than assuring you that they wouldn't bear our constitutional ways and noble independence at Mugby Junction, for a single month, and that they would turn us to the right-about and put another system in our places, as soon as look at us; perhaps sooner, for I do not believe they have the good taste to care to look at us twice.'

The swelling tumult was arrested in its rise. Sniff, bore away by his servile disposition, had drored up his leg with a higher and a higher relish, and was now discovered to be waving his corkscrew over his head. It was at this moment that Mrs Sniff, who had kep' her eye upon him like the fabled obelisk, descended on her victim. Our Missis followed them both out, and cries was heard in the sawdust department.

You come into the Down Refreshment Room, at the Junction, making believe you don't know me, and I'll pint you out with my right thumb over my shoulder which is Our Missis, and which is Miss Whiff, and which is Miss Piff, and which is Mrs Sniff. But you won't get a chance to see Sniff, because he disappeared that night. Whether he perished, tore to pieces, I cannot say; but his corkscrew alone remains, to bear witness to the servility of his disposition.

George Silverman's Explanation

FIRST CHAPTER

IT happened in this wise:

– But, sitting with my pen in my hand looking at those words again, without descrying any hint in them of the words that should follow, it comes into my mind that they have an abrupt appearance. They may serve, however, if I let them remain, to suggest how very difficult I find it to begin to explain my Explanation. An uncouth phrase: and yet I do not see my way to a better.

SECOND CHAPTER

IT happened in *this* wise:

– But, looking at those words, and comparing them with my former opening, I find they are the selfsame words repeated. This is the more surprising to me, because I employ them in quite a new connection. For indeed I declare that my intention was to discard the commencement I first had in my thoughts, and to give the preference to another of an entirely different nature, dating my explanation from an anterior period of my life. I will make a third trial, without erasing this second failure, protesting that it is not my design to conceal any of my infirmities, whether they be of head or heart.

THIRD CHAPTER

NOT as yet directly aiming at how it came to pass, I will come upon it by degrees. The natural manner, after all, for God knows that is how it came upon me!

My parents were in a miserable condition of life, and my infant home was a cellar in Preston. I recollect the sound of Father's Lancashire clogs on the street pavement above, as being different in my young hearing from the sound of all other clogs; and I recollect that, when Mother came down the cellar-steps, I used tremblingly to speculate on her feet having a good or an ill-tempered look, – on her knees – on her waist, – until finally her face came into view and settled the question. From this it will be seen that I was timid, and that the cellar-steps were steep, and that the doorway was very low.

Mother had the gripe and clutch of Poverty upon her face, upon her figure, and not least of all upon her voice. Her sharp and high-pitched words were squeezed out of her, as by the compression of bony fingers on a leathern-bag; and she had a way of rolling her eyes about and about the cellar, as she scolded, that was gaunt and hungry. Father, with his shoulders rounded, would sit quiet on a three-legged stool, looking at the empty grate, until she would pluck the stool from under him, and bid him go bring some money home. Then he would dismally ascend the steps, and I, holding my ragged shirt and trousers together with a hand (my only braces), would feint and dodge from Mother's pursuing grasp at my hair.

A worldly little devil was Mother's usual name for me. Whether I cried for that I was in the dark, or for that it was cold, or for that I was hungry, or whether I squeezed myself into a warm corner when there was a fire, or ate voraciously when there was food, she would still say, 'O you worldly little devil!' And the sting of it was, that I quite well knew myself to be a worldly little devil. Worldly as to wanting to be housed and warmed, worldly as to wanting to be fed, worldly as to the greed with which I inwardly compared how much I got of those good things with how much Father and Mother got, when, rarely, those good things were going.

Sometimes they both went away seeking work, and then I would be locked up in the cellar for a day or two at a time. I was at my worldliest then. Left alone, I yielded myself up to a worldly yearning for enough of anything (except misery), and for the death of Mother's father, who was a machine-maker at Birmingham, and on whose decease, I had heard Mother say, she would come into a whole courtful of houses 'if she had her rights'. Worldly little devil, I would stand about, musingly fitting my cold bare feet into cracked bricks and crevices of the damp cellar floor, – walking over my grandfather's body, so to speak, into the courtful of houses, and selling them for meat and drink, and clothes to wear.

At last a change came down into our cellar. The universal change came down even as low as that, – so will it mount to any height on which a human creature can perch, – and brought other changes with it.

We had a heap of I don't know what foul litter in the darkest corner, which we called 'the bed.' For three days Mother lay upon it without getting up, and then began at times to laugh. If I had ever heard her laugh before, it had been so seldom that the strange sound frightened me. It frightened Father, too, and we took it by turns to give her water. Then she began to move her head from side to side, and sing. After that, she getting no better, Father fell a laughing and a singing, and then there was only I to give them both water, and they both died.

FOURTH CHAPTER

WHEN I was lifted out of the cellar by two men, of whom one came peeping down alone first, and ran away and brought the other, I could hardly bear the light of the street. I was sitting in the roadway, blinking at it, and at a ring of people collected around me, but not close to me, when, true to my character of worldly little devil, I broke silence by saying, 'I am hungry and thirsty!'

'Does he know they are dead?' asked one of another.

'Do you know your father and mother are both dead of fever?' asked a third of me, severely.

'I don't know what it is to be dead. I supposed it meant that, when the cup rattled against their teeth and the water spilt over them. I am hungry and thirsty.' That was all I had to say about it.

The ring of people widened outward from the inner side as I looked around me; and I smelt vinegar, and what I now know to be camphor, thrown in towards where I sat. Presently some one put a great vessel of smoking vinegar on the ground near me, and then they all looked at me in silent horror as I ate and drank of what was brought for me. I knew at the time they had a horror of me, but I couldn't help it.

I was still eating and drinking, and a murmur of discussion had begun to arise respecting what was to be done with me next, when I heard a cracked voice somewhere in the ring say, 'My name is Hawkyard, Mr Verity Hawkyard, of West Bromwich.' Then the ring split in one place, and a yellow-faced, peak-nosed gentleman, clad all in iron-gray to his gaiters, pressed forward with a policeman and another official of some sort. He came forward close to the vessel of smoking vinegar; from which he sprinkled himself carefully, and me copiously.

'He had a grandfather at Birmingham, this young boy, who is just dead too,' said Mr Hawkyard.

I turned my eyes upon the speaker, and said in a ravening manner, 'Where's his houses?'

'Hah! Horrible worldliness on the edge of the grave,' said Mr Hawkyard, casting more of the vinegar over me, as if to get my devil out of me. 'I have undertaken a slight—a ve-ry slight—trust in behalf of this boy; quite a voluntary trust; a matter of mere honor, if not of mere sentiment; still I have taken it upon myself, and it shall be (O yes, it shall be!) discharged.'

The by-standers seemed to form an opinion of this gentleman much more favourable than their opinion of me.

'He shall be taught,' said Mr Hawkyard, '(O yes, he shall be taught!) but what is to be done with him for the present? He may be infected. He may disseminate infection.' The ring widened considerably. 'What is to be done with him?'

He held some talk with the two officials. I could distinguish no word save 'Farm-house.' There was another sound several times repeated, which was wholly meaningless in my ears then, but which I knew soon afterwards to be 'Hoghton Towers.'

'Yes,' said Mr Hawkyard, 'I think that sound promising. I think that sounds hopeful. And he can be put by himself in a Ward, for a night or two, you say?'

It seemed to be the police-officer who had said so, for it was he who replied, Yes. It was he, too, who finally took me by the arm and walked me before him through the streets, into a whitewashed room in a bare building, where I had a chair to sit in, a table to sit at, an iron bedstead and good mattress to lie upon, and a rug and blanket to cover me. Where I had enough to eat too, and was shown how to clean the tin porringer in which it was conveyed to me, until it was as good as a looking-glass. Here, likewise, I was put in a bath, and had new clothes brought to me, and my old rags were burnt, and I was camphored and vinegared, and disinfected in a variety of ways.

When all this was done, – I don't know in how many days or how few, but it matters not, – Mr Hawkyard stepped in at the door, remaining close to it, and said: 'Go and stand against the opposite wall, George Silverman. As far off as you can. That'll do. How do you feel?'

I told him that I didn't feel cold, and didn't feel hungry, and didn't feel thirsty. That was the whole round of human feelings, as far as I knew, except the pain of being beaten.

'Well,' said he, 'you are going, George, to a healthy farm-house to be purified. Keep in the air there, as much as you can. Live an out-of-door life there, until you are fetched away. You had better not say much – in fact, you had better be very careful not to say anything – about what your parents died of, or they might not like to take you in. Behave well, and I'll put you to school, (O yes, I'll put you to school!) though I am not obligated to do it. I am a servant of the Lord, George, and I have been a good servant to him (I have!) these five-and-thirty years. The Lord has had a good servant in me, and he knows it.'

What I then supposed him to mean by this, I cannot imagine. As little do I know when I began to comprehend that he was a prominent member of some obscure denomination or congregation, every member of which held forth to the rest when so inclined, and among whom he was called Brother Hawkyard. It was enough for me to know, on that day in the Ward, that the farmer's cart was waiting for me at the street corner. I was not slow to get into it, for it was the first ride I ever had in my life.

It made me sleepy, and I slept. First, I stared at Preston streets as long as they lasted, and meanwhile I may have had some small dumb wondering within me whereabouts our cellar was. But I doubt it. Such a worldly little devil was I, that I took no thought who would bury Father and Mother, or where they would be buried, or when. The question whether the eating and drinking by day, and the covering by night, would be as good at the farm-house as at the Ward superseded those questions.

The jolting of the cart on a loose stony road awoke me, and I found that we were mounting a steep hill, where the road was a rutty by-road through a field. And so, by fragments of an ancient terrace, and by some rugged out-buildings that had once been fortified, and passing under a ruined gateway, we came to the old farm-house in the thick stone wall outside the old quadrangle of Hoghton Towers. Which I looked at, like a stupid savage; seeing no specialty in; seeing no antiquity in; assuming all farm-houses to resemble it; assigning the decay I noticed to the one potent cause of all ruin that I knew, – Poverty; eyeing the pigeons in their flights, the cattle in their stalls, the ducks in the pond, and the fowls pecking about the yard, with a hungry hope that plenty of them might be killed for dinner while I stayed there; wondering whether the scrubbed dairy vessels drying in the sunlight could be the goodly porringers out of which the master ate his belly-filling food, and which he polished when he had done, according to my Ward experience; shrinkingly doubtful whether the shadows passing over that airy height on the bright spring day were not something in the nature of frowns; sordid, afraid, unadmiring, a small Brute to shudder at.

To that time I had never had the faintest impression of beauty. I had had no knowledge whatever that there was anything lovely in this life. When I had occasionally slunk up the cellar steps into the street, and glared in at shop-windows, I had done so with no higher feelings than we may suppose to animate a mangy young dog or wolf-cub. It is equally the fact that I had never been alone, in the sense of holding unselfish converse with myself. I had been solitary often enough, but nothing better.

Such was my condition when I sat down to my dinner that day, in the kitchen of the old farm-house. Such was my condition when I lay on my bed in the old farm-house that night, stretched out opposite the narrow mullioned window, in the cold light of the moon, like a young Vampire.

FIFTH CHAPTER

WHAT do I know now of Hoghton Towers? Very little, for I have been gratefully unwilling to disturb my first impressions. A house, centuries old, on high ground a mile or so removed from the road between Preston and Blackburn, where the first James of England,[1] in his hurry to make money by making Baronets, perhaps made some of those remunerative dignitaries. A house, centuries old, deserted and falling to pieces, its woods and gardens long since grass-land or ploughed up, the rivers Ribble and Darwen glancing below it, and a vague haze of smoke, against which not even the supernatural prescience of the first Stuart could foresee a Counterblast, hinting at Steam Power, powerful in two distances.

What did I know then of Hoghton Towers? When I first peeped in at the gate of the lifeless quadrangle, and started from the mouldering statue becoming visible to me like its Guardian Ghost; when I stole round by the back of the farm-house, and got in among the ancient rooms, many of them with their floors and ceilings falling, the beams and rafters hanging dangerously down, the plaster dropping as I trod, the oaken panels stripped away, the windows half walled up, half broken; when I discovered a gallery commanding the old kitchen, and looked down between balustrades upon a massive old table and benches, fearing to see I know not what dead-alive creatures come in and seat themselves, and look up with I know not what dreadful eyes, or lack of eyes, at me; when all over the house I was awed by gaps and chinks where the sky stared sorrowfully at me, where the birds passed, and the ivy rustled, and the stains of winter-weather blotched the rotten floors; when down at the bottom of dark pits of staircase, into which the stairs had sunk, green leaves trembled, butterflies fluttered, and bees hummed in and out through the broken doorways; when encircling the whole ruin were sweet scents and sights of fresh green growth and ever-renewing life, that I had never dreamed of, – I say, when I passed into such clouded perception of these things as my dark soul could compass, what did I know then of Hoghton Towers?

I have written that the sky stared sorrowfully at me. Therein have I anticipated the answer. I knew that all these things looked sorrowfully at me. That they seemed to sigh or whisper, not without pity for me: 'Alas! Poor worldly little devil!'

There were two or three rats at the bottom of one of the smaller pits of broken staircase when I craned over and looked in. They were scuffling for some prey that was there. And when they started and hid themselves, close together in the dark, I thought of the old life (it had grown old already) in the cellar.

How not to be this worldly little devil? How not to have a repugnance towards myself as I had towards the rats? I hid in a corner of one of the smaller chambers, frightened at myself, and crying (it was the first time I had ever cried for any cause not purely physical), and I tried to think about it. One of the farm-ploughs came into my range of view just then, and it seemed to help me as it went on with its two horses up and down the field so peacefully and quietly.

There was a girl of about my own age in the farm-house family, and she sat opposite to me at the narrow table at meal-times. It had come into my mind at our first dinner that she might take the fever from me. The thought had not disquieted me then; I had only speculated how she would look under the altered circumstances, and whether she would die. But it came into my mind now, that I might try to prevent her taking the fever, by keeping away from her. I knew I should have but scrambling board if I did; so much the less worldly and less devilish the deed would be, I thought.

From that hour I withdrew myself at early morning into secret corners of the ruined house, and remained hidden there until she went to bed. At first, when meals were ready, I used to hear them calling me; and then my resolution weakened. But I strengthened it again, by going further off into the ruin, and getting out of hearing. I often watched for her at the dim windows; and, when I saw that she was fresh and rosy, felt much happier.

Out of this holding her in my thoughts, to the humanizing of myself, I suppose some childish love arose within me. I felt in some sort dignified by the pride of protecting her, by the pride of making the sacrifice for her. As my heart swelled with that new feeling, it insensibly softened about Mother and Father. It seemed to have been frozen before and now to be thawed. The old ruin and all the lovely things that haunted it were not sorrowful for me only, but sorrowful for Mother and Father as well. Therefore did I cry again, and often too.

The farm-house family conceived me to be of a morose temper, and were very short with me; though they never stinted me in such broken fare as was to be got out of regular hours. One night when I lifted the kitchen latch at my usual time, Sylvia (that was her pretty name) had but just gone out of the room. Seeing her ascending the opposite stairs, I stood still at the door. She had heard the clink of the latch, and looked round.

'George,' she called to me, in a pleased voice, 'tomorrow is my birthday, and we are to have a fiddler, and there's a party of boys and girls coming in a cart, and we shall dance. I invite you. Be sociable for once, George.'

'I am very sorry, miss,' I answered, 'but I – but no; I can't come.'

'You are a disagreeable, ill-humoured lad,' she returned, disdainfully, 'and I ought not to have asked you. I shall never speak to you again.'

As I stood with my eyes fixed on the fire after she was gone, I felt that the farmer bent his brows upon me.

'Eh, lad,' said he, 'Sylvy's right. You're as moody and broody a lad as never I set eyes on yet!'

I tried to assure him that I meant no harm; but he only said coldly: 'Maybe not, maybe not. There! Get thy supper, get thy supper, and then thou canst sulk to thy heart's content again.'

Ah! If they could have seen me next day in the ruin, watching for the arrival of the cart full of merry young guests; if they could have seen me at night, gliding out from behind the ghostly statue, listening to the music and the fall of dancing feet, and watching the lighted farm-house windows from the quadrangle when all the ruin was dark; if they could have read my heart as I crept up to bed by the back way, comforting myself with the reflection, 'They will take no hurt from me,' – they would not have thought mine a morose or an unsocial nature!

It was in these ways that I began to form a shy disposition; to be of a timidly silent character under misconstruction; to have an inexpressible, perhaps a morbid, dread of ever being sordid or worldly. It was in these ways that my nature came to shape itself to such a mould, even before it was affected by the influences of the studious and retired life of a poor scholar.

*

SIXTH CHAPTER

BROTHER HAWKYARD (as he insisted on my calling him) put me to school, and told me to work my way. 'You are all right, George,' he said. 'I have been the best servant the Lord has had in his service for this five-and-thirty years, (O, I have!) and he knows the value of such a servant as I have been to him, (O yes, he does!) and he'll prosper your schooling as a part of my reward. That's what *he*'ll do, George. He'll do it for me.'

From the first I could not like this familiar knowledge of the ways of the sublime inscrutable Almighty, on Brother Hawkyard's part. As I grew a little wiser and still a little wiser, I liked it less and less. His manner, too, of confirming himself in a parenthesis, – as if, knowing himself, he doubted his own word, – I found distasteful. I cannot tell how much these dislikes cost me, for I had a dread that they were worldly.

As time went on, I became a Foundation-Boy on a good Foundation, and I cost Brother Hawkyard nothing. When I had worked my way so far, I worked yet harder, in the hope of ultimately getting a presentation to College and a Fellowship. My health has never been strong (some vapour from the Preston cellar cleaves to me I think), and what with much work and some weakness, I came again to be regarded – that is, by my fellow-students – as unsocial.

All through my time as a Foundation-Boy I was within a few miles of Brother Hawkyard's congregation, and whenever I was what we called a Leave-Boy on a Sunday, I went over there, at his desire. Before the knowledge became forced upon me that outside their place of meeting these Brothers and Sisters were no better than the rest of the human family, but on the whole were, to put the case mildly, as bad as most, in respect of giving short weight in their shops, and not speaking the truth, – I say, before this knowledge became forced upon me, their prolix addresses, their inordinate conceit, their daring ignorance, their investment of the Supreme Ruler of Heaven and Earth with their own miserable meannesses and littlenesses greatly shocked me. Still, as their term for the frame of mind that could not perceive them to be in an exalted state of Grace was the 'worldly' state, I did for a time suffer tortures under my inquiries of myself whether that young worldly-devilish spirit of mine could secretly be lingering at the bottom of my non-appreciation.

Brother Hawkyard was the popular expounder in this assembly, and generally occupied the platform (there was a little platform with a table on it, in lieu of a pulpit) first, on a Sunday afternoon. He was by trade a drysalter. Brother Gimblet, an elderly man with a crabbed face, a large dog's-eared shirt-collar, and a spotted blue neckerchief reaching up behind to the crown of his head, was also a drysalter, and an expounder. Brother Gimblet professed the greatest admiration for Brother Hawkyard, but (I had thought more than once) bore him a jealous grudge.

Let whosoever may peruse these lines kindly take the pains here to read twice my solemn pledge, that what I write of the language and customs of the congregation in question I write scrupulously, literally, exactly from the life and the truth.

On the first Sunday after I had won what I had so long tried for, and when it was certain that I was going up to college, Brother Hawkyard concluded a long exhortation thus:

'Well, my friends and fellow-sinners, now I told you, when I began, that I didn't know a word of what I was going to say to you, (and no, I did not!) but that it was all one to me, because I knew the Lord would put into my mouth the words I wanted.'

('That's it!' From Brother Gimblet.)

'And he did put into my mouth the words I wanted.'

('So he did!' From Brother Gimblet.)

'And why?'

('Ah! Let's have that!' From Brother Gimblet.)

'Because I have been his faithful servant for five-and-thirty years, and because he knows it. For five-and-thirty years! And he knows it, mind you! I got those words that I wanted, on account of my wages. I got 'em from the Lord, my fellow-sinners. Down. I said, "Here's a heap of wages due; let us have something down on account." And I got it down, and I paid it over to you, and you won't wrap it up in a napkin, nor yet in a towel, nor yet pockethankercher, but you'll put it out at good interest.' Very well. Now, my brothers and sisters and fellow-sinners, I am going to conclude with a question, and I'll make it so plain (with the help of the Lord, after five-and-thirty years, I should rather hope!) as that the Devil shall not be able to confuse it in your heads. Which he would be overjoyed to do.'

('Just his way. Crafty old blackguard!' From Brother Gimblet.)

'And the question is this. Are the Angels learned?'

('Not they. Not a bit on it.' From Brother Gimblet, with the greatest confidence.)

'Not they. And where's the proof? Sent ready-made by the hand of the Lord. Why, there's one among us here now, that has got all the Learning that can be crammed into him. *I* got him all the Learning that could be crammed into him. His grandfather' (this I had never heard before) 'was a Brother of ours. He was Brother Parksop. That's what he was. Parksop. Brother Parksop. His worldly name was Parksop, and he was a Brother of this Brotherhood. Then wasn't he Brother Parksop?'

('Must be. Couldn't help hisself.' From Brother Gimblet.)

'Well. He left that one now here present among us to the care of a Brother-Sinner of his, (and that Brother-Sinner, mind you, was a sinner of a bigger size in his time than any of you, Praise the Lord!) Brother Hawkyard. Me *I* got him, without fee or reward, – without a morsel of myrrh, or frankincense, nor yet Amber, letting alone the honeycomb, – all the Learning that could be crammed into him. Has it brought him into our Temple, in the spirit? No. Have we had any ignorant Brothers and Sisters that didn't know round O from crooked S, come in among us meanwhile? Many. Then the Angels are *not* learned. Then they don't so much as know their alphabet. And now, my friends and fellow-sinners, having brought it to that, perhaps some Brother present – perhaps you, Brother Gimblet – will pray a bit for us?'

Brother Gimblet undertook the sacred function, after having drawn his sleeve across his mouth, and muttered: 'Well! I don't know as I see my way to hitting any of you quite in the right place neither.' He said this with a dark smile, and then began to bellow. What we were specially to be preserved from, according to his solicitations, was despoilment of the orphan, suppression of testamentary intentions on the part of a Father or (say) Grandfather, appropriation of the orphan's house-property, feigning to give in charity to the wronged one from whom we withheld his due; and that class of sins. He ended with the petition, 'Give us peace!' Which, speaking for myself, was very much needed after twenty minutes of his bellowing.

Even though I had not seen him when he rose from his knees, steaming with perspiration, glance at Brother Hawkyard, and even though I had not heard Brother Hawkyard's tone of congratulating him on the vigor with which he hàd roared, I should have detected a malicious application in this prayer. Unformed suspicions to a similar effect had sometimes passed through my mind in my earlier schooldays, and had always caused me great distress; for they were worldly in their nature, and wide, very wide, of the spirit that had drawn me from Sylvia. They were sordid suspicions, without a shadow of proof. They were worthy to have originated in the unwholesome cellar. They were not only without proof, but against proof. For was I not myself a living proof of what Brother Hawkyard had done? And without him, how should I ever have seen the sky look sorrowfully down upon that wretched boy at Hoghton Towers?

Although the dread of a relapse into a state of savage selfishness was less strong upon me as I approached manhood, and could act in an increased degree for myself, yet I was always on my guard against any tendency to such relapse. After getting these suspicions under my feet, I had been troubled by not being able to like Brother Hawkyard's manner, or his professed religion. So it came about, that, as I walked back that Sunday evening, I thought it would be an act of reparation for any such injury my struggling thoughts had unwillingly done him, if I wrote, and placed in his hands, before going to College, a full acknowledgment of his goodness to me, and an ample tribute of thanks. It might serve as an implied vindication of him against any dark scandal from a rival Brother and Expounder, or from any other quarter.

Accordingly I wrote the document with much care. I may add with much feeling, too, for it affected me as I went on. Having no set studies to pursue, in the brief interval between leaving the Foundation and going to Cambridge, I determined to walk out to his place of business and give it into his own hands.

It was a winter afternoon when I tapped at the door of his little counting-house, which was at the farther end of his long, low shop. As I did so (having entered by the back yard, where casks and boxes were taken in, and where there was the inscription, 'Private Way to the Counting-house'), a shopman called to me from the counter that he was engaged.

'Brother Gimblet,' said the shopman (who was one of the Brotherhood), 'is with him.'

I thought this all the better for my purpose, and made bold to tap again. They were talking in a low tone, and money was passing, for I heard it being counted out.

'Who is it?' asked Brother Hawkyard, sharply.

'George Silverman,' I answered, holding the door open. 'May I come in?'

Both Brothers seemed so astounded to see me that I felt shier than usual. But they looked quite cadaverous in the early gaslight, and perhaps that accidental circumstance exaggerated the expression of their faces.

'What is the matter?' asked Brother Hawkyard.

'Ay! What is the matter?' asked Brother Gimblet.

'Nothing at all,' I said, diffidently producing my document. 'I am only the bearer of a letter from myself.'

'From yourself, George?' cried Brother Hawkyard.

'And to you,' said I.

'And to me, George?'

He turned paler, and opened it hurriedly; but looking over it, and seeing generally what it was, became less hurried, recovered his colour, and said, 'Praise the Lord!'

'That's it!' cried Brother Gimblet. 'Well put! Amen.'

Brother Hawkyard then said, in a livelier strain: 'You must know, George, that Brother Gimblet and I are going to make our two businesses one. We are going into partnership. We are settling it now. Brother Gimblet is to take one clear half of the profits. (O yes! And he shall have it, he shall have it to the last farthing!)'

'D. V.!'[3] said Brother Gimblet, with his right fist firmly clenched on his right leg.

'There is no objection,' pursued Brother Hawkyard, 'to my reading this aloud. George?'

As it was what I expressly desired should be done, after yesterday's prayer, I more than readily begged him to read it aloud. He did so, and Brother Gimblet listened with a crabbed smile.

'It was in a good hour that I came here,' he said, wrinkling up his eyes. 'It was in a good hour, likewise, that I was moved yesterday to depict for the terror of evil-doers a character the direct opposite of Brother Hawkyard's. But it was the Lord that done it. I felt him at it, while I was perspiring.'

After that, it was proposed by both of them that I should attend the congregation once more, before my final departure. What my shy reserve would undergo, from being expressly preached at and prayed at, I knew beforehand. But I reflected that it would be for the last time, and that it might add to the weight of my letter. It was well known to the Brothers and Sisters that there was no place taken for me in *their* Paradise; and if I showed this last token of deference to Brother Hawkyard, notoriously in despite of my own sinful inclinations, it might go some little way in aid of my statement that he had been good to me, and that I was grateful to him. Merely stipulating, therefore, that no express endeavor should be made for my conversion, – which would involve the rolling of several Brothers and Sisters on the floor, declaring that they felt all their sins in a heap on their left side, weighing so many pounds avoirdupois, as I knew from what I had seen of those repulsive mysteries, – I promised.

Since the reading of my letter, Brother Gimblet had been at intervals wiping one eye with an end of his spotted blue neckerchief, and grinning to himself. It was, however, a habit that Brother had, to grin in an ugly manner even while expounding. I call to mind a delighted snarl with which he used to detail from the platform the torments reserved for the wicked (meaning all human creation except the Brotherhood), as being remarkably hideous.

I left the two to settle their articles of partnership, and count money; and I never saw them again but on the following Sunday. Brother Hawkyard died within two or three years, leaving all he possessed to Brother Gimblet, in virtue of a will dated (as I have been told) that very day.

Now, I was so far at rest with myself when Sunday came, knowing that I had conquered my own mistrust, and righted Brother Hawkyard in the jaundiced vision of a rival, that I went, even to that coarse chapel, in a less sensitive state than usual. How could I foresee that the delicate, perhaps the diseased, corner of my mind, where I winced and shrunk when it was touched, or was even approached, would be handled as the theme of the whole proceedings?

On this occasion it was assigned to Brother Hawkyard to pray, and to Brother Gimblet to preach. The prayer was to open the ceremonies; the discourse was to come next. Brothers Hawkyard and Gimblet were both on the platform; Brother Hawkyard on his knees at the table, unmusically ready to pray; Brother Gimblet sitting against the wall, grinningly ready to preach.

'Let us offer up the sacrifice of prayer, my brothers and sisters and fellow-sinners.' Yes. But it was I who was the sacrifice. It was our poor sinful worldly-minded Brother here present who was wrestled for. The now-opening career of this our unawakened Brother might lead to his becoming a minister of what was called The Church. That was what *he* looked to. The Church. Not the chapel, Lord. The Church. No rectors, no vicars, no archdeacons, no bishops, no archbishops in the chapel, but, O Lord, many such in the Church! Protect our sinful Brother from his love of lucre. Cleanse from our unawakened Brother's breast his sin of worldly-mindedness. The prayer said infinitely more in words, but nothing more to any intelligible effect.

Then Brother Gimblet came forward, and took (as I knew he would) the text, My kingdom is not of this world.[4] Ah! But whose was, my fellow-sinners? Whose? Why, our Brother's here present was. The only kingdom he had an idea of was of this world ('That's it!' from several of the congregation). What did the woman do when she lost the piece of money?[5] Went and looked for it. What should our Brother do when he lost his way? ('Go and look for it,' from a Sister.) Go and look for it. True. But must he look for it in the right direction or in the wrong? ('In the right,' from a Brother.) There spake the prophets! He must look for it in the right direction, or he couldn't find it. But he had turned his back upon the right direction, and he wouldn't find it. Now, my fellow-sinners, to show you the difference betwixt worldly-mindedness and unworldly-mindedness, betwixt kingdoms not of this world and kingdoms *of* this world, here was a letter wrote by even our worldly-minded Brother unto Brother Hawkyard. Judge, from hearing of it read, whether Brother Hawkyard was the faithful steward[6] that the Lord had in his mind only t' other day, when, in this very place, he drew you the picter of the unfaithful one. For it was him that done it, not me. Don't doubt that!

Brother Gimblet then grinned and bellowed his way through my composition, and subsequently through an hour. The service closed with a hymn, in which the Brothers unanimously roared, and the Sisters unanimously shrieked, at me, that I by wiles of worldly gain was mocked, and they on waters of sweet love were rocked; that I with Mammon struggled in the dark, while they were floating in a second Ark.

I went out from all this with an aching heart and a weary spirit; not because I was quite so weak as to consider these narrow creatures interpreters of the Divine majesty and wisdom; but because I was weak enough to feel as though it were my hard fortune to be misrepresented and misunderstood, when I most tried to subdue any risings of mere worldliness within me, and when I most hoped, that, by dint of trying earnestly, I had succeeded.

*

SEVENTH CHAPTER

My timidity and my obscurity occasioned me to live a secluded life at College, and to be little known. No relative ever came to visit me, for I had no relative. No intimate friends broke in upon my studies, for I made no intimate friends. I supported myself on my scholarship, and read much. My College time was otherwise not so very different from my time at Hoghton Towers.

Knowing myself to be unfit for the noisier stir of social existence, but believing myself qualified to do my duty in a moderate though earnest way if I could obtain some small preferment in the Church, I applied my mind to the clerical profession. In due sequence I took orders, was ordained, and began to look about me for employment. I must observe that I had taken a good degree, that I had succeeded in winning a good fellowship, and that my means were ample for my retired way of life. By this time I had read with several young men, and the occupation increased my income, while it was highly interesting to me. I once accidentally overheard our greatest Don say, to my boundless joy, 'That he heard it reported of Silverman that his gift of quiet explanation, his patience, his amiable temper, and his conscientiousness, made him the best of Coaches.' May my 'gift of quiet explanation' come more seasonably and powerfully to my aid in this present explanation than I think it will!

It may be, in a certain degree, owing to the situation of my College rooms (in a corner where the daylight was sobered), but it is in a much larger degree referable to the state of my own mind, that I seem to myself, on looking back to this time of my life, to have been always in the peaceful shade. I can see others in the sunlight; I can see our boats' crews and our athletic young men on the glistening water, or speckled with the moving lights of sunlit leaves; but I myself am always in the shadow looking on. Not unsympathetically, – GOD forbid! – but looking on, alone, much as I looked at Sylvia from the shadows of the ruined house, or looked at the red gleam shining through the farmer's windows, and listened to the fall of dancing feet, when all the ruin was dark that night in the quadrangle.

I now come to the reason of my quoting that laudation of myself above given. Without such reason, to repeat it would have been mere boastfulness.

Among those who had read with me was Mr Fareway, second son of Lady Fareway, widow of Sir Gaston Fareway, Baronet. This young gentleman's abilities were much above the average, but he came of a rich family, and was idle and luxurious. He presented himself to me too late, and afterwards came to me too irregularly, to admit of my being of much service to him. In the end I considered it my duty to dissuade him from going up for an examination which he could never pass, and he left College without taking a degree. After his departure, Lady Fareway wrote to me representing the justice of my returning half my fee, as I had been of so little use to her son. Within my knowledge a similar demand had not been made in any other case, and I most freely admit that the justice of it had not occurred to me until it was pointed out. But I at once perceived it, yielded to it, and returned the money.

Mr Fareway had been gone two years or more and I had forgotten him, when he one day walked into my rooms as I was sitting at my books.

Said he, after the usual salutations had passed: 'Mr Silverman, my mother is in town here, at the hotel, and wishes me to present you to her.'

I was not comfortable with strangers, and I dare say I betrayed that I was a little nervous or unwilling. For, said he, without my having spoken, 'I think the interview may tend to the advancement of your prospects.'

It put me to the blush to think that I should be tempted by a worldly reason, and I rose immediately.

Said Mr Fareway, as we went along, 'Are you a good hand at business?'

'I think not,' said I.

Said Mr Fareway then, 'My mother is.'

'Truly?' said I.

'Yes. My mother is what is usually called a managing woman. Doesn't make a bad thing, for instance, even out of the spendthrift habits of my eldest brother abroad. In short, a managing woman. This is in confidence.'

He had never spoken to me in confidence, and I was surprised by his doing so. I said I should respect his confidence, of course, and said no more on the delicate subject. We had but a little way to walk, and I was soon in his mother's company. He presented me, shook hands with me, and left us two (as he said) to business.

I saw in my Lady Fareway a handsome, well-preserved lady of somewhat large stature, with a steady glare in her great round dark eyes that embarrassed me.

Said my Lady: 'I have heard from my son, Mr Silverman, that you would be glad of some preferment in the Church?'

I gave my Lady to understand that was so.

'I don't know whether you are aware,' my Lady proceeded, 'that we have a presentation to a living? I say we have, but in point of fact I have.'

I gave my Lady to understand that I had not been aware of this.

Said my Lady: 'So it is. Indeed, I have two presentations: one, to two hundred a year; one, to six. Both livings are in our county, – North Devonshire, as you probably know. The first is vacant. Would you like it?'

What with my Lady's eyes, and what with the suddenness of this proposed gift, I was much confused.

'I am sorry it is not the larger presentation,' said my Lady, rather coldly, 'though I will not, Mr Silverman, pay you the bad compliment of supposing that you are, because that would be mercenary, – and mercenary I am persuaded you are not.'

Said I, with my utmost earnestness: 'Thank you, Lady Fareway, thank you, thank you! I should be deeply hurt if I thought I bore the character.'

'Naturally,' said my Lady. 'Always detestable, but particularly in a clergyman. You have not said whether you will like the Living?'

With apologies for my remissness or indistinctness, I assured my Lady that I accepted it most readily and gratefully. I added that I hoped she would not estimate my appreciation of the generosity of her choice by my flow of words, for I was not a ready man in that respect when taken by surprise or touched at heart.

'The affair is concluded,' said my Lady. 'Concluded. You will find the duties very light, Mr Silverman. Charming house; charming little garden, orchard, and all that. You will be able to take pupils. By the by! No. I will return to the word afterwards. What was I going to mention, when it put me out?'

My Lady stared at me, as if I knew. And I didn't know. And that perplexed me afresh.

Said my Lady, after some consideration: 'Oh! Of course. How very dull of me! The last incumbent, – least mercenary man I ever saw, – in consideration of the duties being so light and the house so delicious, couldn't rest, he said, unless I permitted him to help me with my correspondence, accounts, and various little things of that kind; nothing in themselves, but which it worries a lady to cope with. Would Mr Silverman also like to – ? Or shall I – ?'

I hastened to say that my poor help would be always at her ladyship's service.

'I am absolutely blessed,' said my Lady, casting up her eyes (and so taking them off of me for one moment), 'in having to do with gentlemen who cannot endure an approach to the idea of being mercenary!' She shivered at the word. 'And now as to the pupil.'

'The —?' I was quite at a loss.

'Mr Silverman, you have no idea what she is. She is,' said my Lady, laying her touch upon my coat-sleeve, 'I do verily believe, the most extraordinary girl in this world. Already knows more Greek and Latin than Lady Jane Grey.[7] And taught herself! Has not yet, remember, derived a moment's advantage from Mr Silverman's classical acquirements. To say nothing of mathematics, which she is bent upon becoming versed in, and in which (as I hear from my son and others) Mr Silverman's reputation is so deservedly high!'

Under my Lady's eyes, I must have lost the clew, I felt persuaded; and yet I did not know where I could have dropped it.

'Adelina,' said my Lady, 'is my only daughter. If I did not feel quite convinced that I am not blinded by a mother's partiality; unless I was absolutely sure that when you know her, Mr Silverman, you will esteem it a high and unusual privilege to direct her studies, – I should introduce a mercenary element into this conversation, and ask you on what terms – '

I entreated my Lady to go no further. My Lady saw that I was troubled, and did me the honour to comply with my request.

EIGHTH CHAPTER

EVERYTHING in mental acquisition that her brother might have been, if he would, and everything in all gracious charms and admirable qualities that no one but herself could be, – this was Adelina.

I will not expatiate upon her beauty. I will not expatiate upon her intelligence, her quickness of perception, her powers of memory, her sweet consideration from the first moment for the slow-paced tutor who ministered to her wonderful gifts. I was thirty then; I am over sixty now; she is ever present to me in these hours as she was in those, bright and beautiful and young, wise and fanciful and good.

When I discovered that I loved her, how can I say? In the first day? In the first week? In the first month? Impossible to trace. If I be (as I am) unable to represent to myself any previous period of my life as quite separable from her attracting power, how can I answer for this one detail?

Whensoever I made the discovery, it laid a heavy burden on me. And yet, comparing it with the far heavier burden that I afterwards took up, it does not seem to me now to have been very hard to bear. In the knowledge that I did love her, and that I should love her while my life lasted, and that I was ever to hide my secret deep in my own breast, and she was never to find it, there was a kind of sustaining joy or pride or comfort mingled with my pain.

But later on – say a year later on – when I made another discovery, then indeed my suffering and my struggle were strong. That other discovery was — ?

These words will never see the light, if ever, until my heart is dust; until her bright spirit has returned to the regions of which, when imprisoned here, it surely retained some unusual glimpse of remembrance; until all the pulses that ever beat around us shall have long been quiet; until all the fruits of all the tiny victories and defeats achieved in our little breasts shall have withered away. That discovery was, that she loved me.

She may have enhanced my knowledge, and loved me for that; she may have overvalued my discharge of duty to her, and loved me for that; she may have refined upon a playful compassion which she would sometimes show for what she called my want of wisdom according to the light of the world's dark lanterns, and loved me for that; she may — she must — have confused the borrowed light of what I had only learned, with its brightness in its pure original rays; but she loved me at that time, and she made me know it.

Pride of family and pride of wealth put me as far off from her in my Lady's eyes as if I had been some domesticated creature of another kind. But they could not put me farther from her than I put myself when I set my merits against hers. More than that. They could not put me, by millions of fathoms, half so low beneath her as I put myself when in imagination I took advantage of her noble trustfulness, took the fortune that I knew she must possess in her own right, and left her to find herself, in the zenith of her beauty and genius, bound to poor rusty plodding Me.

No. Worldliness should not enter here, at any cost. If I had tried to keep it out of other ground, how much harder was I bound to try to keep it from this sacred place.

But there was something daring in her broad generous character that demanded at so delicate a crisis to be delicately and patiently addressed. After many and many a bitter night (O, I found I could cry for reasons not purely physical, at this pass of my life!) I took my course.

My Lady had in our first interview unconsciously overstated the accommodation of my pretty house. There was room in it for only one pupil. He was a young gentleman near coming of age, very well connected, but what is called a poor relation. His parents were dead. The charges of his living and reading with me were defrayed by an uncle, and he and I were to do our utmost together for three years towards qualifying him to make his way. At this time he had entered into his second year with me. He was well-looking, clever, energetic, enthusiastic, bold; in the best sense of the term, a thorough young Anglo-Saxon.

I resolved to bring these two together.

NINTH CHAPTER

SAID I, one night when I had conquered myself: 'Mr Granville,' – Mr Granville Wharton his name was, – 'I doubt if you have ever yet so much as seen Miss Fareway.'

'Well, sir,' returned he, laughing, 'you see her so much yourself, that you hardly leave another fellow a chance of seeing her.'

'I am her tutor, you know,' said I.

And there the subject dropped for that time. But I so contrived as that they should come together shortly afterwards. I had previously so contrived as to keep them asunder, for while I loved her – I mean before I had determined on my sacrifice – a lurking jealousy of Mr Granville lay within my unworthy breast.

It was quite an ordinary interview in the Fareway Park; but they talked easily together for some time; like takes to like, and they had many points of resemblance. Said Mr Granville to me, when he and I sat at our supper that night: 'Miss Fareway is remarkably beautiful, sir, and remarkably engaging. Don't you think so?' 'I think so,' said I. And I stole a glance at him, and saw that he had reddened and was thoughtful. I remember it most vividly, because the mixed feeling of grave pleasure and acute pain that the slight circumstance caused me was the first of a long, long series of such mixed impressions under which my hair turned slowly gray.

I had not much need to feign to be subdued, but I counterfeited to be older than I was in all respects, (Heaven knows, my heart being all too young the while!) and feigned to be more of a recluse and bookworm than I had really become, and gradually set up more and more of a fatherly manner towards Adelina. Likewise, I made my tuition less imaginative than before; separated myself from my poets and philosophers; was careful to present them in their own light, and me, their lowly servant, in my own shade. Moreover, in the matter of apparel I was equally mindful. Not that I had ever been dapper that way, but that I was slovenly now.

As I depressed myself with one hand, so did I labor to raise Mr Granville with the other; directing his attention to such subjects as I too well knew most interested her, and fashioning him (do not deride or misconstrue the expression, unknown reader of this writing, for I have suffered!) into a greater resemblance to myself in my solitary one strong aspect. And gradually, gradually, as I saw him take more and more to these thrown-out lures of mine, then did I come to know better and better that love was drawing him on, and was drawing Her from me.

So passed more than another year; every day a year in its number of my mixed impressions of grave pleasure and acute pain; and then, these two being of age and free to act legally for themselves, came before me, hand in hand (my hair being now quite white), and entreated me that I would unite them together. 'And indeed, dear Tutor,' said Adelina, 'it is but consistent in you that you should do this thing for us, seeing that we should never have spoken together that first time but for you, and that but for you we could never have met so often afterwards.' The whole of which was literally true, for I had availed myself on my many business attendances on, and conferences with, my Lady, to take Mr Granville to the house, and leave him in the outer room with Adelina.

I knew that my Lady would object to such a marriage for her daughter, or to any marriage that was other than an exchange of her for stipulated lands, goods, and moneys. But, looking on the two, and seeing with full eyes that they were both young and beautiful; and knowing that they were alike in the tastes and acquirements that will outlive youth and beauty; and considering that Adelina had a fortune now, in her own keeping; and considering further that Mr Granville, though for the present poor, was of a good family that had never lived in a cellar in Preston; and believing that their love would endure, neither having any great discrepancy to find out in the other, — I told them of my readiness to do this thing which Adelina asked of her dear Tutor, and to send them forth, Husband and Wife, into the shining world with golden gates that awaited them.

It was on a summer morning that I rose before the sun, to compose myself for the crowning of my work with this end. And my dwelling being near to the sea, I walked down to the rocks on the shore, in order that I might behold the sun rise in his majesty.

The tranquillity upon the Deep and on the firmament, the orderly withdrawal of the stars, the calm promise of coming day, the rosy suffusion of the sky and waters, the ineffable splendor that then burst forth, attuned my mind afresh after the discords of the night. Methought that all I looked on said to me, and that all I heard in the sea and in the air said to me, 'Be comforted, mortal, that thy life is so short. Our preparation for what is to follow has endured, and shall endure, for unimaginable ages.'

I married them. I knew that my hand was cold when I placed it on their hands clasped together; but the words with which I had to accompany the action I could say without faltering, and I was at peace.

They being well away from my house and from the place, after our simple breakfast, the time was come when I must do what I had pledged myself to them that I would do, – break the intelligence to my Lady.

I went up to the house, and found my Lady in her ordinary business-room. She happened to have an unusual amount of commissions to intrust to me that day, and she had filled my hands with papers before I could originate a word.

'My Lady,' – I then began, as I stood beside her table.

'Why, what's the matter?' she said, quickly, looking up.

'Not much, I would fain hope, after you shall have prepared yourself, and considered a little.'

'Prepared myself! And considered a little! You appear to have prepared *your*self but indifferently, anyhow, Mr Silverman.' This, mighty scornfully, as I experienced my usual embarrassment under her stare.

Said I, in self-extenuation, once for all: 'Lady Fareway, I have but to say for myself that I have tried to do my duty.'

'For yourself?' repeated my Lady. 'Then there are others concerned, I see. Who are they?'

I was about to answer, when she made towards the bell with a dart that stopped me, and said, 'Why, where is Adelina?'

'Forbear. Be calm, my Lady. I married her this morning to Mr Granville Wharton.'

She set her lips, looked more intently at me than ever, raised her right hand and smote me hard upon the cheek.

'Give me back those papers, give me back those papers!' She tore them out of my hands and tossed them on her table. Then seating herself defiantly in her great chair, and folding her arms, she stabbed me to the heart with the unlooked-for reproach: 'You worldly wretch!'

'Worldly?' I cried. 'Worldly!'

'This, if you please,' she went on with supreme scorn, pointing me out as if there were some one there to see, – 'this, if you please, is the disinterested scholar, with not a design beyond his books! This, if you please, is the simple creature whom any one could over-reach in a bargain! This, if you please, is Mr Silverman! Not of this world, not he! He has too much simplicity for this world's cunning. He has too much singleness of purpose to be a match for this world's double-dealing. What did he give you for it?'

'For what? And who?'

'How much,' she asked, bending forward in her great chair, and insultingly tapping the fingers of her right hand on the palm of her left, – 'how much does Mr Granville Wharton pay you for getting him Adelina's money? What is the amount of your percent-age upon Adelina's fortune? What were the terms of the agreement that you proposed to this boy when you, the Reverend George Silverman, licensed to marry, engaged to put him in possession of this girl? You made good terms for yourself, whatever they were. He would stand a poor chance against your keenness.'

Bewildered, horrified, stunned by this cruel perversion, I could not speak. But I trust that I looked innocent, being so.

'Listen to me, shrewd hypocrite,' said my Lady, whose anger increased as she gave it utterance. 'Attend to my words, you cunning schemer who have carried this plot through with such a practised double face that I have never suspected you. I had my projects for my daughter; projects for family connection; projects for fortune. You have thwarted them, and overreached me; but I am not one to be thwarted and overreached without retaliation. Do you mean to hold this Living another month?'

'Do you deem it possible, Lady Fareway, that I can hold it another hour, under your injurious words?'

'Is it resigned, then?'

'It was mentally resigned, my Lady, some minutes ago.'

'Don't equivocate, sir. *Is* it resigned?'

'Unconditionally and entirely. And I would that I had never, never come near it!'

'A cordial response from me to *that* wish, Mr Silverman! But take this with you, sir. If you had not resigned it, I would have had you deprived of it. And though you have resigned it, you will not get quit of me as easily as you think for. I will pursue you with this story. I will make this nefarious conspiracy of yours, for money, known. You have made money by it, but you have at the same time made an enemy by it. *You* will take good care that the money sticks to you; *I* will take good care that the enemy sticks to you.'

Then said I, finally: 'Lady Fareway, I think my heart is broken. Until I came into this room just now, the possibility of such mean wickedness as you have imputed to me never dawned upon my thoughts. Your suspicions –'

'Suspicions! Pah!' said she, indignantly. 'Certainties.'

'Your certainties, my Lady, as you call them, your suspicions, as I call them, are cruel, unjust, wholly devoid of foundation in fact. I can declare no more, except that I have not acted for my own profit or my own pleasure. I have not in this proceeding considered myself. Once again, I think my heart is broken. If I have unwittingly done any wrong with a righteous motive, that is some penalty to pay.'

She received this with another and a more indignant 'Pah!' and I made my way out of her room (I think I felt my way out with my hands, although my eyes were open), almost suspecting that my voice had a repulsive sound, and that I was a repulsive object.

There was a great stir made, the Bishop was appealed to, I received a severe reprimand, and narrowly escaped suspension. For years a cloud hung over me, and my name was tarnished. But my heart did not break, if a broken heart involves death; for I lived through it.

They stood by me, Adelina and her husband, through it all. Those who had known me at College, and even most of those who had only known me there by reputation, stood by me too. Little by little, the belief widened that I was not capable of what was laid to my charge. At length I was presented to a College-Living in a sequestered place, and there I now pen my Explanation. I pen it at my open window in the summer-time; before me, lying the churchyard, equal resting-place for sound hearts, wounded hearts, and broken hearts. I pen it for the relief of my own mind, not foreseeing whether or no it will ever have a reader.

APPENDIX

Descriptive Headlines, 1867–8

Headlines at the top of each right-hand page were added in the Charles Dickens Edition. For the selections from *Pickwick Papers* (1867), *Nicholas Nickleby* (1867), *Sketches by Boz* (1868), *American Notes and Reprinted Pieces* (1868), and *The Uncommercial Traveller* (1868), the passage to which each headline refers is indicated here by the opening and closing words of the page in the Charles Dickens text.

The Story of the Goblins who stole a Sexton (pp. 39–49)

'In an old abbey town . . . of his spade with a firmer *Larcenous Goblins*.

'Seated on an upright tombstone . . . my friends want you, Gabriel,' said the goblin. *Gabriel Grub wanted*.

with laughter as he coughed . . . according to the established and invariable *An Exhibition of Pictures*.

'But he was an altered man . . . which Gabriel Grub saw in the goblin's cavern.' *Live and Learn*.

The Baron of Grogzwig (pp. 49–58)

'The Baron Von Koëldwethout, of Grogzwig in Germany . . . There were many strange circum- *Another Story Volunteered*.

'The four-and-twenty Lincoln greens turned pale . . . kicked the two Lincoln greens who were *The New Baroness Von Koëldwethout*.

'"If I had been a bachelor . . . that he threw his cloak *A Spectre calls upon the Baron of Grogzwig*.

these opinions all at once . . . by the laudable example of the Baron of Grogzwig.' *The Spectre Takes Leave of the Baron*.

The Election for Beadle (pp. 93–100)

asperity and determination . . . in his capacity of director *Party Politics*.

in rusty black, with a long pale face . . . Bung was 35 years of age. Spruggins *Nomination*.

Seven Dials (pp. 100–105)

posts. We never saw a regular . . . on a hot summer's evening, and *The Dials in General*.

Meditations in Monmouth-Street (pp. 106–12)

-nary wearers; lines of trousers . . . smart but slovenly; meant to be *Old Clothes*.

regard; and we had got a fine . . . when we heard a shrill, and *A Jolly Pair of Boots*.

A Visit to Newgate (pp. 112–26)

but for his keys, would have looked . . . every now and then burst into an irrepres- *Its Internal Arrangement*.

shelf above. At night, . . . excessively meritorious in getting there at all. We *Its Women and Boys*.

with all their crimes upon their heads, . . . some mitigatory cir- *Its Chapel and Press-yard*.

can know. He has wearied . . . with a speed and lightness, *Its condemned Prisoner*.

A Christmas Tree (pp. 126–41)

I have been looking on, . . . observe in this tree the singular *Christmas-Tree Fruit*.

and coming down, head foremost . . . look out the Wolf in the Noah's *Christmas-Tree Flowers*.

Sultan goes out, giving no orders . . . so suggestive and all-embracing, *Christmas-Tree Theatricals*.

house, full of great chimneys . . . old hall, where a certain *Christmas-Tree Ghosts*.

evening at sunset, when . . . for his little playmate was surely run. *The Orphan Boy*.

A Flight (pp. 142–51)

When Don Diego de . . . Stock Exchange perhaps – City *Travelling Companions*.

Demented Traveller, who has been . . . looking at Enchantress while *No Hurry*.

of soup, little caraffes of brandy . . . was never wanting? Where are the *A Rapid Review*.

APPENDIX

Our School (pp. 152–9)

long and narrow, is a puffy pug-dog ... denied him at breakfast, he
would *We were First Boy.*

The principal currency of Our School ... presents the Latin master as
a colourless *The popular Usher.*

Lying Awake (pp. 159–66)

'My uncle lay with his eyes ... the only result that came of it. *Benjamin
Franklin a failure.*

fire, and the same supper ... with his throat cut, dashing *Rambling
Night Thoughts.*

far lower estimation than a mad wolf ... may prove now to a great
many more. *Obliged to get up.*

Refreshments for Travellers (pp. 168–76)

In the late high winds I was blown ... accursed locality, than I have
read of *A Walworthy Speciality.*

am 'breaking up' again ... where five invalided old *Another Case.*

are rather like his brother ... walls that are too new *Hotel Refreshments.*

Travelling Abroad (pp. 176–88)

I got into the travelling chariot ... so went I, by Canterbury *The very
queer small Boy.*

until – madly cracking, plunging ... picture of the creature; and that
had so *The large Dark Creature.*

jolting through the highway dust ... they slowly and spitefully
Mysterious Conduct of Straudenheim.

About this time, I deserted ... in a German travelling chariot that *The
Journey's End.*

City of London Churches (pp. 188–98)

reader's soul. A full half ... as great a success as was expected?
Meditations in Church.

for a while resists ... help us out. The personage *The Personage.*

their little play in the heart ... They are worth a Sunday-explo- *A
Year's Impression.*

APPENDIX

Shy Neighbourhoods (pp. 198–208)

and meditative nature of their peaceful calling . . . in the same hands and always *A Clever Bird*.

the boards, like a Dutch clock . . . I saw him yester- *Dogs who keep Men*.

tom-cats, and their resemblance . . . as if he were Phoebus in person. *Street Fowls*.

Dullborough Town (pp. 208–18)

It lately happened . . . hitting out at one *Departed Joys*.

greengrocer's house recalled . . . the Thames and other proper *The identical Greengrocer*.

who travelled with two professional ladies . . . at the end of it was a little like- *Its Literature and Art*.

Nurse's Stories (pp. 218–29)

giants, and the refreshed . . . I see no meat.' *Career of Captain Murderer*.

Captain Murderer had a fiendish enjoyment . . . and shipwrights will run *Chips and the Rats*.

smelling at the baby in the garret!' . . . authentication that impaired my diges- *Claims of the Female Bard*.

Arcadian London (pp. 229–38)

Being in a humour for complete solitude . . . having any mind for anything but *The Hatter's Desk and his young Man*.

– and only knows me . . . order-taker, left on the hopeless *Mrs Klem*.

of Adam's confiding children . . . these useful establishments. In the Arca- *A Golden Age*.

The Calais Night-Mail (pp. 238–46)

It is an unsettled question . . . Richard the Third. *Calais*.

'Rich and rare were the gems . . . but still ahead and shining. *Getting across*.

travellers; one, a compatriot . . . I follow the good example. *The little Bird*.

NOTES

In the following annotations, my comments about the selections from *Pick-wick Papers*, *Nicholas Nickleby*, and *Sketches by Boz* are indebted in part to the painstaking notes on these works by T. W. Hill in the *Dickensian*, vols. 44–48 (1947–52). I have likewise been aided in a few other instances by James S. Stevens, *Quotations and References in Charles Dickens* (Boston: The Christopher Publishing House, 1929). Additional references illuminating specific notes are indicated in context. Details of initial publication of each selection are given at the beginning of their respective notes.

THE STORY OF THE GOBLINS WHO STOLE A SEXTON

First published in the tenth monthly number of *Pickwick Papers* (January 1837). In the 1836–7 edition, it erroneously appeared as the second Chapter 28. In 1847 the chapters were renumbered, and the story correctly became Chapter 29. The text here is that of the Charles Dickens Edition of *Pickwick Papers* (1867).

1. (p. 39) *gall and wormwood*. cf. Lamentations 3: 19.

THE BARON OF GROGZWIG

First published in the second monthly number of *Nicholas Nickleby* (May 1838). It appears in Chapter 6 along with 'The Five Sisters of York'. The text here is that of the Charles Dickens Edition of *Nicholas Nickleby* (1867).

1. (p. 51) *Nimrod or Gillingwater*. Nimrod is described in Genesis 10: 9 as 'a mighty hunter before the Lord'. In comic contrast, Gillingwater was a contemporary London barber and perfumier who kept bears underneath his shop and used to advertise in the window, 'another young bear slaughtered this day' – presumably to produce the ingredients for bear's grease, then fashionable on men's hair. See [B. W. Matz], *Dickensian*, vol. 16 (1920), p. 222.

2. (p. 51) *corned*. Preserved by rubbing with salt and soaking in a solution of salt and water.

3. (p. 52) '*Till all was blue*'. According to the *Oxford English Dictionary*, a description of the effects of heavy drinking on the eyesight.

A CONFESSION FOUND IN A PRISON IN THE TIME OF CHARLES THE SECOND

First published in the third weekly number of *Master Humphrey's Clock* (18 April 1840). Dickens omitted the *Clock* material when he published *The Old Curiosity Shop* and *Barnaby Rudge*, the two novels originally presented in this context, as separate works. The text here is that of the first volume edition of *Master Humphrey's Clock* (1840–41).

NOTES

TO BE READ AT DUSK

First published in the *Keepsake* (1852) which provides the present text.

NO. I BRANCH LINE. THE SIGNALMAN

'The Signalman' was first published as part of *Mugby Junction*, the extra Christmas number of *All the Year Round* for 1866 which provides the present text.

1. (p. 79) *a man who had been shut up within narrow limits all his life*. In the first portion of *Mugby Junction*, the central character who uses the name Barbox Brothers after the firm in which his life has been confined until his retirement, becomes belatedly interested in the world from which his job has isolated him. While exploring the railway lines radiating out from Mugby Junction, he gradually undergoes a more natural version of Gabriel Grub's supernaturally induced change of heart. 'The Signalman', as well as 'The Boy at Mugby' and the pieces by the other contributors to this Christmas number, are presented as things which were 'seen, heard, or otherwise picked up, by the Gentleman from Nowhere [Barbox Brothers], in his careful study of the Junction'.

THE ELECTION FOR BEADLE

First published in the *Evening Chronicle* (14 July 1835) and included in the First Series of *Sketches by Boz* (1836). The text here is that of the Charles Dickens Edition of *Sketches by Boz* (1868). For a discussion of Dickens's revisions in successive collections of the *Sketches*, see John Butt and Kathleen Tillotson, *Dickens at Work* (London: Methuen, 1957), chapter 2.

1. (p. 93) *Watching-rates*. Rates levied to pay local watchmen who were subsequently replaced by the police.
2. (p. 94) *the old naval officer on half-pay, to whom we have already introduced our readers*. Described in the second sketch dealing with 'Our Parish', omitted from this selection. 'The Election for Beadle' is the fourth in the 'Parish' section of *Sketches by Boz*.
3. (p. 97) *his neighbour, the old lady*. Likewise described in the second 'Our Parish' sketch.
4. (p. 97) *high-lows*. Laced boots which reached over the ankle, in contrast to shoes, but did not extend so far up the leg as top boots.
5. (p. 98) *envy, and hatred, and malice and all uncharitableness*. The Litany in the Book of Common Prayer petitions for deliverance 'From all blindness of heart; from pride, vain-glory, and hypocrisy; from envy, hatred, and malice, and all uncharitableness'.

SEVEN DIALS

First published in *Bell's Life in London* (27 September 1835) and included in the Second Series of *Sketches by Boz* (1837) [1836]. The text here is that of the Charles Dickens Edition of *Sketches by Boz* (1868).

1. (p. 100) *Tom King and the Frenchman.* Figures in *Monsieur Tonson* (1821), a farce by 'William Thomas Moncrieff' (William Thomas Thomas) based on a poem of the same title by John Taylor (1757–1832). Tom King's coffee house in Covent Garden is depicted in Hogarth's 'Morning' (1738).

2. (p. 100) *Seven Dials.* A district in London so named from the convergence of seven streets at a point once marked by a pillar with six dials, or circular faces, which was removed in 1773. In the first half of the nineteenth century, Seven Dials along with the adjoining area of St Giles was one of the worst slums in London, packed with criminals, vagrants, impoverished immigrants, and more affluent visitors attracted by the low-life atmosphere as well as the ballad-singers and sellers for which the location was famous.

3. (p. 100) *names of Catnach and of Pitts.* James Catnach (1792–1841) and John Pitts (1765–1844), rival printers of street literature whose shops were located in Seven Dials.

4. (p. 100) *penny yards of song.* Songs printed in three columns on sheets approximately a yard in length and sold for a penny. There is an illustration of a long-song seller as well as a discussion of this trade in Henry Mayhew's *London Labour and the London Poor* (1861; reprinted New York: Dover, 1968), vol. I, p. 221.

5. (p. 101) *gordian knot.* Anything intricate or difficult to unravel, like the knot securing the yoke to the wagon pole of Gordius, a peasant who became king of Phrygia. According to legend, whoever could untie the knot would rule over Asia; Alexander fulfilled the prophecy by cutting the knot with his sword.

6. (p. 101) *Beulah Spa.* One of the noted features of this place of recreation, which opened at Norwood in 1831, was a small maze.

7. (p. 101) *Belzoni-like.* Giovanni Baptista Belzoni (1778–1823), born in Padua and educated in Rome, came to England in 1803 to embark upon a colourful career. He won recognition first as a public performer, capitalizing upon his enormous strength and height (approximately six feet, seven inches) and then turned his attention to engineering and exploration. He made numerous journeys within Egypt and became famous for his discoveries of antiquities and his excavations of ancient tombs.

8. (p. 101) *'three outs.'* From the slang phrase 'to drink the three outs', meaning to drink copiously.

9. (p. 103) *put the kye-bosk on her.* Slang for knock out either figuratively or literally.

10. (p. 103) *Blucher boots.* Named after the Prussian field-marshal, Gebhard Leberecht von Blücher (1742–1819). Sturdy boots which reached no higher than mid-calf in contrast to the taller Wellington boots.

11. (p. 104) *increase and multiply.* An allusion to the command in Genesis 'Be fruitful and multiply, and replenish the earth' given at the creation (1: 28) and repeated to Noah after the flood (9: 1).

12. (p. 104) *jemmy.* Slang for a cooked sheep's head.

13. (p. 105) *writes poems for Mr Warren.* The blacking warehouse in which Dickens toiled for a few miserable months as a child bore the name of its

original proprietor Jonathan Warren, a rival of the more famous Robert Warren. Like innumerable other manufacturers both then and now, Jonathan Warren advertised his product with rhyme, and Tony Weller's comments about Sam Weller's valentine in Chapter 33 of *Pickwick Papers* likewise poke fun at these rhyming propensities:

> ' "Lovely creetur," ' repeated Sam
> ' 'Tain't in poetry, is it?' interposed his father.
> 'No, no,' replied Sam.
> 'Werry glad to hear it,' said Mr Weller. 'Poetry's unnat'ral; no man ever talked poetry 'cept a beadle on boxin' day, or Warren's blackin', or Rowland's oil, or some o' them low fellows; never you let yourself down to talk poetry, my boy.'

In *The Old Curiosity Shop* (Chapter 28), the commercial poet Mr Slum persuades the proprietress of Jarley's Wax-work to purchase an acrostic which he has already written for the name Warren but which he readily converts to Jarley.

MEDITATIONS IN MONMOUTH-STREET

First published in the *Morning Chronicle* (24 September 1836) and included in the Second Series of *Sketches by Boz* (1837) [1836]. The text here is that of the Charles Dickens Edition of *Sketches by Boz* (1868).

1. (p. 106) *Monmouth-street*. In London, noted for its second-hand clothing shops.
2. (p. 106) *Holywell-street*. In London, noted for its second-hand book shops.
3. (p. 107) *half-boots*. Boots extending half way up the leg to the knee. Sometimes equated with Blucher boots; see note 10 to 'Seven Dials' (p. 413).
4. (p. 110) *pair of tops*. High boots whose topmost portion was made of a contrasting colour.
5. (p. 110) *knee-cords*. Corduroy trousers ending just below the knee.
6. (p. 110) *Denmark satin*. Smooth surfaced, worsted material used for women's shoes.
7. (p. 112) *imperence*. Slang for impudence.

A VISIT TO NEWGATE

First published in the First Series of *Sketches by Boz* (1836). The text here is that of the Charles Dickens Edition of *Sketches by Boz* (1868).

1. (p. 112) *If Bedlam could be suddenly removed like another Aladdin's palace*. In the oriental tale of 'Aladdin and the Wonderful Lamp', generally considered part of the collection known as the *Arabian Nights' Entertainments*, Aladdin, the son of a poor tailor, acquires a lamp containing a genie who subsequently builds him a palace and enables him to marry a princess. At one point, he temporarily loses the lamp to an evil magician who causes both princess and palace to be transported to Africa, but Aladdin even-

tually triumphs and returns his wife and home to China. Bedlam (the word is a corrupt form of Bethlehem) was long a famous London hospital for lunatics.

2. (p. 112) *Newgate*. A famous London prison, demolished in 1902.

3. (p. 112) *Old Bailey*. The street in which the Old Bailey, the Central Criminal Court, is located.

4. (p. 114) *Bishop and Williams*. The body-snatchers John Bishop and Thomas Head, alias Williams, were hanged on 5 December 1831 for murdering a young boy.

5. (p. 114) *Jack Sheppard ... Dick Turpin*. Jack Sheppard (1702–24) and Dick Turpin (1706–39) were notorious thieves and highwaymen. The former was famous for his daring escapes from prison, but both were eventually hanged, Sheppard at Tyburn and Turpin at York. Both figured in novels by Dickens's contemporary Harrison Ainsworth.

6. (p. 118) *stump bedstead*. A bedstead whose framework ends at the level of the mattress.

7. (p. 119) *Scotch cap*. A brimless woollen cap with two tails.

8. (p. 120) *turn, and flee from the wrath to come!* Matthew 3:7 and Luke 3:7 read 'O generation of vipers, who hath warned you to flee from the wrath to come?'

A CHRISTMAS TREE

First published in the Christmas 1850 number of *Household Words* (21 December 1850) and included in *Reprinted Pieces* (1858) in the Library Edition of Dickens's works. The text here is that of the Charles Dickens Edition of *American Notes, and Reprinted Pieces* (1868).

1. (p. 129) *Barmecide*. In the story of the Barber's Sixth Brother in the *Arabian Nights' Entertainments*, a member of the Barmecide family serves a beggar an imaginary banquet (see Chapter 5 of Edward William Lane's translation).

2. (p. 129) *Punch's hands*. In the Punch and Judy puppet show.

3. (p. 130) *Jack, who achieved all the recorded exploits*. The adventures described here appear in the fairy tales of 'Jack and the Beanstalk' and 'Jack the Giant-Killer'.

4. (p. 130) *ferocious joke about his teeth*. 'The better to eat you with, my dear' – said by the wolf in the fairy tale just before swallowing Little Red Riding-Hood.

5. (p. 131) *Robin Hood ... Valentine ... the Yellow Dwarf ... and all Mother Bunch's wonders*. The exploits of the legendary English outlaw Robin Hood like the adventures of Valentine (raised at court as a knight) and his brother Orson (carried off by a bear and brought up in the woods) which were first recorded in an early French romance, formed part of young Dickens's imaginative diet. The tale of the wicked Yellow Dwarf, who steals a beautiful princess and kills his rival only to have the princess die of a broken heart, is another of the traditional nursery stories, sometimes collected

under the supposed aegis of 'Mother Bunch', which Dickens remembered with delight.

6. (p. 132) *we all three breathe again.* The allusions here, as in the previous paragraphs, are to the *Arabian Nights' Entertainments*, narrated by Scheherazade to forestall her execution by the Sultan: 'trees are for Ali Baba to hide in' and 'cobblers are all Mustaphas', from 'Ali Baba and the Forty Thieves', traditionally considered part of this collection; 'beefsteaks are to throw down into the Valley of Diamonds', from the second voyage of Es-Sindibád of the Sea (Chapter 20 of Lane's translation); 'the Vizier's son of Bussorah, who turned pastrycook', from the story of Noored-Deen and Shems-ed-Deen (Chapter 4 of Lane); 'cave which only waits for the magician', from 'Aladdin and the Wonderful Lamp' (see note 1 to 'A Visit to Newgate', p. 414); 'unlucky date', from the story of the Merchant and the Jinee (Chapter 1 of Lane); 'fictitious trial of the fraudulent olive merchant', from 'The Story of Ali Cogia, Merchant of Bagdad', traditionally associated with the *Arabian Nights*; 'apple ... which the tall black slave stole from the child', from the story of the three apples (Chapter 4 of Lane); 'dog ... who ... put his paw on the piece of bad money' and 'rice which the awful lady ... could only peck by grains', from 'The Story of Sidi-Nouman' (like 'Aladdin and the Wonderful Lamp', 'Ali Baba and the Forty Thieves', and 'Ali Cogia, Merchant of Bagdad', included by Antoine Galland in his early eighteenth-century French translation of the *Arabian Nights* but omitted from many more recent versions including Lane's translation of 1839–41); 'fly away ... as the wooden horse did with the Prince of Persia', from the story of the Magic Horse (Chapter 17 of Lane).

7. (p. 132) *Robinson Crusoe on his desert island.* From *Robinson Crusoe* (1719) by Daniel Defoe.

8. (p. 132) *Philip Quarll among the monkeys.* From *The Adventures of Philip Quarll* (1727), describing the exploits of an imitation Robinson Crusoe, by 'Edward Dorrington' (Peter Longueville).

9. (p. 132) *Sandford and Merton with Mr Barlow.* From *The History of Sandford and Merton* (1783–9) by Thomas Day.

10. (p. 133) *devoted dog of Montargis.* Owned by Aubry de Montdidier who was murdered by Richard de Macaire in 1371. The story of the way in which the dog called attention to his master's assassin, fought him in judicial combat, and forced him to confess his crime was popular in chapbooks as well as on the adult and toy theatre stage.

11. (p. 133) *Jane Shore.* Mistress of Edward IV but later accused of sorcery by Richard III and forced to do public penance. She is the subject of *The Tragedy of Jane Shore* (1714) by Nicholas Rowe.

12. (p. 133) *how George Barnwell killed the worthiest uncle that ever man had.* In *The London Merchant; or The History of George Barnwell* (1731) by George Lillo.

13. (p. 133) *the Pantomime.* For a contemporary account of this form of entertainment in which Dickens delighted, see the description by Francis

Wey, reprinted in *London in Dickens' Day*, ed. Jacob Korg (Englewood Cliffs, N.J.: Prentice-Hall, 1960), pp. 144–7.

14. (p. 133) '*Nothing is, but thinking makes it so.*' cf. Shakespeare's *Hamlet* II, ii, 255–7: '. . . there is nothing either good or bad, but thinking makes it so.'

15. (p. 133) *the toy-theatre.* A favourite nineteenth-century amusement. The sheets of characters and stage fittings could be purchased at toy shops, and, as Dickens notes, hours of labour went into the 'attendant occupation with paste and glue, and gum, and water colours, in the getting-up of' plays such as *The Miller and His Men* and *Elizabeth or the Exile of Siberia* which had been successful in the adult theatres of the day. The actual toy-theatre performance undoubtedly provided a splendid forum for Dickens's youthful imagination since all parts had to be read by the young producer, and the characters were frequently printed in a single attitude in which they necessarily appeared throughout the play, except for 'a few besetting accidents and failures (particularly an unreasonable disposition . . . to become faint in the legs, and double up, at exciting points of the drama)'. Much of the juvenile popularity of *The Miller and His Men*, in which the character of Kelmar appears, was probably attributable to the explosion with which it ended. See A. E. Wilson, *Penny Plain Two Pence Coloured: A History of the Juvenile Drama* (London: Harrap, 1932) and George Speaight, *The History of the English Toy Theatre*, revised ed. (Boston, Mass.: Plays, 1969).

16. (p. 134) '*Forgive them, for they know not what they do.*' Luke 23: 34.

17. (p. 134) *Rule of Three.* In mathematics, 'a method of finding a fourth number from three given numbers, of which the first is in the same proportion to the second as the third is to the unknown fourth' (*Oxford English Dictionary*).

18. (p 134) *Terence and Plautus.* Terence (190?–159 B.C.) and Plautus (254?–184 B.C.), Roman dramatists.

19. (p. 138) *the old King.* George III, who became incurably insane in 1810.

20. (p. 140) *Legion is the name of.* cf. Mark 5: 9.

21. (p. 141) *This, in remembrance of Me!* Luke 22: 19.

A FLIGHT

First published in *Household Words* (30 August 1851) and included in *Reprinted Pieces* (1858), in the Library Edition of Dickens's works. The text here is that of the Charles Dickens Edition of *American Notes, and Reprinted Pieces* (1868).

1. (p. 142) *Deputy Chaff Wax.* An officer responsible for preparing the wax used in sealing documents. The position was abolished in 1852.

2. (p. 142) *Meat-chell.* John Mitchell (1806–74), who had made the St James's Theatre the London location for drama in French at the time of this sketch.

3. (p. 142) *Abd-el-Kader* (1807–83), an Arab leader noted for his skilful battles against the French. In 1847, he was forced to surrender and imprisoned in France until 1852.

4. (p. 142) *Zamiel.* A demonic spirit like Lucifer and Mephistopheles. He appears in Karl Maria von Weber's *Der Freischütz* (1821).

5. (p. 144) *Parliamentary Train.* By Act of Parliament, railways were required to run one cheap train, charging no more than a penny a mile, daily on all major lines; they were known as Parliamentary trains.

6. (p. 151) *statue ... at Hyde Park Corner.* Matthew Cotes Wyatt's huge bronze statue of the Duke of Wellington on horseback, erected at Hyde Park Corner on Decimus Burton's arch in 1846 (and not removed until more than thirty years after Wellington's death in 1852), was a frequent target of contemporary ridicule. Dickens was generally unsympathetic towards the idea of commemorative statues; among his set of dummy bookbacks invented for the library door at Tavistock House was a ten-volume *Catalogue of Statues to the Duke of Wellington.*

OUR SCHOOL

First published in *Household Words* (11 October 1851) and included in *Reprinted Pieces* (1858) in the Library Edition of Dickens's works. The text here is that of the Charles Dickens Edition of *American Notes, and Reprinted Pieces* (1868).

1. (p. 156) *Dog of Montargis.* See note 10 to 'A Christmas Tree' (p. 416).

2. (p. 158) *solemn as the ghost in Hamlet.* cf. I, i, iv, v and III, iv of Shakespeare's play.

3. (p. 159) *So fades ... all that this world is proud of.* From William Wordsworth's *The Excursion* (1814), VII, lines 976–8, loosely quoted.

LYING AWAKE

First published in *Household Words* (30 October 1852) and included in *Reprinted Pieces* (1858) in the Library Edition of Dickens's works. The text here is that of the Charles Dickens Edition of *American Notes, and Reprinted Pieces* (1868).

1. (p. 159) *My uncle ... just falling asleep.* From 'The Adventure of My Uncle' in Irving's *Tales of a Traveller* (1824).

2. (p. 160) '*Get out of bed ... sweet and pleasant.*' From Franklin's 'The Art of Procuring Pleasant Dreams' (1786).

3. (p. 160) *great actor ... playing Macbeth, and ... apostrophising 'the death of each day's life'.* William Charles Macready (1793–1873), noted tragedian and close friend of Dickens. His last performance was at Drury Lane Theatre on 26 Feburary 1851 in the role of Shakespeare's Macbeth. The line quoted here occurs in the context of Macbeth's impassioned description of sleep (II, ii, 35–40):

> Methought I heard a voice cry 'Sleep no more!
> Macbeth does murder sleep' – the innocent sleep,
> Sleep that knits up the raveled sleave of care,
> The death of each day's life, sore labor's bath,
> Balm of hurt minds, great nature's second course,
> Calm nourisher in life's feast –

4. (p. 161) *Mr Bathe.* The proprietor of the London Tavern.

5. (p. 162) *the Mannings, husband and wife hanging on the top of Horsemonger Lane Jail.* On 13 November 1849, George and Maria Manning were hanged for murdering their lodger, Patrick O'Connor. The trial aroused great excitement, and a crowd of approximately thirty thousand people, including Dickens, witnessed the execution. For a discussion of Dickens's reaction, and his attitude toward capital punishment in general, see Philip Collins, *Dickens and Crime*, 2nd ed. (1964; reprinted Bloomington, Ind.: Indiana University Press, 1968), pp. 235 ff.

6. (p. 164) *Cremorne reality.* The Cremorne Gardens in Chelsea, opened in 1845 and closed in 1877, were the site of numerous forms of entertainment including extraordinary balloon ascents. See the contemporary description of Cremorne by Francis Wey, reprinted in *London in Dickens' Day*, ed. Jacob Korg (Englewood Cliffs, N.J.: Prentice-Hall, 1960), pp. 142–4.

7. (p. 165) *like that sagacious animal in the United States who recognized the colonel who was such a dead shot, I am a gone 'Coon.* Frederick Marryat related this anecdote about Captain Martin Scott in *A Diary in America* (New York: D. Appleton, 1839), p. 150.

8. (p. 165) *Pet Prisoning.* Giving more consideration to the welfare of criminals in prison than to the needs of honest men outside the prison walls, the consequence, according to Dickens, of the system of solitary confinement currently being tried at the model prison at Pentonville. Under this system, at the conclusion of *David Copperfield* (Chapter 61), the hypocrites Mr Littimer and Uriah Heep prove to be model prisoners. For a more factual treatment of this theme, see 'Pet Prisoners', *Household Words*, 27 April 1850. Philip Collins has discussed 'the Pentonville experiment' at length in *Dickens and Crime*, 2nd ed. (1964; reprinted Bloomington, Ind.: Indiana University Press, 1968), pp. 140–63.

THE UNCOMMERCIAL TRAVELLER

Dickens published a series of sketches in *All the Year Round* under the heading of 'The Uncommercial Traveller' at intervals between 1860 and 1869. All but the last of the selections presented here appeared in the inaugural group of sketches, published in 1860 and subsequently collected in *The Uncommercial Traveller* (1861) [1860].

HIS GENERAL LINE OF BUSINESS

First published in *All the Year Round* (28 January 1860). The text here is that of the Charles Dickens Edition of *The Uncommercial Traveller* (1868).

REFRESHMENTS FOR TRAVELLERS

First published in *All the Year Round* (24 March 1860). The text here is that of the Charles Dickens Edition of *The Uncommercial Traveller* (1868).

1. (p. 168) *practised thieves with the appearance and manners of gentlemen.* In a similar vein, in his 1841 preface to *Oliver Twist*, Dickens contrasted his own treatment of underworld characters with that of novelists such as Harrison Ainsworth who show 'thieves by scores – seductive fellows (amiable for the most part), faultless in dress, plump in pocket, choice in horseflesh, bold in bearing, fortunate in gallantry, great at a song, a bottle, pack of cards or dice-box, and fit companions for the bravest'. However, Dickens's insistence upon the literality of his own work, whether in *Oliver Twist* or in this particular sketch, cannot be completely taken at face value. As George H. Ford has pointed out, although Dickens 'may have wanted to be considered an accurate social historian, his art consisted in the transmutation of a strong impression, sometimes derived from an actual scene, into convincing illusion' (*Dickens and His Readers*, [1955; reprinted New York: Norton, 1965], p. 134).

2. (p. 169) *Sir Richard Mayne.* (1796–1868), commissioner of the London Metropolitan Police.

3. (p. 172) *like Dr Johnson, Sir, you like to dine.* Boswell says about Samuel Johnson, 'I never knew any man who relished good eating more than he did. When at table, he was totally absorbed in the business of the moment his looks seemed rivetted to his plate; nor would he, unless when in very high company, say one word, or even pay the least attention to what was said by others, till he had satisfied his appetite, which was so fierce, and indulged with such intenseness, that while in the act of eating, the veins of his forehead swelled, and generally a strong perspiration was visible' (*Boswell's Life of Johnson*, edited by George Birkbeck Hill, revised by L. F. Powell, vol. I [Oxford: Clarendon Press, 1934], p. 468).

TRAVELLING ABROAD

First published in *All the Year Round* (7 April 1860). The text here is that of the Charles Dickens Edition of *The Uncommercial Traveller* (1868).

1. (p. 178) '*Blow, blow, thou winter wind.*' From Shakespeare's *As You Like It*, II, vii, 174.

2. (p. 179) *Sterne's Maria.* The half-witted French girl of volume 9 of *The Life and Opinions of Tristram Shandy* (1760–67) who reappears in *A Sentimental Journey through France and Italy* (1768).

3. (p. 185) *nursery rhyme about Banbury Cross and the venerable lady who rode in state there.* From the nursery rhyme which begins 'Ride a cock-horse to Banbury Cross'. In modern versions, the lady is usually described as 'fine', but, in some earlier versions, she was termed 'old'.

4. (p. 186) *a new Gesler in a Canton of Tells, and went in highly deserved danger of my tyrannical life.* Austrian bailiff of the canton of Uri, killed, according to Swiss legend, by William Tell.

5. (p. 186) *Don Quixote on the back of the wooden horse.* From part Two, chapter 41, of *Don Quixote* (1605–15) by Miguel de Cervantes.

NOTES

CITY OF LONDON CHURCHES

First published in *All the Year Round* (5 May 1860). The text here is that of the Charles Dickens Edition of *The Uncommercial Traveller* (1868).

1. (p. 193) *comet vintages*. Wine produced in a comet year, which is supposed to possess unusually fine flavour.
2. (p. 193) *Saint Anthony*. (c. A.D. 250–355) the first Christian monk, noted for his successful struggles against the temptations of secular life.
3. (p. 195) *spencer*. A waist-length jacket.
4. (p. 195) *boxing-gloves*. It appears that the child is wearing mittens.
5. (p. 197) *the church in the Rake's Progress where the hero is being married to the horrible old lady*. Plate 5 of the set of engravings by William Hogarth (1735).
6. (p. 198) *Wren*. Christopher Wren (1632–1723), noted English architect.

SHY NEIGHBOURHOODS

First published in *All the Year Round* (26 May 1860). The text here is that of the Charles Dickens Edition of *The Uncommercial Traveller* (1868).

1. (p. 199) *Mr Thomas Sayers ... and Mr John Heenan*. The pugilists Sayers (1826–65) and Heenan (1835–73) fought a celebrated match in 1860, which was considered a draw.
2. (p. 200) *in the manner of Izaak Walton*. Like the bucolic descriptions in Walton's *The Compleat Angler* (1653, continued by Charles Cotton in 1676), a discussion of the art of fishing.
3. (p. 202) *Green Yard*. A pound for holding stray animals and lost vehicles.
4. (p. 203) *dogs ... who perform in Punch's shows*. A dog called Toby was a traditional figure in the Punch and Judy puppet show, and, according to the showman interviewed by Mayhew, the use of a live rather than a stuffed dog in the performance became highly popular:

> a great hit it were – it made a grand alteration in the hexhibition, for now the performance is called Punch and Toby *as well*. There is one Punch about the streets at present that tries it on with three dogs, but that ain't much of a go – too much of a good thing I calls it (*London Labour and the London Poor*, vol. III [1861; reprinted New York: Dover, 1968], p. 45).

5. (p. 206) *surplus population*. *An Essay on the Principle of Population* (1798) by Thomas Malthus, one of the *laissez-faire* political economists Dickens disliked, predicted that population, if unchecked, would inevitably increase more rapidly than the supply of food.
6. (p. 207) *Mrs Southcott*. Joanna Southcott (1750–1814), English religious prophet.
7. (p. 207) *Chinese circle*. According to an unpublished note by the late T. W. Hill, the 'circle' is apparently a reference to the group to which the fowls belonged. Hill observes that Dickens alludes to several kinds of chickens

in this paragraph: Bantam, Dorking, speckled and Cochin-China (information about Hill's comment kindly supplied by Dr Michael Slater, editor of the *Dickensian*).

DULLBOROUGH TOWN

First published in *All the Year Round* (30 June 1860). The text here is that of the Charles Dickens Edition of *The Uncommercial Traveller* (1868).

1. (p. 209) *S.E.R.* South Eastern Railway.
2. (p. 209) *Seringapatam.* The capital of the Indian state of Mysore at the end of the eighteenth century; it was the stronghold of the sultan Tippoo Sahib, killed when the British captured the city in 1799.
3. (p. 212) *model on which the Genie of the Lamp built the palace for Aladdin.* See note 1 to 'A Visit to Newgate' (p. 414).
4. (p. 212) *Richard the Third ... struggling for life against the virtuous Richmond.* In the last scene of Shakespeare's *Richard III*.
5. (p. 213) *witches in Macbeth ... calling himself something else.* 'Lying Awake' describes an adult recollection of a more sophisticated performance of the same play.
6. (p. 217) *Mr Random.* From *The Adventures of Roderick Random* (1748) by Tobias Smollett.
7. (p. 218) *Pickle.* From *The Adventures of Peregrine Pickle* (1751) by Smollett.

NURSE'S STORIES

First published in *All the Year Round* (8 September 1860). The text here is that of the Charles Dickens Edition of *The Uncommercial Traveller* (1868).

1. (p. 219) *belated among wolves, on the borders of France and Spain.* An episode, like those mentioned in the previous paragraph, from Defoe's *Robinson Crusoe*.
2. (p. 220) *the robbers' cave where Gil Blas lived ... lies everlastingly cursing in bed.* Chapters 4–10 of the first book of *The Adventures of Gil Blas of Santillane* (1715–35) by Alain René Le Sage.
3. (p. 220) *Don Quixote's study ... great draughts of water.* From Part One, Chapters 1 and 5, of Cervantes's *Don Quixote*.
4. (p. 220) *little old woman who ... told the merchant Abudah to go in search of the Talisman of Oromanes.* From the first of *The Tales of the Genii* (1764) by James Ridley.
5. (p. 220) *the school where the boy Horatio Nelson got out of bed to steal the pears ... let down out of window with a sheet.* The anecdote appears in the first chapter of *The Life of Nelson* (1813) by Robert Southey.
6. (p. 220) *Brobingnag.* Correctly spelled 'Brobdingnag' by Jonathan Swift in *Gulliver's Travels* (1726), where, like Lilliput and Laputa, it is one of the countries visited by Gulliver.
7. (p. 221) *Blue Beard.* A fairy-tale villain who murders his wives. His last bride opens a forbidden closet, discovers the bodies of her predecessors,

and verges on the same fate, but her brothers rescue her and kill her husband.

8. (p. 224) 'The Black Cat' ... sucking the breath of infancy, and ... endowed with a special thirst ... for mine. Strikingly similar to the bloodthirsty young man, hungering for juvenile heart and liver, with which Magwitch threatens Pip in chapter I of Great Expectations (originally conceived as a short piece in the vein of these Uncommercial Traveller sketches which Dickens was writing in 1860 – see the letter to Forster of September 1860 in The Letters of Charles Dickens, ed. Walter Dexter (London-Nonesuch Press, 1938), vol. 3, p. 182).

ARCADIAN LONDON

First published in All the Year Round (29 September 1860). The text here is that of the Charles Dickens Edition of The Uncommercial Traveller (1868).

1. (p. 230) a Volunteer. The subsequent details seem drawn from the 11th Middlesex Volunteer Rifle Corps. See Gwen Major 'Arcadian London', Dickensian, vol. 45 (1949), p. 209.

2. (p. 233) chasing the ebbing Neptune on the ribbed sea-sand. cf. Prospero's farewell to his magic in Shakespeare's The Tempest (V, i, 33–5):

> Ye elves of hills, brooks, standing lakes, and groves,
> And ye that on the sands with printless foot
> Do chase the ebbing Neptune ...

3. (p. 234) the Every-Day Book. By William Hone, containing a description of 'the popular amusements, sports, ceremonies, manners, customs, and events, incident to the three hundred and sixty-five days, in past and present times', first published weekly from January 1825 to December 1826.

4. (p. 234) Break. 'A portion of ground broken up for cultivation' (Oxford English Dictionary).

5. (p. 235) taking of Delhi. Recaptured by the British from Indian mutineers in September 1857. William Oddie, 'Dickens and the Indian Mutiny', Dickensian, vol. 68 (1972), pp. 3–15, is a discussion of Dickens's reaction to the insurrection and its reflection in his contributions to The Perils of Certain English Prisoners, the extra Christmas number of Household Words for 1857.

6. (p. 235) New Zealander of the grand English History. An allusion to Macaulay's prophecy that one day 'some traveller from New Zealand shall, in the midst of a vast solitude, take his stand on a broken arch of London Bridge to sketch the ruins of St Paul's'. The prediction occurs not in Macaulay's History of England but in his essay 'Von Ranke', Edinburgh Review, October 1840.

7. (p. 235) to-morrow, and to-morrow, and to-morrow. Shakespeare, Macbeth, V, v, 19.

8. (p. 236) *Agapemone*. Greek for 'abode of love', and the name of a religious community established near Bridgwater c. 1846 by Henry James Prince (1811–99).

9. (p. 238) *Lord Shaftesbury*. Anthony Ashley Cooper, seventh Earl of Shaftesbury (1801–85), English philanthropist active in organizing so-called 'ragged schools' for poor children.

THE CALAIS NIGHT-MAIL

First published in *All the Year Round* (2 May 1863). The text here is that of the Charles Dickens Edition of *The Uncommercial Traveller* (1868).

1. (p. 240) *dogs of Dover bark at me in my mis-shapen wrappers, as if I were Richard the Third*. See Richard's description of himself in the opening scene of Shakespeare's *Richard III* (I, i, 20–23):

> Deformed, unfinished, sent before my time
> Into this breathing world, scarce half made up,
> And that so lamely and unfashionable
> That dogs bark at me as I halt by them –

2. (p. 241) '*Rich and rare were the gems she wore.*' The opening line of one of Thomas Moore's *Irish Melodies* (1808–34) which the Uncommercial Traveller subsequently weaves into his description of his surroundings:

> Rich and rare were the gems she wore,
> And a bright gold ring on her wand she bore:
> But oh! her beauty was far beyond
> Her sparkling gems, or snow-white wand.
>
> 'Lady! dost thou not fear to stray,
> So lone and lovely through this bleak way?
> Are Erin's sons so good or so cold,
> As not to be tempted by woman or gold?'
>
> 'Sir Knight! I feel not the least alarm,
> No son of Erin will offer me harm: –
> For though they love woman and golden store,
> Sir Knight! they love honour and virtue more!'
>
> On she went, and her maiden smile
> In safety lighted her round the Green Isle;
> And blest for ever is she who relied
> Upon Erin's honour and Erin's pride.

3. (p. 243) *Robinson Crusoe . . . in his first gale of wind*. There are other illusions in 'A Christmas Tree' and 'Nurse's Stories' to this fondly remembered novel of Dickens's childhood.

4. (p. 243) *a bull's eye bright*. A bull's-eye lantern.

5. (p. 243) *those Calais burghers who came out of their town by a short cut into the History of England, with those fatal ropes round their necks*. One of

the conditions on which Calais was surrendered to Edward III in 1347.

6. (p. 244) *Calais will be found written on my heart.* Calais was retaken by the French in 1558 during the reign of Queen Mary who is reputed to have said in her final illness, as Dickens quotes in *A Child's History of England*, 'When I am dead and my body is opened . . . ye shall find Calais written on my heart.'

7. (p. 244) *'an ancient and fish-like smell.'* cf. Shakespeare, *The Tempest*, II, ii, 26–7.

8. (p. 246) *Vauban.* Sébastien Le Prestre de Vauban (1633–1707), French military engineer.

9. (p. 246) *such corporals as you heard of once upon a time, and many a blue-eyed Bebelle.* Described in the story contained in 'His Boots', in the extra Christmas number of *All the Year Round* for 1862. See note 1 to *Somebody's Luggage*, below.

10. (p. 246) *Richardson's.* There is a re-creation of a Richardson's Show in 'Greenwich Fair', one of the *Sketches by Boz* omitted from this selection.

SOMEBODY'S LUGGAGE

The monologues presented here were first published in *Somebody's Luggage* the extra Christmas number of *All the Year Round* for 1862 which provides the present text. 'His Leaving it till called for' and 'His Wonderful End' opened and closed the Christmas number while 'His Brown-Paper Parcel' formed one of the pieces which Dickens introduced into this framework. In addition to contributions by other authors, *Somebody's Luggage* also contained a story by Dickens about a little French girl, narrated in the third person and supposedly found in 'His Boots', omitted from this selection. For a further discussion of the contents of Dickens's Christmas numbers, see Deborah A. Thomas, 'Contributors to the Christmas Numbers of *Household Words* and *All the Year Round*, 1850–1867', *Dickensian*, part 1, vol. 69 (1973), pp. 163–72; part 2, vol. 70 (1974), pp. 21–9.

HIS LEAVING IT TILL CALLED FOR

1. (p. 252) *Lord Palmerston.* Henry John Temple, third Viscount Palmerston (1784–1865) British statesman and prime minister.

2. (p. 253) *screws.* Slang for miserly people.

3. (p. 253) *union.* A workhouse.

4. (p. 253) *Consols.* Contraction of consolidated annuities – interest-bearing, British government securities.

5. (p. 257) *calimanco.* 'A cotton and worsted textile, highly glazed, plain or twilled' (C. Willet Cunnington, Phillis Cunnington, and Charles Beard, *A Dictionary of English Costume* [London: A & C. Black, 1960], p. 246).

6. (p. 258) *o10.* Originally divided here at a page end with the notation 'Carried forward . . . £1 4 0' and 'Brought forward . . . £1 4 0'.

7. (p. 260) *Blue Beard.* See note 7 to 'Nurse's Stories'. (p. 422).

HIS BROWN-PAPER PARCEL

1. (p. 264) *'domestic drama of the Stranger, you had a silent sorrow there.'* A translation of Augustus von Kotzebue's *Menschenhass und Reue*. The popular version translated by Benjamin Thompson, first produced in 1798, contained a song by Richard Brinsley Sheridan which began:

> I have a silent sorrow here,
> A grief I'll ne'er impart;
> It breathes no sigh, it sheds no tear,
> But it consumes my heart!

2. (p. 264) *'coining or smashing?'* Slang for counterfeiting, or passing bad money.
3. (p. 265) *'An honest man is the noblest work of God.'* cf. Alexander Pope, *An Essay on Man* (1733–4), Epistle IV, p. 248, and Robert Burns, *The Cotter's Saturday Night* (1786), line 166.
4. (p. 265) *Hunger is a . . . sharp thorn.* Proverbial.
5. (p. 267) *green-eyed monster.* Shakespeare, *Othello*, III, iii, 166.
6. (p. 267) *improve each shining hour.* 'Against Idleness and Mischief', the twentieth of Isaac Watts's *Divine Songs for Children* (1715) opens with the lines:

> How doth the little busy bee
> Improve each shining hour,
> And gather honey all the day
> From every opening flower!

(The second chapter of *Alice's Adventures in Wonderland*, [1865] contains a parody of this by Lewis Carroll.)

7. (p. 269) *Britons Strike . . . Home!* The title of an opera by Charles Dibdin (1803), from a song in Henry Purcell's *Bonduca* (1695).

HIS WONDERFUL END

1. (p. 274) *A.Y.R.* An abbreviation of *All the Year Round*, the journal edited by Dickens in which this Christmas number originally appeared. As explained in the Introduction (p. 26) the number was intended as an elaborate spoof of the difficulties inherent in what had by 1862 become an annual Christmas production. (See the letter to Wilkie Collins, 20 September 1862, in *The Letters of Charles Dickens*, ed. Walter Dexter (London: Nonesuch Press, 1938), vol. 3, p. 304.) Here, as in his footnotes, Dickens is poking fun at his own editorial activities.
2. (p. 275) *the last echoes of the Guy-Foxes.* Fireworks on 5 November commemorating the detection of the Gunpowder Plot in which Guy Fawkes (1570–1606) was one of the leading conspirators.
3. (p. 277) *Basilisk.* A legendary reptile whose gaze was supposedly fatal. The Boy at Mugby, who adds his own inimitable errors to some of Christopher's literary pretensions, likens Mrs Sniff's observation of her husband to that of the 'fabled obelisk' (p. 378).

4. (p. 280) *four-wheeler*. A hackney carriage with four wheels.
5. (p. 280) *Beaufort Printing House*. The printer for *All the Year Round* was C. Whiting, Beaufort House, Strand, mentioned again at the end of the first section of *Doctor Marigold's Prescriptions* (p. 363).

MRS LIRRIPER'S LODGINGS

'How Mrs Lirriper carried on the Business' and 'How the Parlours added a few words' were first published as the framework of *Mrs Lirriper's Lodgings*, the extra Christmas number of *All the Year Round* for 1863 which provides the present text.

HOW MRS LIRRIPER CARRIED ON THE BUSINESS

1. (p. 285) *Airy*. Area, a sunken space providing access to the basement of a building. In *Bleak House*, on her first visit to the Jellyby family, Esther extricates one of the Jellyby children who has caught his head in the area railings.
2. (p. 285) *a man and a brother*. The seal of the London Anti-Slavery Society contained the motto 'Am I not a man and a brother?'
3. (p. 290) *engine*. Fire engine. According to the *Oxford English Dictionary* a common eighteenth-century usage which persisted into the nineteenth century.
4. (p. 290) '*sufficient for the day is the evil thereof.*' Matthew 6: 34, 'Sufficient unto the day . . .'
5. (p. 294) *Sleeping . . . Beauty*. The fairy-tale princess who sleeps for a hundred years.
6. (p. 298) *treasured His sayings in her heart*. Luke 2: 19, 51.
7. (p. 302) *him as sweeps the crossings*. Human crossing-sweepers, like Jo in *Bleak House*, were a familiar sight in Victorian London (see Mayhew's *London Labour and the London Poor*, vol. 2 [1861; reprinted New York: Dover, 1968], pp. 465–507).
8. (p. 302) *L.S.D.-ically*. Slang for monetarily.
9. (p. 304) *Italian iron*. A cylindrical, hollow iron containing a heater, used for lace and frills.
10. (p. 304) *larding-needle*. A needle used to insert strips of bacon into meat and poultry in preparation for cooking.
11. (p. 308) *salad days*. In Shakespeare's *Anthony and Cleopatra* (I, v, 73–5), Cleopatra dismisses the time of her earlier romance with Caesar as

> 'My salad days,
> When I was green in judgment,
> cold in blood,
> To say as I said then!'

MRS LIRRIPER'S LEGACY

'Mrs Lirriper Relates how She Went On, and Went Over' and 'Mrs Lirriper Relates how Jemmy Topped Up' were first published as the framework of *Mrs Lirriper's Legacy*, the extra Christmas number of *All Year the Round* for 1864 which provides the present text.

MRS LIRRIPER RELATES HOW SHE WENT ON, AND WENT OVER

1. (p. 315) *ashes to ashes and dust to dust.* From the order for the burial of the dead in the Book of Common Prayer.

2. (p. 316) '*stump up.*' Slang for pay up.

3. (p. 317) *dressed almost entirely in padlocks like Baron Trenck.* Baron Friedrich von der Trenck (1726–94) imprisoned from 1754 to 1763 in the fortress at Magdeburg. His *Memoirs*, detailing his confinement and, in particular, the heavy chains with which he was loaded, were published in 1787 and quickly translated into several languages

4. (p. 318) *garden-engine.* 'A portable force-pump used for watering gardens' (*Oxford English Dictionary*).

5. (p. 320) *Johnson's Dictionary.* Samuel Johnson's *A Dictionary of the English Language* appeared in 1755 and remained authoritative well into the following century. It was still in use as late as 1870 when Robert Gordon Latham completed *A Dictionary of the English Language . . . Founded on That of . . . Samuel Johnson, as Edited by . . . H. J. Todd.*

6. (p. 320) *Hamlet and the other gentleman in mourning before killing one another.* In the concluding scene of Shakespeare's *Hamlet.*

7. (p. 321) *boned.* Slang for stolen.

8. (p. 326) *Plymouth Sister.* The Plymouth Brethren, an evangelical religious sect which makes no official distinction between clergy and laity, arose c. 1830 at Plymouth, England.

9. (p. 328) *Old Moore's Almanack with the hieroglyphic complete.* Francis Moore's *Vox Stellarum* first appeared in 1700 (with predictions for 1701). The idea and the name became popular, and several almanacs with a variety of prognostications emerged in the nineteenth century under the title of 'Old Moore's'.

10. (p. 329) *Fortunatus with his purse.* In the folktale of Fortunatus (dramatized by Thomas Dekker in 1600), the beggar Fortunatus meets Fortune who gives him a choice of a variety of gifts. He chooses riches instead of wisdom and receives a magic purse from which he can always take ten pieces of gold. Equipped with this purse, he embarks on a series of adventures, at the height of which Fortune terminates his life

11. (p. 333) *Your sin has found you out!* Numbers 32: 23, 'behold, ye have sinned against the Lord: and be sure your sin will find you out'.

12. (p. 336) *dressed in blue like a butcher.* The characteristic colour of butchers' aprons and often other articles of their clothing in the nineteenth century.

13. (p. 337) *Barricading.* In the wave of revolution which engulfed France and

most of the rest of Europe in 1848, militant members of the working class threw up barricades in the streets of Paris and plunged the city into successive riots which drove Louis-Philippe from the throne, ultimately left thousands dead and wounded, and set the stage for Napoleon III and his Second Empire. The insurrection was sixteen years in the past at the time of this Christmas number, but, like many of her contemporaries who congratulated themselves on the relative stability of England during the period of turmoil, Mrs Lirriper evidently still mentally associated France with the possibility of revolution. In 'A Flight', the traveller known as Monied Interest dogmatically insists that 'the French are revolutionary, – "and always at it"'.

DOCTOR MARIGOLD'S PRESCRIPTIONS

'To Be Taken Immediately' and 'To Be Taken for Life' formed the framework for *Doctor Marigold's Prescriptions*, the extra Christmas number of *All the Year Round* for 1865 which provides the present text. *Doctor Marigold's Prescriptions* also contained a ghost story entitled 'To Be Taken with a Grain of Salt', omitted from this selection. Information about the authorship of this omitted piece is contradictory. Although there is strong evidence that a large portion, if not all of it, was written by Dickens alone, the possibility exists that Charles Collins, the brother of Wilkie Collins and the husband of Dickens's daughter Kate, may also have had a share in its composition (see Deborah A. Thomas, 'Contributors to the Christmas Numbers of *Household Words* and *All the Year Round*, 1850–1867', part 2, *Dickensian*, vol. 70 [1974] pp. 26–7).

TO BE TAKEN IMMEDIATELY

1. (p. 344) *Cabbage*. Scraps of material stolen by tailors in the course of cutting out their work and thus slang for a tailor.
2. (p. 345) *hearts of oak*. From a patriotic song in *Harlequin's Invasion* (1759) by David Garrick. The actual description is 'heart of oak', rather than 'hearts'.
3. (p. 346) *Board of Guardians*. Local administrators of the Poor Law. The New Poor Law of 1834 was a triumph of the kind of Malthusian zeal to which Dickens was unalterably opposed. In order to discourage pauperism, the workhouses were deliberately conducted with great severity and, as Oliver Twist discovered, the prescribed diet was kept as marginal as possible. At the time of *Doctor Marigold's Prescriptions*, conditions in the workhouses were still notoriously grim; in *Our Mutual Friend*, the novel on which Dickens was working just before he wrote this Christmas number, an elderly woman named Betty Higden, impelled by her horror of parochial charity, stubbornly resists offers of assistance and wanders over the countryside, with money for her burial sewed into her dress, until she dies.

4. (p. 349) *old lady in Threadneedle-street*. A familiar name for the Bank of England, situated in Threadneedle Street. In 1850, Dickens collaborated with his sub-editor H. W. Wills on an article of this title, reprinted and discussed in Harry Stone's edition of *Charles Dickens' Uncollected Writings from Household Words 1850–1859*, vol. I (Bloomington, Ind.: Indiana University Press, 1968).

5. (p. 351) *Joskin*. Slang for country bumpkin.

6. (p. 355) *the Favourite Comic of Shivery Shakey, ain't it cold*. A popular song, written by J. Beuler, entitled 'The Man That Couldn't Get Warm'. The first verse – quoted by James T. Lightwood in *Charles Dickens and Music* (London: Charles H. Kelly, 1912), p. 94 – warns:

> All you who're fond in spite of price
> Of pastry, cream and jellies nice
> Be cautious how you take an ice
>   Whenever you're overwarm.
> A merchant who from India came,
> And Shiverand Shakey was his name,
> A pastrycook's did once entice
> To take a cooling, luscious ice,
> The weather, hot enough to kill,
> Kept tempting him to eat, until
> It gave his corpus such a chill
>   He never again felt warm.
> Shiverand Shakey O, O, O,
> Criminy Crikey! Isn't it cold,
> Woo, woo, woo, oo, oo,
>   Behold the man that couldn't get warm.

7. (p. 359) *Over the hills and far away*. A traditional refrain; cf. John Gay, *The Beggar's Opera* (1728), I, xiii, air xvi, as well as the nursery rhyme which begins:

> Tom, he was a piper's son,
> He learnt to play when he was young,
> And all the tune that he could play
> Was, 'Over the hills and far away'.

8. (p. 360) *light under a bushel*. Matthew 5: 15; Mark 4: 21; Luke 8: 16 and 11: 33.

9. (p. 363) *eight-and-forty printed pages, six-and-ninety columns*. A description of the format in which this and the other extra Christmas numbers of *All the Year Round* originally appeared. The earlier extra Christmas numbers of *Household Words*, beginning in 1852, consisted of thirty-six pages and sold for threepence; they were printed by Bradbury and Evans whose disagreement with Dickens, stemming from the break-up of his marriage in 1858, led to the establishment of *All the Year Round* published jointly by Chapman & Hall and by Dickens himself.

NOTES

TO BE TAKEN FOR LIFE

1. (p. 364) '*I says the sparrow, with my bow and arrow.*' From the nursery rhyme which begins:

> Who killed Cock Robin?
> I, said the Sparrow,
> With my bow and arrow,
> I killed Cock Robin.

2. (p. 364) *history of David.* 1 Samuel 17 describes David's victory over the giant Goliath.

3. (p. 365) *The Dairyman's Daughter.* The title of a popular tract (1809) by Legh Richmond.

MAIN LINE. THE BOY AT MUGBY

'The Boy at Mugby' was first published as part of *Mugby Junction*, the extra Christmas number of *All the Year Round* for 1866 which provides the present text. See note 1 to 'The Signalman' (p. 412).

1. (p. 371) *Bandolining.* Stiffening with bandoline, a sticky substance used to hold hair in place.

2. (p. 371) *Cooke and Wheatstone electrical machinery.* William Fothergill Cooke (1806–79) and Charles Wheatstone (1802–75) jointly made important contributions to the development of the electric telegraph.

3. (p. 377) *Bright.* John Bright (1811–89), noted orator, member of parliament, and prominent representative of the emerging manufacturing class which exerted an increasing influence on British politics after the Reform Bill of 1832.

GEORGE SILVERMAN'S EXPLANATION

First published in the January, February, and March 1868 issues of the *Atlantic Monthly* which provide the present text; the breaks between serial instalments are indicated here by asterisks. Dickens wrote 'George Silverman's Explanation' as well as a piece entitled 'Holiday Romance', omitted from this selection, for initial publication in America, where he visited, for the second time, from November 1867 to April 1868. The two works subsequently appeared in *All the Year Round*, and 'George Silverman's Explanation' was serialized in the 1, 15, and 29 February 1868 issues of the latter journal.

1. (p. 384) *the first James of England.* James I suffers even more severely at Dickens's hands in *A Child's History of England* where he is repeatedly referred to as 'his Sowship'.

2. (p. 389) *you won't wrap it up in a napkin, . . . but you'll put it out at good interest.* cf. Luke 19: 20–23.

3. (p. 392) *D.V.* Abbreviation for '*Deo volente*', 'God willing'.

4. (p. 394) *My kingdom is not of this world.* John 18: 36.
5. (p. 394) *What did the woman do when she lost the piece of money?* cf. Luke 15: 8.
6. (p. 394) *faithful steward.* cf. Luke 12: 42–48.
7. (p. 398) *more Greek and Latin than Lady Jane Grey.* Lady Jane Grey (1537–54), the ill-fated queen of England for nine days after the death of Edward VI, was noted for her devotion to learning and, in particular, for her fluent command of Latin and Greek.